LACING LISBETH

'We all scrupulously adhere to our dress code, Hilary,' Lisbeth mused, 'petticoat, corset for narrow waist and proper nylons and sussies, but I assumed I needed no hygienic code! Although I'm not sure smelling of passion isn't a clever subliminal sales tool, given that our hotels offer extreme sybaritic luxury. What am I to do with you? You've put me in a deuced awkward position, Hilary. You're one of my best salesgirls, and yet I can't have this sort of indiscipline in my office.

'If I fire you, Amanda and the others will think me a spoilsport and a hypocrite, when our whole purpose is to market sensual pleasure and freedom. I have to think of office morale. You see my dilemma.'

Hilary bit her lip. 'There *is* a way you could punish me, miss,' she whispered. 'It may sound silly, but it's quite effective. When I was a girl, I had a pretty strict upbringing, and if I was naughty, well, I had to bend over, and have my bare bottom smacked. It's more common than you'd think, miss,' said Hilary, recovering some of her composure.

LACING LISBETH

Yolanda Celbridge

This book is a work of fiction.
In real life, make sure you practise safe, sane and
consensual sex.

First published in 2004 by
Nexus
Thames Wharf Studios
Rainville Road
London W6 9HA

www.nexus-books.co.uk

Typeset by TW Typesetting, Plymouth, Devon

Printed and bound by Clays Ltd, St Ives

ISBN 0 352 33912 8

Contents

You'll notice that we have introduced a set of symbols onto our book jackets, so that you can tell at a glance what fetishes each of our brand new novels contains. Here's the key – enjoy!

cp (traditional)

cp (modern)

spanking

restraint/bondage

rope bondage/hojojutsu

latex/rubber/leather/enclosure

fem dom

willing captivity

medical

period setting

uniforms

sex rituals

1

Butting In

'In the *lavatory?*'

'Yes, Miss Lache.'

Lisbeth Lache allowed her lips to purse in a frown, not censorious, but definitely displeased. She stroked her long, snow-blonde tresses, cascading in shiny contrast over her ripely swelling breasts, sharply upthrust by slender scalloped bra cups, under her flounced white blouse of Italian silk. She brushed an imaginary strand from the sleeve of her grey shantung silk jacket before crossing her legs, with a flash of her sheer grey nylons, under the lacy white hem of her silken petticoat, and swivelling briefly, in her tight corset, to gaze out at the summer foliage, shimmering in the heat haze of Sloane Square. She crossed her ankles, allowing the brilliance of her crimson toecaps to dance with the reflection of her petticoat.

'Let us be clear, Hilary,' she said, after some time. 'You were observed ... snogging, is, I think, the polite term, with a young man – a motorcycle messenger – in one of the cubicles, whose door you had neglected to lock. Amanda was an unfortunate choice of witness, as the dear girl is such a gossip. So now Luisa and June and the whole office know you were naked from the waist down – apart from your nylons and petticoat, I hope – with your panties at your ankles, and your head thrust into the lavatory bowl, while you held onto the seat, and the young man ... *snogged* you, from behind. Is that true?'

Hilary nodded, crimson with embarrassment.

'And this event took place this morning?'

'Yes, Miss Lache. I'm sorry – I didn't think anyone would see – it's just that he is so dishy, and I couldn't help myself. I was overwhelmed by passion, Miss Lache. Surely you understand.'

'I'm not sure whether to be amused or appalled,' said Lisbeth Lache, leaning back in her black leather swiveller, and gazing at the traffic, crawling far below in Eaton Square, as the eighteen-year-old girl fidgeted, standing before her desk, with her feet nervously treading the thick-pile Axminster. 'Passion is scarcely the thing, during office hours, unless it is passion to promote Sybarite Resorts. Good heavens, Hilary, I know what passion is – I am only four years your senior – but my passions know their place. That is why I am director, sitting here, and you are standing there, looking uncomfortable, as well you should.'

Pursing her lips, she stared at the red-faced girl, noting the long, coltish legs, in sheer, shiny, black nylons, slithering in embarrassment, under the swaying melons of her black, tight-skirted derrière; the full breasts, trembling slightly, with the big nipple plums straining at the skimpy bra, under their pink satin blouse; waist pinched to pencil thinness by a slender waspie corset, its shape faintly glimpsed under the clinging blouse fabric; the slender neck, wreathed in glossy chestnut tresses. Hilary Warmduff was a beauty, every swelling curve of her body showing good English breeding. Lisbeth licked her lips, then sighed.

'I suppose I ought to fire you,' she murmured, and Hilary paled.

'No, miss, please!' she blurted. 'I've said I'm sorry! I swear, I've never done such a thing before, and promise it won't happen again. Don't send me back to the horrid job centre. They'll say I am voluntarily unemployed, and won't give me any dole money, and ... and I'll starve to death ...' A tear trickled down her cheek.

'Come, Hilary, don't be melodramatic,' Lisbeth purred. 'Nobody starves to death in today's Britain.'

'They do, miss,' Hilary snuffled. 'It's just that the government lies.'

'I assume you've showered, and ... tidied yourself up, since your snogging episode?'

'Why, no, miss. I've been busy seeing corporate clients ever since. It's been quite busy. I've taken some quite juicy block bookings for our resorts in Thailand and South Africa.'

'Without showering? Such passionate encounters tend to be messy, and I'm sure your nylons and bottom area have suffered a little dampness and smelliness. You did wash yourself, down there, I expect?'

Hilary blushed again. 'I . . . I sort of forgot, miss.'

'So you were talking to clients, smelling of you-know-what?' drawled Lisbeth.

'Oh, please, miss, don't,' whispered the crimson girl.

'We all scrupulously adhere to our dress code, Hilary,' Lisbeth mused, 'petticoat, corset for narrow waist and proper nylons and sussies, but I assumed I needed no hygienic code! Although I'm not sure smelling of passion isn't a clever subliminal sales tool, given that our hotels offer extreme sybaritic luxury. The question is, what am I to do with you? You've put me in a deuced awkward position, Hilary. You're one of my best salesgirls, and yet I can't have this sort of indiscipline in my office. After all, it is I who have the task of smoothing things over with Miss Stuart-Bossi. Firing you won't undo the damage caused, and my partner will wish to know how it happened in the first place. Then, if I fire you, Amanda and the others will think me a spoilsport and a hypocrite, when our whole purpose is to market sensual pleasure and freedom. I have to think of office morale. You see my dilemma.'

'Yes, miss,' said Hilary. 'You mean, you aren't going to fire me?'

'I didn't say that,' drawled Lisbeth. 'I mean, I see no alternative.'

'Please, miss, I admit I've been foolish,' Hilary said. 'I deserve some kind of punishment, I can see that. The other girls will be jealous if I get away scot-free.'

'What, then?' replied Lisbeth. 'Fire you, and I'm an ogress. Cut your pay, and you'll be surly and won't perform. It's a pretty pickle.'

Hilary bit her lip. 'There *is* a way you could punish me, miss,' she whispered. 'It may sound silly, but it's quite effective.'

'What, then?' Lisbeth demanded.

'Oh, you'll think I'm strange,' Hilary mumbled, blushing furiously.

'Try me,' said Lisbeth drily.

'Well, miss, umm, you could give me a spanking.'

'*What*?'

'*You* know, miss,' Hilary said, wiggling her bottom, in embarrassment.

'I'm not sure I do.'

'I mean, when I was a girl, I had a pretty strict upbringing, and if I was naughty, well, I had to bend over and have my bare bottom smacked.'

'Well! This is most unusual,' murmured Lisbeth, gazing intently, with sparkling eyes, at Hilary's trembling legs and the big breasts, heaving in their bra cups.

'It's more common than you'd think, miss,' said Hilary, recovering some of her composure, 'and it's an effective way of bringing foolish girls to their senses. That is, we girls know when we are being foolish, but there's something inside us so that we can't help ourselves, and sometimes a good whopping is the best thing to straighten us out.'

'I believe it is the sort of thing certain *men* like,' said Lisbeth, curling her lip.

'It's the spanking that counts, miss,' blurted Hilary. 'A lady's palm hurts just as much.'

'Does it?' Lisbeth drawled. 'But what if I don't *want* to hurt you, Hilary?'

'With respect, miss, I . . . I think you should. You could consider it a duty, if you wished. A good hard spanking would punish me for my insolence, and get you out of your pickle.' She licked her lips. 'I promise that if my bottom's really red and sore and smarting, I'll be an even better salesgirl.'

'What exactly do you want me to do?' asked Lisbeth, crossing her nylons, with a moist, slithering swish.

'It's not *want*, miss,' Hilary said. 'Surely you don't think I relish the idea of pain, and my bum all red and ribbed, and hurting for days? It's the only solution to the problem I can see. You would put me over my knee, and pull my panties down, and spank me as hard as possible, on my bare bottom. She gulped, her whole body trembling. 'I *hate* being spanked, miss,' she whispered. 'That's why I suggest it.'

Lisbeth frowned, biting her lip.

'You give the impression that you are spanked frequently.'

Blushing, Hilary looked down, in silence.

'The bare bottom, you say?' Lisbeth whispered.

'It's the only way, miss.'

'What if I spanked you on your petticoat, with your panties underneath? It would be a trifle more modest.'

'Then it wouldn't really hurt, and more important, I wouldn't feel the shame of a naked bottom. Sometimes we like to put on airs, and a bare-bottom spanking reminds us that we are just naughty little girls. Also, I wouldn't want to spoil my petticoat, or my panties.'

'You're not suggesting I'd spank you as hard as that?'

'It would have to be pretty hard, miss, I'm afraid, hard enough to make my bum really red.'

'And how long would that take? I'm rather busy. In fact, I have to meet Miss Stuart-Bossi in a few minutes.'

'It might take a while, I admit,' said Hilary, 'depending on how hard you spank me.'

'I haven't said I *will* spank you. The idea of smacking your bare bottom – well, don't you think there's something rather intimate about it, some might say, indecent? What would the other girls think?'

'Why, they'd perfectly understand. Heaven, miss, we girls must be – you know – sensuous, to promote our resorts with whirlpools and nude beaches, and fun discos, everything for swingers –'

'Don't use Americanisms. Our clients are sybarites.'

'Sorry, miss. Oh, please, miss, say you will. Go on. Give me a really hard spanking on my bare bottom. Please.'

5

Lisbeth took a deep breath.

'Very well,' she said. 'You may report back to me at four o'clock precisely, when I can give you forty-five minutes.'

'Thank you so much, miss!'

'And don't be late,' Lisbeth warned, 'or . . .'

'Or I'll earn a bare-bottom spanking, miss?' said Hilary, po-faced.

Lisbeth smiled. 'Or I'll *enjoy* spanking you,' she whispered.

Her intercom warbled, and she pressed the button.

'Miss Stuart-Bossi's here, Miss Lache,' said a girl's voice.

'I'm awaiting her,' said Lisbeth, waving Hilary out.

The two girls passed each other outside Lisbeth's office, with the tall, olive-skinned girl glancing quizzically at the pale, rather nervous English rose, who deferentially made way for her.

'Lisbeth – adorable as always,' drawled Sabrina Stuart-Bossi. 'Only true beauty can look fabulous in grey. Who was that? Quite a corker. New girl?'

'Yes. Hilary Warmduff.'

'Of the Shropshire Warmduffs, no doubt. She looked a bit peeved.'

'I had to . . . to give her a bit of a talking to,' Lisbeth blurted.

'Sly fox,' murmured Sabrina.

'Now, Sabrina,' retorted Lisbeth, 'you know I never mix biz with plesh . . .'

'Exceptions are allowed, in mitigating circumstances, and I'd say that *bella figura* is mitigating circumstances.'

'Oh, don't, Sabrina,' pouted Lisbeth, blushing. 'You are such a tease.'

The two girls, Sabrina four years Lisbeth's senior, sat in white leather easy chairs, by a coffee table, in the corner, where two windows allowed them a lofty panorama of Eaton Square, and the distant hubbub of Knightsbridge. Presently, a girl in a coyly frilly French maid's uniform teetered in on perilous stilettos and served them coffee and biscuits on a silver tray. Her bubbies gleamed, almost naked, in a tiny brassiere, under her tight white blouse. She bent over, revealing her buttocks, covered by a skimpy satin thong, snaking almost invisibly between the brimming fleshy arse marrows. Satin straps lashed her seamed black fishnet nylons to a frilly garter belt, glimpsed under her bobbing skirtlet, as she poured coffee from the silver pot. Lisbeth rewarded her maid with two taps to the bare right fesse; the maid stood, blushing slightly, curtsied, and departed. Sabrina raised an eyebrow.

'*That's* not mixing business with pleasure?' she asked, raising her coffee cup to her dark crimson lips.

'That is *pure* pleasure,' Lisbeth simpered. 'I rescued her from some wretched dole queue in Westminster. There are a lot of girls from good schools on their uppers there. Tasty, you must admit.'

'If I shared your sapphic inclinations, I'd agree,' said Sabrina. 'What a plump cooze she has! And covered only by a darling little satin triangle – you can see every fold.'

'Quite so,' said Lisbeth, licking her lips, and biting into a ginger nut. 'But my other girls don't know I'm sapphic, or don't have reason to know.'

'Not even that juicy piece who just left?'

'No ... not yet, at any rate. That's what I'm rather afraid of. You see, she's placed me in a rather ticklish situation, and I'd love your advice.'

Quickly, Lisbeth recounted her conversation with the errant Hilary. Sabrina laughed, slapping her bronze-nyloned thigh, under her cream mini-skirt, ridden up.

'In the lav!' she chortled. 'Girl has vim, eh? And sound sense – a spanking clears the air wonderfully. But you are worried you'll get excited by her bare bottom and give yourself away, or do something foolish.'

'I never do anything foolish, Sabrina,' said Lisbeth, baring her teeth.

'Of course not. Otherwise we wouldn't be partners.'

'But there are signs of excitement, impossible to hide,' Lisbeth added. 'And I'm not sure, but I thought I caught a twinkle in her eye, as if the minx was daring me, provoking me.'

'That's easy. Call her bluff, and give her a really juicy lacing. Make the troll squirm. Nothing like the sight of a juicy bare bum, all red and writhing. Gosh, it would probably turn *me* on.'

'I'm not sure I know how. It's just that Hilary's an awfully good salesgirl, and I really don't want to lose her.'

'Then I'll attend, and help out if necessary. A spanking's more decorous with a chaperone and, actually, I know a thing or two about corporal punishment.'

'You, Sabrina? We all had our bums laced at school, of course, but is there more?'

'When I grew up on Acklins Island in the Bahamas, with a buccaneer Italian daddy and a poor white mummy, who claimed descent from King Charles the Second, you can be sure that my bare bum got lathered, like a proper English lady's, with distressing frequency. It was normal. Half the time we ran around in the nude, even as teenagers, and discipline, for shrieking or splashing, or being "pestilent", as Mummy said, was a rough and ready affair. Usually with a belt, or a stick. It was also quite normal for nude teenagers to masturbate, in public, and whipping never deterred us. We all watched each other strapped on the bare, howling, and it was great spectacle, unless you were the one doing the howling.'

'Gosh,' Lisbeth said. 'For a moment, I had visions of you playing kinky games with some perverse London boyfriend . . .'

'Sounds fun,' murmured Sabrina, licking her lips.

'Oh, you do tease,' blurted Lisbeth. 'But I'd be awfully grateful if you could help me out. Four o'clock all right? I don't really know how long a spanking is supposed to last.'

Sabrina smiled, and sipped her coffee. 'Usually, longer than you expect. But I've nothing else on. Look, Lisbeth, lighten up. It might surprise you to learn that in all the masculine boardrooms I have to look dainty in, and choose my moment to breathe a ladylike word or two about money, spanking an office girl's bottom is considered quite the normal thing, to correct some error on her part. Most girls like it. It's painful, but swift and simple,

8

with no nasty after effects, after she's had a good cry. So don't think this one is teasing you. Spanking is common practice, all over the City of London. I've even witnessed a few, all very clean and modest. Bend over the boardroom table – the pinstripes get a kick out of that – skirt up, knickers down, and the gentleman's palm, or his belt, or even a whippy little office cane, kept specially for this purpose, whop-whop-whop, till the girl's bum is nice and red, then rueful smiles all round, knickers up, and back to work.'

'A cane?' Lisbeth shivered.

'There's a sexual side to it, of course, a girl's naked bottom caned by a clothed – *uniformed* – male, and the piquancy is that the beating is entirely chaste.'

'I can't see the slightest sexual pleasure in caning,' Lisbeth blurted. 'It was horrid at school.'

'Don't be too sure.'

Flaming a long cigarette with her gold lighter, Sabrina crossed her legs, allowing Lisbeth a brief glimpse of her stocking tops and sussies, and the unpantied cooze hillock, gleaming above the nylons. Lisbeth excused herself. 'I'll let you finish your gasper, while I pee,' she said.

Squatting in her private bathroom, Lisbeth sighed, spurting a jet of smoky golden liquid, and watching her bare-shaven quim hillock, peeping from her corset hem – *almost down to nineteen inches!* – as her golden shower streamed. Wiping herself, her fingers slipped between her thighs, and she blushed, realising her quim was moist.

'I can understand rueful, but not the smiles,' said Lisbeth, as she rejoined Sabrina. 'At Bedminster, we girls took awful corporal punishment, caning on the panties, or even bare bum, but it wasn't to make us smile. I got more than my share, for having such a big bottom – "bum-worthy" they called me, amongst other things – and I hate even thinking about it. That's what made me turn to other girls for pleasure. I imagined men, with their stiff tools, were as brutal as our prefects, with *their* rods, and found that doing things with girls was soft and beautiful. I say "sapphic" because I'd hate to be thought a *lesbian* – and

9

I've had enough pleasure with boyfriends to know that I can go both ways. I love the power of a hard sex organ in my pouch, but I'm afraid of men, too, and their will to dominate. My sapphism is a cosy secret possession, something I know I can turn to, for gentleness and affection.'

Sabrina lit another cigarette, and blew a plume of fragrant blue smoke. 'My policy is to make men afraid of *me*,' she said. 'Admit that you do get a thrill from seducing – no, I should say introducing – tasty young girls, like your frilly maid here, to the delights of sapphism.'

'And why not?' said Lisbeth. 'It's sweet to give pleasure to other girls.'

'With you in charge, the dominant.'

'I'm a teacher. Girls must be awakened to their bodies, how every curve and crevice, properly caressed, can raise them to ecstasy. Don't tell me that girls running around naked in the Bahamas didn't delight in exploring each other's bodies.'

'We did, and more – even when whipped for it. Funnily enough, it is our business in the Bahamas I wanted to talk to you about.'

'We haven't any business in the Bahamas,' Lisbeth said.

'Which is about to change. I know I'm the money and you're the marketing, and a jolly good partnership it is, and normally I don't like butting in but, thanks to my Bahamian contacts, I've caught wind of something that could make us even more of a fortune. It means you'll have to take a rather yummy holiday . . .'

After Sabrina had explained her scheme, both girls had to set off for their respective power luncheons. Lisbeth taxied to a restaurant in Knightsbridge, where, amid braying hunky guards officers, she entertained a suave gentleman, something large in the City, who wanted to take his dozen female office staff for a luxury holiday with a difference. He neither winked nor nudged, but his meaning was clear, and Lisbeth sold him on their 'Diggers' beach resort on the remote western coast of Tasmania, near the old convict settlements, where visitors could visit

10

real dungeons, with real chains and shackles. Afterwards, Lisbeth took a walk in Hyde Park, thighs just a bit slithery from her moist cunny, excited at the prospect of spanking Hilary's bare bottom, and nipped into a public loo for a sudden pee. As she evacuated, she wondered what those juicy bum flans would look like naked, and how it would feel to spank them. Well, she concluded, time will tell, and it's not long to four o'clock. She shivered, pulling up her panties, whose gusset was noticeably wet.

Lisbeth's sapphism was an open secret between her and Sabrina, their relationship subtly enhanced by Sabrina's own charm, and the unspoken electricity between them, knowing that only common sense prevented Lisbeth from making a pass. As she strolled in the park, she remembered her own induction to girl–girl love . . . in the fifth form at Bedminster, tired from a strenuous volleyball game, she found herself alone in the showers with an older girl, a sixth-former, who had undertaken to soap Lisbeth's body for her. The girl's fingers stroked and caressed her, as she bathed Lisbeth's tingling bare skin, finally soaping and rinsing her bum crack, and rubbing her pouch lips, so that they swelled, and her clitty began to throb. The girl caressed her buttocks, running her fingers up and down the cleft, with an electrifying tickle of her anus bud, and rubbing her stiffening nipples, then pinching and squeezing them. A tickling finger went into her anus and Lisbeth wriggled, moaning, but did not protest, nor when fingers invaded her wet pouch and began to thrust.

The cooing words had disappeared, and there was only the rushing of the shower to drown Lisbeth's moans of ecstasy, as the older, experienced girl expertly tongued her cooze and clitty, licked and scratched her stiff nips and finger-fucked her both in bumhole and pouch, until Lisbeth exploded in the deepest, most shuddering orgasm she could remember. Masturbating alone, which, from the onset of puberty, she had done every night, had never been like this. Thereafter, they became lovers, sneaking into each other's studies or bedrooms for naked, passionate writhing, their bodies slippery with sweat as they cavorted,

11

each with her lips and tongue sucking the copious come from her lover's cunt. Such liaisons, as at most girls' boarding schools, were unofficially tolerated as 'crushes' or 'pashes' and assumed to be chastely platonic, thus unpunished – when mere possession of a battered cigarette end could earn a girl six stingers with the cane, on her panties pulled tight over the buttocks, or even on the buttocks fully bared.

Later, a sixth-former herself, she found a winning seduction technique was to comfort a younger girl who had recently been caned, stroking the dreadful crimson bruises disfiguring her bottom globes, and whispering words of sympathy and outrage, that beastly prefects could delight in such cruelty. Lisbeth's horrid experiences of being flogged on her bare bottom meant her sympathy was quite sincere. To be caned on the bare, at her age, shamed for wetting the bed! It wasn't something a teenage girl could help . . . she shuddered, thinking of Dorcas Gunn, the prefect from hell, and *aggressively* lesbian, caning her smarting bare bum for 'wetting', while threatening her with the dreaded penance board.

When the time came to lose her 'official' virginity, with an acceptable boy, whose name she scarcely remembered, she had experienced pleasure of a different kind, but already considered herself no longer a virgin, after that magical seduction in the showers at Bedminster. Thereafter, it was a special thrill to play the role of seductress with younger girls, the more innocent the better – like Clara, her scrumptious new frilly maid – the power of her experienced lips and fingers making the innocent twitch and moan and shudder, as her pouch seeped come and her nipples stiffened under Lisbeth's insistent, probing caresses, introducing her to sapphism, another notch on Lisbeth's belt . . .

What would Hilary's bottom look like naked and, more important, how would Lisbeth's own body react? Would she moisten down there at the sight of the bare orbs, completely in her power? The girl would probably be shivering, a little apprehensive, to say the least, and that in

12

itself would be thrilling. Kind words might relax her, but even those would be an expression of the spanker's power. It was hard to tell how a girl's bottom would look, even under a tight skirt as prescribed for Lisbeth's sales staff. All girls' bottoms were different, all yummy, soft and firm at the same time, and so smooth to caress, like so many ripe, swelling fruits – plums, pears, apples, peaches. Some had fesses so large and firm that they could only be likened to lush tropical melons, bursting with juice.

How, then, would Hilary's personal bare feel under the cracking of Lisbeth's palm? Should she spank always in the one area, probably the big fleshy mid-bottom, or paint a tapestry of pink fingermarks all over the bare buttocks? Above all, she must strive to remain impersonal as she spanked the girl, undoubtedly making her squirm in distress: it must not be Lisbeth spanking her, but a mere agent of justice. No question of exacting revenge, for all the schoolgirl welts Lisbeth's own bottom had borne, on Hilary's buttocks, guilty only of foolishness.

Yet such sluttish foolishness! Bending over a lavatory seat, petticoat up and panties down, to take a tupping from behind, like some farmyard animal! Lisbeth's couplings had never involved *that* degradation. Luckily, Sabrina would be there, and would help – Lisbeth was sure Sabrina knew more about spanking than she had admitted, and was certain that, when she was away in the Bahamas, Sabrina would take advantage of her temporary command to spank the salesgirls on the slightest pretext.

Suddenly, a spasm jolted Lisbeth's clitoris, as she imagined Sabrina's own bottom, bared for a spanking: Sabrina, the ice-cold beauty, whose buttocks swayed and slithered under the skimpiest designer silk skirt, like two big chocolate drops, unencumbered by panties, with nothing but the clinging silk between her naked bottom and thin air. Lisbeth herself habitually went unpantied, but her skirts had a sensible absorbent lining, in case of . . . well, drips, when she had to pee hurriedly, or was excited to moisture by a girl's beautiful bottom. Sabrina, with outrageous confidence, got away with being shamelessly unpantied. Lisbeth stifled her longing to see, and touch, Sabrina in the nude – the long, ripely muscled legs, the thrusting bubbies, helped quite unnecessarily by a silk-cupped bra, to jut proud and firm, two ripe melons, rivalling Lisbeth's own; the lustrous caramel skin, and shiny raven tresses.

Those lush bare bum globes would tremble a little, as they pouted cheekily on Lisbeth's nyloned thigh, the cleft teasingly open, to show the downy brown perineum, the anus bud, and the softly swelling quim lips, with the fesses clenching just a little, begging for Lisbeth's palm to spank them. And Sabrina, after her spanking, sitting on Lisbeth's face, her bare spanked bum crushing her lips and nose, as she drank the sweetest come from Sabrina's fleshy pink cunt, glistening between dripping brown pouch flaps, while Sabrina's bare thighs clamped her head. Lisbeth repressed her sudden, terrific urge to masturbate. *Not in public, Lisbeth!* Gasping, she licked her lips, as she walked back to Knightsbridge, her clitty throbbing and her nylons slithering with seeped come, to hail a taxi outside the Hyde Park Hotel. Once aboard, she felt safe from her own longings, and contemplated the Bahamas scheme on the crawl through the traffic.

It sounded an absolute winner, and an adventure, too. Normally, when LaBo Associates, as Sabrina and Lisbeth styled themselves, wanted to acquire a property for their Sybarite Resorts, there was a fair amount of wining and dining, and exertion of both girls' charms, but the bulk of the transaction was rather dull number-crunching and sales forecasts. Not so with Rum Hole, in the Jumentos Cays, a hundred miles from Acklins Island, itself one of the most isolated members of the Bahamas group – seven hundred islands, of which only thirty were inhabited. Sabrina knew of the cays only from her matelot father, whom she described as a 'proper pirate', with a twinkle in her eye. The Jumentos Cays were truly a paradise, a chain of interlacing small islands, low and scrubby, with the most fabulous beaches in the already fabulous Bahamas: turquoise clean sea, all manner of fish and crustaceans, and alabaster-white sand. On one of these, Rum Hole, lay the world's most exclusive hotel, far from any airport, or shipping lane. Supplies of the world's finest wines and foodstuffs, as well as guests themselves, were ferried there by seaplane.

Owned by a mysterious, fabulously rich Englishman, Roger de Hazebrouck, it was so excusive that it had no advertising, attendance was by invitation only, and no tariff was ever published, on or off Rum Hole. Guests were promised the fulfilment of their every desire, and satisfaction of their slightest whim, and when they chose to leave, Roger de Hazebrouck presented them with a bill of his own computation. The slightest question struck the complainant's name off the guest list for ever. Rum Hole was, naturally, for people so rich that they did not even consider themselves rich; curiously, it was for ladies only. Not, Sabrina hastened to add, that it was sapphic, although sapphism was not excluded, and, in fact, male guests were sometimes admitted, as ladies' consorts. Sabrina's task was to gain acquaintance and, if necessary, intimacy, with Roger de Hazebrouck, to persuade him to sell his island. Rum Hole, a few miles long, would lend itself superbly to a Sybarite resort, covering the whole terrain, and not just the environs of Roger's guesthouse.

'I hear he's a dish,' Sabrina had murmured, breathily, 'and hung like an absolute *stallion.*'

Lisbeth blushed. 'So what?' she replied, with feigned coyness. 'Business is business. And I aim to have a jolly good holiday. Mr de Hazebrouck may pamper me to the utmost – after all, we are paying for it.'

A double excitement gripped Lisbeth as she entered the tiny lift to carry her to her penthouse office suite – the prospects of a real Bahamas vacation and of spanking a beautiful teenage girl's bare bottom. She was not sure which excited her more.

2

Constant Squirm

'That's another delicious bottom, ripe for a spanking,' Sabrina murmured, just loud enough for the maid Clara to hear, as she bent over the table, serving steaming oolong.

The girl blushed, but with the hint of a smile, glancing very briefly at Sabrina's thighs. Sabrina lolled in an armchair with her legs crossed, like a man; one ankle perched on her knee, with her flimsy skirtlet ridden up, displaying her inner thighs and unpantied quim, the lips big and ripe, enfolding a sinuously curving slit, gleaming bare, in the skirt's silken shadow. The maid teetered out of the office on her high stilettos, waggling her bottom, Lisbeth thought, a little more than usual. Hand trembling a little, she sipped her tea, herself glancing at Sabrina's naked quim, which Sabrina made no effort to hide; shifting slightly, in fact, and spreading her thighs wider, with studied casualness, so that Lisbeth could not fail to be aware of the bare-shaven hillock and cleft above her nylon stocking tops, and black rubber garter straps.

'Really, Sabrina,' Lisbeth protested, with mild indignation, 'I don't think you should embarrass the girl.'

'Why not? Most hussies like to be teased, if they have lovely big fesses. They know perfectly well how spankable they are, and that men long to spank them. Oh, I forgot – you are trying to turn Clara against men.'

'Not turn,' said Lisbeth hotly. 'Simply let her enjoy a choice – the same choice I enjoy. I must say, Sabrina, I've never heard you talk like this before – about spanking, I mean.'

16

Sabrina lit a cigarette, inhaled, and lazily puffed. 'The subject hasn't come up before. It's *you* who are proposing to spank Hilary, don't forget.'

'I didn't propose it,' Lisbeth blurted, 'she did.'

'My point exactly,' purred Sabrina.

The two girls sipped their tea, as the hand on the rosewood grandfather clock crept closer to four. Outside, the lowering sun cast a mellow glow on the denizens of Eaton Square strolling below, amid red buses and black taxi cabs snarled in the traffic. Slender fingers of light penetrated the office, illumining the lazy blue smoke from Sabrina's cigarette, curling in the air.

'Rather hot,' she said. 'One has a mad impulse to take one's clothes off.'

'It's not as if you are wearing many,' said Lisbeth.

'I know. But it's all Giulio Ferracci.'

Lisbeth whistled appreciatively.

'He's such a hunk to look at, but most of his designs are brutal,' Sabrina said, 'either so flimsy that you're practically naked and never at ease, always embarrassed and having to check what's showing, or else horridly uncomfortable, all wires and straps and wedges, like a form of bondage, to punish us. I mean, his shoes and corsets are positively painful. He must really hate women. But of course, at those outrageous prices, you *have* to wear him. How I admire you, Lisbeth, with your yummy corset and petticoat and everything. It's so *right*.'

'These *are* Ferracci corset and shoes,' Lisbeth said, with a wince. 'They do pinch, rather.'

'I suppose that's the point,' Sabrina drawled.

'Well, I insist on proper dress for my salesgirls, but I'm looking forward to Rum Hole, to relax a bit. I imagine I'll be able to swim and sunbathe in the nude, in some deserted cove. Perhaps be surprised by some fabulous girl, and she'll strip off, too, and, you know . . .' She blushed, with a little giggle.

'Oh, you'll do more than that,' said Sabrina.

At one minute to four, Hilary knocked on the door, and was bade enter. She looked startled at Sabrina's presence,

17

even though Sabrina's thighs were now pressed demurely together, until Lisbeth explained that Miss Stuart-Bossi would supervise her chastisement, and make sure everything was done properly and modestly.

Sabrina laughed gently. 'Miss Lache is far too polite to use the word "spanking", Hilary,' she drawled, 'but that's what you're here for, an't it? A bare-bottom spanking.'

'Why, yes, of course, miss,' stammered Hilary, blushing. 'It's just . . . I didn't know there would be both of you.'

'Miss Stuart-Bossi will be a kind of referee, Hilary, for she has considerable experience in corporal punishment,' Lisbeth blurted. 'Oh, I mean – that is, I didn't mean –'

'It's quite all right, Miss Lache,' said Sabrina. 'I am sure Hilary fully understands. You don't mind my watching, do you?'

'I'm quite indifferent, miss,' said Hilary. 'It's not up to the spanked girl to dictate her punishment.'

'A rare girl, who's indifferent to a bare-bum spanking,' opined Sabrina drily.

'Well, seat yourself and have a cup of tea, before we get to the business,' said Lisbeth.

'Gosh, thanks, miss,' said Hilary, seating herself primly, and accepting her cup.

'I believe you are quite experienced yourself, Hilary,' said Sabrina, offering the girl a custard cream. 'I'm fully aware of your case, and know that this punishment was your suggestion.'

'Ohh . . .' said Hilary, allowing crumbs to cascade down her chin, 'then you know about . . . oh, I'm so embarrassed.'

'So you should be,' said Lisbeth, 'A healthy girl's impulses must be punished, I'm afraid, when they get foolishly out of hand.'

'Hilary has, however, been very sensible,' Sabrina drawled, 'in suggesting a sound spanking . . . on the *naked* bottom. It is always the best way to clear the matter up. You do agree to be spanked bare bum, Hilary?'

'It was I who advised Miss Lache to spank me on the bare,' said Hilary, colouring, and her fingers trembling on her teacup. 'I'm sorry, I'm rather nervous. I've always hated being spanked, and especially on the bare, of course, because it is so shameful, and my bottom tends to wriggle rather a lot. It's quite mortifying, knowing my bare skin is on show, reddening, while I squirm around, gasping and panting, like some silly young girl. I mean, I was spanked quite a lot at school – caned, as well, on the bare – and I'm afraid I didn't put up a very good show. I dreaded that awful moment when you feel your knickers sort of slither down your legs, with a rush of cold air to your exposed bum. I couldn't stand the pain and disgrace.'

Lazily, Sabrina slung her ankle over her knee and sat cross-legged, thighs apart. A shaft of sunlight briefly illumined her full bare cunt hillock, nestling between her rippling, glossy thigh tops. 'Funny thing,' she drawled, baring her teeth in a narrow smile, 'a girl who doesn't merit a spanking from time to time hasn't much pepper in her. Just as in the Royal Navy of old, if a cadet hadn't earned a few bare-bum birchings – at least twenty-four strokes was normal – he wasn't considered officer material.'

Hilary bit her lip, smiling nervously. 'Twenty-four cuts of the birch, on the bare,' she murmured. 'Whipped naked, with all the other boys watching . . . gosh.'

'I'm sure you'll take it like a grown-up,' Sabrina said.

'I'll try, miss,' blurted Hilary, gulping, as she averted her gaze from Sabrina's exposed cooze. 'It depends how you want to take me. Standing up, and holding onto your desk, with my legs apart, is least undignified, but then the spanker has to slice a bit sideways, without the descending slap that you get when the spanked girl is over the knee. Or, I could bend over and touch my toes, if you prefer, with my cheeks really high, which allows a pretty good downward slap. They are the most painful.'

'Then let's get started,' said Lisbeth, briskly. 'Miss Bossi, if you would care to, ah . . . direct?'

'Clearly it's best if you sit, and take her over the knee,' Sabrina said.

Hilary smiled ruefully. 'I was afraid you'd say that, miss,' she murmured. 'Over the knee is really hard, and a clever spanker can switch from palm to slipper, without her victim even knowing.'

'Good idea,' said Sabrina, mischievously. 'Or I suppose a Giulio Ferracci stiletto would do.'

Lisbeth's throat was dry, and she swallowed the last of her tea before moving to the leather sofa and sitting, with her skirt pulled up, to leave an expanse of nyloned thigh for Hilary's belly. The sofa squeaked as she sat down, patting her thigh. 'Place yourself here,' she commanded. 'Lift your skirt and petticoat over your back, then lower your panties.'

'I suggest the panties around the ankles,' said Sabrina, 'with a knot to tighten them. It will stop her legs threshing.'

Balancing her weight on the arm of the sofa, Hilary stretched out and lowered herself gingerly onto Lisbeth's thighs, until her full weight pressed on them. She raised her skirt and tucked it at the small of her back, while Sabrina deftly lifted her petticoat, revealing her knickers, a sliver of pink satin stretched tightly over the full, ripe globes of her bottom, whose cheeks were over half exposed by the skimpiness of the garment. Lisbeth unfastened Hilary's garter straps from her suspender belt, and pushed them, too, up over her back. Hilary applied a trembling hand to her panties, and rolled them down her thighs, the thin fabric clinging stickily to her cunt. Her fesse melons shivered, firm and ripe, with gooseflesh covering their nudity, and her anus bud and cunt lips were visible in the steep arse cleft, between the slightly parted cheeks.

Lisbeth grasped the panties and slid them all the way down her stockinged legs to her ankles, where Sabrina swiftly knotted them in a little bow, tightening it round Hilary's ankles, so that they could not move. She wriggled to get comfortable, and the skirt, petticoat and garter straps tumbled down over her bare bottom. With a moue, Lisbeth swept the clothing back onto Hilary's back, baring the buttocks fully, with the tight band of Hilary's corset just visible, rather cruelly nipping her flesh above her suspender belt. Having pinned the underthings on Hilary's back, Lisbeth raised her spanking arm. Sabrina grasped her uplifted wrist.

'No,' said Sabrina, thoughtfully, 'that won't do. If she bucks, you'll want your hand free to hold her head down, like this.' Sabrina raised her left leg and clamped Hilary's neck in the instep of her stiletto, forcing the girl's head low. 'And those undies will slip over her bum, when it's squirming. The only solution is for her to take everything off – skirt, petticoat and sussies – but leave her stockings and knotted panties at her feet.'

'Yes, you're quite right,' said Lisbeth. 'Get up, Hilary, and take off your things below the waist.'

Hilary stumbled to her feet, bandaged by her panties, and clumsily slithered out of her petticoat, then unpinned her skirt, letting both garments drop to the floor, where the suspender belt followed.

'Please, miss,' she said, 'I think it would be better if I took my blouse off too, otherwise the shirt tail will get in the way of my bum.'

Teetering on her bound feet, she unbuttoned her blouse, letting the full breast melons pop out, scarcely restrained by her narrow bra cups, which only just covered her big strawberry nipples, with half the areolae showing above the cups. Standing in only her stockings, bra and corset, she revealed her naked cooze for the first time, and both Lisbeth and Sabrina gasped, licking their lips. Hilary's hillock sprouted a thick pube-thatch of astonishing density, area and length, extending up her flat belly almost to the rim of her corset, and downwards, between her thighs, to hang profusely past her cunt collops, like tendrils of lush weed. Hilary noted their gaze and blushed.

'Is . . . is something wrong, miss?' she blurted.

'I didn't know you were hairy,' Lisbeth said, 'down there, you know.'

'Well, I can scarcely help it, miss,' Hilary mumbled. 'I'm naturally hairy. I shave my armpits and legs and everything.'

'No, no . . . I meant, I assume, as part of our office dress code, all my girls shave their hillocks. It's part of being

21

ladylike – though unseen, like corset and petticoat, a bare mound is part of our femininity.'

Hilary blushed profusely. 'I . . . I wasn't aware of that, honestly, miss.'

Lisbeth sighed. 'If I'm going to spank you over my knee,' she said, 'your hillock's going to rub my thigh, and I'm afraid such a thick growth will be itchy, even through my nylons. Hilary, would you mind awfully shaving yourself smooth, before I spank you? I know it sounds a bore, but I promise you it will feel lovely and clean and sensuous.'

'Must I, miss?' blurted Hilary.

Lisbeth stood and lifted her skirt several inches, giving the girl a glimpse of her own shaven cooze. Hilary gasped in surprise, as much at her superior's sudden nudity as at the shiny alabaster smoothness of Lisbeth's hairless cunt. Smiling, Sabrina flipped up her skirtlet, with a playful tap to Lisbeth's bare buttocks, and Hilary gaped at two swelling bare cooze mounds, with slivers of pink wet flesh peeping between the naked cunt lips.

'Gosh,' she said, 'I've never shaved that part. It's so pretty!'

'Yes,' drawled Sabrina, 'and quite the done thing, these days, Hilary. For most of civilised history, proper girls were shaven, apart from the ghastly twentieth century. Why not go into the bathroom and use my kit?'

She lowered her skirt, groped in her purse and produced a disposable plastic razor and scissors.

'I'll help you,' Lisbeth said. 'Come on, girl. There's always a first time.'

Sabrina helped the girl clamber out of her pile of discarded underthings and, hobbling awkwardly in her knotted panties, Hilary followed Lisbeth into her private bathroom. She sat on the edge of the bath, and Lisbeth instructed her to part her thighs, as best she could, with her ankles hobbled. Handing Hilary the scissors, she ordered her to commence clipping off her thatch until it was time to shave the remaining stubble. Hilary bent over, and, nervously, began shearing her abundant pubic fleece. Tufts of brown glossy hair dropped to the floor as, biting her lip, she denuded her hillock to a rather ragged lawn of bristles. Lisbeth squatted at her feet, gazing into the spread quim, and directed Hilary's depilation. The girl parted her thighs wider, ankles straining at the panties, as she strove to reach into the cunt sides and the inlet of the perineum. As she stretched, suddenly her left breast popped from its flimsy bra cup and dangled, wobbling, over her corseted belly.

'Oh!' she cried, 'I'm sorry.'

'Don't be sorry,' purred Lisbeth, licking her lips. 'Actually, I suggest you take the bra off, Hilary, as it's an obvious interference. You *are* a big girl, aren't you? I can spank you just as well in only your corset.'

Hilary groped behind her back and unfastened her bra, allowing both bubbies to tremble in the nude, the nipple buds, in their wide, pink areolae, standing erectly to attention. The extreme stricture of her corset made the naked breasts jut full and swelling above her ribcage and exaggerated the curve of her buttock pears, spreading dramatically from the corset-squeezed waist. She bent down, her back arched, to trim behind her cunt lips, and her breasts hung, swaying, inches from Lisbeth's mouth. Sabrina stood in the doorway watching, with a leer curling her lips, as Hilary groped in her arse cleft.

'What a lovely creature,' Sabrina said, lips pursed. 'Such a body – those gorgeous proud titties, big bottom cheeks, and rippling thighs, so adorably tawny. Why, her skin looks like the softest beaten calf leather. The cunny mound is much better shorn, so pale and shiny, like marble – and her nips are quite erect! A lovely touch, in a girl about to wriggle under a spanking. I'm quite envious of you, Miss Lache, getting to spank those delicious arse pears.'

'Shall I shave my cunny close, now, miss?' said Hilary.

'I'll do it,' said Lisbeth quickly, springing to her feet. 'You relax, like a good girl, and keep your thighs wide. Shaving means everywhere – round your bumhole, too.'

She splashed Hilary's shorn cunt with water, then began to rub soap into the hillock, until she had produced a generous foam. The soap slipped over the cunt lips, mashing hard, and touching exposed pink slit flesh, making Hilary squeak that it was stingy. Ignoring her, Lisbeth pressed into the arse cleft and perineum, rubbing the wrinkled anus prune for several seconds, until Hilary's entire cunt basin wore a girdle of foam. Lisbeth squatted, and began to shave the girl's pubis, with delicate, sweeping strokes, rinsing the razor after each slice. Hilary craned to look, as the razor exposed the skin of her mound, smooth and bare. Her bottom, squashed on the side of the bath, trembled at each swish of the blade.

'It's rather exciting,' she said faintly.

Lisbeth delved between the parted thighs, into the arse cleft, then to the anus bud itself, scraping carefully round the big crimson pucker.

'Ooh,' Hilary moaned. 'That tickles.'

Lisbeth hosed her down and stood with her fingers stroking the bare-shaven hillock and playing on her cunt lips, slightly swollen, with the big pink thumb of her clitoris clearly extruded between the upper folds. Hilary breathed deeply at Lisbeth's caress and made no move to close her thighs, which were moist, with several trickles of come from her swollen gash flaps. Lisbeth squelched her nyloned thighs together, feeling a definite seep from her own tingling quim.

'Your clitty looks a tad excited, Hilary,' said Lisbeth, and Hilary blushed.

'Well, it seems erotic to be shaved down there, naked save for my corset and things,' she admitted. 'Perhaps that's why I've been frightened to do it before.'

Sabrina took a bottle of eau de cologne and splashed it on the shaven mound.

'Oh! That stings!' Hilary cried, her eyes watering.

'Cologne,' said Sabrina. 'You still smell of your beastly boyfriend's spunk. Come on, miss, time to spank you.'

Lisbeth rose and helped the shaven girl hobble back to the sofa, where Lisbeth sat, nyloned thighs proffered for Hilary's belly and cunt. Her ankles hobbled in her panties, Hilary stretched over Lisbeth's legs, her cunt mound rubbing the nylons.

'That's better,' said Lisbeth. 'Lovely and smooth.'

She felt moisture oozing from the girl's gash. With a deep breath, she raised her arm and brought her palm hard down on Hilary's trembling bare bum flans. Slap! Her hand left a vivid pink imprint on the delicately tanned skin.

'Ooh,' gasped Hilary, her head jerking up.

Lisbeth put her hand on Hilary's nape, under her tresses, and held her head down for the second spank. Slap!

'Uhh!' Hilary cried, her neck thrusting against Lisbeth's pinioning hand and her legs jerking rigid, with her ankles straining against the knotted panties.

Sabrina was positioned in her easy chair, legs crossed and ankle resting on her knee, with her skirt ridden high over her stockinged thighs, showing her garter straps and unpantied quim, directly exposed to Hilary's gaze. Her hands rested casually on the nyloned skin of her topmost thigh.

'You can spank harder than that, Miss Lache,' she purred. 'I don't think you are really hurting the girl. Ignore her gasps – spanked minxes love to overdramatise. Try closing your fingers and stiffening them into a paddle.'

Frowning, Lisbeth obeyed, and spanked the bare arse with her fingers rigid. Slap!

'Ooh! That hurts!' squealed Hilary, her fesses clenching hard, and beginning to squirm, with her entire buttocks and thighs writhing in a circular motion, which rubbed her moist cunt harder on Lisbeth's thighs.

The pinched flesh strained against her corset, whose stricture seemed tighter and more painful, as her bare bottom reddened and her naked bubbies bounced below her dangling brown mane. Slap! Slap! Lisbeth was panting, her own quim wet with come and her nylons slithering as the cunt juice trickled down her bare thigh skin into the stocking tops. Hilary's bare reddened quickly, the spanked skin glowing against the trembling tan flesh of her unspanked portion. Slap! Slap! Lisbeth spanked on the tender upper buttock.

'Ahh! That *really* hurts,' Hilary gasped.

Slap! Slap! She smacked the fleshy underfesse, and thigh tops, above Hilary's writhing nylon stockings, then

25

spanked hard on each haunch, with Hilary panting and gasping, her head jerking against Lisbeth's restraining hand, until her whole naked bottom was a mottled mass of palm prints and fingermarks. Hilary's legs trembled, rigid behind her, with her panties twitching at her ankles. Slap! Slap! Lisbeth, herself breathing hoarsely, returned to the mid-fesses, now puffing crimson. She paused, to remove her grey suit jacket, revealing her white blouse darkened with sweat at the armpits, with her bra and heaving breasts starkly outlined under the clinging fabric, moist with perspiration. Slap! Slap! She recommenced the spanking, the spanked girl writhing and drooling, with little mewls of distress, and her crimson bottom in constant squirm.

'I can't spank properly if you're going to clench all the time, in that girly fashion,' Lisbeth gasped. 'You will kindly relax your bottom after each spank.'

'Ooh, miss, haven't I taken enough?' Hilary moaned. 'It smarts dreadfully.'

'You insolent minx,' hissed Lisbeth. 'I'll be the judge of that.'

Slap! Slap! Slap!

'Oh! Ooh . . .' Hilary whined, as her glowing spanked arse clenched and squirmed.

Cigarette smoke drifted into Lisbeth's nostrils. Sabrina sat, smoking, exhaling through her nose, with her skirt ridden up almost to her waist, and her hand resting on her thigh, almost at the hip, two fingers lolling idly over her shaven cunt hillock.

'Where did you get the all-over suntan, Hilary?' drawled Sabrina. 'Your bum's lovely and brown – or *was*.'

'Please, miss,' gasped the spanked girl, 'I go up on the roof with Luisa and the other girls at lunchtimes and we sunbathe naked.'

'How sweet,' said Sabrina. 'I suppose you play games.'

'What?'

Slap! Slap! Hilary's bare bum jerked.

'Ooh! Games, miss?'

'What girls do when they are naked. You know.'

'I'm sure I don't, miss.'

Slap! Slap!

'Ohh! Oh, miss, enough, please. It smarts so.'

'I'm sure you do,' drawled Sabrina. 'Girls are lustful beasts – why, you've proved it, with your smutty episode this morning. They are curious about other girls' bodies, and they like being nude, feeling each other's titties and silky skin and crevices. Don't you look at each other, feel each other's bare boobs and cunnies?'

'Well, maybe sometimes, miss, just in fun.'

Slap! Slap!

'Oh! Ouch,' wailed the squirming girl.

'And do you masturbate? Play diddling games?'

Slap! Slap!

'Ohh! Sort of.'

'There's no "sort of". You wank off, don't you?'

Slap! Slap!

'Ooh! Ahh! Yes, miss. Oh, please stop. I've admitted it.'

Lisbeth wiped sweat from her brow and looked through sweat-blurred eyes at her partner. Sabrina sat smoking and coolly masturbating! Her fingers were between her swollen cunt folds, tweaking her enormously enlarged red clitoris peeping through the quim lips, her stockinged thighs shivering just a little as oily come oozed from her gash. Lisbeth's own cunt was dripping, every spank to the girl's deliciously reddened bum sending spasms through her throbbing clitty and making her long to masturbate. She customarily wanked off upon rising and before bed, but Hilary's glorious bare was an extra-special case . . .

'Hilary,' she gasped, 'if you play naked games with Luisa and Amanda and everybody, that means you *know* they have shaved cunnies.'

'Why, yes, miss,' Hilary snuffled, 'that's . . . that's part of the fun. It's so smooth and silky to wank a girl who's bare-shaven.'

'Then you lied. You *did* know shaving is office practice,' Lisbeth snarled. 'Yet you neglected to do so.'

Slap! Slap! Slap!

'Ooh! Ahh! Enough, miss, please.'

'You cheeky madam.'

27

Slap! Slap! Slap!

'Uhh ... uhh ... please stop,' Hilary sobbed.

The girl's reddened bare danced in a squirming spasm of pain, with her shaven hillock sliding in the pool of come dripped from her cunt onto Lisbeth's sopping nyloned thighs. Slap! Slap! Lisbeth spanked her, fingers digging in the soft underfesse and perineum, her spank connecting to the shivering little anus bud, which bore the full force of her blow. Hilary squealed, her buttocks winking and clenching, to show her bare cunt flaps. Slap! Slap! Lisbeth spanked her on the swollen wet quim lips, denuded of downy hairs and glistening red between the writhing cheeks of her bottom.

'Ahh! Oh, please, no,' Hilary whimpered. 'Not there, miss.'

Sabrina smiled, lighting another cigarette, while continuing the blatant masturbation of her own glistening wet cooze, her thighs and shaven hillock gleaming with smeared come. Lisbeth squeezed her thighs, applying pressure on her stiff clit and sending jolts of pleasure through her spine and belly. Slap! Her spanking fingers smacked Hilary's writhing anus pucker.

'Ouch! Ooh! Ahh!' Hilary squealed. 'I confess, miss. I did avoid shaving – I was so proud of my minge, and the others loved to play with it as we wanked.'

'That confession merits an extra spanking,' purred Sabrina, licking her teeth as she masturbated with firm, easy strokes to her dripping cunt. 'I'd be glad to do the honours, Miss Lache.'

Sobbing, Hilary stumbled to her feet, from which Sabrina ripped the knickers. She dragged the girl by her hair towards the sofa.

'Please, miss,' sobbed Hilary, 'may I take off my corset? It hurts awfully, when my bottom's wriggling under spanks. I know it's real shame to be spanked completely bare, but it would be so much more comfortable.'

'You certainly may not,' snarled Sabrina. 'Belly down on the floor, girl!'

'Ooh ... ooh ...' Hilary snuffled, as she stretched face down on the carpet.

Sabrina placed her foot at the small of Hilary's back, then leaned down and began to pull her corset strings, lacing her even tighter.

'Oh! That hurts, miss. I can't bear it,' Hilary gasped. 'I can hardly breathe. For pity's sake, miss.'

'Be quiet,' hissed Sabrina, lacing the girl to the corset's minimum width. 'That's scarcely down to twenty inches. You can take far tighter than that.'

Hilary's trembling bottom and bubbies were thrust into swollen, straining melons by the biting vice of the corset. Dragging the girl by her hair, Sabrina made her bend over, with her arms stretched, hands clasping the back of the sofa and legs spread wide, so that her arse cleft and the dripping cunt lips were on full view. Her dangling breasts trembled, their nipples stiffly erect. Sabrina lifted her skirt and unclipped her garter belt, releasing her stockings from their straps. She perched on Lisbeth's desk and unrolled her come-slimed stockings, then stood, bare thighs gleaming with smeared come below her cunt lips, while she swished her sussies, bunched into a flail. The quirt of four rubber garter straps whirred in the air, their metal buckles flashing.

'Rubber straps? Awfully heavy, for sussies,' Lisbeth said.

'A girl must always be prepared,' Sabrina replied, with a wink. 'Hilary, on tiptoes, please, and hold. Legs absolutely straight back. It's a tiny bit more painful that way, because you can't wriggle quite so much.'

She tapped Hilary's inside stocking top, making her spread wider, until her straightened legs were almost at right angles and the swollen, pendant cunt flaps hung clear of her thighs. Denuded of Hilary's thick foliage of cunt hair, the lips swayed, glistening like dew-fresh rose petals. Hilary's legs trembled, making her stocking tops sag, slowly unpeeling from her shivering bare thigh. She turned to stare at the four rubber garter straps, transformed into a flail.

'Please, miss,' she whined, 'you said a spanking. That's whipping.'

'Do you want to go back to the dole queue?' Lisbeth snapped, her own legs trembling as she gazed at Hilary's upturned bare bottom, glowing red from her spanks.

A seep of come moistened the inside of Lisbeth's thighs, tickling her so that she lowered her hand to scratch, slid it under her skirt, and gasped, as her fingers touched her heavily swollen clitty bud. Oily hot come oozed from her cunt lips over her wrist, as she began to rub the stiff nubbin. She parted her cooze lips, and began to wank off quite blatantly. *There's nothing wrong in diddling. All girls do, and we're all girls.*

'You know I don't, miss,' the girl sobbed.

Making no secret of her masturbation, Lisbeth smiled at Sabrina. 'Then chin up and give us a good show, Hilary,' she murmured.

Sabrina raised her quirt and brought it down hard on the girl's spread bare buttocks. The thongs lashed the shivering meat of her mid-fesse, clinging to the reddened flesh, before sliding away. Thwap!

'Ooh! God, that hurts,' Hilary wailed.

Her bottom clenched and began to wriggle, the naked fesses churning, while her outstretched legs strained on tiptoe, the thigh and calf muscles rippling as she shuddered. Four bright weals marked her bare, with livid indentations where the strap buckles had flogged her. Thwap! Thwap! Two rapid, swirling strokes lashed each haunch in turn, striping the tender skin with deep red bruises. Lisbeth's thumb waggled on her throbbing clitty, her skirt half raised to show Sabrina her naked cunt. Come poured from her winking gash flaps as she masturbated.

'Ahh!' Hilary shrieked, her flogged crimson bare in constant squirm, with the whipped arse globes writhing in a desperate, squelching caress. 'My bum's on fire! It hurts so very much . . . please, please tell her to stop, miss! It's a real whipping, and I've never been whipped before. I really can't take it.'

'I believe you must,' hissed Lisbeth, bending to an inch from Hilary's pain-wracked face. 'And you really want it, don't you?'

Thwap! Thwap! The girl's bare bum jerked in agony.

'Ooh! Oh . . .' she sobbed.

Thwap! Thwap!

'Ahh . . .'

'Don't you?'

Come seeped from Hilary's writhing gash flaps. Thwap! Thwap! The weals wriggled like snakes on her pouting bare cheeks.

'Oh! Ah! Yes, miss, yes . . .'

'Carry on whipping her, Miss Stuart-Bossi,' gasped Lisbeth, masturbating.

3

Gagging for It

Rush-hour traffic growled faintly in the heat haze, far below them. It was that time when London shimmered in an unearthly reality, midway between the bustle of the day, and the mysteries of the night to come. The shafts of waning sunlight illuminated Hilary's bare, wriggling bottom, as Sabrina's whip lashed the crimson globes. Thwap! Thwap!

'Ahh!'

The rubber straps snaked across her buttocks, raising fresh crimson weals on the spanked flesh.

'Ohh . . . have pity, miss,' Hilary groaned, amid her tears.

Her legs quivered on straining white tiptoes, the knees buckling after each cut, then jerking rigid as a fresh lash wealed her bottom. Sweat dripped from her breasts, their firm jellies swaying and bouncing above the corset rim, biting a raw welt into the bubbies' underflesh. Her stockings drooped at her ankles; between her spread bum cheeks, her dangling cunt flaps oozed rivulets of come, dripping onto the carpet and spraying, as her hips and bottom wriggled, to slime her quivering thigh skin. Thwap! Thwap!

'Ooh! Oh, please, miss, I need to piddle. Can't I stop for a wee?'

'Silence, slut,' hissed Sabrina.

'But I'm bursting, miss. My corset is squeezing me so hard, my tummy really hurts, and I don't think I can hold it in.'

Lisbeth paused in her masturbation and placed an empty copper waste bin beneath Hilary's squirming bum. Her own thighs were glazed with come, streaming from her wanked cunt, with her skirt well up and her bottom and gash quivering. Sabrina had her skirt fluttering as she whipped her victim, and her free palm cupping her bare fesses. Lisbeth saw Sabrina's naked cunt, glistening with seeped juice, and frigged her clitty harder. It was all happening so fast! For so long she had yearned to see that bulging slice of Sabrina's, yearned to kneel before it, cover it with kisses and drink her come. But the necessary discretion of her sapphism restrained her. Only once had she lost control, with that teasing lesbian *bitch*, Dorcas Gunn, at school. Just the sight of her nude body reduced Lisbeth's cooze to hot gushing wetness, even as she was squirming under Dorcas's brutal cane, for Dorcas liked to cane in the nude – but she had vowed never to repeat the shame, the hurt, after her cruel betrayal.

Dorcas hoped that, as Lisbeth was a big girl, she bore no hard feelings for her welts. The longed-for invitation had come – a private seduction, in Dorcas's chamber, with Lisbeth all excited and moist in her panties, wearing her Sunday best green uniform, the skirt pleats ironed razor sharp, over her very best white nylon stockings. Anticipation had turned to suspicion as Dorcas led her to a faraway Nissen hut 'for a party'; then horror, as she saw a schoolgirl naked, strapped to the 'penance board', as Dorcas leeringly called it, with a boy, wearing only a bulging jockstrap, flogging her bare bum with a school cane. Other jockstrapped boys watched, chuckling and drooling, and Lisbeth recognised the rugger team, brawny seniors from Bedminster Boys' Academical. Dorcas pinioned her arms, and she watched the rugger men shed their jockstraps, and the first of them mount the squirming red buttocks of the caned girl, parting her flogged cheeks, and plunging his massive cock into her anus!

'No! No!' Lisbeth squealed.

'You're next up, girly,' Dorcas drawled, 'the penance board is yummy fun for gels who play at being lesbos.'

Lisbeth watched the creamy white stuff bubbling from the girl's bum cleft, as the rugger man spurted inside her bum. The male dismounted, and another took his place, to tup her squirming anus just as cruelly. Lisbeth's pleated skirt was lifted, a hand was inside her panties, and Dorcas was masturbating her clitty, throbbing inside her wet cunny folds, with the lesbian's fingers probing her slit. Come gushed from Lisbeth's gash, as she watched the girl buggered.

'You're gagging for it, bitch,' Dorcas sneered.

'No! It's awful!' Lisbeth gasped.

'Your cooze says otherwise, slut.'

Lisbeth moaned as she pissed herself, a heavy jet of steaming pee filling her panties, and flooding her nice stockings, as Dorcas jeered, calling her horrid names. Somehow, Lisbeth broke free, and ran and ran, away from the awful scene, with come and piss slopping her panties as she fled.

She shuddered briefly, casting the vile memory away. Now, Sabrina masturbated coolly before her eyes, and seemed amused, or tolerant, at Lisbeth's own blatant wank. It was harder and harder to control her savage impulse to embrace Sabrina, squeeze her and rub quims in a mutual frot. Did Sabrina feel . . . *that* way? Or was this just girly playfulness? Thwap! Thwap! Hilary's glowing bare bottom squirmed.

'Oh, God! Stop, please!' shrieked the flogged girl.

There was a loud, hissing tinkle as a powerful stream of piss spurted from her cooze and sprayed the sides of the copper bucket.

'Noo . . .' she wailed.

The piddle continued for nearly a minute, filling the pail half full, while her whipping continued. The lashes made her bum quiver so much that a spray of piss wetted Lisbeth's thighs and soiled Hilary's own legs, dribbling down to foul her bedraggled stockings. Sabrina laughed.

'The mucky pup,' gasped Lisbeth. 'Whip her bum raw, Miss Stuart-Bossi.'

'Yes, Miss Lache,' said Sabrina.

As her beating continued, Hilary held position well, despite the constant buckling of her knees, as the rubber tongues etched livid weals on her skin. Her bottom was well puffed up, the crimson bruises darkening to purple, and her whole croup, from haunch to underfesse, mottled with dark scars of the garter straps' buckles. She whined and mewled, sobbing, with drool running down her chin from her lips, tightened in a rictus of agony. Thwap! Thwap! Her legs and back shuddered, as her flogged bum clenched.

'Ohh!' she wailed. 'How much more, miss? I must have taken fifty, at least.'

'Not quite,' panted Sabrina.

Thwap! Thwap! Thwap!

'Ooh! Ahh!'

'There, that's fifty.'

Breasts heaving, Sabrina lowered her quirt, transferred her hand from buttock to quim, and began a vigorous masturbation, winking at Lisbeth.

'Going to come soon?' she panted.

'You know I can't help it, Sabrina,' gasped Lisbeth. 'You are wicked.'

Lisbeth stroked the puffy ridges of Hilary's bottom, her fingernails clawing the deepest welts, so that Hilary squealed.

'Please, miss, is it over? May I dress?' the girl gasped.

'My, you've a blotchy arse,' Lisbeth purred. Her hand slipped between Hilary's thighs, and felt her cunt. 'You're wet,' she sniffed. 'Disgustingly wet, as though your flogging excited you.'

'*Excited* me, Miss Lache? Oh, that's cruel. How could any girl enjoy such pain?'

Lisbeth raised her come-slimed fingers to Hilary's nose, and smeared the girl's juices on her face.

'Oh, don't,' Hilary whimpered.

'Well, it's not over,' Lisbeth said. 'You still stink of your boyfriend's spunk, and now your own water. You need cleaning. Stay standing, with your legs straight.'

She wrenched Hilary by the hair, forcing her to bend double, and pushed her head into the piss-filled bucket. Lisbeth watched Hilary's buttocks quiver, as her head sank under the piss, and rubbed her own clitty, gasping at the electric pleasure from her wank.

'Urrgh . . .' Hilary gurgled, bubbles foaming in the piss.

'At least we've got her quim looking ladylike,' drawled Sabrina, 'but the slut hasn't been punished enough for her deception. Don't you want to be naughty, Lisbeth, before you depart for Rum Hole?'

In the rays of the setting sun, Hilary's nude body gleamed golden, with the welts on her bare vividly outlined in purple and crimson by the warm pink light. Lisbeth's wanked cunt gushed come as she masturbated faster and faster. She pulled Hilary's hair, wrenching the girl's head from the piss.

'Urrgh,' Hilary spluttered, gulping air, until Lisbeth forced her under again.

There was a knock on the door.

'Is that you, Clara?' called Sabrina.

'Yes, miss,' said the maid, from outside.

'Enter,' Sabrina bade.

'Sabrina, wait –' Lisbeth began, smoothing down her skirt over her dripping cunt.

Clara teetered into the office on her high heels and gasped as she saw Hilary's flogged bottom. Quickly, she recovered her composure and, curtsying, demurely handed Sabrina a package in brown paper wrapping.

'I hope you don't mind my running an errand for Miss Stuart-Bossi, miss,' she said to Lisbeth.

Without bothering to conceal her naked quim, Sabrina took over Hilary's immersion, wresting her mane from Lisbeth's grasp, and told Lisbeth to open the package. Trembling, Lisbeth undid the wrapping, and gasped, seeing an enormous black rubber dildo with waist-straps.

'It's for you,' Sabrina said. 'I knew you'd want it, so I sent Clara to a little shop down the King's Road. Don't be shy, put it on. Clara won't mind.'

She chucked Clara under the chin.

'N-no, miss,' said Clara, blushing. 'It was awfully thrilling, going into that shop, and buying it, wearing my uniform. Everybody thought I was one of . . . well, you know.'

'And aren't you?' Sabrina drawled, touching Clara's bare bottom, under her skirtlet.

Clara blushed. Lisbeth stroked the shiny rubber dildo, hard and striated with bumps.

'Might as well remove your skirt, Lisbeth,' Sabrina purred. 'I'm sure Clara's seen it all before. I'll do the same, for comfort. Let's make a meal of it.' She bared her teeth. 'Clara, would you . . .?'

The maid knelt, and unfastened Sabrina's skirt, taking it clean off, to reveal Sabrina's bare arse and cunt, shiny with come.

'I was just having a wank,' said Sabrina, casually. 'Perhaps you'd like to join us, Clara? Hilary has been rather naughty, and is getting what for.'

Clara licked her lips.

'Yes, please, miss, I'd like that very much. If Lis– if Miss Lache permits.'

'Yes,' blurted Lisbeth, 'I permit.'

Her heart thumped: it was true, *all* girls liked sapphic girlplay, wanking off and cuddling and squelching.

'Hilary is gagging for it,' Sabrina said. 'That's why I had you fetch this toy, Clara. Our Hilary is shy but manipulative – she *wants* to be thrashed and tupped. Miss Lache understands, don't you, Miss Lache?'

Lisbeth nodded, licking her lips.

A dream come true. I should resist, but I can't. Clara too! Oh, Dorcas, if you knew . . . I'm not just playing at sapphism, I love girls, the feel of their smooth naked bodies, the taste of their come, the jiggle of their bare bums and breasts. And now this, Hilary, shamed and flogged, with her striped bottom glowing so sweetly, so thrillingly . . . she wants it, I know she does. Why does her beaten bare excite me? I can't resist, don't want to.

Lisbeth panted, not protesting, as her maid loosened and removed her skirt, baring her cunt basin like Sabrina's.

Their quims glistened wet, while their naked arses pouted, pert and full and ripe, with the satin skins shivering.

'Miss's bottom looks awfully beautiful, if I may say so,' Clara said coyly.

'You may, Clara,' Lisbeth blurted, rubbing her bared portion.

Breathing heavily, she allowed the maid to strap the rubber dildo around her hips, feeling the weight, looking at the monstrous protuberance between her thighs and gasping as the secondary knob of the clitty-tickler made contact with her throbbing nubbin. The dildo's lower shaft quickly slimed with Lisbeth's flowing come. Still gurgling and spluttering in the piss-bucket, Hilary spread her thighs, allowing the dildo's tip to nuzzle her pendant cunt flaps. Lisbeth took a deep breath, tightened her fesses and pushed the tube into Hilary's pouch from behind. It slid in easily, oiled by the girl's gushing come. Clara's fingers were discreetly under her skirtlet, flouncing up the frilly chiffon and playing with her own cunt. She smiled at Lisbeth.

'Give her a good seeing to, miss,' she whispered. 'Is it all right if I wank, as you fuck her? And, begging your pardon, when we're alone, I'd love you to do *me*.'

'Yes,' murmured Lisbeth. 'Wank off, Clara, and remove your skirt and panties, if you wish.'

'I'm not wearing panties, miss,' Clara lisped.

'Ahh,' Hilary groaned, buttocks shuddering and teats slapping together, as Lisbeth plunged the dildo hard to her wombneck and began to fuck her.

It all seemed to happen in dreamlike slow motion. The noise of the traffic below was stilled; the only sounds in the office were the gurgling of Hilary's head, as Lisbeth's dildo slammed her wombneck, with the sucking plop of the giant rubber shaft slamming in and out of Hilary's clinging wet gash; the squelching flick of Sabrina's fingernails between her cunt lips, tweaking her swollen pink clitty.

Clara's maid uniform slithered to the carpet and the girl was nude, but for shoes, stockings and corset. She unhooked her bra and let her heavy bubbies spring bare. She knelt behind Lisbeth's buttocks, which heaved, as Lisbeth fucked the whimpering Hilary. Lisbeth squealed as the point of Clara's tongue penetrated her cunt lips, with the maid's face pressed to her pumping bare bum. With little clucks of pleasure, Clara tongued Lisbeth's clitty. There was a rush of liquid and a gasping groan from Hilary, as Sabrina wrenched her head from the piss bucket and applied the girl's dripping face to her cunt.

'Lick me, bitch,' said Sabrina sweetly, lighting a cigarette and blowing smoke on Hilary's face.

Hilary's tongue flickered on the wet folds of Sabrina's gash and began to lick the clitty and slit in long sweeps of her tongue, while her bubbies shook at each thrust of Lisbeth's dildo to her own cunt. She mewled and moaned as her throat bobbed, swallowing Sabrina's come. Her own thighs glistened with the come pouring from her fucked gash. The evening sunlight bathed all the girls in warm, pink softness. Their naked limbs, cunts and buttocks glistened with sweat, forming tiny iridescent rainbows on the bare girlskin.

'Mm . . . mm . . .' Hilary moaned, licking Sabrina, who still puffed casually on her cigarette.

Lisbeth's thighs, slapping as she fucked the squirming girl, smacked Clara's face, pressed to her own cunt lips, and slimed with the juice from Lisbeth's gash.

'Oh, I'm going to come,' Hilary whimpered. 'Fuck me harder, miss, please fuck harder . . .'

Sweat poured from Lisbeth's brow as she pumped her loins, thrusting the come-slimed dildo to the root of Hilary's writhing pouch. Her belly fluttered, as Clara's tongue flicked and caressed her throbbing, swollen nubbin, extruded from the folds of her cunt, like a hot raw cherry. Suddenly, Clara's tongue withdrew, and Lisbeth faltered in her fucking, only to squeal with pleasure, as the girl's tongue slid into her anus pucker and began to probe her squelching anal elastic. Lisbeth wriggled her bum as she felt the tongue penetrate her anus to its full depth, tickling and teasing, until her anal pucker expanded to accommodate the hot pink flesh and clasped the tongue with the sphincter muscle. Behind her, Clara panted hoarsely, with her fingers vigorously masturbating her erect clitty, and come dribbling down her nylons from her squeezed cunt lips. Sabrina growled in her throat as she pressed Hilary's piss-wet face to her cunt.

'Yes,' she gasped. 'Tongue me hard, bitch, swallow my come.'

Hilary's cooze poured with juice; Sabrina held her cigarette end under the girl's fucked cunt, and it fizzled to extinction.

'Urrgh . . .' Hilary murmured, her face slapping against Sabrina's cooze. 'Oh, yes, fuck me, Miss Lache, I'm almost there . . .'

The clitoral tweaker rubbed against Lisbeth's nubbin, sending shudders of electric spasm through her fluttering belly, as her loins slammed the dildo into Hilary's womb-neck. Her blouse was sodden with sweat, outlining her bubbies, heaving and bouncing under the wet, translucent fabric, with her bra cups equally soaked and transparent. Lisbeth's nipples stood erect as huge red plums, while sweat dripped from her brow onto Hilary's writhing corset. The power of her prong electrified her, the power to pound another girl's intimate hole . . .

'Oh, yes,' Lisbeth gasped. 'Yes, tongue me, tickle my bum, Clara, you minx. It's so good . . .'

The maid had her tongue fully inside her anus, and reamed the twitching elastic, probing and tickling, as she licked Lisbeth's copious arse grease. Orgasm welled in Lisbeth's belly, the delicious sweet honey filling her fluttering cunt and setting her titties tingling, as come poured from her gash, spraying her thighs and the wealed, twitching buttocks of the fucked girl squirming beneath her.

'Oh, I'm going to . . . oh, yes, I am,' Hilary yelped. 'Oh . . . oh! Oh!'

'*Ahh* . . .' Sabrina grunted, in her own spasm.

'Mm . . . Mm . . . *Ahh* . . .' mewled Hilary, while the panting Clara squealed in her own wanked climax.

'Ooh! It's so good . . .'

'Do me . . .'

'Ahh!'

'Ooh!'

'Ohh . . . ahh . . .'

'Yes!'

The four girls orgasmed, filling the warm air with sobs, gasps and squeals, as come spurted from their wanked cunts.

Sabrina lit a cigarette, and exhaled noisily. 'Feel chastened, Hilary?' she drawled.

'Oh!' gasped the bedraggled girl. 'Whipped, and drenched in pee, and done with that horrid rubber thing, and swallowing your come, miss? I've never been so humiliated.'

'Not even when your motorcycle romeo was giving you one up the bum?' said Sabrina.

'You know?' Hilary gasped.

Withrawing her dildo from the girl's cunt with a sticky plop, Lisbeth gazed in astonishment at the raw, whipped buttocks, and the powerfully enlarged anal pucker between the arse flans.

'I didn't know,' she said. 'In the . . . bumhole? But that's grotesque.'

'Walls have ears,' Sabrina replied. 'He was buggering her, all right. But, Hilary, wasn't your buggery more shameful than this all-girl submission?'

Hilary's flushed face creased in a coy, sly smile. 'Oh, no, miss,' she said. 'This was *much* better.'

In the aeroplane to Nassau, over the Atlantic, Lisbeth had plenty of time to read or watch a film, and allowed the pretty young stewardess to ply her with a decent dry champagne, so that she felt pleasantly light-headed. The stewardess wore a tight little uniform with a delicious crimson pleated skirtlet, a micro-skirt really, which showed off her long, coltish legs in clinging pink sheen nylons. She was Lusnydd from Carmarthen, awaiting her twentieth birthday. When she leaned over to serve, Lisbeth smelled her powerful animal scent and glimpsed her big tan titties, bare and straining under a tight pink bra. Lusnydd explained that since there were only a few passengers in first class, pampering Lisbeth gave her something to do, and she hoped she didn't mind. The meal was superb, with lobster and crayfish and everything, and a choice of wines, a lovely creamy strawberry pudding, and afterwards more champagne. At every visit, Lusnydd's eyes fixed Lisbeth's, and her big, tightly skirted bottom waggled in front of her face just a fraction longer than was really necessary.

Lisbeth's mind drifted back to the lustful, troubling events of a few days before. The following day, the office had functioned as though the scene had never happened, and even the loyal Clara, in bed with Lisbeth, with her short nylon nightie pulled up to her neck, put her finger over Lisbeth's lips when she tried to mention it.

'Girls will be girls, miss,' she murmured.

Sabrina, going over the details of Lisbeth's Bahamian mission, smiled wickedly, and told a story about two teenage girls found squelching in the nude on Acklins Island: the enraged villagers strung them from trees, caned them naked and invited every boy on the island to fuck them.

'That's terrible!' Lisbeth blurted.

'It certainly cured them of lesbianism,' Sabrina said airily. 'All girls will go that way, especially in hot climates. Look at Hilary – it wasn't your fault you gave way to your lesbian lusts – the slut was gagging for it.'

'Sabrina, I'm *not* a lesbian,' Lisbeth retorted. 'I like to experiment, that's all. I can control myself.'

'Perhaps,' said Sabrina, lighting a cigarette, and eyeing Lisbeth, while casually raising her skirt, to scratch the naked lips of her unpantied cunt.

She laughed as Lisbeth's eyes moistened. Lisbeth unconsciously licked her lips at the sight of Sabrina's juicy, gleaming bare cooze.

'But you aren't a manipulative submissive like her, Lisbeth, are you? So you're in no danger.'

Putting away the memory, Lisbeth frowned. Her brief was to tease and enthral Mr de Hazebrouck with the aid of her luggage of frillies and skimpies and sexy underthings, until he signed on the dotted line for LaBo Associates. She must not give way to temptation, nor reveal any lustful chink in her armour as the cool international businesswoman. A chaste holiday in paradise ... yet, as the aircraft whined, Lisbeth daydreamed of Hilary's luscious bare buttocks, squirming under Sabrina's cruel whipping, and shifted in her seat, conscious of the seeping moisture at her quim.

The images flashed back to her – her glorious feeling of dominance, fucking the whimpering girl's cooze with her monstrous strap-on; Sabrina masturbating, as Hilary tongued her and swallowed her copious spurts of girl come; Clara's tongue reaming Lisbeth's bumhole. Lisbeth began to moan in her doze, and her fingers extended under her travel rug to her naked quim, sopping and knickerless under her cool cotton skirt. As she gazed at the fleecy clouds beneath the aircraft, she felt alone, cocooned in the heat of her growing desire.

Masturbation is no crime. Clara knows I masturbate every day, and Sabrina admits frequent wanks clear her head for business. Spanking's no crime, either . . . . but I mustn't think of perverse things. Perhaps I'll have to wank off even more than usual, at Rum Hole, to quell my lusts.

Lusnydd hovered around Lisbeth's seat, patting her bobbed hair, hitching up her skirt, or lifting it right up to examine her nylons for rips, showing her garter straps and the ripe wedge of her cunt hillock swelling in her pink satin panties. She apologised to the watching Lisbeth with a coy, all-girls-together smile that was not really an apology, as if she *knew* Lisbeth was stroking her clitty – yes, *masturbating* – as she watched the girl provocatively fuss with herself. Lisbeth wore a black business suit, with cream blouse and nylons, and worried it made her look older than her age. Lusnydd tucked her blouse into her skirt, smoothing it down over her flat belly and touching her breasts, as though to adjust her bra cups, which seemed to need no adjustment. The movement emphasised the swelling of her teat globes, with the hard acorns of her nipples just visible through the thin bra fabric.

43

Lisbeth's face warmed in a blush, as lustful juice seeped from her cunt. She tried to return to her book, but it was no use. Lusnydd's pink stockings had lovely crimson seams down the back, waggling as she walked, in time with the swaying of her ripe arse pears. Outside the aeroplane, a brilliant sun in a blue sky shone on the adorable fluffy clouds, as though they were already in the balminess of the tropics. Trembling, Lisbeth put down her book, picked up her purse and asked the girl, slightly shorter than herself, for directions to the lavatory. Lusnydd showed her, lips pouting in a smile and with a toss of her lustrous auburn hair. Their eyes met for an electric moment.

Lisbeth did not lock the door but kicked off her shoes, then stripped off her skirt and blouse. She settled on the seat, wearing only bra, sussies and stockings, for a long, steaming piddle. When she had flushed away her golden pond, she extracted a pink electric razor and cord from her purse and opened the door a fraction. The stewardess was not far away.

'I wonder if you could help?' Lisbeth said. 'My electric razor – where it plugs in – I'm a bit of a dunce at these things.'

Smiling, Lusnydd entered the cubicle, locking the door behind her. She glanced at Lisbeth's naked cunt, and her smile widened at the tube-shaped, obviously phalliform, razor.

'Very sexy,' she murmured.

'It's a designer razor,' said Lisbeth, blushing. 'Giulio Ferracci.'

'Mm . . . expensive. And rather male chauvinist. Men are so good at making girls want toys.'

Her smile made Lisbeth feel so silly! After plugging in the cord, Lusnydd switched on the razor. She waved the buzzing cylinder at Lisbeth.

'Armpits and legs, miss?' she said. 'I'll do you, if you like. All part of the service.'

'Well, not really,' said Lisbeth. 'I waxed yesterday – it's my – down there, you see. I don't wax, but shave.'

'You get a better shave from an old-fashioned razor,

miss,' Lusnydd said. 'These disposable Femshaves are quite good, and I use them myself.'

Amid the free toiletries offered to first-class passengers was a dispenser of wrapped razors.

'I fear I'm a bit clumsy, you know . . . down there,' said Lisbeth, looking the girl in the eyes.

Lusnydd licked her teeth. 'The more reason for me to do you, miss,' she replied softly, putting down the electric razor, still buzzing. 'If you'll lift one leg, and spread your thighs wide – I take it you want full service, shaving the whole crevice.'

'Yes, please,' murmured Lisbeth faintly, 'full service.'

She stood beside the lavatory with her foot on the washbasin and her slit lips stretched wide, showing pink, moist flesh inside her pouch. Already, a trickle of come moistened her thigh backs and perineum, and she knew the girl had seen it. Her clitty bulged, stiffening, through the upper folds of her cooze and began to throb, as Lusnydd's soft fingers stroked her outer cunt lips. She gasped as she felt the fingertips lather the bare hillock of her cunt with shaving foam and stroke, accidentally on purpose, the swelling clitty bud.

Lusnydd *must* have seen the come seeping from her quim. It was thrilling to be bared and somehow defenceless before this beautiful uniformed girl, shining razor in her hands. The blade descended on Lisbeth's hillock, scraping her flesh in smooth, firm strokes, with Lusnydd pausing to rinse it. When the hillock shone bare, Lusnydd went to work on the perineum and arse cleft, tickling Lisbeth as she shaved around the anus bud, with the razor's handle frequently stroking her pucker. She grasped each cooze flap in turn, to shave its base.

'You scarcely needed foam, miss,' she whispered. 'You're lovely and oily. All wet, I mean, from your quim.'

The two girls gazed at each other, lips slack and drooling. Suddenly, Lusnydd's face was between Lisbeth's thighs, her lips on Lisbeth's erect clitty, with her tongue darting in and out of the come-spewing slit.

'Oh! You cheeky bitch! Oh, yes, that's so good,' Lisbeth moaned. 'Do me, Lusnydd . . .'

'I knew you were sapphic, miss,' the girl gasped. 'One of us ... Never heard of the mile-high club? Doing it airborne? Some of the really *dirty* stewardesses keep a score.'

In her Welsh accent, the word slithered out as '*doohty*'. Lusnydd had her skirt up and a hand inside her panties, masturbating, as she licked the squirming Lisbeth. Lisbeth shuddered as the girl expertly tongued her stiff clitty, with slurping sucks on the cunt flaps. Lusnydd's throat bobbed as she swallowed Lisbeth's gushing come.

'I'm not lesbian,' Lisbeth faintly protested. 'I just like ...'

'You like what all girls like,' murmured Lusnydd, gurgling at Lisbeth's gash, with come sliming her nose and lips. 'We all want a good cunt-licking, and ...'

'Oh! Don't stop,' Lisbeth panted. 'I'm coming, oh, do me, yes, *yes* ...'

'And a licking somewhere else,' gasped the girl, as Lisbeth's cunt sprayed come over her face and erupted in a wriggling, fluttering orgasm.

Lusnydd grabbed the buzzing electric razor and slipped the plastic cap over the blades. Jumping onto the lavatory seat, she straddled Lisbeth, pinning her to the mirror, and pulled down her own come-soaked pink panties. Under her hairless hillock, her erect clitty stuck from the folds of her gash like a thick pink worm. She parted Lisbeth's cunt flaps and rammed the vibrating tube into her slit, until it slapped her wombneck. Lusnydd pressed her cunt against Lisbeth's, their erect clitties touching, and began to squelch, grinding her hips against Lisbeth's belly, and pressing the razor so that it disappeared inside Lisbeth's slit. Her bare bum jerked as she clit-fucked, and come streamed down her rippling nyloned thighs. Fucking vigorously, Lusnydd began to gasp harshly, until her come sprayed Lisbeth's cunt, and she shrilled in orgasm. Panting, she got down and handed a pearl-handled hairbrush, bearing the airline insignia, to Lisbeth, who had recommenced masturbating her own clitty with the electric razor buzzing inside her pouch.

'My licking, miss,' she gasped.

'What?'

'Spank my bare,' whimpered Lusnydd. 'I need it so badly.'

'That's a bit kinky,' Lisbeth blurted.

'Please, miss. Go on. All girls need their bums spanked.'

'Oh, gosh. Why? Well, you've asked for it.'

Lisbeth stood, and raised the hairbrush over Lusnydd's trembling bare buttocks, framed by her risen skirt and lowered wet knickers. She slapped hard, in mid-fesse. Vap! A livid bruise instantly pinked the buttocks.

'Uhh . . .' Lusnydd gasped.

Vap!

'Yes . . .'

Vap! Vap!

'Ahh! Gosh, it hurts. Oh, wank me off, miss, *please*,' Lusnydd moaned.

As she spanked the reddening bare, Lisbeth thrust her fingers into Lusnydd's slimy pouch and tweaked her clitty, while ramming her fingers into the wombneck. Lusnydd gurgled as come sluiced from her cunt.

'Yes . . . spank harder, miss,' she gasped. 'I'm gagging for it.'

Vap! Vap!

'*Ooh*! Yes! Gosh, it hurts.'

Vap! Vap!

'Ahh!'

Lisbeth spanked her over sixty slaps, with the heaving bare moons covered in crimson blotches. The razor still buzzed inside her juicing cunt. As she wanked the groaning girl to spasm, she touched her own throbbing clitty once, then twice, yelping, as a fresh climax overwhelmed her, come spurting from her gash to drench her nylons. The aircraft bucked and a sign flashed, ordering them to return to their seats. Lisbeth extracted the razor from her slit and, trembling, dressed herself, while Lusnydd, sighing contentedly, slid her wet panties over her bruised red bottom.

'That makes thirty-nine,' she chortled, blowing Lisbeth a kiss as she slipped out of the door.

Blushing crimson, and with her come-soaked nylons slithering at her thighs, Lisbeth managed to regain her seat and swigged gratefully at her glass of champagne.

The shame! That beastly slut used me for her own perverted pleasure! I must never degrade myself, never, ever lose control again.

4

Shot in Your Juice

Lisbeth was fresher than she had expected, yet had no desire to do anything more strenuous than sip her cold fruit juice and watch the hubbub of Nassau airport as she waited for the connecting flight to Acklins Island. Her black suit, she thought, was perhaps not the right attire for this sun-bright place, with its crowd in gaudy pastel colours. She had no time to be mildly annoyed at a male shadow hovering over her, before its owner sat at her table, announcing that she wouldn't mind his joining her. She looked up, and saw a young black man, her own age, with gold neck-chain and watch, sporting a clinging T-shirt over slab-like chest muscles, and equally clinging jeans, which made no secret of the bulge at his crotch.

'I can see you are a person of worth,' he said, white teeth flashing. 'Not some frivolous fun-seeker, like most of our visitors. Perhaps you are in banking? I am myself, in a manner of speaking. My name is Antoine Windermere.'

Lisbeth could not take her eyes from his bulge. *God, he's massive.* She blurted that she was merely here on holiday.

'A beautiful lady like you, all alone?' he murmured, eyes twinkling, and fastened on her swelling breasts and crossed legs. 'It must be awfully sticky in those nylons – I expect you are anxious to get into your bikini, and take some sea breeze between those pretty toes.'

'I don't wear a bikini,' she said, knowing she sounded awfully snobbish. 'I have a Giulio Ferracci one-piece.'

He pressed his fingertips together.

'I can just *imagine* how lovely it is,' he said.

That was clever – praising her costume, rather than her body. She guessed what was coming, but didn't mind. He was so attentive, so flattering! And he instinctively understood how a girl's nylons would get sticky in this heat. Luckily, she was without knickers, and the air played coolly around her naked quim. Antoine claimed to be a 'beach bunny', who preyed on, or entertained, lonely women.

'Enslaving them to desire,' he said, licking his lips.

He gaily admitted he was broke, that his gold trinkets were gimcrack, and that he got money from ladies, grateful for his attentions.

'But I've never met a lady as special as you,' he drawled, parting his thighs to show his cock unmistakably stiffening.

Blushing, Lisbeth said she was waiting for a flight to Acklins Island. She was not repelled by his come-on – there was something boyishly appealing, even innocent, about his approach. The black men all around seemed to share the same insouciance, and she thought of the men she had bedded, or avoided bedding, back in Europe – exciting at first, but all, eventually, proving large of ego, obsessed with achievement and money. *Big wallet, small dick* – was it Sabrina who had sneered thus? Probably. With the Bahamians, it seemed exactly the opposite.

'Haven't you time to hang loose in Nassau?' asked Mr Windermere. 'I'll show you around . . . go to the best beaches.'

It was so tempting!

'Thank you, no,' said Lisbeth. 'I have a booking at . . . at a rather exclusive resort, in the out islands.'

Thankfully the loudspeaker announced the departure of her flight to Acklins Island. She scooped up her shoulder bag, and said goodbye to Antoine, who dismissed her with a lazy wave and a scratch of his crotch, now swollen to treetrunk proportions inside his jeans. Blushing, Lisbeth cast the bulging cock a parting look, before scurrying to the departure gate, acutely aware of the slithery, oily come that seeped into her nylons from her bare cunt lips. She could not look at the throng of males without the electric sensation that they *all* had huge cocks waiting to penetrate her moist, willing slit . . .

The departure gate was empty save for a tall ebony girl in police uniform, and Lisbeth herself. Outside on the tarmac, scorching in the afternoon heat, stood a small white propeller plane, marked 'Acklin Air'. Lisbeth put her bag on the security conveyor belt and stepped through the portal, which beeped loudly. The police girl frowned, and ordered her to repeat the procedure. The portal beeped again.

'Come this way, miss,' said the police girl, gesturing to a curtained cubicle.

'What is the problem?' Lisbeth demanded.

'I have to search you. Don't worry, he won't take off without you. You're the only passenger. Not much call for Acklin. Some very ba-a-d people in the out islands.'

Lisbeth entered the cubicle, empty, save for a wooden table. In her jaunty blue bonnet, the police girl stood taller than Lisbeth, her uniform skirt and blouse a crisp navy blue, with gold sergeant's stripes, and a short, tight skirt over shiny chocolate legs, bare, and shaved smooth. Her skin was lustrous dark satin, her age scarcely more than Lisbeth's, and her body exuded a sensuous, musky tang, both salty and fruity fresh. The tight uniform emphasised the large gourds of her breasts, firmly restrained, and the ripe pears of her buttocks, bulging under the thin cotton skirt. Her shoes were black, with navy knee-socks pulled up smartly. At her leather belt hung a wooden police baton, two feet long, and two inches thick. Her name badge read 'Sgt Cynthia Placket'.

'Strip off, please,' she drawled. The bared upper portion of her breasts trembled, as she spoke.

'I beg your pardon?'

'Everything off. It is a strip search.'

Lisbeth blushed hotly. 'This is outrageous! What if I refuse?'

Sergeant Placket leered, showing bright white teeth. 'Then I deport your big round ass back where it came from, miss.'

She folded her arms, smiling, as she scrutinised Lisbeth,

who, blushing scarlet, began to undress. She folded her jacket on the table, followed by her blouse. Her breasts trembled like jellies in their skimpy scalloped bra.

'Very nice,' drawled Sergeant Placket. 'The brassiere, I mean. Off with it, please.'

'Oh, really,' grumbled Lisbeth, but smoothly unhooked her bra and let her bare breasts spring free. 'I mean, what could I possibly be hiding there?'

'Big bulbs like that could be all sorts of things,' said the sergeant. 'The rest of it, please. Now.'

Lisbeth unpinned her skirt, and removed it. She stood in her stockings and sussies, while Sergeant Placket's lip curled.

'No panties?' She whistled. 'You must be one of those *degenerates*.'

'I certainly am not!' retorted Lisbeth.

'We'll see,' replied the sergeant, tapping her baton with casual menace. 'Now the stockings.'

Sighing, Lisbeth rolled down her stockings and undid her sussies, until she stood in the nude. Sergeant Placket ordered her to bend over the table with her arms outstretched and legs apart. Lisbeth did so, parting her thighs until she felt a cool draught from the fan caressing the lips of her slit. From her waist purse, the sergeant took a rubber glove and put it on.

'What–?' Lisbeth blurted.

'A strip search, miss. First, your asshole. It'll hurt, but don't squall and I won't take long.'

'Ooh!' Lisbeth cried, as two fingers thrust into her anus, pushing hard, and penetrated the rectum.

The girl probed right to the arse root and the entrance to her colon, and Lisbeth groaned, her bare buttocks squirming.

'Ouch! That hurts!' she panted, tears in her eyes. 'Do you get pleasure in humiliating me?'

'I'm not allowed to say, miss,' replied Sergeant Placket laconically.

She reamed Lisbeth's rectum for over a minute, before withdrawing her fingers with a sticky plop and replacing her glove, soiled by Lisbeth's arse grease, with a fresh one.

Lisbeth gasped as the police girl inserted two hard fingers into her quim, and thrust them right to her wombneck, where she began to poke, reaming Lisbeth's slit in a circular motion. Lisbeth swallowed, her breasts heaving, as her cunt began to juice.

'Satisfied?' she said, her voice trembling.

Placket did not answer, but began to stab Lisbeth's gash, withdrawing her fingers to the tip, then plunging them fully into the moistening slit. She brushed Lisbeth's swelling clitty, making her moan. Her fingers made a sucking, liquid plop as they reamed Lisbeth's pouch.

'Your pussy's wet, miss,' said Sergeant Placket coldly. 'This must excite you.'

'No, really,' lied Lisbeth.

Come trickled down her naked thighs.

'You're a mess of girl juice,' said the sergeant. 'You like a woman fingering you. I think you are one of those *lesbians*. We don't like *them*, here in the Bahamas, and I'm minded to deport you.'

Her finger touched Lisbeth's throbbing clitty, and Lisbeth jumped at the spasm of pleasure, as copious come spurted from her dripping cunt.

'Ooh . . .' she whimpered. 'No, really, sergeant, it's just that I was thinking of a man I met, a . . . a beach bunny. That's why European women come here, honestly. He was quite adorable, so well hung, *you* know, and I can't help getting wet when I think of his . . . his big sex organ. Antoine Windermere, I think his name is . . .'

'*What*?' hissed Sergeant Placket.

With a slurping squelch, her fingers left Lisbeth's cunt. There was a sound of straps unbuckled, and Lisbeth looked round, gasping, to see Sergeant Placket lift her police baton, its polished wood gleaming.

'Eyes front, bitch,' she snapped, pinioning Lisbeth's head by strong fingers on the nape of her neck.

'No . . . wait . . .' Lisbeth whimpered.

Vap!

'Ooh!' she squealed, as the heavy baton smacked her bare buttocks.

Vap!

'Oh! Stop!'

Vap!

'Ouch! Oh, you're hurting me.'

Vap! Vap!

'Ahh!'

Tears sprang to Lisbeth's eyes at the dreadful smarting, and her bottom wriggled helplessly, with her back writhing in the officer's powerful grasp. Vap! Vap! Her legs shot rigid behind her as the baton drubbed her heaving buttocks, searing her bare bum, like white-hot lances. Through her tears, she stared at the curtained walls of the cubicle, her womb of pain. Vap! Vap!

'Ohh! Don't! It really *hurts*,' wailed Lisbeth, through her floods of tears.

'It's meant to hurt, bitch,' hissed the ebony girl.

Vap!

'Ahh!'

'This is to teach you . . .'

Vap! Vap!

'Ooh! Ouch! Please . . .'

'. . . that if you want damn beach bunnies . . .'

Vap! Vap!

'Urrgh! I can't take any more.'

'. . . you leave my Antoine alone, whore!'

Vap! Vap!

'Ooh! Ahh!'

Placket lowered her baton, and Lisbeth slumped, weeping and wriggling, on the table, clutching her bruised bare bottom and slithering in the pool of come which puddled the wood beneath her cooze. Outside, the aeroplane's engines began to whine.

'Ooh! How dare you,' Lisbeth sobbed. 'I've never been so humiliated in my life.'

'There's your flight, slut,' spat the policewoman. 'Just be glad I don't deport your sorry spanked ass.'

She wrenched Lisbeth's hair, lifting her head to stare into her scarlet, tear-glazed face. 'Good luck with the beach bunnies on the damn out islands,' she drawled. 'You might get more than you bargain for.'

Lisbeth walked unsteadily across the tarmac, under the bright sun of late afternoon, and mounted the stairway into the compact aircraft, where she was welcomed by a pretty stewardess, badged as Vimella, in a vivid green tartan miniskirt, white blouse, swelled by pert, conical breasts, and a flounced tartan bow tie. The cropped curls of her sleek, shiny coif clung to her high ebony cheekbones; her long legs shimmered in white silken stockings, with gleaming, silver-buckled white sling-backs. Her waist was so slender that Lisbeth was sure she was corseted – in this heat! – and her pencil waist jutted sharply into broad hips and a pair of beautifully big buttocks, quivering like beach balls, where the waist of the miniskirt hugged her croup.

Vimella curtsied to Lisbeth and said she was the only passenger on the eight-seater plane. Lisbeth settled by a window and Vimella fastened her seatbelt for her. She watched the ground rolling away, faster and faster, until the aircraft soared over a sparkling turquoise sea. Having slept on the transatlantic flight, Lisbeth was not tired – how could she be, with her bottom smarting so abominably? Her bruises from Placket's vicious beating lanced her buttocks with sharp, searing pains, yet her clitty tingled at each throbbing smart, and her nylons were damp with a telltale seep of come from her twitching cooze lips. As she served her a frosted glass of fruit juice, Vimella saw her shift in her seat, and her rosebud lips creased in a smile, showing pearl-white teeth against her smooth ebony skin.

'Not used to the heat, miss?' she purred. 'Perhaps you'd like a shot in your juice? I gather you're bound for Rum Hole. We always give our Rum Hole customers special treatment.'

'I . . . what?'

Did I mention Rum Hole?

'A shot of rum, miss?'

'Oh. Well, why not – yes, please.'

Vimella topped up her glass with a generous pouring from a bottle labelled 'Screech'.

'It's from Newfoundland, miss,' she said, 'seventy per cent strength. It'll give you an appetite for dinner – I can cook you up a goombay omelette, if you like. It's an out-island speciality.'

'Fine,' said Lisbeth, though she was not hungry.

She looked at the gentle heave of Vimella's breasts as she spoke, and the slinky, stockinged curve of her thigh, pressed under its tartan, as she casually leant against Lisbeth's seatback. The smarting of her flogged buttocks mingled with a warm, delicious fluttering in her belly. She thought of Lusnydd's firm body, and the seep of come in her cunt grew stronger. Too much to hope for two sapphic conquests in one day – if, indeed, she had conquered Lusnydd, and not the converse – yet Vimella's lithe, dainty form tempted Lisbeth, as she fussed around the cabin, flicking dust, her ripe, muscled buttocks swaying tastily under the pretty pleated rump of her skirtlet.

From the moment I arrive at Rum Hole, I must be chaste and controlled – but I'm not there yet.

Lisbeth sipped her drink and found it delicious; yet the throbbing of her buttocks would not go away, and the smarts seemed somehow connected to her tingling clitty and the inviting bum of the pretty young hostess. Lisbeth imagined the girl's bottom raised for a beating, the pert globes naked and writhing under spanks. Her hand slipped beneath her purse, perched on her lap, and crept under her skirt hem. Her fingers slid up her stockinged thighs, the nylon becoming increasingly moist as she neared her crotch, and rolled the skirt up just a little. She stifled a gasp as her fingers touched her cunt lips, slimy with her dripped come, then pressed the throbbing clitty. Vimella was at the fore of the cabin, her back turned, and her buttocks aquiver under the tartan skirt.

Lisbeth began to masturbate to the rhythm of the smarting throbs in her whipped fesses. Come gushed copiously over her trembling fingers. She gazed at Vimella's swaying bottom, imagining those ripe ebony globes naked, whipped, and smarting like her own. Vimella furtively raised her skirtlet, and revealed her white lacy panties, very high cut and with the gusset no more than a string, so that almost the whole expanse of bare ebony buttock was exposed. Lazily, she scratched her bottom, each fesse in turn then, parting the nates, delved into her bum cleft, to scratch her anal pucker and perineum. Lisbeth wanked off faster, fingers flicking her swollen clit very rapidly. Suddenly, Vimella spun on her ankles, looked at Lisbeth, and smiled, still holding her skirt up, with her buttocks exposed. Lisbeth blushed crimson.

'Well! The heat *has* taken you,' purred Vimella. 'Lots of ladies get hot, after a shot of screech.'

She began to stroke her bared buttocks with the palm of her hand. Trembling in embarrassment, Lisbeth removed her hand from her cunt and fussed with her seatbelt, which refused to open. Vimella lowered her skirt and approached, bending over to stare Lisbeth in the eyes. She lifted Lisbeth's skirt, very slowly, until her naked quim was bared, then ran her fingertips up Lisbeth's nyloned thighs until she reached the swollen cunt folds, slimy with come, and tickled the pendant flaps. The girl's sultry perfume filled her nostrils and she gazed down Vimella's shirt front at her firm ebony teats. Lisbeth swallowed, moaning. Vimella's fingers crept to her throbbing nubbin, and flicked it with her fingernail. Lisbeth shuddered, closing her eyes.

'Oh . . .' she gasped. 'That's good.'

'You get off on girls' bare butts, miss?' murmured Vimella. 'Or their titties? You can see me bare-ass naked, if you want. But what do you *really* want? Isn't cock what all the ladies come here for?'

'No,' moaned Lisbeth, feebly fiddling with her seatbelt, which wouldn't budge. 'Please . . . I need to piddle.'

'Plenty of time for that later, miss,' said Vimella.

Vimella's fingers penetrated Lisbeth's soaking cunt and began a sensuous fingerfuck, thrusting all the way to her core and pinching the hard wombneck, while Lisbeth's bottom wriggled against the come-soaked lining of her skirt. Vimella's thumb pressed Lisbeth's hard clitty, making her gasp over the squelchy gurgles from her pulsing cunt flaps, as Vimella mashed her swollen flesh.

'Oh . . .' Lisbeth moaned. 'It's so good . . . do me, frig me, Vimella, please . . . I'm so tense.'

'You're really juicing. I think you're a lesbian,' whispered Vimella.

'No! Lisbeth cried.

'In which case, you'll want the real thing.'

Abruptly, Vimella withdrew from Lisbeth's squirming cunt, and marched to the pilot's cabin, licking Lisbeth's come from her fingers. She vanished inside, and Lisbeth heard voices and laughter. Her fingers crept back to her gash and she began to masturbate anew, her belly bursting with the desire to come. Vimella emerged again, followed by a tall young male, swaggering, in jeans and T-shirt, wearing a pilot's cap jauntily pushed back on his head. Lisbeth gasped.

'Meet captain Antoine Windermere, Acklin Air's chief pilot,' said Vimella.

'Acklin Air's only pilot,' said Antoine. 'I believe I already know the lady. What's this? Diddling on board my craft? Upsetting my crew merits a spanking.'

'How about *real* punishment, sir?' Vimella murmured, eyes sparkling.

'Now, look here –' Lisbeth blurted, struggling with her locked seatbelt.

Vimella slapped her face.

'Oh!' Lisbeth gasped.

'We have restraining equipment for fractious passengers,' Antoine drawled. 'Fetch it, Vimella.'

Lisbeth stared at the bulge of his rising erection.

'What . . . what are you going to do to me?' she whimpered.

'Give you what you want,' replied Antoine. 'Even if you don't *know* what you want.'

Vimella returned, bearing her menacing cargo. She was completely nude but for a white lace corset stayed with dark, shiny wooden struts, which constricted her belly, from the top of her full cunt hillock to just below her pouting breasts, whose nipples stood stiff as chocolate cherries. The corset narrowed her belly to scarcely more than a handspan, with its top rim poking her breasts up in a trembling dance. Her bare buttocks waggled insolently before Lisbeth's face before she bent over her, allowing her breasts to rub Lisbeth's nose, which was filled by the naked ebony girl's smoky perfume. She grasped Lisbeth's wrists, suddenly, and forced them behind the seat, where she clicked a pair of handcuffs shut.

'Oh, no ... please,' Lisbeth moaned, as Vimella's deft fingers unfastened her skirt and pulled it off.

The girl's firm hands gripped her stockinged ankles, parting the legs and raising them, despite Lisbeth's feeble kicks. She clamped a wooden yoke, like a mediaeval stocks, across Lisbeth's thighs, then married it with the bottom half, snapping the two halves shut to form a hobble, stretching Lisbeth's thighs painfully apart. She looped a thick rubber strap through a slit in the hobble, and buckled each end of the strap to the grip rail at the top of Lisbeth's seat. Lisbeth squirmed, gasping, pinioned by her seatbelt, with her feet wriggling and her thighs and cunt completely exposed. She was helpless. Vimella completed her task by reclining the seat, so that Lisbeth lay almost prone, with her legs up, trapped by the hobble, and her bare cunt winking between her quivering nylons; then swivelling it, so that the bound girl's cooze faced the aisle.

'Please, no ...' Lisbeth whimpered.

Her thigh backs were fully exposed above the lower half of her wealed buttocks. Vimella touched the bruises on her bare.

'She's taken a whaling already,' she said to Antoine.

'I can explain,' Lisbeth blurted. 'It was a terrible misunderstanding – oh! No, no, no ...'

Antoine was nude, his dark, muscled flesh entirely hairless, and his cock standing stiffly erect – far bigger than the dildo which Lisbeth had used in Hilary's cunt – with the prepuce fully withdrawn back, exposing the gleaming helmet and peehole, winking at his captive. His balls were huge shiny globes, bulging beneath his cockshaft like pomegranates.

'It's what you want, lady,' he murmured.

'No, no . . .' Lisbeth wailed, as the giant ebony cock hovered inches from her spread vulva.

Vimella poked two fingers into Lisbeth's slit, and smeared them on Antoine's glans. 'She's juicing, the bitch,' she said.

'No, please,' Lisbeth sobbed, come trickling down her bum cleft and thigh backs, from her swollen, twitching cunt lips, now glazed in gushing oily fluid.

'Your cooze doesn't lie,' said Antoine. 'You want my cock inside you, slut. Or else, you want to suck.'

His glans moved to her lips.

'Yes, make her suck you,' trilled Vimella.

The girl's hand was at her own quim, masturbating vigorously, with her pert bare buttocks trembling to the rhythm of her wank. Her quivering thighs shone with seeped come.

'No,' said Antoine, 'I can't *make* her – she must *want* to.'

'Please, don't play with me,' Lisbeth sobbed. 'I'm your prisoner, I accept that. Do whatever you wish, but please get it over.'

Antoine grasped Vimella's head, and pushed it down; the girl knelt at his waist, and began to lick his balls.

'And what do we wish, miss?' purred Antoine. 'Please tell us.'

He parted the inner lips of her cunt with his helmet, and held the glans there, bathed in her flow of come. Lisbeth's buttocks wriggled, her cunt lips closing around the stiff glans. Suddenly, with Vimella's tongue on his balls, Antoine drew his cock back.

'Don't tease,' wailed Lisbeth.

Vap! The back of Antoine's palm viciously slapped Lisbeth's naked bottom, on a broad crimson weal.

'Oh! Stop!'

'Tell us, then,' Antoine ordered.

Still masturbating, with come flowing down her bare thighs, Vimella slid her tongue up the shaft of Antoine's cock, and clamped his helmet between her lips. She thrust her head onto the rigid shaft, until her cheeks bulged and her lips were almost at his balls, then began to bob her head back and forth, sucking the cock. Vap! Antoine slapped Lisbeth's naked quim with a squelching sound, as come spurted beneath his knuckles.

'Ooh! You bastard!'

'Tell us what we want,' he said.

'You want to shame and possess me,' she gasped. 'You want to plunge your cock into my mouth, and fuck my throat, and sperm in me, and make me swallow all your cream. You want to push your cock right up my cunny, and fuck me so hard that I scream, and my pouch is gushing with juice, and I beg you to fuck me harder, and my clitty is throbbing so much, I lose all control, and climax, and your big cock makes me come and come, with the most powerful orgasm I've ever had. You want to spank and whip my bare bottom, until I'm in agony, and my pouch juices still more, and I beg you to fuck me again, split my cunny and belly with that horrid, monstrous tool, pounding rock hard, as my pouch drowns your balls in my come, and then you pour your cream into me, so much cream, that it splashes out, all over my belly and thighs, and then I have to lick your cock and balls clean, like a . . . a slave.'

Vimella's lips made a slurping sound, as Antoine pulled her by the ears off his cock, and turned her to kneel with her face at Lisbeth's gash. Her bottom stuck up in the air, and Antoine's finger parted the cheeks wide as the girl, wanking off, plunged her tongue between the folds of Lisbeth's quim. The tongue jabbed in and out of the pulsing cunt, while licking the stiff clitty at each thrust.

'Oh . . . oh, yes,' Lisbeth gasped.

'You want it, don't you?' said Antoine.

'Oh, you brute . . .'

'Want to be fucked, miss . . .'

Lisbeth's buttocks writhed as Vimella expertly licked her. Come sprayed from her tongued cunt, all over the girl's face.

'I need it,' panted Lisbeth. 'I'm so wet. Yes, Antoine, do me, please! Fuck me till I burst, fuck me so hard I scream, I need it, need your horrid huge cock inside my cunny.

Please fuck me, spurt your cream in my slit, then come some more, all over my naked breasts and my face, make me lick it up and swallow all your hot cream, fuck me, *please*.'

Antoine thrust his buttocks hard, and his cock plunged between Vimella's twitching bum flans, right into her anus. Another thrust, and he was in her up to his balls, cock filling her rectum.

'Urrgh ... yes,' groaned Vimella, sucking the lips of Lisbeth's gash. 'Do me, captain, burst my asshole with your cock, I want your sperm hot and creamy, right up my colon.'

Her lips flapped on Lisbeth's clitty as she babbled, and Lisbeth gasped aloud, her bare titties bouncing and quivering, with their strawberry nipples hardened to rigid domes.

'Yes, yes, Vimella, lick my cunny,' Lisbeth moaned. 'Lick me, girl, suck my slit, make me come ...'

Antoine began to bugger the stewardess with swift, powerful jabs to the rectum. As he fucked, he spanked her quivering arse flans with loud, heavy cracks of his palms.

'Fuck my ass, fuck me,' panted Vimella, making Lisbeth's cunt thrill with vibration. 'Spank me hard, spank my ass ... *yes!*'

Her buttocks writhed as Antoine's cock pumped her bumhole, and his spanking reddened her bare buttocks.

'Vimella, no,' groaned Lisbeth. 'You can't be serious, you can't let him fuck you *there* ...'

'Nngh! Nngh!' grunted the writhing girl. 'Cock filling my asshole, splitting me open. It's so fucking *good*.'

She removed her wanking fingers from her cunt and stuck them into Lisbeth's anus, ramming the come-slimed fingers brutally right to her arse root. Lisbeth shrieked, her bum squirming.

'Oh! It hurts!'

'It's meant to hurt,' hissed Vimella, as Antoine's hips slapped against her bare buttocks at each plunge of his cock into her arse pucker.

She began a vigorous fingerfuck of Lisbeth's bumhole, jabbing and reaming Lisbeth's rectum. Lisbeth began to moan, her bottom twitching to meet Vimella's thrusts. Come streamed from her licked cunt to glaze her arse cleft.

'Ooh! Urrgh!' Lisbeth howled. 'Oh, God, yes! It's good! I'm going to come . . .'

'You *do* want it up the ass,' Vimella spat into Lisbeth's cunt lips.

'Oh! I'm so confused,' whimpered Lisbeth through drooling lips. 'I don't know! Oh! Ahh! It's good, right in my belly, I need it, yes, yes, fuck me! Please, Antoine, won't you fuck my bumhole with your cock? Oh, please?'

Antoine continued his buggery and spanking of the squirming stewardess, who sucked Lisbeth's cunt, while her fingers squelched the arse grease oozing from Lisbeth's rectum.

'Ooh, I'm going to come,' Lisbeth moaned. 'Won't you please fuck my bum, sir? Fill my hole with that tool, so big and horrid and monstrous. Split me open with your cock, please, please . . .'

Vimella clamped her teeth on Lisbeth's swollen clitty and Lisbeth howled, a massive spurt of come spraying from her flapping cunt folds.

'Ooh! Yes!' Lisbeth gasped. 'Oh, gosh, I'm coming . . . yes, yes!'

Antoine grunted, and a fountain of sperm bubbled at the lips of Vimella's writhing anus as he spurted at her arse root. Vimella's fingers rammed Lisbeth's anus, while her free hand tweaked her own clitty, sending streams of come splashing on her rippling thighs, and her teeth clamped fiercely on Lisbeth's cunt as she yelped in her climax. Antoine withdrew his cock with a plop from the girl's anus. Vimella rose and presented her bare bum, blushing with spank-marks, to Lisbeth's face.

'You wanted his cream, miss?' she said. With a wiggle of her buttocks, she expelled a stream of sperm from her anus, to splash on Lisbeth's mouth and nose.

'Oh! Urrgh!' sobbed Lisbeth, licking the sticky cream with her tongue. 'I've never been so humiliated in all my life!'

She licked the dripping sperm until her face was clean.

'Isn't it what you wanted, bitch?' said Antoine, donning his pilot's cap.

'Your goombay omelette,' added Vimella.

'Please, let me go,' Lisbeth groaned. 'I really need to piddle.'

Vimella reached up and ripped an oxygen mask and tube from the overhead. She clapped the mask over Lisbeth's quim, then thrust the tube into her anus, pushing it all the way up, until it kissed her colon.

'Ouch! Ooh! That hurts,' Lisbeth squealed, her bum wriggling.

'Piddle, then,' said Vimella.

'You can't be serious – ooh,' Lisbeth groaned, as the girl began to squeeze her belly.

Her quim writhed, and the rubber mask filled with her piss, hissing loudly. She gasped, feeling the hot fluid disgorge into her colon. Lisbeth pissed long and hard, watching the swelling in her belly as her colon filled with piss.

'Oh, no . . .' she moaned.

Vimella removed the rubber tube, and held closed Lisbeth's anus with her fingers.

'That's cruel . . .' Lisbeth whimpered.

'Part of the service, miss,' said Vimella. 'Can I be of further assistance?'

The piss enema was warm and filling in Lisbeth's belly, and she felt her clitty begin to throb.

'Yes,' she gasped. 'Vimella – be nice – wank me off, *please*.'

5

Spanking Panties

'Goodbye, miss, and thank you for flying Acklin Air.'

'Goodbye, Vimella, and thank you.'

Lisbeth blushed as she descended the staircase into the hot tropical night. A strong sea aroma invaded her nostrils, under stars sparkling in a sky of velvet black. What else *could* she say? None of the arrogantly muscled youths lounging around the tiny airstrip would believe the truth. Or would they? She waved back to Vimella, unconsciously licking her lips. Vimella *was* a dish – the way she had tongued Lisbeth's cunny, deft fingers reaming her bumhole, and that lovely wank, while kneading Lisbeth's belly, her colon bursting with hot piss . . .

'See you soon, Vimella!' she cried, waving, and Vimella blew her a kiss.

I didn't have that monstrous tool in my bum . . . he did Vimella, but wouldn't do me. The bastard! I hope Sergeant Placket whips his cheating arse . . .

The heat was stifling. Lisbeth mopped her brow and listened to the rumbling in her tummy. Her portion of sperm had reawakened her appetite.

'Miss Lisbeth Lache?'

She turned to see an ebony gamine, dressed in a skimpy white dress, whose moist fabric clung to her body. Long bare legs snaked below the hem of a skirt that scarcely covered her big buttock pears and ended in white fluffy ankle socks and red sneakers. Her hair, braided in twin plaits, bobbed over hard, jutting breasts, braless, their

65

warm ebony skin largely revealed at the cleavage, plunging between thin shoulder straps. Lisbeth started, thinking for a moment that Vimella had returned, and felt a sudden stab to her clitty, with a spurt of come in her pouch. The girl stood, twirling her waist, with her hands behind her back, the dance of her skirtlet allowing Lisbeth to see a thin thong of white panties crouching in her arse cleft between the big chocolate croup melons. Like Vimella's, her waist was pencil-thin, curving dramatically into the massive ripeness of the arse, yet seemed uncorseted. Big bright eyes shone white in her slender dark face, the rosebud lips extruded in a submissive pout.

'Yes,' Lisbeth said.

'If you please, miss, I'm to take you to Rum Hole.'

Her nimble fingers took Lisbeth's case and she led her to a jetty in the gently lapping water where a rowing boat awaited, with a coiled rope fastening it to a bollard on the dock.

'In that?' Lisbeth gasped.

'No, miss, in that.'

The girl pointed to a small hydroplane bobbing on the sea a hundred metres away. Lisbeth settled in the little boat, and the girl began powerfully rowing until, minutes later, they were under the hull of the hydroplane, where a rope ladder swayed from a lighted hatchway. The girl ascended first, with Lisbeth gazing at her buttocks, almost fully exposed save for the thong snaking between the hard, muscled cheeks, glinting in the reflected starlight. Again, her clitty throbbed, and she felt come moisten her quim. The girl extended a hand, helping Lisbeth up the ladder, and when they both stood on the aircraft's deck, she waved at the shore. The boat receded, pulled on its rope back to land by a pair of uniformed boys, and the girl pulled the hatch door shut behind them.

The tiny passenger compartment was furnished in the style of a hotel room, with low tables and sofa, soft lighting and a sumptuous buffet, with a full bar and champagne in ice buckets.

'Welcome to Rum Hole, Miss Lache,' said the girl. 'I'm Femella Culbutt, and I've done my best to make things nice for you. I'm sorry it's only a cold buffet, but I won't be able to cook, as I have to fly the plane.'

Lisbeth's mouth watered at the sight of the buffet – quails' eggs, foie gras, pheasant, fruits and cheeses, and steaming fresh French bread.

'You, a pilot?' she gasped. 'You are awfully young.'

'Why, I'm eighteen, miss, and my master, Mr de Hazebrouck, taught me,' Femella replied proudly. 'It's very easy – just remember altitude, fuel and speed. My sister Vimella's only an air hostess. You probably met her on Acklin Air.'

'Yes, I did,' Lisbeth said. 'There is a remarkable resemblance.'

'You mean my bottom?' said the gamine, eyes sparkling. 'That's because we're twins, so we have twin bottoms. Would you like to see?'

Without waiting for an answer, she giggled and lifted her skirt to her shoulder-bones with a wriggle of her buttocks, showing Lisbeth her full bare, save for the minuscule thong clamped between the ripe arse cheeks. She turned coquettishly to show her firm, jutting bubbies, which she waggled provocatively at Lisbeth, with their brown conical nipples standing stiff and upright. On her slender gamine's form, the massive ripeness of teats and buttocks sprouted like dark jewels from the earth. Lisbeth gasped as a spurt of come wetted her thighs. She bit her lip, trying to shoo away her sudden desire. *The girl's bum begs to be spanked.*

'I know what you're thinking, miss,' said Femella, coquettishly.

'You do?' blurted Lisbeth, blushing.

'You're thinking I'm a very naughty girl. And I am – but it's only when Mr de Hazebrouck lets a slave leave Rum Hole that she has a chance to talk, and be a bit foolish. Otherwise it's silent obedience at all times. You won't report me, will you, miss, after all the nice food I've prepared for you?'

Lisbeth laughed in relief. 'I certainly *shall* report you, for being such an excellent hostess, Femella.'

'You will? Oh, thank you, miss.'

Femella sprang to Lisbeth and hugged her, planting a kiss on her cheek and pressing her hard bare breasts against Lisbeth's nipples. Lisbeth returned the kiss, holding the girl to her by the buttocks and cupping the warm fesse flesh with both hands. Beneath the soft skin, the muscles of her croup rippled like whipcord. They embraced silently, Lisbeth stroking the girl's bare and plucking at her thong to run her fingertip down the arse crack. Femella clenched her buttocks against Lisbeth's probing finger, giving a soft moan as Lisbeth touched the big extruded prune of her anal pucker.

'Ooh, that's nice, miss,' she cooed. 'You don't think my butt wrinkle's too big? Sometimes Vimella teases me. She is a real bobtail, you know.'

'Bobtail?'

'A rum mot, a proper bit of muslin.'

'I think I know what you mean,' Lisbeth murmured, rubbing the firm bare bottom with her fingers.

'Not like me. I'm a virgin,' Femella declared.

'You've never had sex with anyone?' Lisbeth said, stroking Femella's gash lips, then her anus pucker. 'You've never had a sex organ here, or here?'

'I didn't say that. Of course, people have had sex with me – I'm a slave, after all – but that's not the same thing. I'm a virgin in my heart, trying to be pure and pretty for the master. He insists that all his slaves strive to have perfect buttocks, and sometimes, a girl needs reassurance.'

'I think your bottom's adorable. But what about "slaves"? That's an odd term.'

'It means serving maids, miss. It's the master's whim.'

Lisbeth's finger slipped to the opening of the girl's cunt, which was swollen and juicing with oily come. 'That's adorable, too.'

'Oh, miss, you mustn't tease me.'

'You have the loveliest bottom I've seen for ages,' Lisbeth gasped. 'The loveliest breasts, too, and the juiciest, sweetest – well, Femella, your body is quite superb.'

Femella broke away, panting.

'That's so nice! But you'll give me a swollen head, and

Mr de Hazebrouck will be cross with me, and give me – anyway, this plane won't fly itself.'

She rolled down her dress, and scampered to the pilot's cabin.

'You can talk to me, miss, if you'd like to know all about Rum Hole. Just fasten your seatbelt – don't worry, it unfastens, not like Vimella's!'

When the hydroplane was airborne, Lisbeth helped herself sumptuously to food and wine before venturing into the cockpit, where Femella's face was eerily lit by the green glow of the controls. The hydroplane glided over the waves, sparkling in the starlight, with clumps of landmass sliding past beneath them, on either side. The nearness of the scantily clad gamine and the memory of her smooth bare bum under Lisbeth's fingers made her cunt gush anew. She pondered if her vow of celibacy had to be absolute, and when she could find the willing girl alone. Lisbeth's own bottom still throbbed from the weals laid by Cynthia Placket's baton, and she longed to kiss Femella's naked globes, stroke them tenderly, show the girl the beauty of tender sapphism. Yet her humiliations made her lust for vengeance. It was so confusing! Lisbeth asked the girl if she would like something to eat.

'Why, no, miss!' exclaimed Femella, genuinely shocked. 'Me – to eat guest food? Mr de Hazebrouck would be more than cross.'

'But Mr de Hazebrouck wouldn't know.'

'He would, miss. He has ways,' Femella retorted.

'I look forward to meeting Mr de Hazebrouck,' said Lisbeth.

'You may, and you may not, miss. The master pleases himself, and keeps to himself. But you'll *so* enjoy Rum Hole!'

Lisbeth heard faintly over the roaring of the aircraft's engine that the resort catered for super-rich ladies who valued privacy. There was no enforced communality – the many pleasures on offer were enjoyed discreetly. There were all the culinary and recreational features of a luxury resort, but a lady could remain in the seclusion of her private villa if she wished, enjoying her private beach, with every need satisfied by room servants. Some ladies chose to spend their entire holiday in seclusion, visited only by servants, the 'hole mistress' and, perhaps, the master himself. When Lisbeth asked questions about the resort's finances or its ownership structure, Femella evaded them mumbling that Lisbeth would learn as she went along.

'The hole mistress is Miss Cicatrix Comington, and she'll be pleased to instruct you further,' was all Femella would add.

'Instruct?' said Lisbeth. 'Sounds as if I'm in training.'

'Rum Hole is all about pleasure, miss,' chirped Femella, 'and some ladies need to be trained for pleasure.'

In the distance, a chain of islands emerged, crouching in the velvet sea. Femella told Lisbeth they were the Jumentos Cays, mostly uninhabited. The islands slumbered in the starry darkness, with only a few clusters of light visible. Femella pointed to the brightest and said it was Rum Hole. Lisbeth withdrew and buckled her belt for their descent, which took place with scarcely a tremor, as the aircraft kissed the ocean. Another boat awaited them, piloted by a sturdy black girl, big-bottomed and big-titted, and nude but for a red scarf wound round her head and the same white socks and sneakers as Femella wore. Lisbeth climbed in beside Femella. Without acknowledging their presence, the girl rowed them ashore, moonlight glinting on her huge chocolate nipples, rippling thighs and the lush curve of her shaven quim hillock. *Gosh, I'm feeling so fruity,* Lisbeth thought.

They tied up at a small jetty, surrounded by darkly silhouetted buildings amid lush foliage of flowers and trees, sparsely illumined by overhead lamps strapped to their branches. The night air was sweltering; Lisbeth looked at her watch for the first time since her arrival at Nassau, and found that it was nearly midnight. Awaiting them was a tall, lithe police girl in a similar blue uniform to Sergeant Placket's, but she carried a thin cane instead of a baton. Her bare brown legs gleamed in the darkness, and her full breasts trembled a little under their clinging uniform shirt as she saluted.

'Welcome to Rum Hole, Miss Lache,' she said in a fluting, mellow voice. 'I am Corporal Rodding of the watch. Melanie Nave is your rickshaw girl, who will take you to your villa.'

She gestured at a European girl, waiting in the shadows, with a golden tan skin, and blonde tresses, cropped just above her nipples. She was nude but for a red cap and kerchief, and a corset, which pinched her slender waist very tightly, forcing out her bubbies into round balls, with red nipples spread to saucers, and the pert buds standing firm in their centre. She was shod with thick metal horseshoes; she glistened with sweat as her feet restlessly clapped the ground between the shafts of a rickshaw. The corset, straightened with dark wooden stays, like Vimella's, had a buckle at its rear, through which a thick rubber cord was looped, fastening the girl's body to a similar buckle on the vehicle. The naked black girl efficiently stowed Lisbeth's bags in the rickshaw, then curtsied to the corporal.

'Dugger here gave you no trouble?' said Corporal Rodding, gesturing with her cane to the girl standing sullenly, biting her lip. 'She didn't try to speak?'

'Why, no,' Lisbeth said.

'Good girl,' said Corporal Rodding, somewhat grudgingly. 'You may go to the commissary, and tell the duty officer I permit you a half pot of beer.'

Dugger flashed her white teeth in a dazzling smile.

'Off you go, bobtail.'

The corporal's wrist flicked, and her cane landed – vip! – in a hard cut across the middle of Dugger's bare fesses. The girl winced but curtsied again, still smiling, and scampered into the darkness.

'Low slaves are not permitted speech,' explained the corporal. 'Higher slaves, like Femella here, may speak, within limits.'

'Is my rickshaw driver a low slave?' Lisbeth asked, as Femella helped her climb into the passenger seat.

'Why, of course, miss,' said the corporal, smiling. 'However, she is permitted speech enough to introduce you to your villa. The rickshaw carries a light whip, in case you need to urge her on with strokes to the buttocks. Most guests find it desirable.'

'I'm sure that won't be necessary,' exclaimed Lisbeth. 'She looks like a good girl – aren't you, Miss Nave?'

She received a glowering pout, in return.

'Did you really mean what you said about my body, miss?' whispered Femella.

'Yes, I did.'

'Even after seeing Vimella's?'

'Yes, but ... who told you I saw Vimella's?' Lisbeth blurted.

Femella's answer was lost. The corporal cracked her cane smartly across Melanie's bare buttocks, and with a snort of pain the girl raised her knees and pulled Lisbeth's rickshaw away at a brisk trot. The jetty was soon far behind them as they travelled along a corniche, over-shadowed by palm trees and bougainvillea, with a wide white beach at their side. The few lanterns made it difficult to see, but Melanie seemed to know her path; they trotted past a wide open field, various two-storey houses, a barracks surrounded by a fencework of pointed staves, with two cane-wielding corporals standing to attention outside; then the path curved away from the sea, and between rickshaw and beach was a line of wooden, white-painted villas, secluded behind palm fronds and banana trees. On the other side of the road, to landward, began a dense forest, trees interspersed with lush clumps of flowering bushes.

The night was perfectly still, the silence broken only by Melanie's harsh panting as she trotted. Sweat poured down her spine, funnelling into the pumping crack of her buttocks, which churned at the pounding of her long, coltish legs. Her bare breasts bounced helplessly as she ran. Lisbeth contemplated the girl's croup, glistening with sweat, and the powerful fesse muscles rippling hard beneath the satin skin. She peered more closely, and saw that Melanie's buttocks bore the marks of whipping: thin pink weals, crisscrossing the bare flesh. She reached forward and drew a thin, coiled whip from its pouch, uncurled it and ran the hard leather through her fingers. The whip was half an inch thick and a good six feet long, ample for her to flick Melanie's buttocks without straining; ample, too, to deliver a vigorous whipstroke and draw a new mark on the girl's pumping bare arse melons.

Crack! The whip flashed in the moonlight and Melanie groaned in a whinny, as the tip flicked the air, inches from her bare bum, without touching her. Lisbeth smiled and lashed again, her whip slicing the air above Melanie's bare back. Again, Melanie whinnied, and began to trot faster. Crack! Crack! Lisbeth, too, was lathered in sweat as she whipped the filly on, yet, to her own puzzlement, not striking bare flesh. Fear seemed spur enough, for Melanie was running at breakneck speed, panting and puffing amid her whinnies, as the whipcracks followed her. Lisbeth pressed her nyloned thighs tight as come spurted from her cunt in the excitement of her make-believe lashing, her pouch still hot from her frustrated caress of Femella.

Her clitty began to tingle and swell, hardening and throbbing, as Lisbeth teased and taunted the luscious bare croup, pumping to her command. *Should* she . . .? Should she lash the girl in earnest? Then she would *have* to masturbate, she would be unable to resist flicking her clitty, and she didn't know when the journey would end . . . *No! I'm not here to play games!* Gulping deeply, Lisbeth lowered her whip and, pressing her thighs together, sat demurely listening to Melanie's hoarse panting, and her shoes thumping the packed earth. Soon the rickshaw came to a halt outside an adorable villa, and Lisbeth dismounted by a horse trough filled with water. The road behind was dotted with similar curiosities. A tall female figure stood at the gate, silhouetted by the light from the villa's open door.

'Welcome, Miss Lache,' she said, in a purring contralto. 'I am Miss Cicatrix Comington, the hole mistress, and I anticipated your arrival to make sure all was in order for so honoured a guest.'

Brusquely, she unfastened Melanie from her harness, and the girl busied herself with Lisbeth's bags. As she passed Lisbeth on the garden path, behind Miss Comington, she looked up with warm, grateful doe's eyes.

'Thank you for not whipping me, miss,' she whispered.

'Why, you're English,' Lisbeth exclaimed. 'What on earth–?'

'Ssh!' hissed Melanie, before clanking into the villa – Lisbeth saw that the plates of her horseshoes were nailed together – and depositing the bags at the door, without entering.

Melanie curtsied to both ladies, and removed herself from the house by hobbling backwards. Miss Comington ordered her to use the trough and, moments later, Lisbeth heard a splash as the girl immersed herself.

'The master was kind enough to drop me off here,' said Miss Comington. 'Melanie can give me a ride back. It's always good to freshen up a pony slave with the trough, Miss Lache, even though the mots hate it – shrinks their corsets, d'you see? Let me show you your new home, Miss Lache. You may call me Cissy.'

Cissy Comington was a svelte black woman with a long, smooth raven mane caressing her breasts. She was slightly older and taller than Lisbeth, and wore a black, short-sleeved silk dress with white ruff, the skirt extending no further than halfway down the thighs of her long, bare ebony legs. Her feet were encased in rubber boots with high pointed heels that clicked as she strode. The clinging dress emphasised the swellings of her breasts and buttocks, with no evidence of a panty line or of any brassiere supporting the jutting melons of her teats, which extruded bullet-firm from her lithe frame. Her buttocks swayed as she strolled around the house, and Lisbeth found herself gazing at the firm arse flans, shivering so delicately under the thin silk, with the thigh muscles rippling powerfully beneath the massive croup. Miss Comington's waist was so slender that Lisbeth guessed her to be corseted. A silken waist cord carried a dangling, crook-handled cane.

Fatigued, and drowsily enchanted by Miss Comington's lustrous body, Lisbeth nevertheless thrilled to her new abode, joyously bedecked with flowers. Cissy used her cane to point out the various features, light switches and cupboards. Everything was provided: a choice of bedrooms, cane furniture with cushions in satin, cotton or silk; a refrigerator stocked with delicacies and a complete range of food and drink in the kitchen; a dining room with a rosewood table; three bathrooms; swimming pool, and private beach, perfectly secluded between rows of palm and jacaranda, with the master bedroom's French windows opening onto the beach. Cissy told her that the wardrobe and bathroom were stocked with a few essentials, but that the Rum Hole boutique offered interesting clothes, crafts and sundries for sale. The house smelled fresh and new, salty with the perfume of the sea and fragrant with flowers, and Lisbeth said it was perfect.

'I'll let you get some sleep, Miss Lache. There is the telephone, if you need anything from central, or else press a button to summon a slave. The slaves' quarters are seconds away, across the road, within the forest, and we aim at a complement of four slaves per guest. If any slave displeases you, please let me know, or else, for a minor matter, you may discipline her, or him, as you see fit. I suggest you read the master's welcome pamphlet, but be aware that the Rum Hole guest is supreme, and with slaves, her word is law. They are here to serve your needs in *any possible way you can imagine*.'

Miss Comington emphasised her last six words with six quite resounding smacks of her cane on her own bare thigh. Lisbeth thanked her, and the hole mistress bade her goodnight. Lisbeth sighed happily, flinging open the French windows of her bedroom to look at the velvet sea, sparkling across her own dazzling white sand beach. She undid her clothing and let her things drop to the floor, rolling down her stockings and sussies and standing nude in the door frame to let the gentle breeze caress her bare body. The sea beckoned her and she padded across the warm, fine sand for a naked swim. She heard the rattle of rickshaw wheels, and Cissy's cry of 'Giddy-up!' – followed by a savage whipcrack, then another and another, punctuated by whinnying screams from Melanie Nave. *What is an English girl doing here, working as a slave?* Shivering, Lisbeth slid her body into the warm water, cleaving the sea and immersing herself totally. She stood, her wet skin sparkling in the light of moon and stars, and heard the crack of Cissy's whip on bare girlskin growing fainter in the distance. Her hand clutched her bare quim, and she felt juice oozing from the swollen lips.

'Ooh . . .' she sighed, touching her throbbing clitty.

She stroked the bruises on her bottom, still smarting a little, and as she caressed her weals, Lisbeth masturbated to a shuddering climax, crying and squealing to the sky and the ocean, as come spurted from her twitching cunt to sprinkle the soft Bahamian waters.

Late in the morning, Lisbeth yawned, stretching her nude body inside cool cotton sheets. Birds sang, and the translucent turquoise sea lapped her private sands. In a pure azure sky the sun beamed dazzling white on her beach, still imprinted with her footsteps. She sat up, juggling her bare breasts, which bore pink marks where her sleeping body had crushed them. There was a gentle tap at her French windows, and there stood a girl, silhouetted in the sunlight. Lisbeth instinctively raised her sheet to cover her breasts, and asked who was there.

'Please, Miss Lache, it's Sapphire, your room slave,' said the girl. 'Does miss wish to give me her breakfast order?'

'Why, yes,' said Lisbeth. 'Come in. The doors are open.'

She saw the girl's silhouette – slender and tall, with generously thrusting breasts and a bottom as succulent as Melanie's. Lisbeth dropped the sheet and reclined on her arms with her breasts bare, as the girl entered. Sapphire was young, perhaps eighteen, and wore a pretty maid's costume of white frilly blouse, cut very low to show her trembling ebony breasts, bunched by a too-tight bra; seamed chocolate-brown nylon stockings, and high heels, with a bonnet on her smooth black locks. Instead of a skirt, she wore a ballooned pair of silken bloomers, the pants held at her narrow waist and at mid-thigh by elastic hems. On her arm she carried a basket full of steaming hot

French loaves. Lisbeth tried to be as cool as possible, confronting the clothed girl with her torso naked, but Sapphire kept her eyes modestly to the floor and, if she saw the guest's nudity, revealed no surprise. Lisbeth licked her lips.

'I can cook miss's breakfast, if it pleases her,' said Sapphire.

'Yes,' drawled Lisbeth, and gave her breakfast order, of eggs, juice, coffee and mineral water.

'Than you, miss,' said Sapphire, blinking her lustrous eyelashes.

Lisbeth threw back her sheet and stood in the nude before the maid, to stretch and scratch her bottom, where she felt the faint reminders of yesterday's thrashing. She sauntered into the bathroom and, without bothering to close the door, evacuated noisily, with a string of dark hard dungs plopping loudly into the water. As she reached for the paper, Sapphire appeared in the doorway.

'Please, miss,' she said, almost pleading, with her eyes wide.

'What? Oh, you want to – gosh, very well,' blurted Lisbeth, bending over, and spreading her thighs for the maid to wipe her bottom. 'Ooh,' she giggled, as the soft fingers tickled her anus bud.

'A bath, miss?' said Sapphire.

'No. You may serve breakfast on the patio,' she said. 'I'll have a swim first.'

'Very good, miss,' said the maid. 'If miss wishes to tinkle, she may care to command a chamber pot.'

Lisbeth padded naked past the girl, closer than was necessary, and smelled the musky perfume from the creamy ebony skin. She noticed that her unpantied bottom was covered quite neatly by the bloomers, with each globe delicately outlined, and that the two halves of the garment were separated by a vent, showing the delicate line of Sapphire's naked arse cleft. The two pieces of fabric were joined at her waist by a drawstring, tied in a bow. Lisbeth ran to the water's edge and plunged in for a vigorous swim, after which she emerged, dripping, into a huge fluffy towel held by the impassive ebony girl. Sapphire dried every inch of Lisbeth's body, her slender fingers massaging belly, breasts and bum, and even penetrating the cleft and patting the fount lips dry, yet without any hint of lustfulness. Lisbeth refused the proffered bathrobe.

'I'll breakfast in the nude, I think,' she said airily, provoking no reaction from the girl, save a solemn nod.

Lisbeth felt her nipples tingle and stiffen, thrilled at her insouciant nudity, the true power of a mistress over her slave. Sapphire went into the kitchen and Lisbeth saw a figure wading in the sea, from the adjoining beach, then stepping onto her own sand. It was a young black male, nude, his head and entire body, including the pubis, bare-shaven. The sunlight glistened on his slender, almost girlish, body, which Lisbeth decided was eighteen or nineteen years old, and the enormous cock, which dangled insouciantly, thrillingly turgescent, to halfway down his thighs. He walked a few steps up Lisbeth's beach, then paused, and began to pose, not looking at her, with his head raised in casual arrogance. Pirouetting in slow motion, he showed her his tight buttocks, the huge gourds of his balls, and his stiffening cock, then stood still for half a minute, looking over Lisbeth's head.

'Your pleasure, miss?' he murmured. 'I am your pleasure slave.'

Numbly, in utter confusion, she shook her head, saying nothing; he turned on his heel, and waded back into the sea. When Sapphire returned, he was gone, leaving Lisbeth with a frustrating vision and a cunt dripping come. *A pleasure slave, to do my bidding. A dream come true.*

Her breakfast appeared on the white, wrought-iron patio table: hot, freshly buttered croissants and French bread, perfect eggs, freshly squeezed juice and a newly cut blossom in a vase. Lisbeth clapped her hands in delight as Sapphire poured coffee. The girl indicated a little silver bell on the table which 'miss' might care to ring if she wanted to summon her. Meanwhile, if Miss Lache permitted, Sapphire would attend to her cleaning duties.

'Is my attire to miss's satisfaction?' she murmured shyly.

'Why, yes! You look adorable, Sapphire.'

Sapphire smiled coyly, her wide, dazzlingly white teeth spreading in a sunbeam of pleasure.

'Thank you, miss. I can, of course, change any item, or remove my clothing altogether, if it is your wish.'

'Remove it?'

'Some guests prefer their slaves to work in the nude, miss,' Sapphire said. 'It is perhaps more submissive.'

Lisbeth stuck the knob of a croissant in her mouth and licked it.

'Well, I wouldn't want that,' she drawled. 'Not today, anyway.'

Lisbeth recalled that she herself was nude. *To be bare is to be powerful.* She ordered the slave to bring her the master's pamphlet to read, and Sapphire obeyed. Seconds later the girl was at a crouch, swabbing the floor with a cloth protecting her nyloned knees, and her bottom pointed at Lisbeth. Lisbeth watched the gentle rippling of her arse globes under the flimsy silken bloomers, and the undulating crack of her bare buttocks squeezing and writhing as her bottom moved. Lisbeth shifted her own bottom on her towel, feeling a heavy seep of come wetting her thighs as her nubbin began to swell.

'Your costume is quite adorable, Sapphire,' she said, 'but please tell me the meaning of your curious nether garment. Most maids, I thought, wore little frilly skirts.'

Sapphire leapt to her feet, and curtsied.

'Please, miss, I am not a maid but a slave, and those are my spanking panties,' she said.

6

Turquoise and Ebony

'Spanking panties?' Lisbeth said as casually as she could, leafing idly through the vellum pages of the master's pamphlet. 'Please explain.'

Sapphire hung her head.

'If I'm naughty, miss, you can easily untie my panties and spank me ... or whatever,' she murmured. 'One pull to my drawstring and my panties fall away, and my bottom is bare.'

Lisbeth licked drops of butter and marmalade from her chin to avoid soiling the pages, which she scanned with half an eye:

'The aim of Rum Hole is the pleasure of its guests. Nothing must stand in its way, and especially not the idleness of slaves, as craven a crew of slowbellies, mudlarks, bobtails and scallywags as ever disgraced these Bahamas. For any sloth, rudeness, or dereliction of duty, a slave merits and expects sound chastisement of the naked posteriors, whether slogging, cobbing, whipping, caning or teazing, at the guest's discretion and pleasure. Slaves may not complain at a chastisement, nor question it. They may not speak unless spoken to, but guests should not ask them why they choose a scullion's life of humiliance, albeit well rewarded, for they are forbidden to discuss such matters, even amongst themselves, lest their slavish lust for money inspire them to seek further humiliance, in the hope of earning it.'

Lisbeth lifted her shoulders, rolling them, so that her breasts swayed. Her nipples were tingling, their buds stiff. She took a deep breath, her titties heaving.

'Why would I need to spank you, Sapphire?' she asked.

'Why, miss, for being lazy, or imperfect in my duties,' the girl answered. 'I've been cobbed many times on my bare melons.'

'I can't imagine that,' said Lisbeth, her titties trembling at the thought of the girl's bare buttocks quivering under spanks. 'You seem like perfection itself.'

'You are very kind, miss, but we slaves are idle brutes.'

'So, idleness might earn you a spanking on your bare bottom,' drawled Lisbeth, crossing her naked thighs over the slimy ooze of come from her cunt, whose lips swelled as she looked at the girl's quivering belly. 'Please explain "whatever".'

'It's not for me to say,' blurted Sapphire. 'Miss hasn't looked in her armoire?'

Lisbeth touched her stiff nipples.

'You may butter me another croissant, Sapphire,' she murmured.

As Sapphire bent over the table, Lisbeth slipped her fingers under the billowing panties cloth and touched the skin of the slave girl's naked bottom. She felt Sapphire's buttocks tense, clenching almost imperceptibly, then relax, parting a little to allow Lisbeth access to her steep bum cleft. Lisbeth played her fingers up and down the arse crack as Sapphire buttered her croissant, with her smooth bare bum flesh rising in little goose pimples. The girl's legs trembled. Lisbeth swallowed, panting through flared nostrils, as her cunt began to flow with oily come.

No . . . I must control myself . . .

Trembling, she withdrew her hand and rose, sauntering across the carpeted bedroom to her antique oaken armoire. Her own bottom still smarted a little from Sergeant Placket's flogging, and she thought, almost hoping, that Sapphire could see her weals. As her buttocks pressed together she felt the bruises throbbing dully and was flooded with a wash of anger and a flash of desire to avenge her own bottom's shame on squirming Bahamian buttocks.

Opening the armoire door, she gasped. On the left side hung costumes, shiny and dark, which seemed like swimsuits, only with strange knobs of gleaming metal. On the right was an array of leather, wooden and rubber appliances. There were whips of brown, lustrous leather, beautifully aromatic; gleaming wooden canes; quirts of many-thonged black rubber; cuffs, clamps and bracelets, and even a wooden hobble, like the one in which Vimella had trapped her. Panting hoarsely, and with come streaming from her pulsing cooze down her thighs, Lisbeth slammed the door shut. She stood gulping and watching the globes of Sapphire's bottom, as the girl attended to the breakfast table. Lisbeth's finger crept down her fluttering belly, across the bare expanse of her quim hillock, to the folds of her gash.

She parted the top lips, and touched her clitty, starting as electric pleasure transfixed her cunt. The nubbin was stiff, swollen and throbbing, with an unabashed stream of juice spurting from her slit, over her fingers. She rubbed her clitty, moaning softly with her eyes on the girl's bum globes, clinging to her thin spanking panties in the dazzling sunlight. For several seconds, Lisbeth stood, frotting herself, then, with a shiver, she ceased masturbating and returned, on shaky legs, to her chair. She sat down and saw Sapphire's finger trying to wipe away a stain of butter on the white tablecloth. Sapphire stared at her with wide, frightened eyes, their white orbs delicious against her ebony skin. The girl swallowed and began to shiver as Lisbeth inspected the butter stain.

'An accident?' she murmured.

Sapphire nodded, silently.

Lisbeth patted her bottom, and began to stroke.

'That's all right,' she said. 'Nothing to worry about.'

Sapphire visibly relaxed.

'Nothing, that is –' Lisbeth said, as her fingers jerked the bowstring of the panties, and the cloth fell from the girl's naked bottom '– that a spanking won't put right.'

'Ohh . . .' Sapphire moaned, as her knickers slithered down her legs to her ankles.

Her bare fesses gleamed, shivering in the sunlight, with a myriad tiny dewdrops of sweat glittering on the taut buttock skin. The thick ebony lips of her shaven cunt swelled, pendant between her rippling, parted thighs. The girl panted hoarsely, her breasts, dangling over Lisbeth's breakfast, rising and falling in a jerky rhythm. Lisbeth touched the girl's big bubbies, stroking the nipples under their thin cloth, then squeezing and kneading the soft, rubbery teat flesh. Sapphire's breasts shivered and she moaned faintly. Lisbeth touched her own slit lips, slopping her fingers in the slime of come flowing from her throbbing cunt. She removed her fingers from her slit and touched Sapphire's trembling bare, leaving a glinting smear of her come on the taut bum flesh. Lisbeth's breasts heaved as she panted through her wide nostrils. Her fingers slipped down the crack of Sapphire's arse, across the perineum to the cunt flaps, where she inserted a fingertip between the fleshy folds. Sapphire was wet.

'You may assume position,' Lisbeth ordered, her voice trembling.

'Very good, miss,' said Sapphire. 'Does miss wish to take me here, or inside?'

'Here,' said Lisbeth. 'Lean over the breakfast table with your bottom out and up and thighs spread. Take care not to squirm too much or you'll upset my breakfast things, and I shall really be cross.'

'I promise not to squirm, miss,' said Sapphire, spreading herself over the breakfast, and gripping the far side of the table. 'Would miss prefer I step out of my panties, and present full bare?'

'Um, yes,' Lisbeth replied.

Sapphire kicked off her panties, flicking them up to land draped on her shoulder. She parted her chocolate-stockinged legs, with her bum thrust high and the cheeks well parted, showing her pendant cunt flaps, heavy and swollen, between quivering thighs. The naked, sun-kissed globes of her bottom were prettily framed by her tight turquoise garter belt and straps, biting into the ebony skin, with her turquoise adornment mirroring the bright ocean. There was a droplet of juice at the outer lip of her cunt petals which fell with a plop to the patio floor. Lisbeth positioned herself beside the upturned buttocks, and raised her arm. Smack! Her palm fell on the fleshy mid-fesse, which trembled a little. Smack! She repeated the stroke, and was pleased to see her faint palm print, glowing on the ebony bumskin. Smack! Smack!

'Uhh . . .' Sapphire gasped, as her arse cheeks clenched. Smack! Smack!'

'Ooh . . .'

Sapphire's bottom began a delicate wriggle, the cheeks squashing and squeezing as she clenched. Smack! Smack! Lisbeth's titties bounced, as she spanked harder and faster, raising a blush on the girl's squirming bare. Sapphire gasped, teats flapping, at each smack to her naked derrière, as large drops of come plopped from her gash. Lisbeth, too, panted, sweat dripping from her heaving titties, her belly and quim glistening with moisture. As her hips swivelled for each spank, her thighs and cooze lips rubbed, squeezing droplets of come from her own cunt, to mingle with the spanked girl's. Smack! Smack! Sapphire's brow wrinkled in pain and her lips stretched in a rictus over her clenched teeth, teats wobbling and her bare buttocks, dewed with sweat, jerking at each spank.

'You haven't asked how many spanks you're to take, or for how long,' panted Lisbeth.

'Please, miss, I have no right to question you,' gasped the quivering girl. 'A guest may chastise me as she sees fit.'

Lisbeth paused to stroke the hot buttocks.

'It is your fault, for having such tempting fesses,' she murmured.

'Thank you, miss.'

Smack! Smack!

'Ooh!'

Lisbeth spanked the girl for ten minutes, until her bottom glowed fiery with the prints of her palms and fingers. Twice she paused, to gulp orange juice, offering a drink to Sapphire, who asked for water. Lisbeth served her from the jug, with the water slopping over Sapphire's blouse, drenching her titties so that their dark bulbs appeared through the translucent fabric. Lisbeth's hand grasped her pubis and rubbed her throbbing clitty, pressing a squirt of come into her palm. Panting as she gazed at the girl's blushing bare, she began to masturbate, flicking the stiff nubbin for several seconds, until Sapphire asked if there was anything wrong.

'No . . . no . . .' blurted Lisbeth. 'My hand hurts from spanking, so I'll get something harder. Don't move.'

She sped to the armoire and selected a paddle from the rack. Trembling and openly masturbating, she lifted the heavy wooden tongue over Sapphire's buttocks and brought it cracking down. Whap!

'Ooh!' gasped the girl.

Whap!

'Ahh!'

Whap!

'Uh! Uhh . . .'

Sapphire's flogged buttocks reacted fiercely, wriggling and clenching between smacks of the wood; yet she didn't make the breakfast table tremble, all her agitation being expressed in the violent shaking of her titties, bum and thighs. Her thighs, below her cunt flaps, glistened with trickling rivulets of come. Lisbeth, constantly masturbating, beat her for five minutes, then, pouring with sweat, gasped: 'Aren't you going to beg me to stop?'

'No, miss!' blurted Sapphire, her voice cracking in a sob. 'I must take everything you give me. It is the master's order. Slaves must be striped, and Miss Comington inspects our bares regularly. Only a wet bitch like Melanie squeals and cajoles to get out of stripes. That's why she's a rickshaw girl, where she can't avoid them.'

Lisbeth stroked Sapphire's glistening cunt lips and withdrew her fingers, slopped in come. She thrust them to Sapphire's nose. '*You're* not a wet bitch?' she murmured.

'If it pleases, miss,' blurted the spanked girl. 'Miss knows a girl can't help juicing when her bare bottom's whopped.'

Lisbeth returned to the armoire and took her time choosing her next implement, feeling and weighing flogging tools of leather, rubber or wood. She selected two: a short, whippy English school cane, and a quirt of four square rubber thongs, two feet long. Showing them to the trembling victim, she asked which hurt more.

'They both hurt dreadfully, miss,' gasped Sapphire. 'The cane stings more, the quirt welts more.'

Lisbeth picked up the jug of orange juice and poured the liquid over Sapphire's buttocks. 'Good for the skin,' she said, 'and cooling.'

She lifted the quirt and began to thrash Sapphire's arse, the four sinewy thongs spreading in a fan all over the quivering buttocks with wet, crushing thwaps as they lashed the soaked skin.

'Ooh . . .' panted the flogged girl, her thighs rippling at each cut and her striped bottom wriggling violently. 'It hurts so much more on the wet, miss. Thank you.'

Come dripped steadily from the girl's cooze. Lisbeth gasped as she wanked off, whipping her bare bum. After four minutes of the quirt, Lisbeth switched to the cane. Vip! Vip! She lashed the bare buttocks in mid-fesse, already glowing with bruises, and dark stripes mottled the ebony skin.

'Ahh! Ooh!' sobbed the wriggling maid, clenching her buttocks tight.

Masturbating vigorously, Lisbeth sliced twenty strokes of the cane on the girl's wet, sticky bare. Her fingers poked inside her streaming pouch, jabbing her wombneck while she rubbed her clitty with her come-slimed thumb. Gasping, she felt her belly flutter as her orgasm approached. The turquoise sea and white sand, bathed in dazzling sunlight; the quivering flogged orbs of Sapphire's naked bottom; the bright stripe of her turquoise sussies, shimmering against her skin; the livid bruises of whipping on the ebony nates – all mingled in a rush of power and desire. Sapphire's bum was twitching, like her own cunt flaps, spewing a torrent of copious come. Lisbeth masturbated, stroking the whipped bottom, as her cooze squirted oily juice, and she began to whimper in her climax. As pleasure overwhelmed her, she clawed the weals she had raised on Sapphire's bare, making the girl whimper.

'Ooh ... ah ... *ahh* ...' Lisbeth gasped, her belly exploding in a shuddering spasm.

Her fingers slid down the crease of Sapphire's arse cleft into her cunt folds, and touched the nubbin. It was stiff and swollen. Sapphire tensed, her legs jerking rigid, and her breasts shuddering.

'Ahh ...' she moaned, as her cunt sprayed come, her belly and nates quivering in a long, yelping orgasm that outlasted Lisbeth's own.

'You vile slut,' Lisbeth hissed. 'Beating made you come. You tricked me.'

'I couldn't help it, miss,' Sapphire whimpered. 'A flogging on the bare always excites me.' She turned her head and waggled her bottom, sending a spray of come from her dripping cooze, and smiled a slow, coy smile at Lisbeth. 'Sometimes it's the only way I can get off, miss,' she whispered.

Lisbeth paled. 'Why, you – you manipulating bobtail,' she hissed. 'Is *that* why you choose slavery?'

'Miss, you know I may not answer that,' blurted the girl, 'except that a slave of Rum Hole has the best life there is, and any girl would fight rather than say otherwise. Miss, surely you enjoyed your wank? Didn't whipping me give you pleasure?'

'You devious hussy,' Lisbeth spat.

'May I assist your pleasure, miss?' purred a gentle voice.

A figure loomed into Lisbeth's sweat-blurred vision. It was the young male pleasure slave. How long had he been watching? His nude body was almost dry of seawater, and his cock was now fully erect, standing from his lithe ebony thighs like a tree. He posed, with his hands behind his neck. Lisbeth gaped at the massive tool and trembled as she felt a gush of come flood her cunt.

'You were watching us,' she accused.

'Certainly not, miss, for it is forbidden. I averted my gaze. Is there aught you desire, miss?'

Sapphire's head hung low, dripping sweat, but she maintained her punishment position, with her thighs wide apart.

'Yes,' said Lisbeth. 'This wench must be chastised. Whipping achieves nothing. I want you to ... to shame her. *Do* her.'

Lisbeth's heart pounded.

'I must swive the slave, miss?'

'Yes.'

'In which hole?'

'Why ... you know, the normal one.'

The youth bowed, and stepped up to Sapphire's buttocks. He pressed his fingers to her cunt, slopping them with her come and anointing his cockshaft with the lubricant. Grasping her hips, he thrust his buttocks and his cock penetrated her bumhole. Lisbeth's jaw dropped. *The normal hole ...!* The boy's cock pushed in for several inches, then stopped, ramming hard, until Sapphire moaned, and his cock slid into her rectum, her buttocks slapping against his balls. He began to bugger her, his upper body scarcely moving, but his buttocks a blur, and his balls clapping like bells, so rapidly did he fuck.

'Ohh! Oh, no, please don't,' Sapphire whimpered. 'Ahh! It hurts me so much, I can't bear it. Miss, tell him to stop, or he'll split me open.'

The boy's hips slapped Sapphire's writhing arse flans with a dry, staccato thud, as his gravid cock, shiny with the girl's copious arse grease, withdrew several inches from her anus before plunging in, right to the balls, in each fresh penetration. At each thrust, Sapphire wailed that he was bursting her hole, and she couldn't take it. Her cheeks were glazed with tears and her body wriggled violently, impaled on the giant spear of the boy's cock. Lisbeth watched his shiny, pumping buttocks and began to masturbate, come sliming her thighs, to drip onto her ankles and feet. As she tweaked her clitty, familiar swooning pleasure fluttered in her belly.

'Ooh!' wailed the buggered girl. 'He's splitting me in two. Have pity, miss.'

'Do her harder, boy,' hissed Lisbeth, masturbating vigorously. 'Or it'll be your arse for a whipping.'

Suddenly, the boy pulled his cock, with a loud plop, from Sapphire's squirming bumhole, and grabbed Lisbeth by her hair.

'Wanking off, miss?' he said pleasantly, wrenching her hair, and forcing her to her knees.

'Ouch! Oww! You're hurting me. Let go! How dare you!' Lisbeth spluttered. 'You beastly slave, I'll have you flogged.'

'That would be an honour, miss,' panted the boy, 'but as a pleasure slave, I must first give you what you want.'

His swollen tool, dripping with Sapphire's arse grease, hovered an inch from her lips.

'No, no!' she whimpered. 'You can't be serious. How can you know what I want?'

'It is my job to know,' he said.

'I forbid you to – urrgh!'

Lisbeth gagged as the giant stiff cock filled her mouth. His ebony buttocks pumped as he thrust his cock deeper, and began to throat-fuck her.

'Mm! Urrgh!' Lisbeth gurgled.

Her lips fastened on the shaft of his cock and she began to suck powerfully. The boy eased his strokes, withdrawing his whole cockshaft, to let her suck and nibble his shiny glans, before he plunged the organ to the back of her throat. Lisbeth's fingers were a blur on her extruded stiff clitty as she masturbated. Her face crimson, she clung to the massive cock, sucking hard and squealing, her cunt flowing with wanked come. She felt cool hands on her quivering bum flans, prising the cheeks apart, then a wet, wriggling tongue licking her arse cleft, and flicking her anus bud.

Sapphire, crouching under Lisbeth's buttocks, tongued her anus as Lisbeth masturbated her cunt. The slave girl's stiff tongue poked an inch inside, reaming Lisbeth's bumhole, until Lisbeth squeaked with pleasure, as she slobbered the slave's cock. Lisbeth felt the glans tremble, and knew he was about to spurt. She tweaked her clitty hard, slicing it with her thumbnail, and squealing at the sudden, thrilling pain, as orgasm convulsed her cunt.

'Mm . . . mmm,' she groaned, gurgling and swallowing, as the slave's hot cream jetted into her throat, and her own wanking fingers were drenched in a spray of her come.

Sapphire's tongue was fully up her anus, the girl's nose pressed in her cleft, and Lisbeth swallowed the flood of hot boy-come, spurting to her gullet as her body quivered in its orgasm.

'Oh,' she whimpered, releasing the softening tool. 'Oh, what have I done . . .?'

A shadow darkened the patio. Lisbeth looked up and saw pair of long, bare ebony legs rising into the bulging crotch of a turquoise swimsuit. Water dripped from the girl's body onto Lisbeth's hair.

'I trust you are settling in well, Miss Lache?' said Cicatrix Comington. 'Norbert and Sapphire are taking care of your needs? I often take a morning swim around this part, so thought I'd call in.'

Lisbeth rose, smoothed back her hair, then wiped sperm from her lips. She smiled, showing her teeth and tongue, glistening with the slave boy's cream.

'Yes, everything is satisfactory,' she blurted.

How long has the bitch been here? Did she see my shame . . .?

'I am glad you enjoy life in the nude,' said Miss Comington. 'So much more relaxing and, of course, our slaves may not notice. Perhaps we shall see you at afternoon tea, in the Cat and Crossbones? That's our bar and restaurant.'

'Will I meet the master?' enquired Lisbeth.

'That is a rare honour,' replied the hole mistress. 'But –' she scanned Lisbeth's nude body '– you seem to be a rare lady, miss.'

Her breasts trembled with secret amusement, beneath the v-shaped cleavage of her swimsuit, low at the bosom and cut very high at the waist, to show naked skin right up to her ribcage. Her bare feet glistened with toenails polished turquoise, like the sea.

'I see Sapphire's spanking panties are down,' she said pleasantly, 'and, from the looks of her fesses, you've had occasion to discipline her. Sapphire, you may report to my office when Miss Lache dismisses you. You're due another punishment – turquoise garters, indeed! You know turquoise is for me alone.'

Sapphire's face crumpled.

'Well,' Lisbeth said, 'I did lay it on rather hard, and I rather think the poor girl has been whopped enough.'

Miss Comington ambled back towards the sea, her taut bum pears wiggling – a little provocatively, Lisbeth thought. And the turquoise swimsuit so stunningly offset her lush ebony skin . . .

'Thank you, Miss Lache,' she said. 'A guest's wishes are, of course, paramount. Happily, there are plenty of *other* punishments available. Report to me, Sapphire, for the insertion of your choke pear.'

Sapphire blanched, then murmured, 'Of course, mistress,' with tears misting her eyes.

Suddenly, Lisbeth was bursting to pee. She ordered Sapphire to fetch a chamber pot, and the girl brought a fine porcelain vessel, the bowl painted with scenes of flagellation – girls whipped on their bare bottoms, with comically exaggerated expressions of dismay. Inside were painted a voluptuous pair of naked female buttocks, spread to show the anus pucker and open pink quim. Sapphire crouched, holding the pot just beneath Lisbeth's gash, which released a steaming jet of piss, half filling the receptacle, with several droplets spraying Sapphire's face.

Lisbeth coolly dismissed her two slaves, then sat down to the rest of her breakfast, now cold, and ate ravenously. She thought of the slave boy's cock, sliding into the tight brown pucker of Sapphire's anus . . . how huge his meat, how dreadful to take it in *that* hole! Yet, Sapphire had seemed to find a curious pleasure in her ordeal. She fingered the fading welts on her own bottom, and wondered if Miss Comington had observed Lisbeth's shameful fellatio of the slave boy. Did it matter?

She licked the last of her bacon and eggs from her plate and padded into her bedroom to the armoire. There, in a drawer, was a selection of dildos and vibrators: strap-ons, ticklers, butt plugs. Panting, she selected the biggest dildo, a monster in black rubber, nearly as big as Norbert's cock, and smeared it with come from her juicing cooze. She crouched on the bed with her bottom in the air and a towel under her spread thighs, just in case. She gasped as the tip of the dildo penetrated her anus, but pushed it further, biting her lip against the pain. She pressed it hard, feeling the gnarled shaft work its way into the elastic walls of her anus, until it seemed to be stuck, refusing to budge. She gave a fierce push and, suddenly, the dildo slid smoothly, right to her arse root, making her gasp as it filled her rectum, seeming almost to split her belly.

She squeezed her sphincter on the shaft and received a shock of pleasure, with a copious spurt of come from her cunt. Grasping the dildo's base, she began to ram it inside herself, fucking her own bottom in swift, urgent strokes, and reaming her rectum with circular thrusts. Her face sank to her pillow, moaning, as her fingers found her throbbing clitty, and Lisbeth began another frig. Closing her eyes, she imagined Femella Culbutt's ebony bare bum swaying, tantalisingly close, then sitting on her face, crushing her, as Lisbeth tongued her gushing pink slit and swallowed her squirted come.

Then, dream-Femella had a cock – real flesh or a strap-on, Lisbeth wasn't sure – but Lisbeth was clutching Femella's pumping bare arse, as the ebony girl fucked her anus. Faster and faster she buggered herself with the hard rubber tool, with come pouring over her masturbating fingers, until she howled into her pillow, as her belly exploded in an orgasm so powerful she almost fainted. Groaning, she withdrew the dildo from her anus, leaving an ache, but also a pleasant sensation of absolute fullness. *So that's what a bumming feels like.* She rose and walked on trembling legs onto the beach. Scampering into the sea, to wash away her shame, she vowed to be celibate. *From now on.*

Lisbeth spent the rest of the day in the nude, lounging, sunning, swimming and reading. For a late luncheon, she summoned a maid, and Rose, a luscious dark creole girl, appeared, wearing spanking panties like Sapphire's, but Lisbeth did not yield to the temptation of discipline. The girl prepared her a delicious dish of oysters and lobster, seeming unconcerned by Lisbeth's nudity. As Lisbeth sipped champagne, she answered questions dutifully enough, revealing that she was a clandestine migrant from Haiti, like many of the slave girls.

'We come from all over, miss,' she said, in charmingly halting English. 'Europe, or Jamaica, oh, everywhere in the world.'

Having piddled copiously in the potty, held by Rose, whose unblinking face was splashed by the force of Lisbeth's stream, she dismissed the slave girl.

After luncheon she took a nap, then summoned another slave, this one Melissa, a tall, raw-boned Jamaican girl, with arse and titties bursting exuberantly from her slave's costume. Melissa made Lisbeth a delicious tea, with watercress sandwiches, and set to cleaning the unmuddied house, while Lisbeth sat down by her pool to study the master's pamphlet. On a whim she ordered the Jamaican girl to strip off and work in the nude, and the young slave complied without a murmur. Lisbeth feasted on her gleaming ebony croup and firm, thrusting bare bubbies, relishing the seep of come in her cooze, yet congratulating herself on keeping her hands chastely off.

The master wrote:

'The female of the species learns to know and relish her subservient place in the world, apart from those few who have risen to riches and prominence. They are the guests of Rum Hole, and must not err in thinking slaves resent their position. On the contrary, slaves love to serve, hoping that the beauty and power of their mistress will rub off on them, especially if their bottoms are made to tingle with well-deserved stripes. A slave well disciplined is a happy slave.'

For the next few days she kept to her vow of celibacy, although, beguiled by the tropical heat and the beauty of her various slaves, she masturbated several times a day and took especial delight in unconcernedly frigging in full view of her slaves, either male or female – casually lifting a thigh to expose herself – and was pleased when the sight of her open frigged cunt, its pink flesh glistening with juice, made the males' cocks instantly erect. There was extra pleasure in her exhibitionist masturbation, a casual display of her power, like the coolness with which she pissed into a slave girl's proffered potty. Sometimes she masturbated while pissing, her swollen clitty inches from the girl's splashed face, or did without the potty, ordering a nude slave boy to lie on his back, for her to piss on his buttocks or balls. Alone, she masturbated with the fearful rubber dildo in her anus, bringing herself to delicious comes of pleasure mixed with pain.

Rum Hole was restfully old-fashioned, with no distractions from sensuous relaxation. Slaves provided every service, and Lisbeth was daily visited by a quimicure girl, usually Cuban, who attended to the perfect shaving of her cunt hillock. Excitements were small, but relished: the passage of a rickshaw girl, or a post girl, who cycled in the nude but for a fetching red cap and kerchief, the bicycle saddle being merely a metal bar, like a horizontal dildo. Many guests cycled, and Lisbeth obtained a bicycle from Miss Comington's commissary for a trip to nearby Gibbet Town, the island's only settlement.

She rode, knickerless, slopping the saddle tube with her come, across the dense scrubland, chirping with birds and reptiles, to a large clearing, where a few dusty shacks lolled in the sunshine. The few people were young and sleek with ebony beauty, the males shirtless, the girls with short flimsy dresses, their big breasts and bottoms evidently naked beneath the thin gaudy cloth. There was a store, a rum shop and the courthouse, a two-storey structure, more imposing than the rest, with a dark, muscled young man in policeman's uniform shorts and cap, but bare to the waist, standing at the door, a coiled whip at his belt. This must be Eldridge Perkins, the catchpoll, Lisbeth thought, and waved to him, receiving only a frosty stare in return.

She stopped for a glass of rum in the shebeen and was served politely, the young people clustering, yet not crowding her, gazing at her unpantied bottom with coy, amused gleams in their eyes, shy but somehow knowing. Lisbeth *was* rather fruity from her bicycle ride, and felt her come-soaked skirtlet sticking to her buttocks, her quim throbbing for a frig. The males thrust their muscled chests, and the girls rippled their braless breasts and unpantied croups. She asked what they did for a living, and received the reply that they worked 'for the master' – the girls in the corset factory, or the canewood plantation which supplied it, while the males had 'duties'.

'*Your* bottom looks ripe for canewood, miss,' trilled a mischievous, elfin girl with a ragged dress that scarcely covered her lithe bare body. 'It's as big as any of ours, and a lovely shape.'

'Well!' gasped Lisbeth, reddening. 'Thank you. I don't think any of the girls at Rum Hole would dare compliment me like that.'

The minx pirouetted, letting her dress flutter up to show Lisbeth her lushly tight bare buttocks, the dark velvet skin soft and quivering in the dusty sunshine. Lisbeth's pouch seeped come.

'Nor should I, miss. Mr de Hazebrouck owns the entire island, including Gibbet Town,' she whispered. 'And all the bottoms in it.'

7

Pole Position

At beach, restaurant, bar, pool or sauna, the lady guests of Rum Hole greeted each other with a certain reserve, smiling coyly in the knowledge that each pursued her secret sensual agenda. One or two remained nude, even outside their villas, but most delighted in dressing up in frocks and tops of exotic and expensive frothiness. Lisbeth found that the days passed easily with swimming, sunbathing, reading and feasting. She frequented the Cat and Crossbones, a huge, airy chamber with immaculately laid tables and a handsome mahogany bar, where she reached a nodding or small-talk acquaintance with several of the lady guests, amid murals depicting a blonde girl flogged with a cat-o'-nine-tails at the mainmast of a pirate barque, with the flag of the skull and crossbones fluttering above her wealed nude body. Sometimes the subject was whipped on the buttocks, sometimes on the back, but in all her head was turned and mouth open to her male chastiser. In the Rum Hole handcrafts boutique, as well as paintings, pottery, sensuous frocks, corsets and underthings, guests could purchase replica items from the island's colourful past: whips, hobbles, branks and other torture implements.

Small talk centred on the master, with all the guests excited by the prospect of meeting him, whenever he should return. His presence, apparently, heralded exciting events, like spearfishing or doe hunting. The petty assizes in Gibbet Town would also come up shortly, the administration of out-island justice being a major guest attraction.

After girl-talk at the bar, each lady had her own dining table, exquisite with linen, silver and fresh flowers. The service was provided by frilly maids and slave boys in tight black evening wear, amongst whom Lisbeth recognised Norbert, who did not return her smiles.

At the beginning of the meal, the slave boys waited on tables at random but, by the meal's end, some curious affinity meant that each guest was served by one slave, sometimes two or even three, who then accompanied her home after her meal. Everyone seemed to retire early, and Lisbeth walked home alone, or rode by rickshaw. Melanie was often on duty and her face lit up when Lisbeth took her. The girl prattled happily as she trotted, about England, and her travels, but was coy about her reasons for remaining at Rum Hole, except to say she couldn't feel at home elsewhere.

'You are so kind, miss,' she panted after one journey. 'You don't whip us.'

'But others do,' Lisbeth retorted. 'Surely you don't *have* to be a slave, so cruelly beaten.'

'I wouldn't know, miss,' answered Melanie.

Lisbeth scanned her bare bottom, faintly wealed with numerous whipmarks, and felt the sudden desire to humiliate the happy slave. With the on-board whip, she lashed Melanie four hard strokes across the naked buttocks, making the girl squeal and sob, her eyes wrinkled in pain, as she rubbed her wealed bare.

'Oh, miss,' she wailed, 'what was that for?'

'For taking me for granted,' replied Lisbeth.

One evening Lisbeth's table adjoined that of a sleek, ash-blonde, thirtyish lady, whom she knew noddingly, and who accompanied a slender, slightly younger male, whom Lisbeth also recognised. Both wore evening dress, the lady a skimpy black cocktail dress, with spaghetti straps like Lisbeth's, but her nylons were turquoise, while Lisbeth had black eight-denier seamed sheens.

'Excuse me,' Lisbeth murmured, leaning over, unable to prevent the male from looking down her cleavage. 'Isn't that Jeremy Bonslitt, the Formula One driver?'

The lady smiled.

'Yes, he's my husband. I'm Tanya Bonslitt. The master permitted me to bring him, for he's apt to misbehave if left alone. All those racing groupies, you know.'

'I do love your stockings,' said Lisbeth.

'Yours are *awfully* moisture-making,' purred Tanya.

Lisbeth was happy to join their table, and talked of the home counties, and property prices in Ascot and Virginia Water, with Jeremy preening himself at Lisbeth's attention and unashamedly ogling her breasts.

'It must be so exciting to be a racing driver,' she said.

'He's retiring soon,' Tanya said curtly, then smiled. 'Twenty-seven, you know! Too old. Not like Gregor, here.'

Jeremy glowered. Their servant was a young slave, with the same supple frame and lustrous ebony skin as Norbert. He also possessed the same notable bulge at his crotch. After much wine, it did not surprise Lisbeth that Gregor must accompany the married couple to their villa, a few doors from Lisbeth's, nor that she should be invited for a nightcap. They took a rickshaw back to the Bonslitts' villa, a few doors from Lisbeth's, with Jeremy making liberal use of the whip on the rickshaw girl's bare back and bottom. The girl's whimpers and sobs shrilled above the clacking of her horseshoes.

'Oh, Jeremy,' drawled Tanya, 'I do wish you wouldn't show off. This isn't a racetrack. Besides, it's awfully cruel.'

'Nonsense, girl,' snorted Jeremy. 'It's the only language girls understand. Anyway, life's a racetrack, and if you're not cracking on, in pole position, then you go under. It's all about domination, Lisbeth. A filly respects a man who shows her he's the boss.'

Tanya rolled her eyes as Lisbeth suppressed a giggle. Gregor helped the ladies dismount and led them into the villa, while Jeremy busied himself with a final few lashes to the quivering bare bottom of their sobbing rickshaw girl.

'Gave the filly a good lesson,' he said, rubbing his hands. 'Now, sit ye down, Lisbeth. The boy can fix us some drinks. Gin and tonic for you?'

'Oh, Bonslitt, how primitive you are,' pouted Tanya. 'Just because you're too cheap to offer her Scotch.'

'G and T is what girls drink,' said Jeremy.

'Gin and tonic will be fine,' Lisbeth said.

'Nonsense,' said Tanya. 'Boy, bring us two large Scotch and sodas. Oh, and one for Bonslitt, I suppose.'

Pouting, Jeremy sat beside Lisbeth on the sofa, while Tanya placed herself in an armchair opposite. Her black dress rode several inches up her nyloned thigh, revealing a ripely curved naked cunt hillock, shaved, and unpantied, framed by frilly turquoise lace sussies.

'Like the frillies?' said Tanya. 'I got them from Miss Comington, and my nylons too.'

'Tanya, you're showing off,' said Jeremy, reddening. 'What if Lisbeth's a lesbo? Most unmarried girls are, really – just waiting for the right man to tame them – and in that case, you're unfairly exciting her.'

'What if I am?' said Tanya, accepting her drink from the slave.

'I'm not a lesbo, as you put it, Jeremy,' said Lisbeth, blushing. 'I may have had some sapphic experiences, like any normal girl, but it's not the same.'

'Isn't it?' said Jeremy, eagerly. 'So it's true that all girls are lezzies under the skin? Gad, won't you tell us . . . you know, what you get up to? Or show us, even better. That's the whole point of Rum Hole, an't it? Girls free to indulge their fancies. Tanya's partial to a spot of rug-munching, and I indulge her. Why not? I'm a generous chap. Nothing wrong with a pair of fillies squelching, eh? I mean, if you two felt like putting on a show . . .' He leered, drooling a little.

'Bonslitt, don't be gross,' said Tanya.

'Freedom's not the same as showing off,' Lisbeth riposted sweetly.

'You might say that Gregor here is showing off,' drawled Tanya.

Her fingers brushed the prominent bulge at his groin, emphasised by his tight black evening suit. The slave boy remained impassive, as he served Lisbeth and Jeremy.

'He *is* superbly hung, isn't he, Lisbeth?' Tanya continued, licking her lips.

'Tanya, really,' huffed Jeremy. 'Now who's being gross?'

'Well, he is a pleasure slave, after all,' retorted Tanya, stroking the boy's buttocks. 'And such a lovely tight bum. Oh, look. How splendid.'

Gregor's bulge had grown, as she stroked his bottom.

'I'll bet it's an absolute monster when it's fully stiff,' said Tanya. 'Wouldn't you like to see him naked, Lisbeth?'

Lisbeth blushed, yet could not help the seep of come wetting her panties, as she eyed the slave's rising cock.

'I suppose so,' she replied, smiling, with an apologetic glance at the sulking Jeremy.

Tanya hoisted her left leg onto her seat and hugged her knee, letting her skimpy cocktail dress fall right to her hips and displaying the full expanse of bare cunt basin to Lisbeth and the saturnine pleasure slave. Her long, pink slit, the lips swollen, the bud of the clitty peeping from its soft folds, glistened with a film of seeped come. Jeremy blushed profusely. Gregor fluttered his long, girlish eyelashes but remained aloof, his lips creased almost imperceptibly in a smile. Tanya took a long pull of her drink.

'Twelve inches, at least,' she bubbled, her face flushed. 'Wouldn't you love him to do you, Lisbeth? I mean, that's the beauty of Rum Hole. Ladies have absolute power. We may command any pleasure we want.'

'Really!' Jeremy growled.

'And whose money pays for all this?' sneered Tanya. 'Mine.'

'Money,' spat Jeremy. 'You mildewed hussy, is that all you think about?'

'It was all you thought about when you married me,' retorted Tanya, gesturing for more Scotch. 'You didn't have a pot to piss in.'

Gregor freshened all their drinks, his crotch now bulging unashamedly and his eyes blatantly fixed on Tanya's exposed bare cunt.

'And what did *you* think about?' snarled Jeremy. 'Getting a name! You were plain Tanya Dole-Mingent, fruit of some scabrous dalliance of Charles the Second. A whore from a whore's lineage! The Bonslitts came over with William the Conqueror.'

'You dare call me a whore,' hissed Tanya. 'After all those racetrack groupies you've pronged.'

'As if you weren't the horniest!' said Jeremy. 'Every driver's cock was in pole position, and I was last out of the pits.' He turned to Lisbeth. 'The drab didn't marry me, she married the Bonslitt coat of arms,' he said accusingly.

'Now, now,' said Lisbeth. 'We are supposed to be here for pleasure.'

'*Her* pleasure,' muttered Jeremy. 'To humiliate me, she lets me tag along on her outing to this knocking shop for randy rich cunts!'

'Jeremy, I think that's a bit steep,' said Lisbeth.

'You think I haven't seen you ogling those pleasure girls?' said Tanya. 'Dreaming of your cock up their hot slimy holes? Fucking them, for all I know, while I'm out.'

Jeremy leered. 'Swiving the serving maids is an aristocrat's prerogative, my dear,' he said. 'Something *you* are ignorant of.'

'Swive them?' sneered Tanya. 'With what? That tiny apology for a tool?'

Jeremy rose, scarlet with rage.

'You've gone too far,' he hissed. He grabbed her glass and splattered the drink down her front.

'Bonslitt! How dare you?' cried Tanya.

Jeremy tore the thin silk from her breasts, exposing the heavy bare bubbies, heaving with rage, their pert nipples stiffly erect. He leered, then ripped the rest of the dress from her, leaving her naked but for stockings and sussies, and the pearl choker at her neck.

'That frock was a genuine Giulio Ferracci! You'll pay for it out of your allowance,' she blurted.

Jeremy spat on her breasts. 'That rag-snipping gigolo,' he snarled. 'I suppose he's fucked you too.'

'Ooh!' she squealed. 'You're disgusting.'

He grasped her hair, twisting it round his fist.

'Ouch! Ooh! Stop, you're hurting me,' gasped his wife.

'I've had enough of your lip,' said Jeremy. 'You're all bloody mouth and no bloody trousers, you shameless hussy. Now you're going to get a lesson. Gregor! Open the armoire.'

He dragged Tanya by her hair to the rosewood dining table. The nude girl kicked and screamed but was unable to prevent the wrenching of her long mane as he forced her to bend over the table. On Jeremy's instructions, Gregor selected a long, thin rattan cane from the array of tools in the armoire. Tanya's ripely swelling bare buttocks churned as her titties thumped helplessly on the table, and her ankles threshed the air.

'This is monstrous,' she gurgled. 'Gregor, I forbid you ... Lisbeth, aren't you going to do something?'

'It is unseemly to interfere in a marital dispute,' purred Lisbeth, sipping Scotch. 'And you *were* just the tiniest bit provocative, Tanya.'

'Oh!' gasped the scarlet-faced girl. 'I can't believe this!'

Gregor deftly wrapped each wrist in a rubber cord, which he bound to the table legs. When he had repeated the process with her ankles, and all four limbs were securely fastened, Jeremy let go of her hair. Tanya's nude body trembled in a right angle, her legs spread wide with her buttocks parted, showing her anus and pendant gash flaps, and her arms stretched, spreadeagling her torso on the tabletop.

'Oh, please, Bonslitt,' she whimpered, 'don't flog me.'

'I shan't,' said Jeremy.

'Oh, good. You've given me enough of a scare, you rotter.'

Jeremy spat into her arse cleft, right on her anus pucker.

'Ooh!' she squealed. 'Don't be revolting, Bonslitt.'

'Since you are so fond of pleasure boys, Gregor is going to thrash you,' Jeremy murmured. 'See what pleasure you get from *that,* harlot.'

Gregor swished the cane in the air, inches from her face. The bulge at his crotch was huge.

'No ...!' she wailed, struggling frantically at her bonds.

'And, just to show you, Gregor is going to deliver your caning in the nude,' said Jeremy, licking his teeth. 'You will see that his tool stands, not for the chore of fucking your slimy loose box, but for the pleasure of flogging that big pale arse.'

With the ghost of a smile, Gregor slid from his garments and stood nude, cane in hand, at Tanya's head. She strained to look up at the giant stiff cock, inches from her face, and the massive ball-gourds tight beneath his pole.

'Oh, God . . .' she moaned.

Gregor lifted his cane to quiver over her naked buttocks.

'Oh, Bonslitt, please,' Tanya begged. 'I didn't mean it. You can't . . . you wouldn't . . .'

Vip! The cane lashed her hard across her quivering bare mid-fesse.

'Ahh!' she screamed.

Vip!

'Ouch! Ooh!'

Vip!

'Oh, stop, please.'

Vip!

'Ah! Bonslitt, tell him to stop. I can't take it.'

'That's what we shall see,' hissed Jeremy.

Vip!

'Uhh . . . uhh . . .' Tanya moaned, drooling.

Her flogged buttocks clenched tight and squirmed against the table, whose surface glistened with a smear of come at her jerking cunt. The slave boy's muscles glistened, rippling, as he caned the woman's arse with sinewy force, his massive stiff tool swaying like a branch. He caned for several minutes, working his way from haunch to under-fesse, until Tanya's wriggling bare croup was a dark, blotchy mass of weals.

'See how pretty her bum is now, against her turquoise things,' said Jeremy.

'Oh, Bonslitt, please, honestly, that's enough,' Tanya whimpered. 'It hurts dreadfully. My bum's on fire.'

Gulping scotch, Lisbeth could not ignore the copious ooze of come in her own slit as she watched the girl's naked arse wriggle in torment. She let her skirt ride up a fraction, showing her stocking tops, and slid her hand up her thighs to the wet swollen gusset of her panties. Pushing in two fingers, she penetrated her slit through the cloth, shuddered as she tweaked her throbbing clitty, and began to masturbate. Beside her, Jeremy was tense, his teeth bared in a rictus of delight and his crotch bulging with his erect cock. Vip! Vip! The cane sliced its flashing arc to kiss Tanya's reddened bare fesses, wriggling on the table, while the whipped girl drooled and whimpered, her head shaking from side to side and her bare bubbies bouncing on the rosewood with a squelching sound.

'Oh! Oh! It's agony. Oh, please, Bonslitt, I beg you, stop. Haven't you shamed me enough?'

Her bottom took its fortieth canestroke before Jeremy ordered Gregor to stop.

'Shamed, you say, m'dear?' he murmured.

'Yes! To have my bare exposed like this, and my cunny and bumhole . . . oh! What must our guest think? Please release me.'

Jeremy glanced at Lisbeth, who was masturbating vigorously, and remarked that she seemed to thoroughly enjoy the spectacle. Lisbeth's tongue lolled, drooling, as she frigged her clitty, and come trickled into her nylon stocking tops. Abruptly, Jeremy ordered Gregor to cease the flogging and release his wife from her bonds. Freed, she stood, shivering, weeping, and snuffling.

'Oh! Oh, the shame . . .' she moaned, rubbing her striped bare. 'My bum's a mess, and smarts so frightfully.'

'Shame? You don't know the meaning of the word, you bitch,' snarled Jeremy, grabbing her by the hair.

'Ooh!' she squealed. 'Let go. What are you doing to me?'

'You'll see,' he said, and began to drag her by the hair into the bedroom.

Lisbeth rose and followed. Tanya did not resist as he flung her on her back on the queen-sized counterpane.

'Now, slave, I want you in pole position,' Jeremy said.

'Sir?' asked Gregor.

'Tup the slut,' he commanded.

'Very good, sir,' purred Gregor, flicking the massive hard helmet of his cock. 'And in which aperture?'

'Why, the most *shameful*,' said Jeremy, chuckling.

'No!' shrieked Tanya, struggling, but powerless to rise, as her husband wrenched her hair to the pillow.

She moaned and burbled as the slave's giant cock approached her writhing cunt basin. Gregor straddled her and pushed her thighs apart, then nestled the bulb of his cock at her juicing cunt, sliming his glans with her come before stroking her arse cleft with his tool as it slid to her anal pucker. His buttocks jerked, he thrust savagely, and his glans disappeared inside her anus.

'Ahh! No,' Tanya shrieked.

Watching, Lisbeth lifted her skirt right up and thrust her whole hand inside her come-sodden panties, drooling as she powerfully masturbated her dripping cunt. Gregor thrust again, and two more inches of cock penetrated the girl's bumhole. She writhed, impaled on his huge stiff cock, and Gregor thrust again, this time driving his entire shaft to the root of her rectum, burying his cock inside her, with only his balls showing at her anal entrance. His dark buttocks gleamed, flickering, as he buggered Tanya in strong, rapid thrusts.

'Oh! Oh! God, it hurts!' wailed the buggered girl. 'How can you see your own wife shamed, you bastard? Another man's cock inside her!'

'Does sir wish me to discharge inside miss, or continue her treatment without sperming?' panted Gregor.

'Do not sperm till I command,' said Jeremy. 'Fuck her till she screams for mercy.'

'Very good, sir.'

Lisbeth watched the slave's muscled buttocks ripple, and the huge tool emerge briefly, glistening with Tanya's copious arse grease, before plunging to the hilt once more, to constant shrieks and moans from the buggered girl. A stream of come spurted from Tanya's cooze, dribbling down her thighs and wetting the bed. After several minutes' vigorous buggery, the bedspread under Tanya's pumping buttocks was soaked in her come. Tanya's shrieks softened to panting moans and her legs rose. Her pubis began to thrust against the impaling cock-thrusts and she wrapped her legs round his back.

'Yes! Oh, yes!' she gasped. 'That's so good. Bugger me, fuck my arse till it splits. Get your belly down low, so I can rub my clitty on your pube bone. Yes, that's it. Oh, feel how wet I am, I can't stop spraying! Ah . . . ah . . . it's so good, your giant cock in my bumhole, fuck me, fuck me harder, split me with your gorgeous stiff tool . . .'

Tanya's fists thumped the bed as her bum writhed on the slave boy's tool. Lisbeth's fingers were a blur, masturbating her sopping wet cunt.

'That's right,' gasped Jeremy. 'Punish the bitch, give it to her really hard.'

'Fuck me, fuck my arse harder . . .' whimpered Tanya. 'You're all man . . .'

'Hurt her, make the slut squeal,' Jeremy panted.

'Oh, your cock hurts so, it's such a monster, it's *so* good,' moaned his wife, her legs clinging to the slave's jerking back as he rode her.

'Look how strong the fellow is,' Jeremy drawled. 'Really ramming it hard up her slut's arsehole. By gad, she's taking a pounding. I'll bet that excites you, eh, Lisbeth? Sapphically, I mean. My wife, fucked senseless by a virile young stud?' Jeremy's flushed face stared at Lisbeth's cunt. 'I like it, I like it,' he hissed. 'Wanking off, filly? Let me assist, I'll tongue your cooze to come, while my wife has to watch, for more shame.'

'I'm quite content,' Lisbeth gasped.

'Nonsense,' said Jeremy, groping for her cooze.

She slapped his hand away, then removed her fingers from her panties.

'Sir, I think that impudence earns *you* a thrashing,' Lisbeth said icily.

'You can't be serious,' Jeremy blurted.

Lisbeth looked at his bulging crotch.

'Chastising an errant wife is one thing,' she said, 'but getting some smutty pleasure from it, quite another.'

She picked up the cane, still warm from Tanya's bottom, and stroked it, with a sly smile. The caneshaft gleamed with her smeared come.

'Let's have your kit off, Jeremy,' she purred.

'Now, wait a minute,' Jeremy blurted.

'Are you a man or a mouse?' gasped Tanya, writhing

under buggery. 'A gentleman who offends a lady must take her punishment.'

'Damn you! I suppose so,' Jeremy grumbled.

'Oh! God, yes, my darling,' Tanya shrilled, 'fuck me harder, fuck me, fuck my hole . . . ooh!'

Jeremy licked his lips, staring at his wife's buttocks squirming under her buggery by the rippling nude slave.

'All off, Jeremy,' rapped Lisbeth, swishing the cane in the air. 'I want you in the full nude.'

'Yes, of course,' he mumbled.

Within seconds, he was nude, his lithe, muscled body seeming overbalanced by his erect cock.

'That's scarcely tiny,' Lisbeth murmured. 'You're quite disgustingly rampant, sir.'

'Gregor, my darling,' Tanya gasped, 'let me switch round and take it doggy. I want to watch my hubby being beaten by a girl.'

Without removing his cock from her bumhole, the slave flipped Tanya and straddled her at the crouch. Her scarlet face was wrinkled in pain, her bum high in the air, writhing and clenching, as the boy's hips slapped against her. His cock slammed in and out of her anus with a squelchy, plopping sound, as come streamed down her thighs from her gushing cunt. Supporting herself on a single elbow, Tanya thrust her fingers between her thighs and began to masturbate as he buggered her.

Lisbeth ordered Jeremy to bend over, hands on his knees, like a schoolboy, and he complied, seeming to know the drill. She looked at his naked arse – *quite tasty, really* – and felt the weight of her cane. To thrash a man, naked and helpless beneath her rod, bound by his code of honour to take her punishment! Her cunt spurted come as she lifted the rod. Vip! His arse clenched, trembling, as she laid a fierce cut across his top buttock. Vip! Lower down, this time, on the mid-fesse. Vip! A tasty slice to the underfesse. Vip! Vip!

His bum's squirming nicely.

'Ahh!' gasped Jeremy. 'Gosh, that's tight, Lisbeth.'

'Hurting you much?'

'Smarts like the dickens!'

'Good.'

Vip! Vip!

'Ooh! Ahh! Gosh, I bet you've caned dozens of chaps. You're an expert.'

His cock wobbled stiffly, at full erection, as Lisbeth caned his trembling bare arse. Vip! Vip! Vip! She lashed him three times without pause.

'Ooh! Ah! I say, steady on. My arse really smarts.'

'Give it to him harder,' panted Tanya, writhing under Gregor's cock. 'His tool is still stiff, the filthy beast.'

'We'll have to whip that away,' Lisbeth snapped.

Vip!

'Uhh . . .'

Vip!

'Oh!'

Vip! Vip!

'Ahh!'

His buttocks squirmed violently, livid with crimson weals, yet his cock refused to soften.

'It's no good,' panted Tanya. 'Gregor will have to beat him. He's stronger. Lisbeth, you are probably holding back a little, scared to whip a male.'

'I am not,' retorted Lisbeth hotly.

Vip! Vip!

'Ahh! Ooh! Stop, please,' whimpered the wriggling male, his squirming bare buttocks dark crimson with deep, puffy welts.

With a plop, the slave withdrew his cock from Tanya's anus, sprang to Lisbeth's side and, gently smiling, took the cane from her. He approached Jeremy's proffered buttocks with his member detumescent and dangling limply at mid-thigh.

'No – no – that's not fair,' Jeremy protested, as the slave boy raised the cane. 'It's a beastly shame – I can't – I won't –'

Vip-vip-vip-vip-vip!

'Ooh! Ahh! Oh, gosh, that hurts!' shrieked Jeremy, dancing on tiptoe with his welted arse wriggling. 'It's worse than a beating at school!'

His cock was limp. Her teeth bared in a fierce grin, Tanya perched on the bed with her leg raised, so that her spread cunt faced him, and she began to masturbate – firmly and luxuriously.

'You don't mind if I frig off, darling, watching your bum lashed, by a *slave boy*, and your face all creased in pain?' she cooed. 'It is *so* satisfying.'

'You bitch,' sobbed Jeremy. 'You absolute bitch.'

Vip!

'Ooh, stop . . . stop . . .' he moaned.

Vip! Vip!

'Ahh!'

Gasping, Lisbeth and Tanya both masturbated, observing the male's flogging, the lithe body of the slave putting all his weight into the canestrokes, and his soft tool, slimed with Tanya's arse grease, bobbing in counterpoint to the rhythmic descent of the rod on Jeremy's bare. The boy flogged her whimpering husband to over thirty strokes until Tanya ordered him to resume her buggery as she was too hot to wait. He smiled, with a glance at Tanya's proffered bare arse, and his cock stiffened at once to full erection. Watching the huge ebony tool rise, Lisbeth felt a new spurt of come from her gushing cooze. *Such marvellous control . . .!* Leaving Jeremy to sink, sobbing, on the sofa, rubbing his flaming buttocks, Gregor straddled Tanya anew, and rammed his cock into her anus.

'Ooh! Yes! Look at us, Jeremy,' Tanya gasped. 'Don't you want to see me shamed?'

Jeremy raised his eyes to the slave's slimed cock pounding into his wife's bumhole, while her buttocks twitched and thrust, sucking the massive tool into her rectum.

'Gosh, it's super,' Tanya panted. 'Oh, what it is, to be fucked by a *real* man! Are you going to come, darling? I think you are, I can feel it. Come in my mouth, darling, so my husband can see me swallow all your lovely cream.'

Gregor's tool plopped from her hole and, dripping with her arse grease, penetrated her open mouth. Tanya's lips nibbled artfully at the huge ebony glans of the slave's cock, her tongue licking the peehole and corona and frenulum, until Gregor began to pant hoarsely, his bulb half in and half out of Tanya's slurping, teasing mouth. Lisbeth masturbated faster, nearing her climax. Jeremy gazed at the scene, his face twisted in utter hatred.

'You filthy slut,' he hissed.

'Mm!' cried Tanya, as a huge jet of sperm spurted into her mouth.

Her lips puckered, pressing on the glans, to milk the boy of come. It spurted so hard that creamy white globules drooled from her lips, down her chin and onto her quivering bare breasts. Tanya rubbed the sperm into her nipples, cooing in delight, as the shuddering cock bucked in spasm, delivering its heavy cargo of cream. Lisbeth's own gasps, as she wanked herself to climax, joined Tanya's pants of delight as she fingered her nipples and clitty to come, and her husband's growls of incandescent rage. Yet, as he watched his wife drink another male's sperm, Jeremy's cock stood as stiff as ever. When Tanya had licked and swallowed every drop of sperm from her chin and nipples, she turned to the impassive slave.

'Time to freshen up our drinks, I think, slave,' she said.

Tanya decided that to complete his punishment Jeremy must wear a pair of her knickers. Jeremy donned the proffered pink frillies, wincing as the cloth touched his wealed arse, and sat, sulking, in the high-cut silken panties, which did not conceal his rigid erection. Tanya elected to remain nude. Lisbeth was glad she had masturbated to climax, for otherwise the sight of a hugely stiff cock, imprisoned in bursting girl's knickers, and two purple flogged bottoms would have forced her to do so. However, the rest of Lisbeth's visit proceeded with studied elegance, as if nothing had taken place. They made small talk, discussing forthcoming events on the Rum Hole calendar, such as the great doe hunt, and the petty assizes in Gibbet Town. Gregor was dismissed and, after a few more drinks, Lisbeth solemnly thanked them both for a lovely evening and let herself out.

Scarcely halfway down the garden, she heard a furious racket from the house and rushed back to the window, fearing mayhem by one or the other disgruntled spouse. She peeped through the curtain to see both spouses nude, with Jeremy on top of his wife, his stiff cock ramming her anus. Come sprayed from her wet cooze as she met his thrusts with heaves of her cane-striped buttocks.

'By gad, you're hot, you luscious creature,' gasped Jeremy. 'You're the sexiest bitch there is!'

'Oh! Yes! I'm going to come!' yelped Tanya. 'Fuck my bum, darling, give me all your hot spunk, oh, *yes,* you animal! *Nobody* does it better, you're the world's best fuck, when you're angry. Do me, darling, do me hard!'

'I will, you filthy rampant beast! See if I don't!'

'Oh . . . oh . . . oh . . . I'm coming . . . *ahh!*'

Lisbeth turned away and walked the short distance back to her own villa.

I've kept my vow of celibacy. I didn't have sex, I wanked off, that's all . . .

She thought of Gregor's hard cock plunging into Tanya's anus, and her evident relish; of her self-buggery with the rubber dildo; of her thrill of power at caning a male on his bare buttocks; most of all, she imagined beating a slave boy's juicy naked bottom, his huge cock stiff under her whipping, and the slave powerless to protest or resist, when she commanded that cock to impale her bumhole . . .

8

Judicial Whipping

Gibbet Town was busy. It seemed that almost everyone on the island of Rum Hole, resort guests included, turned up for the petty assizes, and Gibbet Square was crowded with elegant women with parasols, sunglasses and bright, expensive summer dresses fluttering in the light sea breeze. Most were accompanied by a slave girl or boy, while Lisbeth chose to stay beside Tanya, Gregor and Jeremy. Rickshaws trotted the dusty roadway, and Lisbeth espied Melanie, her golden body decently covered in sky-blue shorts and halter top. The local people thronged the street in force, lounging gaily in the sinister shadow of the gibbet in the main square. Among them were several European faces, though obviously locals, with their skin a lustrous tan, and the sultry females dressed in the same flowery sundresses as the ebony girls. The males slouched while the females eyed each other with sullen, sensuous envy.

'White Bahamians,' Jeremy explained. 'Been here for centuries, on the out islands. Pirates, runaways, d'ye see? Quite a melting pot.'

'They look rather ... sexy,' said Lisbeth, and Tanya murmured agreement.

'Everybody here is sexy,' she said, stroking Gregor's bottom. 'The outcasts of the islands spent hundreds of years with little to do but fish, copulate, and whip each other's bottoms for rude behaviour or amusement. When the loyal English refugees from the thirteen rebellious colonies arrived with their slaves, they found the land no use for cotton-pickers and cane-reapers, so chose their servants for beauty, not brute strength. Tupping, smuggling and rum-bibbing, that's Bahamian history.'

'Sun's over the yardarm,' Jeremy pronounced. 'Time for a snifter, eh, girls?'

They entered the crowded grog shop, and Jeremy called for glasses of rum and soda.

'I suppose there was plenty of the lash,' murmured Lisbeth.

Tanya's eyes sparkled.

'Yes,' she said, licking her lips. 'The old justice of the whip, slicing luscious, rippling backs and bottoms of bare girlskin . . . yum yum.'

'The only language fillies understand,' trumpeted Jeremy. 'Pity old Chas isn't here, it would open his eyes.'

'Charles Gee-Toole? Your old school chum?'

'Yes, he has an island here somewhere. So many dashed islands, though. Chas was always a bit of a do-gooder. He used to own up for whoppings by our fearful matron for things he hadn't done, because he felt sorry for the chaps that had. Wouldn't approve of tickling fillies or assorted lewdness.'

'Oh, I don't know,' drawled Tanya. 'As I recall, he's *awfully* well hung. Or perhaps it was his manservant. Sometimes I forget who's tupping me, in the dark.'

Jeremy reddened, scowling, and gulped his rum.

'It's not just about whipping fillies,' said Lisbeth, glancing at Gregor, whose lip trembled. 'There is something awfully thrill-making about a man being whipped. He has to take it, you see, be brave, even as his bare bum's wriggling under strokes. Can't blub like a girly, eh, Jeremy?'

Jeremy blushed as Tanya nodded agreement, licking her teeth.

'A man's buttocks are only really attractive when they're striped and squirming,' she purred.

'What about them?' Lisbeth asked. She pointed to a group of tall, slender girls, their skins a burnished copper bronze, who were drinking by themselves, away from the melee. They wore short skirtlets in subdued colours of olive or maroon, which showed curving long legs, gleaming bare, a rippling reddish-bronze sheen. Their faces were austerely handsome, with high foreheads and cheekbones, wide, sensuously full lips, long noses and bare necks laced with precious stones, and each wore a high turban coiled on her head, giving the illusion of a pointed, subtly elongated skull. Their breasts and buttocks jutted in firm, ripe contours below their thin clothing; the arm and leg muscles were well extruded, rippling and glinting in the sunlight. Lisbeth thought they looked like female bodybuilders.

'I believe they are,' Tanya said. 'They are called Lucayans, and keep to themselves, in their village, only showing up here to witness judicial punishments or sell slaves. The Lucayans are supposed to be the original inhabitants of these islands. They call themselves redskins, meaning the superior ones.'

'They have lovely muscly figures,' Lisbeth said. 'Those bottoms! So big and pear-shaped . . . I'd love to see them in the nude.'

The drinkers were subdued and apprehensive, especially when catchpoll Eldridge Perkins strode in, boots gleaming, whip in hand, wearing a spotlessly creased uniform. The crowd parted and he bellied up to the bar, where a tall glass of rum appeared before him. He drank it down in one, and was immediately replenished. Lisbeth sipped her drink, feeling the sweat clammy in her light white sundress, and beginning to regret wearing bra and knickers, which were becoming visible as her light cotton frock moistened with sweat. She looked at the muscular figure of the young law officer, and licked her lips, blushing as he returned her gaze, baring his teeth in a dazzling white smile.

'You must be catchpoll Perkins,' she murmured.

He snapped to attention, and saluted. 'Eldridge Perkins, catchpoll, magistrate and public executioner, at your service, miss,' he said.

'I haven't seen you with your shirt on before,' Lisbeth said, eyeing him over the rim of her glass. 'Either way, you certainly are a fine public figure.'

His chest swelled. 'I aim to satisfy, miss.'

'Surely you don't publicly execute people,' she exclaimed. 'That's barbaric.'

'Of course I don't execute *people,* miss,' he replied, smiling, 'I execute *punishments.* The out islands are a long way from Nassau, and they rely on catchpolls to enforce summary justice. The people respect and like it. Why, look what a crowd we have – townsfolk, the master's guests from Rum Hole, even the red folk from upcountry.'

Lisbeth shivered. 'Does summary justice mean whipping?' she asked coyly.

'Mostly,' said Perkins. 'What else but a good whipping knocks sense into a warmint?'

'And you perform the whippings yourself?'

'I have deputies to help me. My arm would be plumb worn out if I had to discipline every rogue in Gibbet Town. The master says that if they're old enough to vote, drink rum and be hanged at the yardarm, they are old enough for a cobbing on their wicked bare asses.'

He scanned the room, nodding grimly, and several girls and young men sheepishly bowed their heads. Lisbeth saw the cheeky elfin girl from her previous visit. The girl tossed her hair, pouting.

'Elvira O'Malley,' murmured the catchpoll. 'She's one of the worst. Brawling, whoring and gambling. Yet the more stripes her bare bottom takes, it seems, the more she invites.'

Lisbeth ogled the policeman, particularly the prominent bulge in the crotch of his shorts with the crimson stripe down the sides. He laughed heartily.

'The master's guests don't come for the assizes,' he guffawed, 'they come for what's after.'

She decided she liked him: young enough to be yummy, old enough to be wise.

'I suppose so,' she agreed. 'There is something shiver-making and awesome, about ... you know ... a public flogging. So you whip girls as well as men?'

'Of course, miss,' replied Perkins, 'for they are ten times as wicked. All punishments, and tools of punishment, are approved by the chief magistrate, Mr de Hazebrouck. Since you seem so interested, miss, I invite you to my office, to look over my instrument cabinet.'

'Interested?' blurted Lisbeth, blushing fiercely. 'Oh, I don't know.'

'The catchpoll does, Lisbeth,' said Tanya. 'Off you go, you lucky girl.'

Escorted on the catchpoll's arm, Lisbeth strode across the sunbaked square to admiring or envious glances from the local girls. Perkins ushered her into the shadowy, surprisingly cool police station, where a number of uniformed police girls sat at old-fashioned typewriters. They wore tight cotton uniforms, like Cynthia Placket's, with handcuffs, batons, and also whips coiled at their belts. Their lapelled shirts tapered well down their half-bared breasts, sometimes with a peep of lacy white bra; short skirts rode high on bare, lustrous ebony thighs, the naked dark skin of exposed thigh and breast flesh gleaming in the dusty sunlight.

'My deputies,' said Perkins. 'Girls, this is one of the master's guests, come to inspect.'

The girls rose as one and curtsied to Lisbeth, the swelling tubers of their teats bobbing under thin cotton blouses. They gazed at Eldridge Perkins with adoration mingled with jealousy of his new female.

'Candace, please unlock the punishment chest,' ordered the catchpoll.

A shapely deputy swayed, bottom wiggling, into the next room, with a winsome smile at Lisbeth. There was a clank of keys, the creak of a heavy door pushed open, and footsteps echoing on stone flags; then, a rattling of bars, a grunting and whining of voices, and smart whip cracks, with Candace's barked command of silence – followed by a very loud whiplash, and a girl's scream. Eldridge smiled.

'That's my Candace,' he said. 'We can go now.'

Lisbeth followed the catchpoll through an empty chamber, which he said was the courtroom, then into a gloomy stone corridor, one side being the prison wall and the other a long, barred cell, or cage, open to view. Narrow slits in the prison wall admitted a refreshing breeze and dim light, which revealed the crouching occupants, their eyes glowing in the shadow. The prisoners, males and females, were all naked and each was fettered, chained to a bolt in the floor. Lisbeth gasped: the males were chained by fearful clamps around their balls, while the girls were fastened to double teat-clamps, each end of a short metal strut pinned to its nipple. All the prisoners were young, none, seemingly, older than Lisbeth herself. Two of the female prisoners were white Bahamians: one sobbed, crouched in a corner; the second was a tigress, her lush mane ash-blonde and her clamped teats thrusting firm and ripe above her flat, muscled belly, strongly extruded shaven mound and a giant peach of firm, muscled fesses, quivering as she clawed the cell bars. She bore a fresh, livid whip weal across her naked breasts.

'That slut cobbed my tits! You'll rue this, Perkins!' she spat at the catchpoll in her singsong Bahamian accent. 'I'll have your balls for breakfast.'

'It's no good, Nell,' said Perkins. 'You're a dirty bobtail whore, and must pay for it.'

'Ha!' she snarled, parting the lips of her quim to show pink moist slit flesh. 'You only wish *you* were man enough to butter my slice!'

The prisoners laughed and slapped palms.

'Nell is incorrigible,' said Perkins, as he led Lisbeth into a small chamber where an opened glass case overlooked a table spread with the instruments of judicial chastisement.

'You are going to flog her?' asked Lisbeth in a trembling voice, shifting her thighs as a seep of come moistened her panties.

'Unless she can come up with some plea of mitigation,' he said. 'But that's most unlikely.'

'In the nude?'

'Of course, miss.'

The catchpoll locked the gnarled door behind them, pocketing the key from the gaping antique keyhole.

'And are all of them going to be flogged?'

'Mostly flogged with whips, or laced with a cane on the bottom. Of course, I am judge and jury in this court, so unless some tricky advocate appears . . .' He shrugged.

117

'Gosh,' said Lisbeth, biting her lip. 'Such beautiful bare bodies – it seems so horrid to think of those fine skins marked by the whip.'

'The warmints are used to whipping, miss. But there are implements of different strength, you see. This one is a stinger cat, with twenty-four thongs, but very thin –' he pressed the whip into her hands '– and I call it a pussy cat, for it makes a terrible hissing sound, and leaves quite a blush, but doesn't bruise deeply. It's more for show. This one is a three-thonged pigskin whip for the more serious warmint.'

Lisbeth uncoiled the braided leather thongs, shiny and copper-coloured, and stroked them, right down to the splayed tip.

'This one is similar, but the thongs have knots, and the tip is weighted – I call it the bruiser,' said Perkins.

Holding two sinewy whips, Lisbeth pressed them to her breast, her face flushed, and her teats heaving, as she breathed hard.

'And these are the Scottish tawse,' Eldridge said, showing her a flogger of two flat leather tongues, two feet in length, with forked splayed tips. 'Those good old tawse are real painful on the bare ass, with a kind of delayed action afterburn. I should know, for my mum was Scottish.'

'Excuse me – it seems awfully hot,' she blurted, undoing one, then two buttons of her blouse, so that her deep breast cleavage and the lacy edges of her scalloped bra were revealed.

'Might as well be comfortable,' drawled Perkins.

Deftly, he loosened his shirt and stood with his naked chest gleaming.

With a coy smile, Lisbeth lifted her skirt with a whip handle and fanned her thighs and bottom, showing the policeman her white thong panties, the gusset darkly stained with moisture from her gash. The whip thongs swayed as she fanned her skirtlet up and down. His eyes fixed on the curve of her hillock and the deepening smear of come between her thighs.

'Now, this one,' he drawled, 'is for severe warmints. It's a Jamaican stock-whip, eight foot long, single strand of braided cowhide, and it stings hard, with a pretty good bruise. A warmint whipped with the old curmudgeon, as I call it, bears the marks and the smarts for a long time.'

Cradling the whips, Lisbeth stroked the gleaming leather with trembling fingers, her mouth slack, and her breath heavy.

'They are very well kept,' she murmured.

'Yes, Candace keeps them oiled. Like them?'

'Liking is scarcely the word,' she replied. 'They have such an awesome beauty, and power – to think of the pain they can cause . . .'

'Go on, try one,' said Perkins. 'We have a practice cushion.'

Lisbeth steadied herself over the foam rubber mattress stretched on the table; she lifted the cat high, and lashed out. The leather thongs whistled, before thudding onto the rubber with a loud 'vap!'.

'Gosh,' she said, and lashed again.

She flogged the practice cushion harder and harder, making the inert rubber writhe like flesh; her breasts bounced heavily as she flogged, and a third button of her blouse popped open, revealing her bubbies in their entirety. Panting, she took the second flogger and continued to lash for over a minute; then she took the heavy stock-whip. Perkins took her waist and positioned her well back, so that, when she lashed, the whip writhed in the air with a loud whistle, before striking the target. Her face was flushed and her teeth bared in exultation.

Her bottom and bubbies swirled as she pirouetted, to lash the very centre of the cushion, the whip's heavy tip biting into the rubber. Her blouse was drenched in sweat as her skirt fluttered up at each stroke, showing her quivering buttocks and the come-soaked thong separating her arse cheeks. Vap! Her bra sprang open, and her naked breasts popped from its flimsy cover, yet Lisbeth carried on flogging, pushing the useless bra down her belly and leaving her bare teats to bounce, dripping sweat from the nipples, as she pounded the target.

'That rubber would be shrieking, if it was alive,' observed the catchpoll. 'You're a born whipper, miss. I'd say you wanted to practise on a real body. You ever been whipped yourself? I know English folk are fond of disciplining their youngsters that way.'

'Certainly not,' panted Lisbeth, then thought of Sergeant Placket's baton. 'I mean, I've been severely laced on my bare bottom, of course –' she pouted '– but not exactly *whipped*. It's awfully scary. I can't imagine the pain . . .' She looked up at him, running her tongue over her teeth.

'But you are keen to try it out on the bottoms of my miscreants?'

'Could I? Would you . . .?' she blurted, eyes sparkling, oblivious to her trembling naked breasts thrust towards the man's gaze.

Perkins smiled.

'Lean against the wall, miss, with your arms stretched up as far as they'll go. Spread your legs, and stand on tiptoe.'

Trembling, Lisbeth obeyed. 'Like this?'

'Yes. Now you're in position for a full judicial flogging, or the way sailors were punished at sea. Imagine you're naked, and the whip is whistling, to land on your bare back or bottom and scour you with knotted tongues, knocking the breath from you as it sears your bare flesh. And before you've recovered from the dreadful smarting of the first lash, another follows, scalding your weals, the tongues wrapping round your ribs, to lash your naked breasts, and then another, and another, until your nude body is wriggling in agony, and you piss yourself, shrieking for mercy . . .'

Lisbeth's face was scarlet, her thighs and belly trembling, and her nipples erect. Come streamed from her gash and sodden panties in shiny rivulets down her legs. Her eyes were tightly closed. 'It's too awful,' she moaned. 'I can't bear a whipping.'

'But you could whip a miscreant's naked flesh.'

'I know I could,' gasped Lisbeth. 'Please! I so want to . . .'

He grasped each of her bared teats in a hand and slowly, deliberately, began to knead and squeeze the bare flesh. Her nipples stood tingling and erect.

'Oh . . .' Lisbeth moaned, 'what are you going to do to me, officer?'

One hand dived between her thighs, and mashed her wet cooze.

'Uh . . . uh . . . please don't hurt me,' Lisbeth drooled.

'You're all wet, miss.'

'I can't help it.'

'You're like all women. Whipping turns you on.'

'Mm . . .' Lisbeth gasped as he poked her clitty, extruded from her gash folds and throbbing through the wet cloth of her panties.

He took her by the neck, guiding her to the whipping cushion, until Lisbeth lay face down, her legs and arms splayed, and her face pressed to the rubber. She panted hoarsely as the policeman's fingers raised her skirtlet and pulled down her panties to mid-thigh, where the thong quivered, stretched in a bridge. Lisbeth moaned, thrusting her bared buttocks up.

'Are you going to whip me?' she whimpered.

'Mm,' he answered.

There was a rustle of clothing as Eldridge stripped entirely naked. The sound muffled another furtive rustling of skirts lifted, and panties snapped down, beyond the steel door.

'Please be gentle,' she moaned. 'Please don't hurt me . . . too much.'

Eldridge laughed. 'You want it, miss,' he murmured. 'You round-ass bitches are all the same.'

Lisbeth twisted her head to see the nude male, with the three-thonged pigskin flogger raised, and his cock a stiff pole, jutting over his belly, the shiny glans inches from the whip's swaying thongs.

'Oh . . .' she panted. 'You're stiff! You brute . . . whip me, redden my bum . . .'

'Is it really your first time, bitch?' he demanded.

'Yes . . . oh, please, whip my bum hard, I need to know . . .'

Vap!

'Ahh!'

Lisbeth's buttocks jerked, clenching, as the thongs cracked across her trembling bare fesses, raising three long pink weals. Vap!

'Ooh! Oh, gosh, it hurts,' she gasped.

Vap!

'Oh! *Ouch!* Ooh . . .'

Her whipped bare bottom began to squirm, its tracery of pink weals brightening the shadows. Beneath her writhing quim, come dribbled from her gash flaps, sliming the rubber.

Vap!

'Ahh . . . please, not so hard . . .'

Vap!

'Ooh! It smarts. It's the worst pain I've ever had. Oh, gosh, I can't take it.'

'Bite the rubber, bitch, to stop your squealing,' the catchpoll ordered.

Lisbeth got a large hunk of rubber cushion, mingled with a hank of her hair, between her teeth and bit savagely, as the next lashes stroked her squirming bare buttocks. Vap! Vap!

'Nngh . . . nngh . . .' she gurgled.

She grasped the edges of the cushion, her knuckles white, as her flogged buttocks wriggled, with her legs jerking rigid behind her at each slice of the scourge on her seared flesh. Her bottom was a crimson mass of blotched, puffy weals, crisscrossed on her writhing skin and darkening to livid purple as Eldridge rhythmically flogged her. Come gushed from her squirming gash, slopping the rubber cushion so that her hips and cunt mound slithered in her own slime. Tears streamed from her eyes; her voice was an anguished gurgling squeal, deep in her throat, as her teeth bit through their rubber. Vap! Vap!

'Urrgh!' she sobbed, drool spewing from her shuddering lips. 'Oh, I can't take any more . . .'

Vap! Vap!

'Ahh!'

Panting, Eldridge laid aside his whip, running his fingernails over her puffy welts and mashing her arse cleft and wet cunt lips. He poked two fingers into her anus, thrust deeply, and began to ream her rectum.

'Ouch! That hurts,' she whimpered, her pierced bum squirming. 'What . . . what are you going to do to me?'

'What you want, bitch. My big black shovel in your coalhole. You are gagging for it,' hissed the male.

'No . . . no . . . please, no . . . ahh!'

His giant cock cleaved the gripping wrinkle of her anus pucker and thrust in, right to his balls.

'Ahh . . . you're splitting my bum. It's agony.'

Lisbeth's wails of protest, as Eldridge penetrated her anus, grew to shrieks of wriggling pleasure as his massive cock filled her rectum.

'Oh, yes, *yes* . . .!'

Straddling her flogged buttocks, he buggered her from behind with powerful plunging strokes, his glans ramming the root of her colon, as her buttocks writhed and squirmed on his impaling cockshaft. Come gushed from her flapping cunt.

At last, a real man shaming me, taking me in the arse . . .

'Yes,' Lisbeth gasped, 'fuck me hard, hurt me, split me, fuck my hole, fuck me, fuck me, *fuck me* . . . yes! Oh! I'm coming! Ahh, ahh . . . *ahh*!'

Eldridge bared his teeth in a grin and continued to fuck the spasming girl. He buggered her for several minutes, twice more bringing her to orgasm, until he grunted, his glans ramming her colon, and a creamy froth of sperm sprayed from her arse-greased anus to dribble down her bucking thighs. Withdrawing his turgid cock with a loud plop from her bumhole, he grabbed Lisbeth's hair and pressed her mouth to his balls. Gasping, she licked the arse grease and sperm from his tool, until he pronounced it clean.

'Whipped and buggered,' he mused. 'You *were* gagging for it, weren't you, miss?'

'Yes, damn you,' she panted, grimacing as she rubbed her wealed bottom, her face as crimson as her arse. 'Oh! I'm sorry . . . I've got to pee.'

The catchpoll placed a bucket beneath her and she

squatted, sighing, as a heavy golden jet steamed from her cunt. He watched, licking his lips, and sniffing her fumes.

'Most mots get taken short, after a seeing-to,' he drawled. 'Anyway, you've earned your place as my whipping deputy.'

She rose, squeezing the drips from her cunt with her hand. 'You mean, I can lash a miscreant?'

He nodded, and Lisbeth clapped her hands.

'You've really hurt me,' she gasped, 'and my bum feels on fire, inside and out. The worst thing – oh, you beastly brute! – is that after your whipping, and your cock up my bumhole, I shan't want ordinary fucking ever again.'

Dressing herself and pouting coquettishly, her face glowing with satisfaction, Lisbeth waited for the catchpoll to open the door for her. The door's opening surprised deputy Candace, eye pressed to the keyhole, skirt up, panties down, and masturbating her come-slimed cunt.

'Oh,' she said, beaming, slowly withdrawing her fingers from her slit with a loud, squelchy plop, 'that was one of your best ever, sir. I had a fabulous frig, watching the bitch squirm . . . *and* piss.'

She put her come-soaked fingers in her mouth and licked them, leering at the blushing Lisbeth.

'The court awaits you,' she murmured.

In the cavernous justice chamber, Lisbeth had only a few moments to explain her new role and her silver deputy's badge to Tanya and Jeremy, before Eldridge called the court to order.

'You're walking bow-legged,' murmured Tanya. 'Have you been whipped or bummed?'

Lisbeth pouted, licked her lips, and said 'Sshh.'

Proceedings were surprisingly swift, the catchpoll acting as sole authority. A succession of sullen young prisoners, mostly girls, paraded before him, their nudity covered by sacks, and received their charges: spitting, chewing gum, ligging, liming, scrunting and 'hanky-panky', most of them a mystery to Lisbeth, although they seemed not too serious. All pleaded guilty, eschewing their right to counsel. Eldridge rapped out his sentences briskly: four youths and four girls were sentenced to the gibbet and whippings on the bare buttocks, ranging from fifteen to forty lashes. Several girls were not to be whipped but caned a dozen, then 'laced and choked' for a set period of days. Those punishments were carried out on the spot.

After bending over the courtroom table, legs apart and bare bums raised, the nude girls received a flogging of a dozen with a deputy's short, whippy cane. Immediately, the girls, sobbing and crying, were placed nude on the courtroom table, their legs held open held by deputies. Under each girl's back was a corset with long canewood stays, and this was fastened over her belly with a deputy girl standing on her ribs to lace the corset far beyond the bounds of comfort. The girls screamed, wriggling, as their bellies were laced tighter and tighter until they gasped for air and pierced the air with wails that they couldn't take any more. The deputy girl ignored them, straining until the corset enclosed the victim's flesh to pencil thinness, when the ridge of lace-holes was fastened in a padlock. Meanwhile, a choke pear was inserted into her slit, her gash flaps held open in the fingers of two deputies.

The choke pear was a shiny steel cylinder with sharp bolts recessed along its length. The pear slid easily into the cunts of the girls, and then a deputy turned a key in the base of the pear, making the girl buck and scream, her corseted belly heaving and bare buttocks slamming the table. Tanya explained that, once inside the orifice, the spikes sprang out, pinning the device very painfully to the inside of the slit, and only retractable with further insertion of the key. The miscreant was able to pee with some straining, but had to keep the choke pear inside her, night and day. The laced and choked girls were allowed to dress and depart for their period of discomfort, while the spectators filed out into the sun to observe the harsher chastisements.

The crowd buzzed as four young men and four girls, their nude bodies draped in sacks, shuffled to the waiting gibbet. The males were led by ball-harnesses, the females by tit- and cunt-clamps, all on long thin chains. When they stood under the wide crossbar of the gibbet, the males were chained to the guardrail by the stem of their balls, and the females by their teats and coozes. When Eldridge's whip-wielding deputies roughly pulled off the sacks, the males were revealed to have expressions of sullen defiance, while the females sobbed loudly, tears running down their cheeks and bathing their naked breasts – all except one elfin girl, who pranced and pouted, jangling her nip-chains and cunt-clamps, with her breasts bouncing and head held disdainfully high. The clamps held her vulval lips wide showing glistening pink slit flesh, with unmistakable trickles of fluid creeping down her rippling bare thighs. That was Elvira O'Malley, haughty in her lithe nudity, curly black tresses fluttering round her grinning face, with the big brown apples of her titties and arse writhing in a tease.

The eight bodies stood naked in the sun. In addition to their genital clamps, all eight had their arms stretched high and wrists bound in ropes knotted to the gibbet bar.

'Heavens, my cunny's a lake, I'm juicing so much at those luscious bottoms about to squirm,' said Tanya in a loud voice, producing smiles from everyone who heard her, including Lisbeth.

Lisbeth stood, whip in hand, beside Eldridge and six deputies, including Candace. They held whips of varying size, from slender floggers to the catchpoll's own monstrous stock-whip.

'Which backside do you want, miss?' he said.

Lisbeth surveyed the row of bare bottoms.

'Him,' she said, licking her lips and pointing to a male of about nineteen, whose powerful back and buttock muscles rippled as he vainly struggled in his bonds. 'He looks the most fractious.'

And his bum the juiciest.

'Agreed,' said Eldridge. 'That's Jerome, a serious warmint whose cock never tires of poking gash, so you'll need a heavier whip. Candace, change whips with the miss.'

Glowering, Candace exchanged her powerful nine-thonged scourge for Lisbeth's three-thonger.

'The warmint is due forty strokes for aggravated liming and scrunting,' Eldridge said, leering at Lisbeth's own bottom. 'I'll bet you're smarting for revenge on some male behind after the whopping I gave yours.'

'You know I am, you beast,' hissed Lisbeth. 'My bum's smarting horribly, all throbbing and burning.'

'Are you wearing panties?'

Lisbeth blushed hotly.

'Why, what a question,' she blurted. 'As it happens, I left them off. My bum's much too painful to have cloth tight on my skin.'

Eldridge nodded approvingly. 'None of my gels wears panties for a whipping. Saves you getting all hot and bothered down there, and lets the cheeks move freely. Gels generally get a bit slippery in the cooze when they whip bare ass.'

Lisbeth positioned herself a few feet behind Jerome's naked ebony body, and beside the other whipping girls in a row. Eldridge stood at the end of the gibbet before the squirming arse of the spitting white slut, Nell, but kept his whip coiled. At his signal, the floggings commenced: seven scourges rose, flashing in the baking sunlight, and seven bare bottoms shuddered, as the whips fell on the unprotected skin of miscreant buttocks.

'Ahh! Ooh!' the cries and gasps rose, as the nude bodies began to wriggle in their bonds, feet kicking, flogged bums clenching tight.

Lisbeth's first stroke lashed a juicy set of pink weals across Jerome's ebony buttocks. He gasped and rewarded her with a wriggle of his clenching arse cheeks as the watching crowd rippled with excitement.

9

Basted on Bare

Lisbeth's body was drenched in sweat as she whipped the squirming ebony bare, dancing before her blurred eyes. Vap! Vap! At each crack of the thongs on Jerome's naked fesses, he jerked in his ropes, his body swayed by the scourge's weight, and the tight pears of his arse clenched frantically, squeezing the cheeks, striped with raw red weals. His head lolled, drooling and moaning, to jerk sharply up at each new lash to his squirming buttocks. Lisbeth's unpantied cunt dripped come as her belly fluttered, seeing the naked male wriggling in her power. Perspiration soaked her dress to translucence, the skirt clinging to the sticky weals on her bum.

She was *sure* her welts from Eldridge's flogging were in full view of Tanya and the other spectators, but didn't care. In addition to the excitement of flogging a helpless naked male, it was strangely thrilling to know the marks of her own punishment were exposed. The long-headed Lucayans, grouped to one side of the gibbet, stared intently at Lisbeth's croup and Jerome's wealed, wriggling bare fesses. Their hands were under each other's lifted skirts, showing lustrous shaven quims flowing with come. Their eyes glazed, lips curled in fierce smiles, the glistening bronze girls blatantly masturbated each other. The slut Nell twisted her head to scan the bums squirming beside her with a leer, as she waggled her own unflogged buttocks in heartless mimicry of their torment.

'Your turn will come, Nell,' hissed Eldridge, tight-lipped with anger. 'You're the filthiest whore on Rum Hole, opening your legs for any jackanapes with a stiff cock and a glass of rum. Three or four, one after the other, on the floor of the grog shop! I'll thrash the hide from you.'

Nell spat. 'I've had so many fine cocks pounding me fore and aft, I shan't even notice a tickling from a milkweed like you,' she snarled.

Petite Elvira writhed, like the others, under her own lashing, but her mouth gaped open, taking deep lungfuls of air and gasping aloud, while her pert buttocks opened and closed in an unseemly dance with the striping quirt. The firm bullets of her titties bounced high at each whipcrack to her naked buttocks. Vap! Vap!

'Ooh!' she squealed. 'Ahh . . . my poor bottom.'

Her wriggling thighs glistened with heavy streams of come from her shaven cunt, winking to show bright wet pink inside her slit. As Lisbeth's whip spun Jerome's body, she saw that his cock was fully erect. Through his tears, he leered at her. She redoubled the force of her lashes, to no avail; his huge cock remained proudly stiff, even as she approached her fortieth and final stroke. She paused, wiping sweat from her eyes, to see that Candace was gone, her flogged victim hanging limp. So were the others, save for Elvira's whipper. Lisbeth delivered her last three strokes – vap! vap! vap! – at a run, striping Jerome's wriggling arse to a furious glow, yet still her victim's cock stood. Panting, Lisbeth lowered her whip in time to observe the last strokes of Elvira's flogging.

The girl's belly fluttered, come spurting from her cunt, and her whole body spasmed, as she mewled, gasping louder, and at last shrilled, 'Ooh! How it hurts! My croup's on fire! Oh . . . oh . . . oh . . . yes! *Yes* . . .'

At the last crack of the whip on her flamed bare fesses, the girl writhed and shuddered, unmistakably in orgasm, come spurting from her cunt. The Lucayans wanked off faster until they, too, cooed in high-pitched gasps as come streamed down their jerking bare thighs, and they brought each other to climax.

'Catchpoll Perkins,' Lisbeth blurted. 'Those girls are *masturbating*. Aren't you going to punish them?'

Eldridge glowered. 'Those Lucayans are a law unto their selves,' he grunted. 'They enjoy the master's favour.' He lifted his stock-whip. 'Now, Nell, you slut, time for your slut's wages,' he said.

Nell's body hung, legs and arms outstretched, her arse cheeks well parted, and swollen bare cunt flaps pendant. She waggled her buttocks at the catchpoll and a powerful jet of piss hissed from her gash, puddling the deck with steaming golden liquid. The crowd laughed, then gasped as Eldridge lashed his first stroke. Thwap! The heavy leather tongue snaked across her fleshy mid-fesse, and cracked on her skin, raising a deep pink weal right across the fesse meat.

'Ahh!' screamed the pissing girl, her flogged buttocks clenching hard. 'Do your worst, Perkins, you two-faced bastard. I know you've been fucking that English whore because Candace told me. You've had your cock up her pudding hole, *and* thrashed the slut's melons.'

The crowd rippled with laughter. Thwap! The whip flogged her back, leaving a ragged diagonal welt from shoulder to hip.

'Ahh! Ooh! Ooh!' the girl screamed, dancing on tiptoe.

Thwap! The whip lashed her top fesses.

'Uh . . .' she gasped, drooling.

Thwap! A stroke to the left haunch wrapped around her belly, the whip's tongue lashing her navel. Whap! Wealing the right haunch, the tongue wrapped on the slant, flogging her bare nipples.

'Ahh!' screamed the girl. 'Not so hard, Perkins, I beg you.'

Smiling grimly, the catchpoll spat on her wealed buttocks and lifted the whip above his shoulder. Whap! The tongue snaked between her thighs, cracking on her open, dripping bare cunt and wrapping up her belly to stroke the naked bouncing breasts.

'Ahh! No!'

Eldridge stepped back and lashed again between her legs, this time allowing the flickering tip to catch the girl directly on the clitoris, visible, swelling and extruded between her bruised red gash flaps.

130

'Oh! My nubbin, no . . . no . . . please, catchpoll, no . . .,' she sobbed, her cunt basin jerking as her reddened buttocks clenched and squirmed.

Whap! The flogging continued, pitilessly, for over ten minutes, the leather striping her back, buttocks and naked cunt. The Lucayans crooned with lustful pleasure as they masturbated, rubbing their bare copper-bronze buttocks and dripping pink cunts.

'Give her what for,' cheered Tanya.

Lisbeth gasped as she watched the squirming bare bum reddening with cruel stripes under the cracking of Eldridge's merciless whip. Sun baked her; rivulets of sweat tickled her skin under her wet dress and from her quivering gash spewed a torrent of come. Lisbeth's clitty throbbed rock-hard. Moaning, she dropped her flogging arm to let her fingers touch the stiff nubbin and whimpered as electric pleasure filled her belly. As the whip thrashed the girl's back and bare, Lisbeth began to masturbate with sure, powerful strokes, in time with the rhythm of the lash. She looked back at Tanya to see that she, too, was frigging, her teeth bared in a fierce smile. Both the flogged Elvira and Jerome, her own whipping boy, gazed at Nell's squirming bare buttocks – Elvira licking her lips, with her slit spewing come, and Jerome's cock insolently rigid.

From the chamber perched above the courtroom, a pair of glinting dark green eyes surveyed the whipping. Under a Roman nose, white teeth were bared and licked.

'A tasty scene,' the man murmured. 'My Lucayans are pleasuring themselves, and many of my dear guests, too, especially that new girl, Lisbeth. Look at her masturbate! She will be a most sensuous addition to my flock. Such long legs, and those rippling thighs, the breasts a sculpture, and those buttocks, so big, firm and fruity, she could be from these islands! Her bottom has been basted well, and freshly. What do you know of this, Candace?'

His robe lay open, revealing his hairless, sleekly muscled nudity, and massively erect cock, arching over his belly. Candace removed her lips from his swollen glans.

'The catchpoll flogged her, master,' she gasped.

131

'Is that all?'

'He fucked her in the anus, master. I watched.'

'A deep penetration?'

'Why, yes, master. He was in her right to the balls, and that big cock must have touched her colon.'

'You masturbated, I suppose?'

'Of course, master. She has the most succulent fesses. If I can't have Eldridge's cock in my own hole, then I just *have* to relieve myself by frigging myself as he pleasures another bitch.'

'And she likes outsize cock in her rectum ... yet, apart from a certain *folie* on arrival, her conduct at Rum Hole has been chaste and demure. She whips admirably – that boy's arse is quite raw, and such is her power, his cock still stands. I wonder what she wants, or hopes to gain, by suppressing her sensuality? Miss Cicatrix Comington will surely find out. Well, bitch? Are you asleep?'

Whap! He slapped the bare breasts of the crouching girl.

'What are you waiting for, you idle slut? You may wear the horned dildo in your rectum for three hours, after I dismiss you.'

'Yes, master, as you command,' she blurted.

Candace's head dived, her lips enclosing the master's cock, taking his glans to the back of her throat.

'Urrgh ... mmph ...' she gurgled, her face flushed, as she powerfully sucked the massive stiff tool.

Below, Eldridge laid aside his whip, after over fifty strokes to the naked body of the miscreant Nell, whose moans and sobs penetrated the luxuriously furnished spyglass room where Candace gurgled, her mouth sucking Roger de Hazebrouck's cock. The Lucayan girls surged forward and cut down Elvira and Jerome from their bonds. Carrying the pair, they laid them on the deck and positioned the boy's rigid cock above Elvira's come-slimed cunt, open and winking with glistening pink flesh.

A Lucayan girl grasped Jerome's wealed buttocks and pushed his cock between Elvira's cunt lips. He began to buck, slamming his cock right to the balls into her dripping wet pouch. The Lucayans, Tanya, Lisbeth and many other guests masturbated openly as they watched the two whipped ebony bodies writhing in a fierce fuck.

Aloft in his eyrie, the master clapped his hands. 'A cunt-swive,' he murmured, 'splendid – although they neglect Elvira's juicy little dunghole.'

'Nngh ...' Candace grunted, her naked breasts bouncing as her head bobbed, sucking powerfully on the master's cock with flicks of her tongue to his peehole.

'Ahh ... yes,' grunted the master as his cock bucked and cream slopped from Candace's sucking lips, while her throat bobbed, swallowing his sperm.

Lisbeth masturbated to climax as Jerome's whipped buttocks pumped, and he spermed inside Elvira's bucking cunt so copiously that his cream bubbled from her gleaming black cunt lips and slimed her writhing thighs, mixing with her own trickles of cunt juice.

'What fabulous marks you've made on Nell, catchpoll,' Lisbeth gasped, as come spewed from her jerking gash. 'She'll not misbehave again for a while, I'm sure.'

'No chance,' said Eldridge. 'She's the best slut in Gibbet Town, and she'll be fucking and sucking and on her back as soon as some varmint fills her up with rum, and then I'll have to baste her on the bare again. I know her too well.'

'From lacing her so often?'

'More than that,' he said, with a hint of pride. 'That rum bobtail is Mrs Perkins, my wife.'

'Get all the sand off before you spit out,' Lisbeth ordered. 'Every last grain – between my toes, too.'

Squeezed and shimmering in her one-piece turquoise designer swimsuit – the marks of Eldridge's lacing, four days previously, still showing faintly on her bum – Lisbeth stretched her suncreamed legs, reclining lazily, as the crouching slave boy licked her feet clean. The slave girl Melissa's naked bottom swayed in the air as she washed the bedroom floor, using her bare breasts as sponges.

So restful, my new celibacy, however eccentric, with lots of lovely frigs every day, thinking of that powerful Perkins, and his monster of a cock bursting my bumhole ... yet I have

133

*every right to pleasure, and that slave boy's delicious bare
bum is just too tempting. Nobody seems to have seen the
master, if he's here, so he shan't know. And what if he does?
The slaves need discipline.*

She rose, kicking the boy's face away, and stretched
herself, her breasts nearly popping from their skimpy
surround. The slave boy's eyes fastened on her swelling
teats, and his cock became rigid. Lisbeth pointed an
accusing finger. 'An erection,' she hissed. 'You beast.'

'No, miss, honestly,' blurted the slave boy, 'it's just the
breeze.'

'Don't lie to me. I'm afraid I shall have to baste you,
boy,' said Lisbeth, licking her teeth. 'On the bare buttocks.
It will be very painful, I'm afraid.'

Bardolph, the nineteen-year-old slave boy, looked at her
with wide, frightened eyes, their long lashes fluttering, and
a tremble at his knees. The slave girl Melissa raised a hand
to cover her gaping lips.

'There is nothing improper about this,' Lisbeth went on.
'I am not one of those guests who demand ... services
from their slaves. But I am a firm believer in discipline –
your gaze was undeniably impudent, and your work has
been unpardonably sloppy. You seem too much interested
in the person of Melissa, and I have observed your pego
stiffening when you work alongside her.'

She brushed an errant blonde tress from her moist brow.
Melissa's lips pursed in a smile, despite the fear in her eyes.

'You have been caned before?'

'Y-yes, miss,' the slave boy murmured.

'On the bare?'

'Yes, miss.'

'Then you may bend over, and touch your toes – unless
you'd prefer holding onto the sofa,' she ordered.

Both Melissa and Bardolph were nude, their silky ebony
bodies pearled in perspiration. For the four days after the
petty assizes at Gibbet Town, Lisbeth had worked her
slaves in the full nude – save those errant slave girls
sentenced to the corset by Miss Comington – yet, true to
her vow of celibacy, had contented herself with at least

134

thrice-daily masturbation, usually while contemplating the naked bottom of a slave girl, or a slave boy's cock, tumescent at Lisbeth's bare body. She invited the slaves, boys or girls, to masturbate naked for her watching pleasure while she stroked her clitty to stiffness and rapid orgasm, convinced that it was not venery but hygiene.

The first masturbation of the day, apart from a rapid frig during her nude wake-up plunge in the ocean, was after breakfast, when the delicious young quimicurist came to shave her mound, lubricating her razor with Lisbeth's come while Lisbeth caressed her own clitty and that of the slave girl, pantieless beneath her skirtlet. When her mound was shiny and perfectly smooth, she let the slave girl lick her come off while she masturbated both their quims to climax. The Cuban girl panted, drooled and groaned in Spanish, shaking her titties as her cunt poured come over Lisbeth's wrist. That was not sex but healthy recreation.

'At your command, miss,' Bardolph murmured.

He bent over, buttocks tightly pressed, and hands clutching the back of the sofa.

'You've been getting on my nerves all morning,' Lisbeth drawled. 'Dumb insolence, sloppiness, and . . . and walking around with your tarse waving at Melissa, half stiff, without permission – a disgusting impertinence. Now we have all afternoon until teatime for me to skin those insolent buttocks of yours.'

'Please, miss,' he murmured, 'I honestly cannot help it if I get stiff, looking at *you*. You are so . . . so beautiful, miss.'

Melissa's face tightened in anger.

'More impertinence!' Lisbeth snapped. 'It is not for a slave to find me beautiful.'

She rubbed her bottom, tightly encased in her Giulio Ferracci swimsuit – at that Bond Street price, it just *had* to be worn, whatever Miss Comington might think – whose high-cut derrière covered *most* of her whip weals. His cock dangled, still turgid, between his quivering thighs. *It is quite a whopper*, she thought. *The beast.*

She licked her lips.

'Please, miss,' he said, 'I watched you whip my cousin Jerome in Gibbet Town. He's a rude boy, and deserved his thrashing. You won't be so hard on me, will you?'

'Won't I?' she snarled. 'You don't know what's in store for you, sir. I'm going to whip those juicy fesses to the bone, young man. Twenty stingers on that bare bum.'

'Then, I beg you, please begin quickly, miss. I'd like to get it over with.'

'You impudent – giving me orders!' she cried, raising her rattan cane. 'You'll take thirty, for that.'

Melissa tittered. Vip! The cane thrashed the naked slave boy squarely across the fesses; he quivered, his cheeks clenching and his teeth bared in a rictus.

'Uhh . . .' he gasped.

Vip!

'Ooh . . .'

Vip!

'Oh, miss . . .'

His naked buttocks began to squirm, their smooth ebony skin marred by the vicious weals of Lisbeth's cane. Melissa pressed her hands gleefully, her lips curled in a sneer.

Vip!

'Ahh!'

The slave boy trembled, his legs jerking straight as each cut of the cane placed a fresh weal on the entire expanse of his writhing bare arse: haunches, top fesse, underfesse and centre – not an inch of his croup was unwealed. Lisbeth panted, sweat dripping from her heaving breasts, bulged under the soft top of her swimsuit, and from the high-cut crotch, where the sweat mingled with seeps of come from her quim. Her come glistened on her thighs, golden against the shiny turquoise, like the rest of her body tanned in the nude.

Melissa watched the slave boy flogged, with one hand covering her naked cunt and her fingers discreetly poking between the slit lips to tweak her swollen pink clitty, visible outside the ebony cunt flaps. Vip! Vip! Melissa licked her lips, masturbating as tears coursed down Bardolph's cheeks and his caned bottom squirmed. Lisbeth's titties bounced up and down in her swimsuit, threatening to escape from their shiny covering as her arms and thighs rippled with exertion. Vip! Vip!

'Ahh! Ooh . . .' Bardolph whimpered, gasping hoarsely as his bottom clenched and his stiff cock shuddered at each cut to his bare.

Melissa crooned to herself as she masturbated, drool seeping from her slack mouth while come sprayed from her cooze, writhing under her tweaking fingers. Lisbeth's tongue hung out, her own gash leaking come, faster and faster as the slave boy's bare bum coloured with angry weals. His cock, half stiff at the commencement of his beating, now rose in full erection, almost to his navel.

'Your pego's disgracefully stiff, slave,' Lisbeth panted.

'Oh, miss, I can't help myself,' he moaned.

'You really think me beautiful?' she said.

'Yes, miss.'

'With your bottom so sore?'

'Because of that, miss. You are such a powerful lady. It is an honour to take your strokes.'

Melissa glowered.

'Impudent beast,' Lisbeth spat.

Vip! Vip!

'Ahh!'

'Please, miss?' murmured the slave girl.

'Yes, Melissa?' panted Lisbeth, without looking round.

'If miss is tired, then I should be happy to whop him for lying to you.'

'Melissa!' cried the flogged boy. 'How can you say that?'

'Quiet, sir!' Lisbeth snarled.

Vip! Vip!

'Ahh! Ooh!' he squealed, his arse squirming frantically, the cheeks now mottled with puffy mauve weals.

'Lying?' Lisbeth demanded.

'His pego was stiff because of me, miss,' pouted Melissa. 'We are engaged to be married, you see, and I won't let him have a portion until catchpoll Perkins has performed the legal ceremony. A girl must be a virgin for her husband, and he for her.'

Vip!

'Ooh!' sobbed the squirming slave boy.

'It is scarcely normal for a slave to remain virgin,' panted Lisbeth.

'Our duties don't count, miss,' said Melissa gravely. 'We are virgin to each other.'

Vip! Lisbeth delivered the final strokes to the slave boy's squirming bare. Vip! Vip!

'Ooh!'

Vip! Vip!

'Oh ... oh ...'

'Yes,' hissed Melissa, masturbating hard. 'Make the rude boy squirm, miss.'

There was a loud plop as a spurt of come dripped onto the floor between her bare feet. Lisbeth looked round and gasped.

'Did I give you permission to masturbate?' she rasped.

'Oh! No, miss. I'm sorry, miss,' stammered Melissa, withdrawing her fingers from her cooze with a loud squelch and a spray of come over her quivering ebony thighs.

Vip! Vip!

'Ahh!' squealed the shuddering slave boy, as Lisbeth, panting, lowered her cane.

'That's the boy done,' she said, 'but what about *you*, Melissa, you impudent minx?'

'Please, miss, *she* deserves a whopping, the rotten bitch,' sobbed Bardolph, rubbing his welted bottom.

He rose, grimacing, his pego still fully erect and shadowing his heaving belly. Lisbeth gazed at the stiff ebony cock and come oozed from her swimsuit, sodden at the crotch. She touched herself between her thighs and gasped, feeling the clitty throbbing hard.

'You are both impudent,' she gasped. 'And liars. Must I believe you don't pleasure each other? Absurd.'

'Oh, miss, we wank each other off,' said Melissa, 'but that's all. It would be quite wrong to fuck.'

'Bardolph seems a forceful boy,' said Lisbeth, gazing at the slave's stiff cock, 'so how can you restrain his ardour, Melissa?'

'Why, I wank him off three times every day, miss,' said Melissa, blushing.

'With your mouth?'

'No, miss!' she blurted. 'That's *sex*.'

'You may bare up, Melissa,' Lisbeth ordered.

'You're going to thrash me just for masturbating, miss?' said Melissa, her eyes suddenly moist. 'Surely a girl can't be blamed for frigging when she sees a boy beaten with his lovely juicy bare all squirming?'

'Not I. Your future husband shall thrash you.'

'Ohh . . .' wailed Melissa, trembling. 'At your command, miss. When I'm married, I know I'll get regular bastings if he truly loves me.'

She bent over with her bottom thrust high and the pink meat of her slit clearly visible between her parted, pendant gash flaps. Bardolph took the cane from Lisbeth, smiling as he swished the tip near Melissa's face.

'Sure, I'll baste you, cheeky bitch,' he murmured.

She cringed, shutting her eyes as the cane whistled, and smacked her buttocks. Vip!

'Ooh!' she squealed, bare ebony teats wobbling violently as her arse cheeks clenched and wriggled.

Vip!

'Oh! Gosh!' she gasped.

Vip!

'Ooh . . . uhh . . .'

The flogged girl began to sob, tears moistening her face, as her croup jerked and squirmed under the cane's hard slices. The bare velvet fesses, taut and firm, now writhed, pink with fiery weals. She raised her face, twisted in pain and streaked with tears.

'Please, miss, tell him, not so hard.'

Legs spread, Lisbeth settled back to watch, unfastening the button at the perineum of her swimsuit and raising her crotch flap, blatantly baring her naked cunt. She parted the lips, showing pink to both the caned girl and her caner. Bardolph's stiff cock trembled as he licked his lips, his eyes on Lisbeth's glistening pink cunt flesh as she lazily began to masturbate.

'I can't interfere,' Lisbeth said. 'You are his fiancée, Melissa.'

Vip! Vip!

'Ahh!'

Lisbeth rubbed her throbbing clitty, watching the girl's arse wobble and squirm under the smacks of the rod. She slipped a hand under her swimsuit and began to tweak her nipples, bringing them rapidly to tingling erection.

'Hurt much, Melissa?' she asked.

'Yes, miss! It smarts horribly,' sobbed the wriggling slave girl. 'I can't believe you're masturbating, watching my poor bottom lashed.'

'For her insolence, you may take your bride-to-be to forty strokes, Bardolph,' Lisbeth drawled.

'At your command, miss,' panted the slave boy.

Vip! Vip!

'Ooh! He's hurting me so. I can't bear it. '

Vip! Vip!

'Ahh!'

Tears streamed down the cheeks of the writhing Melissa, her face twisted in agony as Bardolph, his cock a rigid pole, mercilessly flogged her bare bottom. Lisbeth's fingers poked into her gushing cunt as the two sweating nude bodies rippled before her. As her caning progressed, Melissa's squeals softened to a dull, bleating whimper, her titties rising and falling with each hoarse breath, and a trickle of come streaking the insides of her quivering bare thighs. Come bubbled at her winking cunt flaps, shiny in the sunlight.

'Does it please you to be caned by your master, Melissa?' panted Lisbeth, her fingers tweaking her throbbing clitty.

'Uhh . . . no, miss,' gasped the slave girl. 'He's too hot for hurting me.'

'Then why is your cunny juicing?'

'Oh, miss, a girl cannot control her cunny,' Melissa moaned.

'Nor, it seems, a slave boy his pego,' Lisbeth murmured.

Bardolph took his future bride to the full forty, her naked bottom a blotched mass of crimson and purple welts. At the final few strokes, Lisbeth masturbated herself to orgasm, come spurting from her cooze mouth as she wriggled on her bottom, her belly and gash fluttering, and drool trickling from her slack lips. Panting, the slave boy laid down the cane and, pressing his face to the girl's flogged bottom, covered the wealed fesses in kisses.

'I'm sorry, Melissa,' he blurted. 'I didn't mean it . . .'

Lisbeth sprang to her feet. 'Cease this disgusting exhibition,' she hissed. 'Slaves acting without orders? Girl, you will position yourself on the rug, crouching, with your buttocks apart.'

Trembling, Melissa obeyed, squatting doggy fashion with her striped croup glowing, and the wet pink meat of her open cooze glistening in the sunbeams. Lisbeth ordered Bardolph to straddle her, and he obeyed, his cock tip just touching the winking pucker of her anus.

'Now, fuck the slut,' rasped Lisbeth.

He inserted the glans of his massive cock between the lips of her anus, and the girl moaned.

'Not there,' commanded Lisbeth. 'Fuck her as a man fucks his wife.'

Bardolph stared in shock. 'In her gash, miss?' he quavered. 'But we are virgins . . .'

Vip! Lisbeth laid the cane across his bare. 'Fuck her,' she hissed.

Panting hoarsely, the slave boy let his cock slide from the girl's anus to her cunt flaps, inserted the tip, then bucked, until the full shaft slid into her wet passage, right to his balls. Melissa moaned, sobbing, her face pressed to the floor as he began to fuck her cunt with hard, ramming strokes, his hips slapping wetly on her wealed bare bum. Lisbeth relaxed and began to frig anew with her cane across her thighs, pausing now and then to whip the slave boy's pumping arse, urging him to fuck his bride harder. After a minute's vigorous masturbation, Lisbeth rose and knelt before Melissa's face, lifting her head by the hair and pressing her mouth to Lisbeth's wet cooze.

'Tongue me, slave,' she murmured.

Lisbeth moaned as the fucked girl's eager tongue found her hard, throbbing clitty, and began to bite, sucking and chewing as she licked the pulsing gash mouth.

'Mm ... mm ...' gurgled Melissa, as she swallowed Lisbeth's gushing come.

The Jamaican girl's velvet body shuddered at the male's fucking, the powerful cock thrusts slamming her face against Lisbeth's cunt. Lisbeth clasped her head, pressing her tightly against her quivering belly until her come bathed the girl's nose and mouth. Melissa gasped for air as she gulped the wash of Lisbeth's cunt juice. Bardolph began to grunt, his body stiffening as he approached his spurt. Lisbeth ordered him to withdraw from his bride's cunt without spurting.

As Melissa continued to tongue Lisbeth's gash, Lisbeth clutched the slave boy's buttocks and pressed his cock to her face. She licked his tight ball gourds, taking each one into her mouth to suck hard. His tool trembled, rigid and slimed with Melissa's cunt fluid. Panting, Lisbeth opened her mouth wide, ran her tongue up the length of the cock and slid her lips over the engorged stiff glans; her tongue flickered on his peehole, and her lips sucked the helmet before she lowered her head and took the full cock right to her throat.

As Melissa continued to chew her clitty and swallow her copiously pouring come, Lisbeth slid her mouth back and forth on the massive ebony cockshaft, sucking powerfully and clutching the slave boy's buttocks, her fingernails clawing at his weals. The slave boy moaned, shuddering, his cock bucking as Lisbeth tasted the first drops of cream at his peehole. She licked the peehole, and the corona and frenulum of the throbbing glans, and the slave boy whimpered in pleasure, as his sperm began to spurt, filling Lisbeth's mouth with a massive jet of hot creamy spunk. She gurgled, swallowing his copious ejaculate and stroking his quivering balls as they pumped their hot, sticky fluid into her throat.

'Oh ... oh ... I want to come ...' gasped the slave girl as she swallowed Lisbeth's juices.

Melissa's groans vibrated against her tingling nubbin as the slave girl's fingers threshed between her thighs, masturbating her own dripping gash.

'Urggh . . .' gurgled Lisbeth, her belly fluttering as climax welled in her tongued cunt, and her throat filled with the slave boy's massive sperming. 'Uhh! *Uhh!*'

She bucked in orgasm while Melissa masturbated, her bare titties swinging wildly as come poured from her gash, and she moaned, lips fastened on Lisbeth's nubbin.

'Mm . . . mm . . . Ahh!' Melissa squealed, Lisbeth's come dripping down her chin as her body shuddered in spasm.

Lisbeth wriggled on the girl's tongue as she drank the slave boy's massive ejaculate, hot cream bubbling from her lips and drooling to slime her teats and swimsuit.

'Oh . . . oh . . .'

'Ooh . . .'

The orgasmic girls gasped as Bardolph spurted the last of his sperm into Lisbeth's throat and slowly disentangled. Lisbeth's swimsuit was wet with her own come and the slave boy's cream. A shadow darkened the sunlight and Lisbeth looked up to see the ebony figure of Miss Cicatrix Comington, dripping wet, in her own turquoise swimsuit.

'Disciplining the slaves, eh, Miss Lache?' she drawled. 'Most rewarding to watch the boy fuck his bride, and so gracious of you to drink his sperm before he can bestow it in her cunt! Curious how often our ideas of discipline express our own hidden needs.'

She flicked Lisbeth's left breast.

'A turquoise swimsuit, just like mine.'

'It's a designer swimsuit, Miss Comington,' Lisbeth blurted. 'A genuine Giulio Ferracci.'

'Bah! You let a brute male design your woman's body, to satisfy his sadistic fantasies?' she snapped. 'It's all wet, miss. I suggest you take it off.'

10

Split to Burst

'You'll be more comfortable in the nude,' purred Cicatrix Comington. 'I'm really quite jealous of your swimsuit. I was *sure* it was a Giulio Ferracci. For a male supremacist, he certainly knows the female body – almost as well as the master.'

Miss Comington tapped her cane. Her suggestion of nudity was, unmistakably, a command. Lisbeth gazed at her steely eyes – at the ripe, jutting breasts, rippling thighs, swelling curve of the cunt hillock and firm arse melons, left almost nude by her own high-cut swimsuit. The hole mistress carried a waterproof pouch and, on a waist strap, several cords and thongs of shiny leather and rubber, swaying against her bare thigh like tree fronds as she moved. Lisbeth shivered, blushing, as she wiped the glaze of sperm from her lips, and hurried to strip naked. Miss Comington inspected the wealed bottoms of the two shivering slaves.

'You've blistered them well,' she said. 'Slaves are idle, uppity creatures, and their fesses need regular flenching.'

Lisbeth stood naked, as nonchalantly as possible, under Miss Comington's inspection, acutely aware of her nipples stiffening and the seep of come in her gash. Miss Comington extended a hand and stroked Lisbeth's nipples with soft fingers. Lisbeth blushed a deeper red and let out a little gasp, but did not resist the kneading pressure as her nipples hardened to full erection.

'And, you know, miss, we are all slaves sometimes,' purred Miss Comington. 'You're very pretty, for a tribade.'

144

'What?' cried Lisbeth. 'I . . . how did you know?'

'The master knows,' said Miss Comington. 'Rum Hole is the ideal place for a dominant, predatory lesbian to satisfy her needs, isn't it? Or to diversify – I admired your excellent sucking of the slave boy's cock.'

Miss Comington's fingers strayed down Lisbeth's quivering belly to the shaven porcelain mound of her cunt, and entered the gash folds, slimed with new come.

'You enjoyed catchpoll Perkins, too,' she murmured, two fingers sliding into Lisbeth's dripping pouch and lightly brushing her swollen clitty. 'His big cock fucking your dunghole – a lovely excuse for revenge, whipping poor Jerome.'

'You know everything,' Lisbeth gasped. 'Look – see how brutally the beast flogged me. And being fucked in my arse – it was so shameful, and hurt dreadfully.'

She half turned to show her bare bottom.

'The marks are almost gone,' said Miss Comington. 'And don't pretend you didn't come, with Eldridge's tool pounding your colon. A girl relishes her bottom more, Miss Lache, if it is properly seen to.'

She nodded and the two slaves pinioned Lisbeth's arms.

'Wait – what –'

Miss Comington pinched her clitty very hard between the nails of finger and thumb.

'Ooh! That hurts! Stop, please!'

'Many girls don't really know what they want,' she said, 'and Rum Hole helps them find out.'

'Please,' moaned Lisbeth, 'please, no . . .'

Miss Comington displayed a bag of simple clothes pegs and, removing them one by one, pinned them sharply to Lisbeth's flesh, ignoring her squeals and sobs, until her naked body was covered in clothes pegs, sharpened at both ends. She moaned, wriggling, held down by the two slaves, as Miss Comington put the finishing touches to her adornment.

'Oh, please . . . it hurts,' Lisbeth gasped, her words distorted by her torture pegs.

This can't be real. It's a nightmare.

The vicious pins pinched her flesh to white bubbles. Her breasts were circled in pins, with an extra-large clamp on each nipple, stinging Lisbeth hideously. Worse, her cooze was opened with a row of three clothes pegs pinned to each cunt flap, and one pinning her clitty bud. A ceinture of pins extended around her back and belly, with garters of pins on her thighs, preventing her from closing her legs. Rows of pins studded each buttock in a crisscross, and the flap of skin between each toe was pinned with another crisscross across the bare soles of her feet. Clothes pegs disfigured her ears, cheeks and nose, with three pins to each lip, and two clamping her tongue.

'Please, miss, I need to go to the lavatory,' Lisbeth stammered. 'I'm really bursting.'

God, I sound like myself as a silly schoolgirl.

Miss Comington smiled, placing a gallipot before Lisbeth's cunt. A heavy stream of piss hissed from her cooze, filling the pot, as Lisbeth sighed in relief. Her sigh became an anguished squeal as Miss Comington poured the piss over her breasts, letting it trickle down her belly and onto her cunt hillock until her body glistened with the acrid fluid.

'Ooh! Mm!' Lisbeth gasped, tears moistening her eyes.

The swimsuited ebony girl threaded strings through the holed ends of the clothes pegs, drawing the strings together, to hold Lisbeth trapped like a puppet. She jerked the strings, now one, now another, wrenching breasts, cunt flaps, belly or soles until Lisbeth sobbed, whimpering, with tears pouring.

'Ooh ... it hurts so much,' she gasped, 'it really, really hurts.'

Miss Comington showed her two strips of burnished brown leather, bound together in a handle, with the flat tongues a foot in length.

'The Scots tawse,' said the hole mistress. 'They are most suitable for close-up work, and have the interesting property of afterburn, that is, they sting like the devil when applied to naked flesh but, shortly afterwards, surprise the subject with a dreadful smarting, worse than the original sting, and long-lasting. You can apply them bunched, like this –' she lashed Lisbeth's left breast, just beside the nipple pin '– or splayed, like this –' lashing the two tongues apart, on either side of the nipple.

'Urrgh! Ooh!' Lisbeth howled, as her breast flesh coloured pink.

'My dear Miss Lache,' said Miss Comington, lifting the tawse across her rippling breasts, 'don't complain. You might have fallen into the hands of the Lucayans with their bizarre rituals and, unlike us, they do not have your pleasure at heart.'

Groaning, Lisbeth was wrenched by her hair to stand, shivering, in the warm sunlight. Miss Comington took two hinged wooden pieces from her pouch, slapped one on holes bored in the wall and affixed it with a screwdriver; squatting, she screwed the second device into holes in the floor some feet away.

'Finger stocks,' she said. 'Part of our rich colonial heritage. They'll help you take a good flenching.'

The wood was grooved with finger-sized notches. Lisbeth moaned as her fingers were inserted into the holes, the top half fastened and screwed shut over the trapped fingers; then her toes were fastened in the minuscule stocks screwed to the floor. Her pegged body stretched helpless at a slant to the wall, with her spread legs straining on tiptoe to escape the pricks of the sharpened clothes pegs clamping her soles. Miss Comington licked the tawse before lifting the twin tongues over Lisbeth's buttocks. Vap! The tawse whipped Lisbeth on the wide portion of fesse left bare by her rows of clothes pegs.

'Ooh!' Lisbeth squealed, her bum wriggling with a rattle of pegs.

Vap! A second stroke to the bottom made her piss-wet cheeks clench. Vap! Vap! Miss Comington, breasts heaving under her swimsuit, flogged Lisbeth's naked buttocks until she had etched an intricate pattern of weals between the rows of clothes pegs, which swayed like reeds as her bottom squirmed, sprinkling stray droplets of piss. Vap! Vap!

'Oh ... oh ...' Lisbeth moaned, sobbing, as her skin reddened.

Vap! Vap! Nates clenched tight, her naked body shuddered and wriggled in the imprisoning finger stocks, with the forest of clothes pegs whirling and rattling, as her titties shook and her bum and cunt basin writhed. Her slit flesh glistened deep pink, oozing come which trickled down her thighs. Miss Comington lashed her on the buttocks for several minutes, until the open flesh was livid crimson. The two slaves stood demurely, hands at crotch, with Bardolph's cock trembling into new stiffness as, licking his lips, he watched Lisbeth's bottom wriggle.

Miss Comington handed miniature floggers – rubber quirts, with six square tongues, a foot long – to each slave, and ordered them to attend Miss Lache's forward parts. She continued to baste Lisbeth's raw bottom while the slaves whipped her artfully on the unpegged portion of her breasts, on her thighs and belly, Melissa delicately flogging her between the cunt pegs in her pink wet slit.

'Ahh!' Lisbeth screamed, as Melissa's quirt sliced her swollen clitoris.

'You like it, miss, don't you?' hissed Miss Comington. 'Like *me* flenching you ...'

Vap! Vap! The tongues of her tawse flashed, slapping Lisbeth's livid bare fesses.

'Ahh! Ouch!'

'You like it.'

Vap! Vap!

'Oh! Oh, how it hurts! I don't know why, I'm so ashamed ... I don't like it, I *need* it, miss,' Lisbeth whimpered, as her tears streamed, and her bum and teats bounced in her agony.

Lisbeth was whipped for thirty-five minutes. Her teats, thighs, and belly glowed with tiny crimson welts, with her inner thighs, cradling her pegged cunt lips, heavily bruised, and the vulval whorl puffily swollen. Come sprayed from her whipped gash, dripping in shiny rivulets down her legs. Miss Comington placed a finger in Lisbeth's slit and licked the oily come coating her fingertip.

'You are juicing, miss,' she purred. 'You are a submissive tribade.'

'No ... no ... no ...' Lisbeth blurted, helplessly shaking her head, her fingers and toes wriggling in their prisons as the tawse and quirts recommenced their lashing.

'You see,' Miss Comington panted as she whipped Lisbeth, 'there are two kinds of tribades – submissive and dominant. Our monitoring shows you cruel and predatory, but secretly begging for your own punishment. Like most so-called lesbians, you *really* crave fucking and severe humiliance from virile males, and especially anal penetration from outsize cocks.'

'Mm! Mm!' Lisbeth whimpered, violently shaking her head.

After a further two minutes of flogging, at Miss Comington's signal, her beating ended. The hole mistress pulled the string tethering Lisbeth's arse pegs. With a loud snapping, the pegs were ripped from her flesh, one by one, with Lisbeth dancing in pain.

'Oh! Ouch! Stop!' she screamed. 'Oh, it's agony.'

'Bardolph's cock met your requirements, miss. Swallowing his sperm was your act of imagined dominance, but now he shall have revenge.'

The slave boy's cock a rigid pole, he mounted Lisbeth's flogged buttocks, parting the cheeks to insert his glans into her quivering anal pucker.

'No ... no ... I beg you ...' Lisbeth sobbed.

His buttocks tightened as he thrust, penetrating her anus to half the length of his massive cock.

'Ahh,' Lisbeth moaned. 'It hurts dreadfully.'

Grunting, he thrust again, penetrating Lisbeth's rectum right to his balls. With his balls slapping against her raw bum bruises, he began to bugger her vigorously.

'Ooh! How can you take pleasure, miss, in shaming me so?' whimpered Lisbeth, her arse writhing under the slapping of the slave boy's hips. 'I expect you'll frig off at my pain. Don't *you* want to play with me? I admit, I *am* a tribade ... *oh*! He's hurting me!'

'My pleasure is following the master's will,' hissed Miss Comington.

As Lisbeth wriggled and sobbed, dancing on tiptoe, the slave boy's cock slammed the root of her rectum, withdrawing after each penetration, his shaft gleaming with her arse grease, before ramming her anew. Melissa gazed at Lisbeth's buttocks impaled on her fiancé's cock and began to tweak her clitty until she was vigorously masturbating, with come sluicing from her twitching ebony cooze.

'Ahh!' Lisbeth shrieked. 'He's too big, he'll split my bum.'

'Isn't that what you want, miss?' purred the hole mistress.

'Oh! Oh! I don't know ... his cock is so cruel and big and hard, I'm afraid he'll burst my belly open. He's right up me, almost into my colon. God, I'm split to burst. It feels so strange ... I'm so ashamed.'

'I know what you told Eldridge after he tupped you,' said Miss Comington.

'He blabbed?' groaned Lisbeth, her buggered bum churning under the slave boy's thrusts. 'Why, the beast ... ooh! Ooh, yes, that's good. Oh, yes, fuck me harder, do me, split me to bursting.'

Her hips danced, slapping her buttocks against the slave boy's balls. Melissa, masturbating hard, crouched under Lisbeth's writhing cunt basin, pressing her hair to the buggered girl's squirming cunt mound, and began to lick the slave boy's balls as his cock rammed Lisbeth's shiny greased anus. Her tongue slid from his bucking balls to the wet slit of Lisbeth's cunt, licking the cunt lips and tonguing the swollen, extruded clitty. Come gushed from Lisbeth's gash, slopping Melissa's face, and the girl opened her mouth wide to drink the juice. The slave boy panted, ramming Lisbeth's back passage harder and harder.

'Oh, yes!' gasped Lisbeth. 'I'm split to burst! Fuck me hard, slave, give me your cream in my bumhole ...'

Bardolph grunted and a bubble of creamy sperm spurted from Lisbeth's anus.

'Yes!' Lisbeth shrieked. 'I'm coming! Spunk hard, give me all your cream, burst me with your cock! Ooh! Oh! Ahh ...'

Her belly trembled as her cunt spurted copious come into Melissa's mouth, which also swallowed the sperm overflowing from Bardolph's quivering balls. Melissa's lips and chin were drenched in sperm and girl come, the mess slopping onto her erect brown nipples and glazing the bare ebony melons of her breasts. Her fingers tweaked her clitty and from her own cooze a fountain of come dripped onto her quivering thighs.

'Uh . . . uh . . . uh . . .' she groaned as her belly, cunt and come-slimed titties shook in her spasm.

A bicycle bell rang outside, followed by a timid scratching on the villa's front door. Miss Comington barked permission to enter and the nude, sweating figure of Rose, the Haitian slave girl, hobbled into the room, clutching herself at the cunt, with her face twisted in distress. She proffered a silver plate upon which lay a letter, sealed in wax, and addressed to 'Miss Lisbeth Lache'. The girl showed the letter to Lisbeth, lowering her eyes from Lisbeth's flenched bare body. She grimaced, rubbing her bottom and pendulous cunt flaps which dripped with come.

'What is the matter?' panted Lisbeth.

'Please miss, I've been made post girl, and the bicycle saddle is awfully sore on my private places,' lisped Rose, curtsying. 'That is, it's not really a saddle, just a bar. It tickles me . . . down there, and I'm all wet. I'm sorry, miss.'

'Bah!' said Miss Comington, snatching the letter. 'Shall I open it for you, Miss Lache?'

Lisbeth gasped her assent.

Miss Comington opened the letter and thrust it under Lisbeth's eyes.

'Well,' said Lisbeth excitedly. 'The master wants me to dine with him tonight! Oh, my . . . I haven't a thing to wear.'

'I recommend something light and girlish,' Miss Comington said. 'A short dress, bare arms, perhaps. And you shall be adorned with certain aids to affection.'

'I don't understand,' Lisbeth said.

She dismissed Rose with a slap to her bare buttocks, and

151

the girl hobbled back to her bicycle while the slaves released Lisbeth, groaning, from her finger stocks.

'You don't mean I should go dressed in these horrid clothes pegs?' she gasped.

'Certainly not,' said Miss Comington. 'I shall unzip you at once.'

She pulled the strings, one after the other, revealing her skin bruised purple where the pegs had pinched.

'Ouch! Oh!' cried Lisbeth. 'Stop. Please, no, it's agony.'

The machine-gun snapping of the pegs went on until she stood nude and crying, as Miss Comington delved in her bag. Melissa and Bardolph pinioned Lisbeth, who moaned but did not resist. Miss Comington fastened two thick rubber garters to Lisbeth's upper thighs, one an inch above the other, and two inches from her lowest quim flaps. The garters constricted her thighs tightly, plain black on most of their circumference, but on the inner side gleamed two-inch high steel metal spikes, as thick as bristles on a brush. Miss Comington locked the garters in position, explaining that, so tightly did they clamp Lisbeth's thighs, they were impossible to roll off.

'You will be obliged to keep your thighs well apart whether walking or sitting, or else get a nasty prickle,' she said. 'A rolling gait is the sign of a sensuous girl. The master likes that.'

Melissa held Lisbeth's thighs wide, while Miss Comington held up a thick wooden tube, phalliform, yet bigger than Bardolph's cock; studded with nodes and deeply striated, with hooks carved at the base and the tip.

'You have heard of the horned dildo,' said Miss Comington sweetly.

'Oh, no,' Lisbeth gasped. 'Please, no.'

Miss Comington slid the dildo into Lisbeth's cunt, rotating and churning it as she rammed it right to the wombneck.

'Ahh!' whimpered Lisbeth. 'I've never felt anything so huge. It hurts . . . ooh!'

'Would you rather have it in your anus?' grunted Miss Comington, 'or a choke pear?'

Lisbeth squealed as the lower horn pressed against her clitoris, and a spurt of come sprayed from her slit lips. Miss Comington slapped a thong of meshed wire filament around her waist and cunt basin, drawing it tight, to Lisbeth's moans of discomfort, and locking it with a tiny padlock. The thong held the dildo clamped inside Lisbeth's pouch, Miss Comington explained, with the lower horn slicing against her clitty, so that every movement would stimulate her.

'You can piss, of course,' she added, 'but aim carefully. It's a tight hole.'

Lisbeth took a few steps, rubbing her wealed bottom and breasts, and abruptly shuddered.

'Ooh, my clitty,' she gasped. 'If I walk too far, I'll ... I'll come.'

'The master likes that,' said the hole mistress.

After the departure of Miss Comington and the two slaves, Lisbeth spent a long time in the bathroom, rubbing her wealed body with zinc ointment, linseed oil and lime juice. Despite wincing, as her fingers touched the raw welts of her flenching, the pain was commingled with the electric thrill at her clitty and wombneck from the touch of the horned dildo at her every movement. The glow of her blistered skin seemed one with the fluttering of her filled cooze, and the come seeping down her thighs.

For her rendezvous with the master she selected a skimpy white silk cocktail dress, held up by spaghetti straps over her golden bare shoulders, and scarcely covering her braless breast melons; no stockings, and barefoot, with shiny gossamer panties to cover the wire mesh thong imprisoning the dildo in her cunt. A single choker of pearls covered her throat. Having made sure the dress covered her weals, she had to walk with a rolling mariner's gait, legs apart, to prevent her spiked garters slicing her thigh flesh, and when she erred, she winced at the stabbing pain inches from her pendant gash lips.

So cruel to lock me in these horrid panties and garters. Yet her cruelty makes me tingle, and it's strangely exciting,

*being in thrall of that lustrous black girl and hoping she will
flog me again . . .*

Darkness fell, cloaking the island in fragrant velvet. Night
birds and insects chirped over the purring of the waves, as
Melanie's rickshaw arrived to transport Lisbeth to the
master's lodge. She stepped barefoot into the carriage,
holding her purse against her skirtlet, which – too late! –
she realised was *shorter* than short, just covering her
bottom, and the beastly spiked garters keeping her thighs
apart.

'Miss looks sumptuous, if she will forgive me for saying
so,' Melanie murmured.

'Why, certainly, I forgive you,' Lisbeth replied.

The rickshaw girl set off at a brisk trot, horseshoes
clattering and sweat beading her naked body.

'It is the first time miss has visited the master?' she
panted.

'Yes,' said Lisbeth. 'Aren't you risking my whip, speaking without being addressed?'

'I know,' said Melanie. 'But I just wanted to . . . to warn
you, miss.'

'Warn me?'

'The master knows and owns everything in these islands.'

'So?'

'He will get the better of you, miss, as he always does. I
advise you to be careful.'

'You, a slave, advise me to be careful?' spat Lisbeth.

'Many a tribade has ended up a slave of the Lucayans,
miss.'

'Impertinent hussy.'

She uncoiled the whip from the rickshaw's side and
cracked its tip savagely across the girl's bare bottom. Vap!

'Ooh!' Melanie yelped.

Vap!

'Ahh . . .'

Vap!

'Oh! Oh, miss, it hurts,' bleated the girl, her buttocks
writhing and darkening with crimson welts.

154

Vap!

'Uhh . . . uhh . . .'

Melanie began to sob, snuffling and moaning, as Lisbeth kept up the whipping until they drew up the driveway of the master's villa, girdled with flowers, trees and bushes. Vap! Lisbeth lashed Melanie's buttocks a final stroke as they stopped, and the master's front door opened.

'There!' Lisbeth panted. 'See what you've earned by your impertinence, slave. I'll bet you're sorry you spoke out of turn.'

'No, miss,' sobbed Melanie. 'That was the cruellest whipping I've ever had, because I thought *you* were kind. But I'm not sorry, for I've done the right thing by an English girl.'

A maid, long ebony legs sheathed in shiny chocolate nylons under her frilly costume, welcomed Lisbeth to the master's house. Lisbeth smiled, recognising her pilot, Femella Culbutt, and mouthing a silent hello, but received a stony, obeisant glower in return. Femella's stiletto heels clacked on the ochre flagstones as her pert bottom swayed under its bouncing tutu. The vestibule was a mass of fragrant, lush house plants, the white walls festooned with paintings depicting scenes from the island's colonial and maritime past. There were pictures of sailing ships, pirates, great houses and sea monsters, and most featured a naked whipping, either as a vignette in the corner of the frame or as the main theme.

Aboard pirate ships, it was men who were flogged with the cat-o'-nine-tails; on land, by the jacarandas, parakeets and turtledoves of the great house, it was a nude female – ebony or peaches-and-cream – who writhed under lashes, with a crowd of elegant ladies and gentlemen as spectators. The largest painting uniquely depicted a nude young blonde woman hanging from her wrists and tethered hair in a whipping gibbet, her face contorted in agony as her striped buttocks and back took the whip of a naked black slave boy. The whipper's cock was fully erect with his balls tethered by a rope in the hand of a smiling mistress, as blonde as the flenched victim.

155

'Like it?' purred the master, sidling up behind her.

He smiled warmly, from a Roman-nosed, raw-boned face that struck Lisbeth as quite ugly, save for his gleaming green eyes and aura of absolute power, which made him seem sinister. He wore black silken pyjamas, lazily draped from his gaunt frame, their very informality drawing attention to the crotch, big with a dangling sex organ, that Lisbeth thought could not be real; it was evidently flaccid, hanging monstrously over his thighs, a giant tube of firm, menacing flesh.

'Oh . . .' Lisbeth blurted, blushing. 'Yes, it's very powerful.'

'A great-something aunt of mine,' he said. 'She made the mistake of forming an attachment to one of her pleasure slaves. So her husband ordered her flogged by her paramour, before his own flenching. The slave's balls are controlled by the miscreant's cousin, who herself desired his body – see how well he is hung. Justice was necessarily brutal in those days – it was acceptable for a lady to bare her anus for a bumming, but not done to form a sentimental attachment to the cockwielder. Do come in. Femella will get us drinks.'

He ushered her into a large sitting room whose panoramic windows looked out on the ocean, with a green sward between, fringed with blossom. Lisbeth sat in an easy chair opposite the master and smiled nervously, aware that her short skirt was up almost to her hips and, with her thighs forcibly parted by her garter spikes, her pantied crotch must be fully visible. She thought her black rubber garters must look silly with no stockings to hold up. Femella brought a tray with rum, fruit juice and ice, and mixed Lisbeth and the master tall glassfuls. The master sipped, gazing at Lisbeth with those hypnotically twinkling eyes over the rim of his glass, and suddenly Lisbeth felt completely nude.

'You are enjoying Rum Hole, Miss Lache?' he said. 'Feeling fulfilled?'

'Very much, sir,' she replied, mentally slapping herself for calling him 'sir', like some silly schoolgirl.

'No doubt you find the name curious. It has an obvious derivation, as it was an entrepôt for smuggling rum from Cuba ever since the days of my ancestor, also Roger de Hazebrouck, granted the Jumentos Cays in perpetuity by his majesty King Charles the Second. Roger was rather a bounder, I'm afraid, and probably relished the alternative derivation – "rum", in our English language, used to mean good or splendid. Our colonial ancestors were a sensuous crew, and imported slaves who were physically sumptuous, for *jouissance* rather than industry. I try to carry on that tradition and share it with my discerning guests.'

Lisbeth blurted that he did so with excellence, and their small talk continued until it was time for supper. The master allowed Lisbeth to precede him, after Femella, who led them to the candlelit refectory. Around the walls were more paintings, these depicting scenes of whipping and torture of naked girls, some slaves and some, apparently, wives or mistresses, with the actual instruments – stocks, yoke, rack, pincers branks, hobbles and Spanish boots amongst them – adorning the sides of the refectory.

One painting, a triptych, showed a nude couple fucking on a four-poster bed while another man, in seventeenth-century wig, lace and ruffles, peeped, frowning, through an open door. In its second panel, the nude woman was caned on the buttocks by the peeper, while her paramour, his enormous tool fully erect, looked on. Lastly, the gentleman watched his whipped wife, weeping and rubbing her crimson bottom, cane her paramour's bare buttocks.

'My ancestor,' purred the master. 'He was a rather lusty youth, and His Majesty Charles the Second paid him to swive certain ladies of the bedchamber, while the king observed, then affected an outraged entrance, with an excuse for pleasant chastisement of his errant mistress. This picture – perhaps scurrilous – shows Henrietta herself, his lustful Portuguese queen, in one such *accouplement*, and taking the consequences. It seems Roger de Hazebrouck was also caned, but I dare say he found it easy to bare up for handsome reward.'

Before them, in a wooden pillory, stood a naked girl,

157

back arched and head hooded, with her bare ebony buttocks presented to the dining table. Her ankles were fixed in a hobble, raised several inches on the pillory's shaft, and obliging her to stand on tiptoe. Her nude body shivered, beaded with sweat, as she stood, legs wide apart, exhibiting her pendant quim lips and the tight brown bud of her anus, freshly distended. Her waist was wrenched to impossible thinness by a turquoise corset shimmering against her velvet skin.

'My most devoted slave girl,' said the master. 'A true submissive, it is her pleasure to suffer, publicly, while her master feasts.'

Sapphire, Rose and Dugger, dressed as maids, curtsied as Lisbeth sat at the head of the table, opposite the master. Wine was poured, soup ladled and lobsters cracked; Lisbeth ate and drank hungrily, listening to the master's reminiscence of ancestors, slave girls and whippings. She was mesmerised by the scents of the flowers, the warmth of the tropical night, good food and drink and the master's suave authority, radiating power embodied by the trembling nude girl, helpless in her pillory of shame. Lisbeth's pulse quickened and her filled cunt moistened as she scrutinised the bare ebony buttocks, begging for the cane.

'I have observed you, Miss Lache,' purred the master. 'You are not like the others.'

Lisbeth's quim spurted come and her cunt writhed, squeezing the dildo against her clitty and wombneck.

'I confess to having compared your form to that ideal of female loveliness which all connoisseurs of beauty know. The buttocks, ripe, firm and tenderly succulent, the most important part of a female, silken to the touch, and their gently quivering globes of creamy flesh just begging for the kiss of a cane; the mystery of the cleft, hiding the wrinkled pucker of the anus, portal to the clinging soft *volupté* of forbidden parts; springy, supple haunches, the naked skin soft over whipcord muscles, hinting at delicious buckings; from them, the appraising palm may stray to pleasingly wide, powerful thighs, narrow waist, hard, flat belly, and swelling curve of the cunt mound, its alabaster skin shaven smooth as the bottom, above the divine orchid of the cooze lips, sensuously moist, swelling and beckoning to the wet pink pouch within. You, Miss Lache, I beg to imagine, from the delicate morsels of flesh you deign to show me, possess all this beauty to perfection. Long legs tapering to slender, smooth-soled feet, the toes so dainty and suckable, with deliciously big, firm teats, mirroring the croup, topped with ripe plums for nipples, glossy and hard with desire, complete the picture of loveliness, for beyond that – what may, or may not, be in a girl's pretty little head – the devotee of the female form has scant need to go. The curve of buttock and haunch, fragrance of skin, perfume of *coynte,* purling its juices of desire, all conspire to make any male rigid with power, his orbs tingling to anoint the wet pouch with their cream.'

'You flatter me, sir,' blurted Lisbeth, blushing.

Her quim was gushing come. She instinctively tried to press her thighs together and jerked, with a little gasp, buttocks rising from her seat, as the spikes of her garters pronged her inner thigh skin.

'Words are one way to penetrate the female . . .' he said. 'And now, to begin our post-prandial entertainment, it is time to cane the pudding slut.'

Sapphire pulled the hood from the pilloried girl's head, and Lisbeth saw the face of Miss Comington.

11

Pudding Slut

Lisbeth's mouth drooled crumbs, juice and cream as she absolutely *gobbled* her peach fool. She did not refuse a second helping, washing the feast down with a delicious sweet Sauternes, and without taking her eyes from the spectacle of Miss Comington's caned arse. Vip! Vip! Dugger and Femella lashed the hole mistress's squirming bare buttocks with springy three-foot canes, as the tethered girl soundlessly writhed, limbs wrenching at her pillory, legs jerking straight back at each lash to her bottom, bare breasts bouncing and toes wriggling in her dance of pain.

'I understand Miss Comington has tested you,' murmured the master.

'Tested?' Lisbeth blurted. 'Oh . . . I see . . .' She laughed ruefully. 'You know everything, sir. Yes, she tested me. Rather hard. I . . . I let her do it. I don't know why.'

'You have exercised your whip during your stay with us,' he said, 'but you have also run the gamut of submissive pleasures – thrashed and buggered by catchpoll Perkins and others, flenched by Miss Comington with every indication of relish. Your sapphic nature desires Miss Comington, of course.'

Lisbeth blushed, feeling her clitty throbbing.

'I feel I have been the victim of misunderstandings,' she stammered.

'Victimhood being itself a submissive pleasure,' purred the master. 'I also know the *real* reason you have graced Rum Hole with your presence, Miss Lache.'

Lisbeth's jaw dropped and a mouthful of fool fell between her breasts. The master watched, lip curled in amusement, as she tried to mop it with her napkin, making her breasts wobble, the left teat spring naked from her dress. Crimson with embarrassment, she pushed the floppy bare breast back beneath its stained covering.

'I confess to being intrigued,' the master continued. 'What can you possibly hope to offer me for my property?'

Lisbeth sat up straight, all businesslike, despite the voluptuous filling of her cunt with the horned dildo which tweaked her clitty and wombneck as she sat, making her wince and shiver. Vip! Vip! The caning of Miss Comington's wealed bare buttocks continued as Lisbeth composed herself.

'Sir,' she said, 'you can't think it wrong for me to test the waters before committing ourselves to an offer. You are deuced hard to contact, you know.'

He smiled. 'I do know,' he murmured. 'Please answer my question.'

He drew his chair back, glancing at Miss Comington's squirming bottom, and Lisbeth gaped, seeing the bulge at his groin risen, even at semi-erection a frighteningly huge member. Vip! Vip!

'Ahh ... ahh ...' The hole mistress's breath was wrenched from her in hoarse, groaning pants by each cane lash. Her ebony titties bounced in a frenzy and sweat poured from her writhing body as come sprayed from her flapping gash. Lisbeth's own gash oozed come as she watched the welts forming on the bare bum globes, then glanced at the master's stiffening, enormous tool.

'Well,' she said. 'On the basis of ... of my experiences, I think LaBo Associates would make you a very generous offer, in cash.'

'You are too kind,' he said. 'But what would I do with even more cash than I already possess?'

'You could name your price,' she blurted.

He placed his fingers together, seemingly oblivious of his rising cock. 'There would be constitutional difficulties,' he said. 'My ancestor Roger de Hazebrouck was, amongst many other things, Bishop of Looe, in Cornwall – a defunct bishopric, rather delightfully pagan, in fact, dating back to the Dumnonii of Roman times, and not subject to the Church of England, but one which the merry monarch was pleased to recognise. Technically, I am the hereditary Bishop of Looe, and Rum Hole belongs to the bishopric, so it is not really mine to dispose of.'

'Oh, I'm sure an arrangement could be made ...' Lisbeth began.

'You would have to recognise the Bishopric of Looe, and its prerogatives.'

'But of course.'

'Certain ancient customs prevailed, of which my ancestor was happy to take advantage, especially when he found himself in the new world and master of these islands. The bishop traditionally had the right to deflower virgins on their wedding night, witnessed by their bridegrooms, who were obliged at once to swive their wives' cunts, still dripping with the bishop's sperm. My ancestor was fond of that, especially as numerous housewives craved his subsequent visits. The folk of Gibbet Town today eagerly submit to sacred custom. In fact, they call me the master because they believe that a powerful, arrogant man should act like one. By allowing me to defile the cunts and dungholes of their womenfolk and whip their bare bottoms, they believe some of my power will rub off on their own persons.'

He snapped his fingers. The girls ceased flogging Miss Comington who was released, groaning and sobbing, from her pillory. Dugger drew back the flap of the master's pyjama bottoms, revealing his cock – nude, hairless, and fully erect. Lisbeth gasped, her mouth open and drooling, as come spurted from her dildoed cunt.

It's not fair. Such a monster ...

Miss Comington stood, naked and shivering, her eyes streaming with tears as she rubbed her welted bottom. 'Master, accept my submission, please ...' she sobbed.

The master nodded and the ebony girl sank to her knees, her face at his crotch. Her mouth closed over the engorged tool, taking the cockshaft right to her throat, with her mouth pressing his balls. Her head bobbed up and down as she sucked with little gurgling whimpers. The master sat back, smiling pleasantly at Lisbeth, and allowed Sapphire to place a lighted cheroot between his teeth. Fragrant cigar smoke filled Lisbeth's flaring nostrils. Her hand dropped between her thighs to rub the soaking gusset of her panties, pushing the horned dildo firmly against her throbbing clitty.

'You wish to masturbate, Miss Lache?' drawled the master, emitting a lazy plume of cigar smoke. 'It is your privilege as a guest. Or would you rather I exercised *my* privilege, as Bishop of Looe? Your submission would be infinitely more persuasive than any offer of vulgar cash.'

Lisbeth swallowed. 'You know what I crave,' she whispered.

The master slapped Miss Comington's bare titties and she relinquished his cock with a whimper of disappointment. She crouched on the floor, licking his balls while masturbating her dripping cooze and squeezing and flicking her erect velvet nipple plums.

'You may strip and approach me, Miss Lache,' the master commanded.

Lisbeth obeyed, slipping off her shoulder straps and wriggling out of her dress, which fell to the floor.

'You have been well flenched,' he said, licking his teeth as his eyes passed over her weals. 'You make an admirable pudding slut.'

'I've . . . I've got this *thing* in my cunny,' she blurted. 'Don't you want to do me there?'

The master smiled and shook his head. Nude, with her cunt squelching with come at each trembling step, she approached his huge stiff tool. He grasped her nipples, pinching them hard so that she whimpered, then spun her and seated her atop his glans, oiled with Miss Comington's drool. The flogged girl continued to lick his balls as she masturbated, while the master pulled Lisbeth's nipples sharply down, ramming her arse cleft onto the tip of his cock, with the glans penetrating her anus to half an inch. Lisbeth winced, her face wrinkling in pain.

'Ohh ... sir, please, not so fast. It's too big, it'll never go in. You'll split my bumhole, sir. *Ahh*!'

The master tugged firmly on her nipples, stretching her titties white and forcing his cock three inches inside her anus. Lisbeth's buttocks wriggled on the impaling tool and she gasped, clenching her cheeks and trying to open her rectum.

'Ooh! It's so huge,' she panted. 'I don't think I can take it, really, sir ... ooh! Ah!'

With a single thrust of his hips, and pulling Lisbeth's jerking body towards him, the master sank his cock right to the balls into her rectum. He began to tease her erect nips, pulling them up and down like puppet strings so that Lisbeth's bumhole was obliged to rise and fall on his cock. At full penetration, the master gave a little buck, plunging his glans to the hilt, and Lisbeth shrieked.

'Gosh, it hurts. Ooh! I've never been fucked like this before.'

Her impaled arse threshed on his balls and come poured from her cunt. She extended her hand to her split cunt lips, and began to frig her clitty.

'Oh, yes! Fill me up, sir ... it's so good ...'

She began to bounce up and down, slapping her buttocks on the master's balls, licked by the masturbating Miss Comington. Her hand clasped her swollen, lumpy belly.

'I can feel your cock inside me, sir, fucking my belly,' she panted. 'Yes, do me harder, sir, do me ...'

Her buttocks jerked and wriggled, squeezing the giant cock impaling her anus with gurgling plops of her arse grease at each thrust to her root. Come flowed from Lisbeth's cunt, dripping onto the bare back of the crouching Miss Comington, whose lips slapped the master's balls. The master clawed Lisbeth's stiff nipples, scratching the titties raw and pinching the squeezed buds, while slapping the naked teats together like balls, with a wet cracking noise. He used her teats to steer her, rolling her buttocks round and round in a grinding motion, with the tip of his cock reaming her colon.

'Ooh,' gurgled Lisbeth, masturbating vigorously. 'Bugger me, fuck my arse, do me, I'm going to come . . . oh, yes, yes!'

She yelped as her belly fluttered in orgasm, with come spurting from her cunt, to be lapped up by the ebony girl's eager tongue.

'You . . . you didn't sperm in me, sir?' she whimpered, rubbing her sweat-blurred eyes.

The master lifted her from his cock, which slid from her anus with a loud sucking plop.

'Rather impudent, miss,' he murmured, as Miss Comington licked his balls and cock clean of Lisbeth's glistening arse grease.

'I've submitted to you, sir,' Lisbeth blurted, 'so can we talk business now?'

'Vulgarity upon impudence,' he sneered. 'You have submitted when I decide, pudding slut. Miss Comington! Secure her.'

The girls dragged Lisbeth by her hair, pinioning her on the floor. Miss Comington unlocked her panties and ripped the horned dildo from her cunt. She thrust the dildo into Lisbeth's mouth and commanded her to suck it dry of come. Trembling, Lisbeth obeyed, swallowing her own fluid, some of her come dribbling onto her breasts, bruised by the master's mauling. Parting her gash flaps, Femella squatted over Lisbeth's face with her frilly skirtlet held up to reveal her naked arse and glistening pink cunt flesh. She sank towards Lisbeth's nose and lips, the ebony perfume of her cunt and anus filling Lisbeth's nose.

'You've always had a thing for your pilot girl, miss, haven't you?' she cooed. 'Like something to wash down your pudding?'

'Oh, yes, Femella,' Lisbeth gasped.

'I've always had the hots for you, miss,' Femella said. 'If the master permits . . .?'

The master nodded.

'I've dreamed of this,' whimpered Lisbeth.

Femella lowered her buttocks to crush Lisbeth's face with her cunt and anus. Writhing on Lisbeth's squashed mouth, she masturbated by rubbing her clitty on Lisbeth's eager tongue. Lisbeth took Femella's cunt fully between her lips, sucking the gush of come, until Femella's bare arse shuddered and she gasped in a heavy, spurting orgasm. With both hands, she clamped Lisbeth's jaw open and pressed it to her cunt, crushing Lisbeth with the full weight of her buttocks. Lisbeth writhed, gurgling, as a jet of piss spurted straight to her throat. Femella did not release her until she had pissed her full bladder and Lisbeth had swallowed it all.

'Oh! How could you?' spluttered Lisbeth, sobbing.

Miss Comington held her down by her hair, while Femella and Sapphire raised her thighs across her belly, with her toes at her mouth, and bound her wrists tightly across the backs of her knees, her forearms overlapping, and wound in a long rubber cord. Lisbeth was helpless, unable to move her legs or arms, with the broad expanse of her fesses exposed, stretching open her cunt, arse cleft and anus bud. Miss Comington knotted her hair to the base of the pillory, then pulled the dildo from her mouth, slapping it once, smartly, on each buttock. Lisbeth was left hog-trussed, feebly kicking and whimpering.

'What do you mean to do with me, sir?' she moaned.

The pink fleshy orchid of her slit glistened with come trickling down her arse cleft and into her anal pucker.

'Please you, Miss Lache,' said the master. 'Isn't that why you are really here?'

'How can torture be pleasure for me?' wailed Lisbeth.

'It is for you to tell us,' he replied.

'Sir, I accept being used naked – it's what every girl secretly craves – but to be treated as a casual plaything, a mere pleasure animal, is cruel.'

'Exactly. If naked *abuse* does not meet your craving, miss, you have only to terminate your residence, and depart.'

'Monster! That's even crueller.'

Smartly uniformed, Corporal Rodding entered, leading Jerome of Gibbet Town, nude, by a rope looped round his balls and cock. She curtsied to the master's stiff tool, then flicked the leash to urge her charge into position, above Lisbeth's bared thighs and croup. The boy's cock stirred and began to rise, swelling to full erection, when the corporal handed him her cane.

'I expect Jerome has been dreaming of revenge,' the master purred.

'No! Please,' Lisbeth shrieked as, at another twitch of his ball-leash, Jerome lifted the cane.

Vip! The whippy cane slashed a raw pink weal across Lisbeth's buttocks, just below her cooze flaps.

'Ooh,' she squealed. 'Oh, no.'

Vip!

'Ahh!'

Vip!

'Oh, gosh, it hurts. Please stop.'

'Stop what you crave, Lisbeth?' murmured the master. 'Isn't pleading part of submissive pleasure?'

Vip! The cane sliced upwards into her cleft, stroking her anus bud.

'Ahh!'

Vip!

Another vertical stroke landed with a squelching thud between her wet cunt lips, right on the tender pink meat of her gushing slit.

'Ahh! Ooh!' Lisbeth screamed.

Jerome's erect cock swung from side to side as he continued to baste Lisbeth's reddening thighs and buttocks. Her pink weals rapidly darkened to crimson, then puce, as he artfully repeated his strokes to her existing weals, raising the skin to livid puffy ridges.

'One's duty is to pleasure a female,' purred the master, 'but not to heed what females *think* their bodies want. One simply knows, without consulting their adorable little brains.'

Vip! Vip!

'Ooh! Ahh!'

Lisbeth threshed in her bonds, her feet wriggling, her stretched bottom unable to squirm to dissipate the pain of caning. Her thigh backs and buttocks were a mottled patchwork of blotchy puce and crimson welts, with livid bruises on the outer and inner lips of her cunt.

'Legs up, and bottom exposed – a curious variation of the normal upright caning position, is it not?' said the master. 'I learned it, rather uncomfortably, at my boarding school in Mevagissey. The masters and prefects allowed us the dignity of bending over and hiding our tearful faces, for a bare-bottom flogging. Not so the cruel matron, all the crueller for being young and pretty – a vicar's daughter from Newquay, and the object of every boy's desire. She would flog us exactly as Jerome is flogging you, Miss Lache, stripping us naked, making us lie holding our legs up by the backs of our knees, then caning our bare thighs and croups. She loved to see the pain in our eyes, with the added thrill that our precious balls were exposed and, if we wriggled too much, a slip of the cane might ... well, as a girl, you are spared that worry. If our cocks stiffened, which mine always did, it meant the caning was prolonged until we softened, or spurted. Matron herself used to masturbate after flogging a boy – it was common knowledge – and in my final year she took to masking our eyes in one of her petticoats so that we could not observe her masturbating, skirt up, during the caning itself.

'I taught myself to weep copiously at the pain, for then my tears would wet her filmy petticoat to translucence, and afford a view of her masturbating her naked quim, shaved bare, with the juicy pink flesh squirting come all down her blue nylon stockings. The sight of girl come, glistening on shiny navy blue stockings! Quite heart-stopping. It was not often I failed to spurt my cream, just watching her come to orgasm with stifled little gasps and shrieks. When this lady insisted on caning me for some trifle, on the very last day of my final term, I knew what she really wanted. I consented to the caning – a corker of thirty strokes – but did not spurt when she came.

'Instead, I rose and took her in my arms in a loving embrace, then ripped off her skirt and petticoat and knickers and striped her thirty on the bare bum with her own cane. She wriggled and howled over the surgery table with her head painfully raised, hair tied to a stethoscope on the rack above. Her cooze was flooded with come. I fucked her in the anus for quite a long time until she orgasmed repeatedly, at which point I deigned to spurt my cream in her rectum. She was sobbing with gratitude as she licked my organ clean. Thereafter, I had occasion to spend a few months at Looe, on Episcopal business, and she travelled on the bus every weekend for my buggery and bare-bottom thrashing. I used to flog her on the sands of Looe harbour when the tide was out, then rub her weals with sand and, after a sound buggery, bury her alive and entire in the tidal mud, leaving her to extricate herself. She always came back for more.'

Vip! Vip! Lashed hard, Lisbeth's bum jerked and squirmed.

'Ooh! Ouch!' she gasped. 'That's disgusting. It's perverted.'

The master chuckled. 'A female's greatest charm is to find all sensuous pleasures disgusting, except when she herself enjoys them.'

'I'm not enjoying this,' Lisbeth sobbed, squirming. 'My bum smarts horribly and Jerome's cock, swaying above me, is so horrid and menacing. Oh, why do I have to look?'

'For the pleasure of anticipation,' the master purred.

'What! No ... surely not. Sir, please!'

A flick of Jerome's ball-leash brought the caning to an end after the thirtieth stroke. He straddled Lisbeth, poking his tool two inches into her cunt and lazily reaming the pouch. Her clitty brushed against his cockshaft and soon stood, stiff and pink, extruded from her caned cunt folds.

'Oh!' she gasped. 'Don't tease ...'

Jerome withdrew his cock, oiled with her come, and pressed his peehole to her anus bud.

'Sir! I'm hurting in there,' Lisbeth wailed. 'You did me so hard, I can't take another bumfuck. Ooh!'

Jerome thrust brutally, sinking his giant cock halfway into her rectum; a further thrust, and he penetrated her to his balls. His buttocks began to pump as he delivered a vigorous buggery at her arse root.

'Ooh, oh, he's bursting me . . .' Lisbeth moaned, yet her buttocks began to rise, meeting his thrusts, her wealed cheeks slapping against his balls.

Come poured from her slit, over his cockshaft and balls, as his huge, glistening ebony tool rammed in and out of her straining anus bud. Lisbeth's eyes screwed shut as, red-faced, she vigorously slammed her bum against his cockthrusts, her anus bud winking and squeezing the penetrating tool. Jerome began to gasp loudly.

'Yes,' she moaned, 'fuck me harder, fuck my bum, more, more . . .'

'I am reminded of a favourite mistress,' the master mused, his own cock rigid as he watched the boy fucking Lisbeth's arse. 'One of my choristers. She was a vixen – what female is not? – and craved a veritable plethora of cocks, even when she earned my vengeful whipping thereby. I soon learned how our two pleasures could coincide, with me watching in delight as a succession of naked slave boys, sometimes a dozen in number, poked her rectum with their sex organs and, from my demure choir girl, she became a snarling, howling animal, consumed by naked lust. After I had flogged her buggered arse quite soundly, I eagerly bumfucked her myself, my tool penetrating her wonderfully elastic arsehole, still slimy from the spunk of a dozen cocks, to which I was pleased to add my own.'

Jerome began to gasp and his cock bucked. A dribble of hot cream bubbled at Lisbeth's anus.

'Oh, yes . . . yes . . . yes!' she squealed, writhing in orgasm, as the boy filled her rectum with his copious sperm.

He withdrew his cock and the master doffed his clothing. Nude, he straddled Lisbeth, licking his lips, his massively swollen tool at her buggered anus. He penetrated her rectum with one thrust, and began to bugger her for the second time, slamming hard against her whip-streaked buttocks for several minutes and bringing her twice more to orgasm before he smiled, licking his teeth, and spurted his cream into her, his copious ejaculate bubbling from her bumhole to mingle, on her threshing fesses, with Jerome's spunk and the come sluicing from her cunt. Lisbeth writhed, howling, as she climaxed once more. The master withdrew his dripping cock from her hole, and ordered the sobbing Lisbeth to lick the tool clean, before Miss Comington wiped it with a hank of Lisbeth's hair.

'Oh, I've never been so shamed,' Lisbeth blurted.

Miss Comington held the master's cock over Lisbeth's body, and he pissed long and copiously over her face and breasts. Lisbeth burst into tears.

'Ooh!' she spluttered. 'You're vile. I shan't stay here a moment longer.'

The master shrugged, accepting a silken robe from the hole mistress. 'Miss Comington, please have a girl fetch Miss Lache's statement of account,' he ordered.

Lisbeth was released from her bonds and stood, trembling and red-faced, to receive her bill, presented by Femella on a silver plate. Sperm still dripped from her bumhole to trickle in glinting streams down her thighs. She opened the folded paper and gasped, her eyes wide.

'What is this, sir?' she said fiercely. 'Some kind of joke to add to my humiliation?'

'No joke,' said the master.

'It's impossible.'

'You know that our accommodations do not come with vulgar tariffs. We judge the satisfaction received by our guests.'

'I've been a victim – bumfucked, gamahuched, throat-fucked, whipped, flenched and now pissed on! You've used me for your pleasure in my naked shame. It's abominable ... it's not fair.'

'Exactly. Ten million dollars seems modest.'

'You know I can't pay such a sum.'

'Cannot, or will not?' said the master.

'It's ... it's preposterous,' Lisbeth blustered.

'Which I take to mean "will not". In that case, according to our laws, you place yourself in *feoffage extrême, sans droit d'escutage*, until you have worked off your debt with your person.'

'Wait!' shrieked Lisbeth, as all the girls pinioned her.

Corporal Rodding cracked her cane across Lisbeth's bare breasts, marking the flesh and nipples with an angry stripe. 'Silence, whelp,' she hissed.

'You may convey the new drudge to the slaves' quarters,' murmured the master.

'No ... no ...' wailed Lisbeth, sobbing and squirming as she was dragged away. 'Please ... I'm sorry. I'll do anything ... *anything*.'

'I know you will,' said the master.

Outside, in the fragrant darkness, Melanie's rickshaw awaited. Femella roped Lisbeth's wrists behind her back while Miss Comington fastened her naked body in a trident harness, a heavy triple quirt with a long handle, the tip of each tongue equipped with a clamp, one for each nipple, and one pressing the cunt flaps together. Miss Comington smartly clicked the clamps in place, the metal pincers squeezing Lisbeth's nips and quim to white slivers of flesh, then fixed the handle's tail loop to the rear of the rickshaw.

Climbing in, she cracked her whip over Melanie's bare bum and cried, 'Giddy-up, bitch.' At once, the vehicle moved away, Melanie trotting briskly in her clattering horse shoes, pulling Lisbeth behind, unable to slow without risking worse pain in her clamped extremities. The path was painful on her bare soles, and her breasts bounced uncomfortably as she panted, trying to run in time with the speeding rickshaw. She had to skip and jump over tendrils or rocks, and once tripped, stumbling into her tethering ropes and losing her footing, so that she was dragged along by her teats and quim for over ten agonising seconds before she could regain her balance.

The sea twinkled so temptingly as Lisbeth stumbled in agony behind the rattling rickshaw! They passed villas with their lights on, and she thought that one of the friendly guests might emerge to stop this nightmare. There was the villa of Tanya and Jeremy; there was her own, fully lit, as though she were at home ... the rickshaw plunged between the trees, across the road, and onto a rutted side track where Lisbeth stumbled to keep her balance, with the vicious clamps straining her nipples and cunt flaps, throbbing with pain. After a short distance they came to a clearing with a long, low barracks hut. Rickshaws were parked at the edge of the savannah, next to a gibbet, stocks and flogging frames, all empty.

Lisbeth sobbed miserably as Miss Comington freed her from her bonds. A uniformed guard emerged from the shadows, saluted, and asked Miss Comington if the new slave was to be pilloried, whipped, or put in the stocks until morning.

'No,' said Miss Comington, stroking Lisbeth under her chin, 'she's had quite a vigorous day, as you can see from her body.'

'She's certainly marked with ample welts, miss,' said the guard, peering at Lisbeth's lash-pocked skin. 'Shall I put her straight into the general population?'

'Yes,' replied Miss Comington. 'Give her a palliasse beside Melanie's. When Melanie has finished her duties, she can show the new slave the ropes.'

The guard flicked her cane on Lisbeth's buttocks, urging her through the barracks door, as Melanie's rickshaw trotted away with Miss Comington. The guard took her to the far end of the room, which was lined with palliasses, and drove away a naked sleeping girl with her whip, freeing her palliasse for Lisbeth. Lisbeth sank down, exhausted yet tingling. She looked round at the candlelit chamber, foetid with sweat and food.

All the slaves, males and females, were nude, including the scattering of European girls, who eyed Lisbeth's whipped body with trembling curiosity. A number of them sat at a trestle table, devouring bowls of soup and bread. The food seemed plentiful and smelled appetising, yet Lisbeth was still sated from dinner with the master. Others lay on their beds, sleeping or talking. A guard sat at each end of the barracks, cane in hand. By the door was a bank of telephones which rang frequently, causing a scramble of slaves to answer them. A task and villa number would be called and, if the guest had not specified a particular slave, the guard would despatch one at random.

173

Beside each palliasse was a makeshift canvas armoire with maids' costumes, work clothes, swimsuits and corsets; the chosen slave, if female, would attire herself appropriately, often cursing as she forced herself into an ultra-narrow corset of pastel hue. If male, his clothing was minimal, and some male slaves were summoned to appear in the full nude. The rickshaw girls were notable for the horseshoes they frequently left nailed on, and the fierce whip scars on their backs and buttocks. Even nude, the slave girls satisfied their vanity, preening before the plentiful mirrors, arranging their hair, rubbing linseed oil and lime juice into freshly caned croups or shaving the quims and armpits of other girls.

Only one incident marred the ambience of bustling tranquillity: two black slave girls quarrelled over a bowl of soup, snarling insults. Suddenly the soup tureen was overturned, soaking both of them in the mushy green liquor, and the two nude girls fell to the floor, kicking, gouging and struggling. Their combat was merciless, as they kicked between the legs, ripped hair and clawed nipples. The guards stood over them, leering, until the two combatants seemed to tire, wriggling in their mess of soupy slime, squealing and howling, as a vicious punch or kick connected with wobbling teat or gaping cunt flesh. A guard pulled each by her hair and began to flog her, while dragging her to the door. Lisbeth followed the crowd to watch.

'Locked and licked for catspatting,' panted one of the guards.

Outside, the catspatters were locked in the pillory, forcing them to stand on tiptoe with their breasts weighted with heavy lumps of metal suspended from their clamped nipples. Equal weights were fixed to their cunt flaps, which were stretched viciously, causing the pilloried girls to sob, gasping in their imprisonment. The guards began a casual flogging of their buttocks, to which the girls responded with pleas for mercy, while their titties and cunts swayed, banging the weights together. The nude bodies writhed in the starlight, their cries added to the chirps and squeals of

174

the forest enclosing them. To Lisbeth's astonishment, the audience of slaves was jubilant rather than sullen, actually cheering the whippers, with some of the slave girls quietly masturbating.

'There is no honour amongst slaves,' said a girl's voice.

Lisbeth turned to see Melanie. Intent on the whipping, she had not noticed the return of the rickshaw girl.

'Oh . . .' Lisbeth gasped.

The two nude girls stared at each other, hesitantly, in the pale light. Melanie held out her hand and touched Lisbeth's cunt lips.

'What . . .?'

She lifted her fingers, showing them sparkling with come.

'You are juicing, miss, at the sight of girls whipped,' she said. 'The master is right – we slaves are all the same – low, sensuous animals. Do you wish to masturbate with me?'

'I . . . I'm not a slave,' Lisbeth blurted. 'There's been a dreadful mistake.'

'It's hard at first,' Melanie said, 'but you'll learn soon enough. I haven't forgotten how cruelly you whipped me earlier, but I'm willing to be your friend, Lisbeth.'

'You should call me "miss",' Lisbeth retorted. 'I'm a guest!'

'*Were* a guest, Lisbeth. So were many of the girls here. So was I,' Melanie said. 'It happened to me, too. But it's not so bad, being a slave girl. Deep down, a submissive girl is happy in her naked shame. And we have each other.'

She put her hand into Lisbeth's wet pouch and began to frig her clitty. Lisbeth moaned and caressed Melanie's quim, the rickshaw girl's copious come slopping over her fingers, as the two slave girls kissed each other's lips and silently masturbated in the velvet night.

12

Rude Bitch

'You *are* tasty,' gasped Melanie, writhing as she sucked juice from Lisbeth's gushing cunt. 'Gosh, yes, you're a rum mot. I knew it as soon as you climbed into my rickshaw, with your lovely big bum rippling. I thought, I'd love to tongue her out.'

The two nude girls gamahuched on Lisbeth's palliasse in the shadows of the darkened barracks. Lisbeth lay beneath Melanie's squirming, muscular body, her mouth sucking Melanie's come, spewing from her wet, fleshy cooze, while Melanie's head bobbed up and down, chewing Lisbeth's clitty and fucking her soaking slit with her angular nose. She made Lisbeth gasp when she moved her tongue to her anus and stuck in its whole length, waggling in the soft anal elastic. Her belly rubbed against the erect tips of Lisbeth's tingling nipples.

'They've really flogged you, haven't they? You're covered in welts and it's quite a turn-on. I hope we can be wanking chums,' Melanie murmured, making Lisbeth's quim vibrate with her lips.

'Mm . . . mm . . . yes . . .' moaned Lisbeth, swallowing the come spewing from the tribade's flowing gash.

'Just like at school, eh?' said Melanie. 'I expect you were at boarding school.'

'Bedminster,' murmured Lisbeth. 'This is scary, like my first night in dorm, with the pres in their green pleated skirts, swishing their canes, only I had no wanking chum.'

'I was at Totnes Gentlefolk,' said Melanie. 'They called me a bold, sexy girl because I wanked all the time. We had turquoise uniforms, with lovely tight panties, really pinching, and it made me feel sexy. I got dreadfully caned, bare-bum, for wanking so much. Or pegged, which was awful – clothes pegs on my nips *and* stuck inside my bumhole or cunny, pinching the insides! I suppose that's what brought me here – I realised I had come to crave it. The master is so *wise*.'

The only light came from the two guards' cabins at each end of the long hall; both guards occupied one, from which issued sounds of laughter and the chink of bottles. All around the slippery, writhing tribades came groans, whimpers and coos of lust and the slapping of nude bodies as the slaves pleasured each other in the darkness. Melanie's belly began to buck, and Lisbeth knew she was coming to orgasm, so took her swollen clitty between her teeth, bit, then sucked the whole distended organ into her mouth, where she tickled it with her tongue tip. Melanie's cunt poured come over Lisbeth's lips and nose.

'Urrgh . . . urrgh . . .' Melanie groaned, her own lips sucking Lisbeth's entire cooze.

'Mm . . .' Lisbeth gasped, as her own cunt and belly exploded in orgasm, a copious stream of come spurting into Melanie's mouth.

Both girls sucked and swallowed the come, until Melanie slithered up Lisbeth's body to cuddle her, breasts pressed together.

'I've come a lot today,' Lisbeth gasped, 'and I was so ashamed – but that was super, Melanie. The guards don't bother us?'

'No,' said Melanie, stroking Lisbeth's bottom. 'We're not badly looked after: the food is plentiful and we can squelch and diddle as we like. It's just that we are *slaves*. But I've been the master's slave for a year now, and I wouldn't know what to do otherwise. Girls are made to be slaves! I came here thinking I was to be a schoolteacher, but really, I wanted to be caned. The master *knew*. Of course, there are the Lucayans, too . . .' She shivered, as her fingers pressed the weals on Lisbeth's bare buttocks.

'Heavy welts,' she murmured. 'You'll take more in the

next few weeks – in the corset factory, spearfishing, perhaps pulling a rickshaw. After that, it's plain sailing, and your bruises will seem part of you. But *these* welts – you are a brave girl, and have suffered enough today. Let's hope the welcome gang ignores you tonight.'

'The what?'

'You'd rather not know.'

Naked bodies loomed from the darkness beside Lisbeth's palliasse. Ebony slave boys smiled, their bare cocks shiny and fully erect. Pushing Melanie to the floor, one of them grasped Lisbeth's hair. Lisbeth was turned on her belly, and her thighs pushed wide apart.

'Please,' she whimpered, 'I've been fucked so much today . . . ahh!' She shrieked as a huge stiff tool penetrated her anus.

'No, please. It hurts,' she gasped.

The tool thrust into her rectum, slamming her arse root.

'Ooh!' Lisbeth groaned. 'Oh, stop, I beg you, stop . . .'

The slave boy laughed as his buttocks pumped, flashing in the glimmering starlight, driving his huge cock into Lisbeth's rectum. Lisbeth squirmed on the smelly straw palliasse, her buttocks writhing under his fierce buggery, and his hips and balls slapping on her wealed bare bumskin. Sometimes, at a particularly hard thrust, her back arched, her head thrown back and her lips drawn in a rictus, drool sliming her trembling chin. The slave boy fucked her for over a minute before spurting. Then he gasped and Lisbeth felt a hot jet of cream at her colon, so copious that it dribbled from her cock-stretched anus, down her crack, and into the lower cunt lips, themselves oozing come from her juicing slit.

'Ahh . . .' she gasped, slumping on the palliasse, her legs still parted, come oozing from her crevice.

She moaned softly, panting as another male mounted her. Again, a massive ebony cock penetrated her open anus, driving hard to her rectum and beginning a vigorous arse-tooling. Lisbeth squirmed, impaled by the cock, her head shaking from side to side and her teeth biting the pillow. Her fucked arse moved in time with her buggery, the writhing globes thrusting upwards to press the boy's balls. Peering through tear-blurred eyes, she saw Melanie watching her buggery and masturbating while sucking cock, the male's balls at her lips, with his glans bulging in her throat. When the second slave boy had spunked at Lisbeth's colon, Melanie's mouth slipped from her tongued tool, her hand grasped his buttocks and, still masturbating, with a lustful smile on her lips, she pressed him into Lisbeth's bumhole.

'Oh . . . ahh . . .' Lisbeth gasped, as the third cock began to pound her arse root. 'Oh, yes . . .'

The slave boy fucked over two minutes before spunking, washing her rectum with hot, creamy sperm which oozed from her squirming arsehole into the mess of come and spunk, slippery beneath her writhing cunt hillock. Melanie was sucking a fourth naked male, his muscles rippling as she tongued his ebony glans and peehole. Primed by her tongue, he slipped into Lisbeth's anus the moment it was vacated, still slimy with the sperm of his predecessors and Lisbeth's copious arse grease.

'Uhh . . . yes, do me,' she moaned, her fingers scrabbling at her juicing cunt. She squeezed her throbbing clitty and gasped aloud. 'Yes, fuck me, bugger my hole, come inside me, pour your hot spunk . . .'

He buggered her powerfully as Lisbeth masturbated herself to orgasm, squealing and drooling, her fucked arse threshing on the palliasse. She spread her buttocks wide for the fifth cock to penetrate her, and masturbated continuously, bringing herself to another orgasm.

'Oh, yes,' she gasped. 'Do me hard, fuck my bum, spunk in me . . .'

Seven cocks in all fucked her bumhole, while the watching Melanie masturbated herself twice to orgasm. There were other spectators, too: a gaggle of nude European girls, their hair sun-bleached and skin bronzed, who twittered excitedly as they frigged each other off. Lisbeth knew her ordeal was over when Melanie's arms encircled her cunt basin and her lips kissed Lisbeth's hot bare bottom. A cool sponge rose, dripping, from the pail of water beside her palliasse, and Melanie washed Lisbeth's raw anus of its slimy cargo.

'Every girl has a buggery sponge beside her bed,' she whispered. 'You've done awfully well, Lisbeth, and everyone is very taken with you. I just *knew* you were made to be one of us.'

A shadow darkened them. Lisbeth looked up and saw Corporal Rodding.

'Settling in all right, bitch?' she drawled.

'Yes, thank you, miss,' said Lisbeth.

Corporal Rodding's cane mashed the straw of the palliasse, soaked in sperm and come. She wrinkled her nose. 'Well, get a good night's sleep,' she said. 'After breakfast tomorrow, you've a session in the caning stocks.'

'But . . . why?' Lisbeth blurted.

'For wetting the bed, bitch,' snapped Corporal Rodding.

Lisbeth did manage to sleep, her bare body tossing and turning in the heat, to be awakened by a cut to her bare buttocks from the duty guard. She followed the other slaves to the communal washroom, where males and females squatted to dung at a long toilet channel, before hosing each other down with cold water. Breakfast was taken in the nude, a copious meal of porridge, milk, fruit, fish and boiled eggs; afterwards, the slaves busied themselves dressing in their costumes of servitude. Lisbeth's armoire contained a generous variety of clothes. She was sorting through them when a guard's hand tapped her bottom.

'Outside at the double, bitch. You've a session in the caning stocks.'

Lisbeth was obliged to trot, knees up and arms at her sides, out of the door and across the savannah to the sinister array of gibbets and flogging horses. She was halted at a wooden frame of two posts, with parallel crossbars pierced by holes for wrists and ankles, and beams slanting from the foot of each post to form a triangle. At the apex of the triangle was a saddle, a pole three feet from the ground with a circular ledge about nine inches across and, rising from it, a wicked cylinder of gnarled wood, polished and worn by use and gleaming in the bright morning sunlight. Lisbeth gasped, her face paling; it was the image of the dreadful horned dildo. The guard slapped a handful of linseed oil onto the wooden shaft.

'She'll slide up you like a tuna,' she said. 'What are you waiting for? Squat, bitch.'

'On that . . .?' Lisbeth blurted.

'Of course. In the anus.'

Under the brandished cane, Lisbeth straddled the greasy tube, parted her bum cheeks and lowered herself onto the tip of the tube until it poked and inched into her anus. Tears sprang to her eyes. Grimacing, and with a shudder that made her breasts bounce, she lowered herself in a rush onto the dildo, gasping loudly as she felt it penetrate her innards. The top half of the split crossbar rose and, meekly, she placed her hands in the slots. The crossbar fell with a crunch, imprisoning her wrists. The guard fastened her ankles in the same way, leaving Lisbeth painfully bent over in a V shape, breasts dangling and bare buttocks thrust outwards, with only minimal support from the narrow wooden ledge, and the massive dildo poking her colon.

'You've an hour's session,' said the guard before striding away. 'Enjoy, bitch.'

Lisbeth was alone, under the sun, her wrenched body shuffling with groans of pain. Sweat dripped from her face and breasts to be absorbed at once into the baked earth. Slaves passed across the savannah to take up rickshaws, or proceed to their duties as summoned. They glanced sympathetically at Lisbeth, who recognised the bodies that had fucked her in the darkness, but no more, although Melanie, strapped to her rickshaw, managed to give her a furtive thumbs-up.

Rather than shift her buttocks to try and maintain her balance on the ledge, it was tempting for Lisbeth to let the massive anal shaft take her weight, despite the agony of the gnarled wood filling her belly. Yet after several minutes, the pain in her rectum was such that she reverted to her precarious buttock-balance on the ledge. It was uncomfortable to keep her head high, and the rising sun made sweat blur her eyes, so she let her head droop over her breasts, despite the pain in her wrenched shoulder blades. After half an hour of constantly shifting position, Lisbeth's whole body was in agony. The guard came, placing a cup of water between Lisbeth's parched lips, and letting her drink it dry.

'Thank you,' Lisbeth gasped. 'I can't imagine my crime of bedwetting merits such suffering.'

The guard laughed.

'New slaves must be broken in,' she said. 'And if you're suffering now, just wait till I cane you.'

'A caning?' blurted Lisbeth.

'Always, before a miscreant is released from the stocks. I shan't say I'll go easy on you, for I won't. You've the juiciest fesses I've seen in a long while, bitch, and I'll enjoy making them squirm.'

The minutes went agonisingly past until the guard reappeared, carrying a rough, unpolished cane which she swished in the air with relish before Lisbeth's frightened eyes. A crowd gathered, some slave girls in maid's attire, males slouching in tight, crotch-hugging shorts, some nude and rubbing their bare bottoms, with moist eyes as, already, many bore stripes from a guest's morning chastisement. Melanie was there, nude, and still wearing her horseshoes, with long whip weals streaking her back and buttocks. She clapped her hands together as the guard lifted her cane behind Lisbeth's upthrust bare.

Vip!

'Ahh . . .' Lisbeth groaned, as the wood sliced fire on her naked bottom.

Vip!

'Oh! No . . .'

Vip!

'Ooh!'

'Vip!

'Ah! Please, no!'

The caning continued, hard and rapid, despite Lisbeth's anguished squirming, her buttocks clenching madly on the dildo rammed in her rectum. At each stroke her bottom

182

bounced up the dildo's shaft, which slid halfway from her anus until her quivering, bruised fesses thumped down again, driving the dildo once more deep inside her anus. Lisbeth's body shuddered as the guard's cane wealed her bare; her stocks rattled, her hobbled wrists and ankles thudding against the wood at each stroke. New welts appeared on her heaving fesses, dark and shiny, over her fading bruises of the previous day, and reawakening those marks, to puff up with new crimson lividity. The guard was careful to stripe her on every part of her spread buttocks, including the cleft, stretched taut, so that the whole expanse of Lisbeth's bare glowed in a patchwork of puffy weals.

Vip!

'Oh!' she moaned, crying and sobbing in a long, drawn-out wail. 'I can't take it. Oh, please stop.'

Yet her cooze, threshing on its platform with the gash flaps slapping wetly against its wood, slimed her impaling pole with come, spurting copiously from her slit. Vip!

'Ahh!' she screamed, and a long jet of piss erupted from her gash, spraying the ground.

The slaves brayed with laughter as Lisbeth wept at her shame. Vip! Vip! Still the cane lashed her bare bottom until the last drop of piss had sprayed from her writhing cunt, and only her shiny come spurted from the flapping gash lips. After forty strokes, the guard lowered her cane and wiped the sweat from her brow.

'Enough,' she grunted. 'One of you slaves tend to her so that she's fit for work.'

Melanie fetched linseed oil and lime juice and rubbed the soothing balm into Lisbeth's buttocks, her fingers straying more than once between the fleshy wet folds of the cooze.

'Gosh,' she whispered, 'you're dripping, Lisbeth. You really are one of us – you relish a good lacing on the bare.'

'How can you say such things?' sobbed Lisbeth. 'It's agony. My bum smarts so much, it feels as if it's on fire.'

'Be glad it was a simple caning,' retorted Melanie. 'A whipping on the bare back – now *that* smarts like fire.'

The guard released Lisbeth from the stocks and said the master had ordered her to work in the factory. Groaning,

Lisbeth was fastened in a yoke with holes for her neck and wrists, which she held balanced on her shoulders, her arms trapped. Her ankles were fastened in a wooden hobble, two feet long, with the hobble on a rope, held by her guard. Like this, Lisbeth began her journey to the corset factory.

'Must I always be nude?' she gasped, as they stumbled through scrubland amid groves of canewood trees, where naked slave girls clambered, plucking the choicest branches for use in the corset factory, or to be pickled for canes of punishment.

'Costume is for proven slaves,' grunted her guard. 'Until you are broken in, you are no more than a rude bitch. Don't speak again, bitch.'

The corset factory was a long shed in a clearing, inside which naked slave girls toiled to sew the cane rods into heavy slabs of rubber, brocade or elastic, which other slaves had cut and trimmed into corset shape. The slave girls were roped together on a long tether lying across their laps and studded with quim-clamps, fixing their gash flaps to the rope. If a girl wanted to piss she did so in the bucket beneath her bench, the contents of the buckets serving to wet those bottoms due an eight-stroke summary caning for idleness.

The corsets were immersed in giant tubs of coloured dye outside the shed for several hours, and then hung out to dry, the finished corsets being itemised according to colour, material and size and loaded into rickshaws, for transportation to the warehouse by the jetty. Certain corsets of each batch were tested on the bodies of the lowest slave girls and, over the weeks that followed, Lisbeth had to endure many agonising sessions as corsets, already far too small for her, were knotted round her belly to their last and tightest eyelet. Her eyes would water as she gasped for breath, with plentiful strokes of a guard's cane on her buttocks to remind her that a rude bitch had to take it in silence.

Fractious bitches who fell into a catspat were restrained in a double yoke, called a 'bitches' bridle', with holes for two heads and two pairs of wrists. Confined head to head in the bridle, the two miscreants were whipped on the bare, after which they were obliged to spend hours in restraint, glowering at each other. When the guards were not looking, bridled girls would recommence fighting, using their feet in a savage form of combat known as 'purring'. They would pound each other's cunts, titties and bellies with high, flying kicks, faces twisted in rage and pain, yet not emitting the slightest squeal for fear of alerting the guards and earning a bare-back whipping in the pillory.

It was just the beginning of Lisbeth's long weeks of agony, the drudgery of her breaking-in mollified only by the caresses of Melanie, with whom she snuggled every night, naked and sweating on the grubby palliasse, for mutual masturbation. As a rude bitch, she had to offer anus or cooze to the ever-stiff cocks of the male slaves, with anal penetration the norm, and, as her bottom grew used to wriggling under vigorous buggery, she came to crave the nightly invasion of her come-slimed palliasse. Sometimes Melanie would gasp beside her, as both girls writhed, holding hands, under a double bumming.

After her most vigorous multiple penetrations, her rectum awash with sperm, a guard would haul her by the hair to the plush guest room where cheroot smoke announced a familiar robed figure. The master's tool, already erect, would plunge into her spunk-slimed anus, fucking her arse hard until, at the last moment, he would withdraw his tool and made Lisbeth suck his dripping cock, to swallow his massive spurt of cream, while his fingers clawed the cane-welts on her buttocks.

Wordlessly, the master would depart, leaving Lisbeth to hobble back to her palliasse, wiping her mouth and rubbing her impaled bumhole. Melanie always kissed her, then, full on the lips, in a slimy, deep-throating French kiss, sucking the master's spunk from Lisbeth's mouth. Whenever the master deigned to spunk in Lisbeth's rectum, Melanie would French-kiss Lisbeth's anus, sucking the master's sperm and, afterwards, kissing her mouth so that the two girls shared the cream.

English slave girls also visited, coy at first, yet eager to tongue Lisbeth's cooze or bumhole. The English girls liked to lick and chew the weals on a freshly flogged bottom, the puffier the tastier, and Lisbeth soon came to relish this practice, sucking the hot blotchy cane-welts on a girl's bare arse. All told the same story – lured to Rum Hole by its promise of pleasure, then seduced into slavery by the master.

'It's not really bad,' panted Linda, a sensuous convent girl from Bishop's Stortford, as she sucked Lisbeth's cunt flaps and clitty, 'as long as you don't get sold down the islands.'

'Sold?' gasped Lisbeth, her gash spewing come over Linda's eager mouth.

'There is a traffic in slaves. They have auctions, and if you displease the master you'll have a far rougher fate than this. Even worse than being sold is to be kidnapped by the Lucayans. They aren't like normal people.'

'Surely the master wouldn't allow such a thing.'

'He turns a blind eye. It keeps the Lucayans quiet and us on our toes. You'll have to do your turn at spearfishing – gosh, that's a bind. We have to lie in the sea while the guests – oh, well, you'll find out. But a girl finds a certain joy in being a man's slave, jumping to order, her own will absolutely crushed. She's not *confused* any more.'

Lisbeth did find out about spearfishing. A score of nude slave girls in light bondage were ferried out to sea and pushed into the water, where they had to float, just under the surface, their faces protected by heavy rubber masks, equipped with a single breathing tube stuck in the mouth; legs stretched painfully wide with balsa wood hobbles, and titties floated by coconuts, while the guests took pot-shots at them with arrows tipped in foam rubber. Points and prizes were awarded for accuracy of aim: an arrow in the cunt or anus might win a genuine antique dildo or cat-o'-nine-tails.

At intervals, corset girls were sent to the canewood groves to pick branches. The girls scampered nude up the stubby canewood trees, and Lisbeth rapidly learned which were the choicest branches for pickling. The work was refreshing, the open air and sea breeze soothing on the bare skin, free of fetters, the only drawback being that one girl out of the squad had to bend over and test the selected canes. It was Lisbeth's turn more often than she thought fair, but she took it with bitten lip and good grace. Sometimes one of their number would disappear, and hushed whispers said the slave girl had been selected for the doe hunt, in which the prey was human.

When caught, the doe was thoroughly scourged, then sent for sale at auction to one of the neighbouring islands, the welts borne on the naked body serving to show the slave's powers of endurance. The master, it seemed, liked to 'cull' his slaves from time to time. No one wished to be culled, for the regime in other slave domains was rumoured to be far harsher than Rum Hole's. As the weeks passed, Lisbeth grew hard of body and subservient in spirit, forgetting her mission, London and the outside world, and conscious only of the food in her belly, the nightly come in her gamahuched or fucked cunt and the daily canestripes on her bare. Linda was right, there *was* something reassuring in the mindless submission of a slave girl.

The day came when Corporal Rodding told her she was broken in and no longer a rude bitch, but promoted to costume slave. Lisbeth could imagine no greater joy. That night Melanie gave her an extra-special gamahuche, licking her all over her nude body for over an hour while masturbating her gushing cooze, so that Lisbeth just came and came. There followed a septuple arse-fucking, as on her first slave night, and this time, Lisbeth's anus responded with lustful glee to the penetrating cocks, milking the slave boys of their sperm, which she held in her rectum and squirted into Melanie's mouth. In the morning she was harnessed and shod as a rickshaw girl – costume of a sort.

Soon her thighs rippled with muscle. She learned to respond to telephoned commands with utmost speed; to idle, seeking a client, near the areas where guests congregated; to bear the whipstrokes to her buttocks and back, as she trotted, knees pumping, to pull her carriage. Melanie showed her how to lessen the agony of nipple and quim clamps by inserting a kind of moss found at the base of canewood trees and lubricating her parts with linseed oil. She listened with a cabbie's ear to the lady guests giggling over the prowess of their sex slaves – how long they could last, fucking in the anus, and how copious was their sperm – realising that, to her nightly paramours, her anus was only the fourth or fifth of the day.

Amongst many, she came to know Mademoiselle Belsenor of Lausanne, Miss Thatchpole from Ascot, Mrs Wemys of Bangor, Frau Schlick of Leverkusen, Miss Doherty of Harrogate; the ladies concurred that anal sex, from a slave boy, was supreme pleasure, surpassed only by an invitation to dine – a sound whipping and vigorous buggery as dessert – with the master himself. Guests commended her, and Melanie sulked, sometimes, as Lisbeth's speed was better than hers. At last, after several weeks of rickshaw-pulling, she could don her frilly maid's costume and await room summonses as a house slave.

Her companions were Melissa, Rose and others who had previously bowed to her imperious commands, and whose bottoms had felt Lisbeth's own cane. Curiously, they seemed to bear her no resentment, as if *that* Lisbeth was a different animal from the sleek, superbly muscled and suntanned slave girl who helped them with zips, straps and pins, swapped knickers and stockings, rubbed her wealed bottom in rueful comparison and joined them in giggling wanks as they caressed each other's welts.

She learned to cook, scrub and mop, her thonged or bare bottom bobbing under the lustful eyes of a guest, and knowing that a spanking at the very least awaited her, for some trumped-up miscreance. She learned to kneel after her bottom was wealed and smarting, to tongue the flowing cooze of her chastiser; to writhe, slippery with come and sweat, gamahuching a mistress, with her own quim licked and chewed as she moaned in feigned, or sometimes real, passion.

One day, she presented herself, meek in her French maid's uniform, at a familiar villa.

'I think the slut's arrived,' drawled Tanya Bonslitt, from her bedroom, 'disgracefully late – that earns her a bum a whipping!'

'Absolutely,' said Jeremy.

'First,' Tanya commanded, 'you may get naked, gel, and polish the floor with those big titty bulbs, well smeared in brown polish. Then you may clean the loo with your quim, while I select a cane to thrash that bare.'

Lisbeth began to strip and, when nude, peeped into the bedroom. She saw Tanya, panting as she crouched, her arse presented to Norbert the slave boy, vigorously buggering her while Jeremy watched, his cock stiff, in his wife's panties.

'Tanya,' she murmured, 'it's me, Lisbeth.'

'The bitch dares to speak,' gasped Tanya, over the sound of Norbert's grunting, as his balls slapped her buttocks. 'She *does* need a lesson. Bonslitt, give her what for – round here where I can watch. I want to see her bum wriggling under your cane as the slave boy spunks in my bumhole.'

Jeremy picked up a whippy little ashplant cane, smiling, as he swished the air. Lisbeth gaped, her titties wobbling in fear.

'But Tanya,' Lisbeth begged, as Jeremy wrenched her hair, forcing her to bend over, 'don't you remember –'

Vip!

'Ooh!'

Jeremy's cane lashed her, full on the bare mid-fesse.

'Tanya, please . . .'

Vip!

'Ahh! It hurts!'

Vip!

'Ouch!'

'Vip!

'Oh, please stop.'

'The rude bitch *is* lippy,' panted Jeremy, cock straining at his girl's panties.

Vip!

'Ooh . . .'

Lisbeth's caned bum quivered, clenching, as the male rained strokes on her naked skin. Tanya watched the punishment, licking her teeth and drooling down her chin and heaving teats as Norbert buggered her. Come gushed from her cunt onto the counterpane.

189

'My,' she gasped, 'blonde, golden, big titties, an arse to die for *and* it speaks proper English. It *is* Lisbeth. I always knew she was a beastly sub.'

Jeremy caned Lisbeth thirty canestrokes, until Lisbeth's squirming bottom was bright crimson with weals. Snarling, he threw aside the cane, lowered his wife's panties and rammed his erect cock between Lisbeth's arse cheeks so hard that she sank to the floor in a crouch. Jeremy palmed his wife's dripping come and oiled his cock before penetrating Lisbeth's anus. Her teats and face squashed to the floor, she pleaded for mercy, but Jeremy ignored her, straddling her body to plunge his cock deep inside her bumhole. He began to fuck fiercely under his buggered wife's eyes.

'Oh,' Lisbeth moaned, 'you're hurting me.'

'You love it, sub,' spat Tanya. 'We all do. Fuck me harder, Norbert. I'm nearly off . . .'

The two buggered girls writhed under their males, Tanya's eyes glittering lustfully while Lisbeth's face was contorted in pain as Jeremy's tool slammed her arse root.

'Please,' she whimpered, as her burning arse cheeks squirmed, '*please* . . .'

'Yes,' panted Tanya, 'fuck me with that lovely cock of yours, Norbert, give me all your creamy hot spunk, right up me . . . Bonslitt, watch me come, as the slave boy fucks me. What a tool! Oh, yes . . . I can feel his spunk coming . . . it's there! Spunk in me, Norbert. Oh, yes! I'm coming! What a man, what a hot load, more than you can shoot, Bonslitt. Oh . . . oh . . . *ahh* . . .!'

'You fucking cow,' Jeremy rasped. 'The shame, having to watch my own wife buggered! *I'll* show you. Wank off, bitch.'

Lisbeth slid a hand down her belly to her pulsing wet cunt and squealed as she tweaked her throbbing clitty, already stiff, and bathed in her gushing come. She masturbated hard as Jeremy continued to bugger her and, as she felt the hot droplets of his sperm wash into her, she gasped, biting the rug with its gaudy pattern of flowers and parrots, and exploding in a fierce, belly-fluttering orgasm. She heard her own voice, mewling: 'Yes, sir, fuck my hole, spunk in me, please, spurt your hot load right up me. Oh! Oh! *Oh,* I'm coming . . . yes!'

Jeremy grunted as his copious spunk filled her rectum, bubbling from her stretched anus to dribble down her thighs. The two males, cocks softening, disengaged from the girls' bumholes with gurgling plops, and streams of sperm and arse grease trickled down Tanya's and Lisbeth's quivering thighs.

'That was good,' declared Tanya, 'and now we'll give the rude bitch what she really wants.'

13

Slave Meat

Vip! Tanya's cane idly flicked Lisbeth in her spread bumcleft, and she groaned, licking away her tears. Tanya laughed, and told her to polish harder. She squatted cross-legged on the sofa, eating a peach, caressing her spread cooze, with the whippy ashplant in her hand. Peach juice drooled down her chin and dripped onto her erect nipples. Her bottom squashed Jeremy's face. He lay across the sofa, his tongue trapped, fully inserted in his wife's anus with the bulge of his erection stretching Tanya's panties. From time to time she wriggled her bottom on his face, making him groan.

Lisbeth's breasts hurt dreadfully, the nipples stinging from the gnarled wooden floor as she rolled her titties over the planks, polishing them to a sheen in which she saw her own pain-wracked face. Her breasts were greasy brown from the dollops of polish applied to them by the sneering slave boy, and her mouth was acrid, having taken his slimy cock inside to lick him to new erection. Her quim stung too from the sponge soaked in disinfectant with which she had cleaned the lavatory and shower cubicle, using her hips and cooze to wipe up the guests' mess. She groaned as the body of Norbert shifted, riding the small of her back. She felt his balls rubbing the top of her arse cleft, and his slimed tool, massively stiff, squashed to her back whenever he leaned forward.

'We've become altogether quite friendly with the master,' Tanya drawled. 'In fact he's having us to tea, later on. That is, he'll have me, while poor Bonslitt has to watch another powerful tool split my bum. I can't get enough of *real* men.'

Jeremy groaned miserably and his wife flicked the tip of his cock with her cane, causing him to whimper.

'Really!' exclaimed Tanya. 'What a noisy pup you are, Bonslitt. You need a lesson.'

She lifted her buttocks and his tongue slid from her anus, with a loud plop, while Norbert leapt from Lisbeth's back.

'No, please,' Jeremy begged, but was helpless as the slave boy turned and pinioned him; Tanya ripped down his panties.

'Enough shame, darling,' Jeremy whimpered, as his wife raised her cane.

Vip! Vip! The cane lashed his bare buttocks.

'Ooh!'

Vip! Vip!

'Ahh! Stop!'

Vip! Vip! Jeremy's bare wriggled as his wife's cane striped him.

'Ooh!' he gurgled. 'This is too shameful. Before a slave girl, Tanya?'

Tanya ordered Lisbeth to rise; she did so and, smiling at her husband, Tanya passed her the cane.

'Give the beastly boy a tanning,' she commanded. 'I take it you haven't forgotten how.'

'It's been a long time, miss,' blurted Lisbeth, and her hand trembled as she held the cane over the male's quivering bare arse.

Vip!

'Ooh!' Jeremy squealed as she lashed him a hard stroke in the underfesse, just below his balls and stiff cock, which bucked between his clenched arse cheeks.

Vip!

'Ouch!'

Vip!

'Oh! Oh! You *bitch*.'

Lisbeth's titties swayed as she caned, and she began to gasp at the rush of come drooling from her cunt. Tanya

193

sprang onto the floor and placed her foot on her husband's neck, pinioning him, while she clutched the slave boy's buttocks and drew his cock towards her in full view of Jeremy's reddened face.

'Mm . . .' she sighed, taking the slave boy's cock in her mouth and licking the peehole.

Vip!

'Oh! Tanya, don't . . . the shame! Don't suck him in front of me.'

'That's the whole point, you whelp,' murmured Tanya, pushing Norbert's bare bum to take the cock right to the back of her throat.

She began to suck the stiff cock, sliding her lips back and forth from glans tip to balls, gurgling with pleasure while her hand flicked at her swollen clitty.

Vip! Vip! Lisbeth's hand slipped to her gushing cooze and she too masturbated, gazing at the flogged bottom squirming below her.

'Cane him until that beastly cock softens,' ordered Tanya, her voice muffled by the ebony tool throbbing in her mouth.

Lisbeth caned hard, with her clitty swollen and tingling under her vigorous wank, as Jeremy's bare turned crimson with heavy welts. He sobbed, moaning and writhing, his buttocks clenching tight at each stroke; yet his eyes remained fixed on his wife's mouth, sucking the slave boy's cock.

'Uhh . . .' he sobbed. 'Such humiliation . . .'

Lisbeth took him to over twenty canestrokes, her belly fluttering as she wanked, rapidly approaching come. Abruptly, Tanya slid her lips from Norbert's cock and ordered him to lay her husband on the floor.

'His horrid erection simply won't go away otherwise,' she said, still masturbating.

Jeremy was pinioned face up on the parrot rug, his tool stiff in the air. Tanya ordered Lisbeth to straddle him and Lisbeth obeyed, squatting over his tool until the glans tickled her anus pucker. Tanya took hold of her polished brown breasts, squeezing fiercely, and tugged the nipples

194

down, forcing Lisbeth's anus onto her husband's tool. Lisbeth squealed as the cock penetrated, then, as Tanya pushed her down, filled her rectum, right to Jeremy's balls. Lisbeth lay back on Jeremy's body as his hips began to twitch, his cock reaming her colon in short stabs. Tanya spread Lisbeth's thighs wide and Norbert straddled her body, his tool poised at her cunt mouth. Lisbeth groaned as he thrust into her slimy pouch, his hard glans slamming her wombneck. Tanya squatted over Lisbeth's face, with Jeremy's beneath it, and pressed her cunt onto Lisbeth's mouth.

'Like being the filling in a sandwich?' she drawled. 'Tongue me, slut, and drink all my juice.'

Norbert, his back arched, began to fuck Lisbeth's cunt, while Jeremy poked her anus from below and her own lips fastened on Tanya's swollen clitty. Lisbeth tongued Tanya's cooze, throat bobbing as she swallowed her copiously spurting come, while her belly and buttocks writhed, fucked in cunt and arse by the two males squeezing her. Jeremy's face was inches below his wife's tongued slit, and her juices dribbled into his mouth.

When Norbert had cunt-fucked Lisbeth for over five minutes, on Tanya's command, he withdrew and knelt on Lisbeth's titties, presenting his cock to Tanya's mouth. She slurped his come-slimed glans, then took his cock to her gullet after ordering him to fill her belly with spunk. Lisbeth moaned as his cock left her gash, and began to masturbate, her anus wriggling on Jeremy's impaling tool and her throat jerking as she swallowed Tanya's come. She slapped her buttocks up and down on Jeremy's balls, milking his cock, hearing his panting grow harsher as his cock trembled, nearing his spurt.

'Yes, yes, yes,' she groaned, 'come on, spunk your load in my bumhole, fill me right up . . . yes . . . oh, yes . . .'

Norbert was grunting, his balls tight, as Tanya's mouth sucked his cock, playing with her tongue at the peehole, then taking the whole shaft rapidly to her throat. Her come filled Lisbeth's gamahuching mouth. Suddenly, Lisbeth gasped, gurgling, as a stream of piss erupted from Tanya's cunt, filling her mouth. She gagged, swallowing the hot piss mixed with come. Tanya gurgled, as the slave boy's cock bucked, splashing his spunk between her eager lips with spurts of cream drooling down her heaving titties, onto Lisbeth's and Jeremy's piss-soaked faces. Jeremy groaned as Lisbeth felt the first spurt of cream at her arse root, and then his cock filled her rectum with hot spunk. She gasped, orgasm flooding her cunt, and her lips chewed Tanya's clitty until Tanya too panted and trembled in orgasm, swallowing the slave boy's sperm.

'Oh, Tanya,' Lisbeth gasped. 'How could you? Pissing on me?'

'Insolent little thing, isn't she?' Tanya drawled, wiping her cunt on Lisbeth's hair. 'There's a doe hunt tomorrow – I'm due a tupping by the master later on, and I'll recommend *her* as the prey.'

Jeremy pushed Lisbeth rudely, to the floor, his turgescent cock plopping from her anus in a shower of sperm and arse grease.

'Let's deliver the bitch well flenched for the hunt,' he hissed. 'I haven't forgotten how she flogged me.'

'Bonslitt, that was ages ago,' Tanya drawled.

'The shame still rankles,' he growled, picking up the cane.

'No,' said Tanya. 'We must deliver her with a smooth bum for the master's pleasure. So much more fun when she's flenched after the hunt.'

'Tanya, you can't mean it,' blurted Lisbeth. 'I appeal to you, as one English girl to another.'

'Be off, slut, before I change my mind and let Bonslitt tan your cheeky arse,' snapped Tanya.

Lisbeth stumbled, sobbing, back to her quarters. That night she slept chastely. Word had spread of her morrow's ordeal at the hunt. Even Melanie contented herself with a wistful kiss to Lisbeth's bottom.

'Be brave,' she whispered, patting the bare cheeks.

Shortly before dawn, Corporal Rodding came to awaken Lisbeth from her fitful sleep and escort her to the beach in front of Lisbeth's own villa. Miss Thatchpole was now in occupation. Together with a crowd of guests, she watched eagerly as Lisbeth bowed before the master, splendid in hunting pink. Lisbeth looked at the serried, smiling faces of ladies brandishing whips. The Bonslitts were there; she recognised Mademoiselle Belsenor, Frau Schlick, Mrs Wemys, Miss Doherty and all those who had whipped her bottom on rickshaw service, now licking their lips at the prospect of Lisbeth's ultimate humiliance: hunted as human prey until her inevitable capture and torture.

Dugger and Femella distributed crossbows to the guests, each with a quiverful of arrows tipped in rubber suction pads, and named for each guest. The master explained that the pads were smeared with a powerful adhesive, and that guests scored favours for hitting the fleeing slave's back, legs or buttocks, with the best prize going to a bull's-eye – a direct hit to the anus. Lisbeth trembled as her wrists were clamped in metal cuffs behind her back.

'Don't think you can hide in Gibbet Town, Lisbeth,' the master said. 'Eldridge Perkins and his people are going to join the chase. I'd wish you good luck were we back in hypocritical England but, since you won't have any, I shan't. You can run, hoping, against all odds, to prove me wrong. Go!'

With a five-minute start, Lisbeth ran, barefoot, across the road and into the scrub. She passed the slaves' quarters, hiding in the bush, then was out into open country, her galloping bare feet stumbling over roots and creepers, past ponds and thickets, scratched by thorns, and squashing insects. Her handcuffs thumped on her pumping buttocks; sweat poured from her, spraying from her bouncing teats and thighs. Behind her she heard a whooping roar as the hunters set off. Her only hope was to hide until darkness, when the hunt would be over; but where? No thicket was dense enough.

Her mind whirled, thinking that, if she could reach the sea, on the far side of the island, she could find a cave, or even a boat, and smash the handcuffs on a rock till she was free. The whoops were growing louder behind her. She crossed the road to Gibbet Town, hoping to skirt the village, until she saw a new crowd, led by Nell Perkins: Candace, Jerome, Elvira O'Malley, faces and bottoms she knew from her whipping scenes at the gibbet, all pounding into the bush on her trail. They hadn't spotted her, so she doubled back and passed the town on the other side. On and on she stumbled, the sun rising in the cloudless azure, her throat parched, her limbs dripping with sweat.

'Oh!' she screamed.

Her left buttock stung, a suction arrow quivering at mid-fesse.

'Ah!'

Another struck her between the shoulders, another on the right haunch. She groaned as arrow after arrow stung her. Her body quivering with the clinging darts, she dived into a coppice and ran, with thorns and briars lacerating her naked flesh. Emerging, she found a savannah and sprinted across it, to no avail: more arrows found their target and, when she gained the next protective scrub, the shafts waggled on her body like a porcupine's quills. Each arrow tip smarted dreadfully, its adhesive sucking at her skin.

Time passed, her bouncing breasts slapping painfully on her ribcage, and her breath searing her throat in short, anguished pants. The horrid whoops of her pursuers never seemed far behind, no matter how hard she ran, stumbling and frequently falling, her face crashing into spiky fronds. At last the hue and cry faded and she smelled the ocean. Slackening her pace, she found a thicket of taller trees, and spied a tree stump where she could rest in the shadows. The pack was going the other way! Blissfully, she sank to her knees, until the matted foliage seemed to give way beneath her and tendrils, sharp as whipcords, wrapped her ankles.

'Ahh!' she screamed as the tendrils sprang up, hoisting her into the air, to dangle helplessly by her ankles, upside down, from an overhanging tree branch.

She hung four feet from the ground, her arms flailing helplessly, unable to grasp. Her ankles were lashed tight, her body quivering with arrows, and her hair streaming to the foliage beneath, where worms and beetles invaded her swaying tresses. Her titties hung upside down, her nipples at her mouth. Lisbeth began to cry, sobbing helplessly as she wriggled upside down, her tears soaking her hair beneath her.

'What's this?' panted a male voice. 'A pretty little hedgehog, stuck with quills, and all mine.'

Lisbeth twisted and looked up to see Jeremy brandishing a scourge of five canewood rods.

'Please, let me go,' she whimpered.

His smile turned to a rictus of hatred.

'No, my dear,' he rasped. 'You've a thrashing due. Tanya might not approve, but I can run faster than that lazy slut. Pity your bum and back are covered, so it'll have to be a front-whipping.'

'No! Please, no!' she screamed.

Jeremy lifted his scourge and lashed her bare breasts. Thwap! The rods striped deep crimson trenches across her teats and nipples.

'Ooh!'

Thwap! He lashed her belly.

'Ahh! No, no!'

Thwap! The rods sliced her between the thighs, lashing her open cunt lips.

'Ahh! Ahh! Oh!' Lisbeth screamed, her flogged bare body flailing and wriggling.

Suddenly she heard a whoosh, and her cries were joined by Jeremy's own.

'What the devil!' he ejaculated, stumbling back, his body trapped in a huge net.

Into the glade sprang a group of females, naked but for turquoise girdles decked with weapons: canes, spears and scourges. Beneath their girdles their bare pubic mounds swelled powerfully, glistening with oil. The split quims revealed huge, extruded pink clitties, like tiny cocks. Their bare, copper-bronze teats jutted massively from powerfully enlarged pectorals; their abdomens were knotted slabs of muscle, and their thighs huge and rippling beneath narrow whipcord waists. They lifted the struggling Jeremy from his net prison, contemptuously ripped off his clothing and roped him naked to a tree with his hands bound and his back and buttocks exposed. The leader of the females slashed Lisbeth's rope, sending her tumbling to the ground, and two others held her wrists, smashing the chain of her handcuffs with rocks, until her arms snapped free. At once, her arms were pinioned behind her back.

'I am Emmeline,' said the leader, 'and you are my meat.'

'You're Lucayans,' Lisbeth blurted.

The girls were bare-headed, their shaven copper-hued skulls gleaming in the dappled sunlight, and the long cylinder of each dolichocephalic head bobbing in excitement as they unstrapped nine-thonged leather quirts from their girdles.

'I say,' Jeremy blurted. 'Let me go, damn it.'

The Lucayan girls lifted their quirts.

'No!' Jeremy squealed, struggling uselessly against his bonds. 'What are you going to do? This is an outrage – the master will – ahh!'

Thwap! A quirt lashed him hard across his bare buttocks. Thwap! Another followed at once, on his back. Jeremy's body thudded against the tree at the force of the lashes, which rained on his bare, from the Lucayans' eager whips. The girls' breasts quivered as they flogged the naked male; their wide purple nipple domes stood erect, and gleaming trickles of come seeped from their dark, massive gash flaps.

'Ahh!' he screamed. 'The pain! I can't take it.'

'You sprung my trap, and misprised my slave meat,' said Emmeline, 'and shall be punished for it.'

Lisbeth watched, her tongue hanging out, as Jeremy's naked body squirmed under a myriad whipstrokes, the skin of his wriggling bare buttocks and back laced in a patchwork of crimson stripes.

'Ahh!' he shrieked, as lashes thudded on his bare, 'Please, no. Ooh! Ahh! I can't take any more.'

'But I think you can, Bonslitt,' said Tanya, stepping from behind a tree.

She wore a high-cut turquoise swimsuit, white fluffy

ankle socks and tennis shoes; her body sweated, titties heaving, from the hunt.

'Lazy slut, eh?' she trilled.

'Are you his female?' growled Emmeline.

'Yes, I certainly am,' said Tanya, 'and the worm has a thrashing well due. Carry on, girls. My, you are handsome beauties – such muscles, good to flog a wretched male.'

'That is our calling, miss,' said Emmeline.

Thwap! Thwap!

'Ahh!' Jeremy gurgled.

Under the lash, his cock rose, fully erect. Tanya licked her lips and pushed her fingers under the seam of her turquoise swimsuit.

'You don't mind if I do myself, ladies?' she purred. 'I love to watch a male's bare arse squirm, especially when it belongs to me.'

Masturbating, her exposed cunt drooling come over her thighs and her teeth bared in a rictus of pleasure, Tanya watched her husband's naked body wriggle as his buttocks and back reddened under the strokes of the nude Lucayan girls. His cock still stood rock-hard. After forty lashes, Emmeline ordered the beating stopped and presented Jeremy's own scourge to Tanya. Emmeline led the way out of the thicket, as Lisbeth was frogmarched behind her swaying bare bottom.

'Mistress, an't we going to take these trash?' said one of the girls.

'Watch your mouth, Lulu, or you'll get a whipping on that cheeky rump,' snapped Emmeline. 'Those folks are guests – this one is my slave meat.'

Behind them, in the whipping thicket, Jeremy's cries redoubled at the vigorous thwap-thwap of the scourge on his skin.

'Take that, you fucking animal!' shrilled Tanya.

Above his cries, the noises of the hunters grew louder until there was a burst of shrill female whoops, and Jeremy's shriek: 'No, no, please, no! Not the horned dildo . . . ahh!' Lisbeth stumbled with her captors into another thicket, where the Lucayans swept aside a carpet of brush to reveal a gaping hole in the earth. A passage led down, its wooden floor sloping sharply, and, after the party had entered, the girls replaced the brushwood covering. The Lucayans lit candles and in the flickering smoky light they descended, the air growing hotter until they were bathed in sweat. The passage levelled out and they marched for several minutes, past intersections where further channels branched off to left or right, until the floor sloped upwards again.

Lisbeth saw the glimmer of daylight; this entrance was not concealed, although it was guarded by two Lucayan girls, armed with uncoiled whips. They emerged in the central square of a village of long, low wooden huts. In the centre of the square stood pillories, stocks and whipping frames. One of the pillories was occupied by a naked blonde girl, her deep bronze bottom pink with spank marks and her face streaked with tears under her matted tresses. The sun was high and scorching, and the several Lucayan girls populating the square stood in shadow, all of them nude but for turquoise girdles or sashes, vivid on their lustrous coppery skin, and all armed with canes. Their shaven, long-skulled heads gleamed darkly bare in the harsh sun. They looked at Lisbeth, festooned as she was with suction arrows, with mild curiosity before returning to their tasks of supervising young, naked males, who crouched, scrubbing clothes, polishing canes and whips, or preparing food. The servant males stared at Lisbeth's naked body, licking their lips, and exchanging eager glances.

Lisbeth was taken into a bath house where, amid clouds of steam, she saw Lucayan girls sitting or lying on slabs, sponged and massaged by nude slave boys, several of whom had blatant erections, as they kneaded the bare flesh of their mistresses, or licked them up and down their bodies, including their titties, bumholes, and quims, as if in an everyday massage. The Lucayans gossiped naturally, seeming unconcerned by their servants' erections, nor excited by the intimate licking between their thighs, save to reward an assiduous masseur with a tickle to his balls or bottom. Lisbeth sank gratefully into a huge steaming tub, fragrant with oils and vapours. Emmeline explained that the herbal bath would loosen the glue of her arrows, as well as restore her strength. Her arrival excited momentary interest, before the massaged girls returned to their gossip.

'What are you going to do with me?' she blurted as one of the naked slave boys – this one with a particularly juicy erection – solemnly massaged her belly and titties under the water.

'You are slave meat,' replied Emmeline.

'So I have exchanged one slavery for another,' Lisbeth said. 'I suppose I shall be whipped.'

'No,' said Emmeline. 'We don't wish to mar that lovely skin – unless you are a real warmint – but to heal you, and fatten you up. You will have pleasant work – unless you are a sapphic tribade, like so many of the master's guests.'

Lisbeth gazed around her at the shining ebony cocks swaying like poles, the trim, muscled bare bums, etched with vivid canemarks, and felt a seep of come in her gash.

'No,' she said, 'no, I don't think I'm a lesbian.'

One by one, the arrows floated from her skin, and she fell into a doze. When she awoke, Emmeline and her posse themselves were nude, shorn of girdles and weapons, and taking steam and massage. Emmeline sat, cross legged, with the erect tool of a slave boy clamped between her lips, his cock penetrating her throat to his balls, which her lips brushed as she powerfully sucked the cockshaft. The slave boy kneeling before her trembled, gasping, and Emmeline slid her lips to his glans, where her tongue played on his quivering peehole. He spurted a powerful jet of sperm, which she caught with her tongue, and promptly enclosed the glans fully with her mouth, to suck and swallow every drop of his spunk. His spend was evidently copious, for Emmeline's throat bobbed for a long time before her mouth released the softening cock. She licked the last drops of ejaculate from his glans, then rubbed her lips and gave a satisfied grunt.

'That was good nourishment, boy,' she drawled. 'How many today?'

'My fourth, mistress,' panted the slave boy.

'Keep it up, and we may promote you to full slave,' she said.

Observing Lisbeth awake, she detached herself from the bathers and approached her, ordering her to rise and follow. They left the bath hut, emerging into the harsh heat of the day, which steamed the water from their bodies in seconds.

'I am your mistress, girl,' Emmeline said, licking sperm from her lips. 'Your name?'

'Lisbeth, mistress.'

'You may not speak, slave Lisbeth, except to me, or to another officer when addressed, and never, ever, to another slave. Slave talk earns a whipping, and we do not like whipping girl slaves. Minor miscreance puts you in the stocks or pillory, after a hand-spanking on the bare buttocks.'

They entered a small hut numbered thirty-four, and Emmeline told Lisbeth she was to sleep there. It contained a wooden bunk bed, table, chair and water jug, but no armoire as, Emmeline explained, slaves remained nude at all times.

'I'll give you your first day's massage here to get you used to it,' she said. 'Slave girls must take at least one massage a day as part of their duties.'

'Please, mistress,' Lisbeth said, 'what are my duties?'

Emmeline smiled. 'You'll learn by practice,' she said. 'I believe I have already set an example. Lie face down on the bed.'

Beneath the washstand stood a large tub of brown, pungently aromatic grease. Emmeline scooped a palmful and began to rub it into Lisbeth's buttocks and thighs. Lisbeth tensed.

'Stingy?' said the Lucayan.

'Yes, mistress,' Lisbeth gasped, for the unguent stung like fire.

'You'll get used to it,' said Emmeline, kneading Lisbeth's shoulders and back. 'It's called slave's butter. Fattens you up, tones your skin. Has to be applied everywhere.'

She rubbed the butter all over Lisbeth's legs, between the toes and on her soles; her fingers delved into Lisbeth's arse cleft, then rubbed her anus and cunt lips. Lisbeth's cunt basin quivered, writhing softly as her clitty began to swell at the gentle pressure of the dark girl's fingers. She gasped as tongues of fire streaked through her quim. Yet already her buttocks, massaged first, glowed with a friendly warmth, the stinging having ebbed. Emmeline ordered her to turn over. She rubbed the dark butter into Lisbeth's breasts, under her arms and on her belly and thighs before again approaching her cunt lips, now swollen and trickling with a seep of come. Lisbeth's clitty was visible, stiff and extruded from the gash folds, and she gave a little yelp when Emmeline touched it.

'Oh!' she cried. 'It does sting, mistress. But it's awfully nice afterwards.'

Emmeline licked her lips and removed her girdle. She stood completely nude over Lisbeth, and Lisbeth's eyes widened, seeing close up the developed musculature of her mistress's body. The veins were clearly defined in a delicate purple tracery on the luminous, copper-bronze skin across her rippling thighs, buttocks and the powerful slabs of her titties, seeming to mirror the graceful elongation of her burnished skull. Between her massive cunt folds, her clitty was a swollen pink thumb.

'You seem intelligent, for slave meat,' Emmeline murmured, her fingers slapping grease in Lisbeth's cunt and furrow, 'and I haven't seen such a tasty body in ages. Those teats and those firm buttocks, and such a big juicy clit . . . you tempt me, slave.'

She slid onto the bed and flipped Lisbeth over across her thighs. Without a word, she spanked Lisbeth's bare – a hard, rapid spanking that made Lisbeth's bottom squirm, her writhing cunt lips and clitty leaving a slime of come on Emmeline's thigh.

'Uh . . . uh . . .' Lisbeth gasped as pain suffused her naked bum globes, but she bit her lip and did not cry out, even as the spanking went to over fifty slaps.

Panting, Emmeline laid her back on the bed and resumed massaging her cunt with butter.

'You take it like a good slave,' she murmured.

Her own gash glistened with flowing come. Lisbeth's whole body was smeared with the dark butter, its warmth – after the initial stinging shock – radiating all over her skin. Emmeline's fingers dallied at her moist gash, no longer rubbing butter, but masturbating Lisbeth's clitty with slow, firm tweaks. Her massive breasts heaved as she breathed low and hoarsely.

'Mm . . .' Lisbeth moaned, her cunt basin squirming as come began to trickle from her slit.

Emmeline penetrated her pouch with three fingers, slamming her nails against Lisbeth's wombneck, and Lisbeth gasped, beginning to pant harshly.

'Oh . . . yes . . .' she gasped.

With her thumb kneading Lisbeth's throbbing clitty, the dark girl fingerfucked her cunt, sliding the come-slimed fingers rapidly in and out of the slit which flowed with come. Suddenly, she sprang onto Lisbeth, straddling her, her shaven cunt mound gleaming inches from Lisbeth's face, her head between Lisbeth's thighs.

'Eat me, slave,' she commanded.

She pressed her cunt down, the full weight of her hips on Lisbeth's mouth, and plunged her own lips and nose into the slimy folds of her heavily juicing gash. Lisbeth began to tongue the girl's stiff nubbin, letting the gush of copious come slide down her throat, and swallowing. Emmeline moaned, as Lisbeth chewed her bulbous nubbin, and responded with a vigorous tonguing of Lisbeth's slit, her teeth brushing the clitty and making Lisbeth writhe under her mistress's weight. She clasped Lisbeth's buttocks, clawing fiercely as Lisbeth's fingers pressed Emmeline's hard arse globes towards her face, abandoning herself to the crush of the Lucayan's quivering loins. Come spurted from Lisbeth's cunt and trickled down her thighs and bum cleft,

'Urrgh . . .' Emmeline growled.

She lifted Lisbeth's thighs hard up and began to stab her anus with her tongue, a monstrous appendage – much longer than any normal girl's, and stiff as a cock. The tongue penetrated Lisbeth's rectum, slithering right to her colon, and Lisbeth moaned, her cunt gushing come over Emmeline's face, as she drank her mistress's torrent of cunt juice. Emmeline's tongue, slicked with Lisbeth's arse grease, shifted to her slit, and began a fierce fucking of her writhing pouch, the tongue tip licking her wombneck at each stabbing thrust. Emmeline panted harshly, her voice rising to yelps as her belly squirmed in on Lisbeth's, and Lisbeth's own cunt pulsed, fluttering into a spasm.

'Ah ... ah ... oh! *Ohh*!' Lisbeth moaned, as she came.

Mistress and slave orgasmed together, their slippery bodies writhing in fierce gamahuche, Lisbeth's throat gurgling with her mistress's come. They continued to kiss each other's cunt for several minutes after their climaxes, until Emmeline rose, licking her lips.

'Such a beautiful gash,' she murmured, 'all pink and bright against that golden skin. But you won't be golden much longer, slave. You'll be like us.'

14

The Punishment Shack

'Bare up for a spanking, slave Lisbeth.'

'Gladly, mistress. It seems silly – I'm already bare.'

'After five weeks as my slave, you should recognise a figure of speech.'

Lisbeth positioned herself on Emmeline's silky bare thighs, licking her lips in anticipation of the spanking to come. Smack! Smack! Emmeline's palm descended hard on Lisbeth's naked bottom, sending the familiar shock of pain through her arse and cunt basin. Smack! Smack!

'Oh . . . yes,' Lisbeth groaned, her bum squirming, her shaven cooze rubbing on the spanker's thigh. 'You are very kind to spank me, mistress. I need it so badly . . .'

'I know you do. Of all the master's slaves addicted to bottom pain, you are quite the worst. Your daily spanking is not for pleasure, but to get you hot and improve your performance at duty.'

Smack! Smack!

'Ooh! It hurts! Thank you, mistress.'

Lisbeth's bare nates wriggled as they reddened under the spanks. The mistress's crimson palm prints overlaid Lisbeth's skin, now burnished to a reddish copper-bronze. Smack! Smack!

'Ooh!'

Emmeline's bare breasts bounced as she spanked. Lisbeth squirmed in a growing puddle of her own come, spurting onto her spanker's thigh, as the reddening of her bottom made it wriggle faster. The spanks mounted to fifty, then sixty.

'I'm not sure you aren't manipulating me,' panted Emmeline. 'Even without spanks, you're the most lustful duty slave we have. Your sperm count is more than impressive.'

Smack! Smack!

'Ouch! I grew used to sucking the master's organ and drinking his sperm, mistress. Perhaps I crave it.'

Smack! Smack!

'Ooh! Gosh, it smarts, mistress. You really know how to hurt a girl.'

Emmeline released Lisbeth, who promptly crouched at her feet, tongue hanging out.

'Does my mistress wish me to tongue her?' said Lisbeth coyly.

'Later, you hot minx,' said Emmeline. 'You are intimate with no one else, I hope. I don't mean slaves, who don't count, although serious tribadism would mean a flogging – or worse – in the punishment shack. If you were enthralled by another guard – I know you wrestle every day with Lulu – well, it . . . it would go amiss for you.'

'Does my mistress think I could be intimate with someone who hurts me so much?' murmured Lisbeth innocently.

'Of that, I'm not sure. Best hurry to work. See if you can overdo your quota.'

'I always overdo, mistress,' said Lisbeth, rubbing her spanked nates and licking her lips.

A few minutes later she sat on her throne in the sperming house. The throne's arms were extra wide and padded, to act as knee rests for the slave boys and guest workers queuing to kneel and present their cocks to Lisbeth's lips. Their hands were roped behind their backs, and their ankles cuffed to the arms of the throne to prevent mischief, or excess passion. Their dark bodies gleamed, completely shaven. Before males were permitted to give sperm, they must submit to a careful shaving of their cock and balls by the slave girls, a task which Lisbeth relished, as the pressure of her razor invariably made the cocks rise to throbbing stiffness.

'Come on, you big girl, spunk like a man,' she would whisper, as her lips touched cock; it seemed to excite them.

Clasping the boy's bare buttocks, she would press his cock into her mouth and suck powerfully, until she tasted his first spurt of cream, at which point she withdrew her lips and masturbated his glans with her fingertips until she had collected a brimming palmful of spunk. This went into a surgical jar on a rack beside her throne. The jars would be collected periodically by the white-sashed sperm mistress. Lisbeth was permitted to take the subject's spunk into her mouth if she ejected it promptly into the correct receptacle. Sperm slaves were encouraged to masturbate, as they worked, to maintain their lustful ardour, and Lisbeth took full advantage, casually exposing her wanked cunt to her sister slaves masturbating beside her in a row.

Lisbeth knew them by sight, to nod to, despite the ban on speech; or she knew their bodies from naked combat in the muddy wrestling arena. Some, she was sure, were English, and she longed for conversation. Her time as a Lucayan slave had passed dreamily, tinged with melancholy, as she had no one but the guards to talk to. They were spirited, if haughty, and eager to indulge her, so she did not mind the lonely nights in her hut, masturbating herself quickly to sleep, exhausted by her sperming duties, the hard daily regime of exercise in the gymnasium and her wrestling tuition by the hard-bodied Lulu.

Lisbeth's body rippled with sleek muscle; she could do three hundred press-ups, and swim – under boat escort – the three miles to Flogger's Cay, the adjoining islet. After daily baths of slave's butter, her skin shone a copper bronze colour, approaching the richness of the Lucayans' own, a skin which seemed to change hue magically, like a kaleidoscope, with every flickering shaft of sunlight. Her hair was bleached a glorious blonde, as shiny as starlight, her titties and thighs grown bigger and firmer, rippling with muscle. Between her gash folds her clitty peeped, swollen like a new marrow, and newly sensitive, with just a few tweaks sufficing to bring her off in her numerous

210

daily frigs. Lisbeth could no longer remember what she had looked like as a pale London girl.

As her body blossomed into a burnished copper flower, so grew her need for orgasm. She masturbated on waking, then in almost every free moment; all slave girls did, and sometimes, in the washroom, they would furtively masturbate together, never speaking, but flushed with excitement, as their comes gushed over each other's fingers. Frigging off was not exactly an offence for the punishment shack, but still, the threat of it made their joys the more urgent. She made crude wooden dildos, their gnarled surfaces hurting her rectum as she masturbated alone, anticipating her tribadic embraces with Emmeline and, lately, the guard Lulu, who consented to bumfuck Lisbeth with a home-made wooden strap-on, although she refused to whip her, fearing that jealous Emmeline would see the marks. Lulu's clitty was even bigger than Emmeline's, and Lisbeth loved to suck it as though it were a lollipop.

The slave boy whose cock she tongued began to groan. Deftly, Lisbeth slid her mouth back, keeping her tongue on his peehole, until she felt his cock buck. She gasped his glans between finger and thumb, milking him by stroking his frenulum and corona, and collecting his heavy spurt of cream in her palm, held several inches away. When he was done, she slid from her throne, indicating to the guards that, for variety's sake, she would take the remaining queue of a dozen males at the crouch, as was permitted. The sperm mistress wheeled a mobile rack of sperm jars and, thighs wide and gash gaping wet and pink, Lisbeth squatted before the first erect cock, pleased to see that the whole line of slave boys were already stiff.

She licked his balls and, with her fingers in her cooze, began to wank herself off, as her mouth engulfed the huge stiff tool. Her fingers, bathed in her gushing come, tweaked the new bulk of her swollen clitty. As she tongued the slave's cock, he advanced his hobbled foot and began to poke her dripping pink cooze flesh with his toe. Lisbeth directed the toe to her clitty and, as he rubbed her throbbing nubbin, she slid a gun of three fingers into her pouch and gave herself a hard fingerfuck. The slave boys watched her masturbate, eyes wide, stiff cocks trembling.

'Mm . . .' she sighed contentedly, peeking at the rank of bodies awaiting her pleasure, her cunt spurting come, as she wanked and sucked; she *was* becoming one of the red folk.

That was what the Lucayans of Rum Hole called themselves: the red folk – a tribe of young, female warriors, survivors of an ancient empire, older than history; their numbers replenished by kidnapping from other islands or continents, whenever their spies – females past twenty-five years of age, who were expelled to breed, in the wider world – recognised one of their own, a genetic throwback, with copper skin, long skull and nose and slender face.

The ancient Mayans, Toltecs and Egyptians divided humanity into three peoples: the red, white and black skins, of which they, the redskins, were superior – colonies of Atlantis, whose empire spread across North Africa, Cro-Magnon Europe, the Atlantic islands, the Americas and the Caribbean. The Asians came to the Americas, then the Europeans, with their guns and horses, decimating the red folk and reducing them to survivors in scattered pockets, like the Basques, Maya or Touareg. After millennia, the redskin gene had learned to hide: it was transmitted, and physically apparent, only in the female, and a redskin who bred would not produce another redskin until the second or third generation.

The Rum Hole redskins traded slaves, fished and raided. Male slaves did menial work and gave them the sperm they needed. The red folk lived on sperm, drinking it daily, mixing with their salves, unguents and foodstuffs. They taught that such a diet, and the constant nourishment of slave's butter, would bring out the latent redskin gene in any female. For ancient Atlantis was a female empire, controlled by an aristocracy of girl warriors, mating with innumerable husbands or male slave concubines, ruled by the whip, rack, pillory and the hardest tortures females could impose. Daily, Lisbeth inspected her naked body, burnished to a glowing copper hue, and felt her skull, sure it had grown in length, like the tingling bulb of her clitty.

The males of the village were permanent slaves, drudges or guest workers. The latter were islanders, who gave their sperm in return for a slave girl's tonguing. Drudges, too, must give sperm at least twice daily, and heavy creamers won promotion to full slaves, pampered with aphrodisiac pleasures to ensure their continuing fecundity. Those slaves were on fixed occasions permitted to have penetrative sex with the warrior girls. Slave girls, whether discards of the master or individually ensnared, were not permitted fucking in order to keep them lustful for their daily duty of multiple fellatio.

Lulu explained that there was a world market for pleasure slaves, who fetched enormous prices: not bedraggled victims of loathsome slaving gangs, but females honed to physical perfection, and utter submission, who *relished* the traditional female role of pleasure slave. The master taught that a perfect slave is she who desires to be a slave: it was his accord with the red folk.

'Lisbeth,' Lulu said, 'aren't you happy in slavery, obedience, and humiliance? The pleasure you get from the pleasure you give? Would you not crave slavery, if deprived of it?'

'I hadn't really thought of it,' Lisbeth replied, blushing. 'It seems so natural for girls to be slaves – I can hardly imagine when I wasn't.'

As Lisbeth's wrestling teacher, Lulu subjected her to punishing exercises, yoga contortions and practice bouts, in which Lisbeth suffered the full array of holds, jabs, twists and gouges – for the red folk practised all-in wrestling – which led to Lisbeth's rapid prowess in the slave girls' wrestling league. Her cunt juiced at the strain of wrenched muscles, the crushing of nude female bodies and the stench of slippery girlsweat, slopped with the mud they writhed in. She wanted to punish these drooling, snarling slave girls for daring to arouse her lust.

She graduated to wrestling males, naked slave boys, proud of their muscles and huge cocks, although the rules forbade any attack on cock or balls – unless the male was aroused and his tool erect. Lisbeth easily stiffened her opponents, showing pink wet slit meat while licking her lips. Once they were stiff, it was easy to use their cocks as levers, to slam the groaning males into the mud floor, with her thigh crammed a hair's breadth from their balls; the threat of what Lisbeth's knee *could* do, in defiance of rules, gained easy whimpered submissions.

In training, Lulu slyly observed that as Lisbeth writhed in choke holds or under her teacher's pummelling, and kicks to teats, belly and groin, her cunt nevertheless spewed come into the mud. The two naked girls rolled in the ooze, their slippery bodies locked in brutal caress, and Lulu too was wet of gash, as Lisbeth's big bare breasts slapped her face, or her thigh ground Lulu's quim lips.

'Yes,' gasped Lulu, 'kick my cooze, do it hard, make me scream, wench. You must want to win, to dominate, to crush!'

In a short time they became lovers, gamahuching clandestinely in bushes, or secluded coves, far from the jealous Emmeline.

'It's only because of you that I've regained my will to dominate,' Lisbeth confessed, embracing Lulu's naked body on a sunny beach. 'I have this dreadful yearning to be crushed, to be a slave for ever.'

'And you shall be,' hissed Lulu, her tongue flicking Lisbeth's throbbing clitoris. 'That is the beauty of combat. For a moment, you are a queen, yet, after the bout, you are back in chains, with a bitter-sweet memory of your aggressive glory.'

'What you *do* to me,' Lisbeth gasped, her cunt drooling come over her gamahucher's face. 'I was a ... an aggressive lesbian – the master's cock cured me of it – but I still relish ... you know, a girl's caress. I so love submission, and want to be in *your* chains, Lulu.'

'That can't be,' retorted the redskin girl. 'You're being fattened up for the slave auction, remember?'

'Oh ... yes. I was trying not to think of that. What will I do, away from Rum Hole?'

'You could go anywhere – probably Europe, or America. Once you're a hardbody, you're fit for sale – unless you earn your red skin.'

'I must have earned that – I'm so high in the league, wrestling girls, and males.'

'There is more, to prove yourself a true *dominant* mistress.'

Lulu reached for her whip, coiled on her neatly folded girdle. She handed it to Lisbeth.

'There are slaves who merit not only stocks or pillory, but severe bare-bottom thrashing,' she said. 'You remember Jerome, squirming under your lash at the gibbet?'

Lisbeth stroked the whip's shiny leather. 'You mean I must learn to whip again . . .' she murmured.

'Yes. And you may start with me,' Lulu said, rolling over, parting her thighs, and thrusting her naked buttocks high.

Her voice became breathy, wheedling and coy. 'I've been a very naughty girl – not least for stealing Emmeline's slave meat. I deserve a bare thrashing. All girls do.'

'Meat? Is that all I am to you?' Lisbeth spat.

She raised the four-foot whip over Lulu's bare bottom. Vap! The tongue lashed her on mid-fesse, its metal-weighted tip curling around her quivering haunches, to leave a deep welt.

'Ooh . . .' gasped Lulu.

Vap!

'Ahh!'

Vap!

'Oh! You flog hard, Lisbeth.'

Lulu's copper-bronze buttocks clenched and began to squirm as the heavy whip lashed her naked skin, squashing her breasts into the sand. Vap!

'Ahh! How many must I take?'

'It depends how naughty you've been,' Lisbeth panted, with a fierce smile.

Vap!

'Ooh . . .' Lulu wailed, the force of the whipping driving her belly to the ground. Her nude body squirmed and writhed in the snow-white sand like a giant red worm.

'Buttocks up, and hold them, bitch,' Lisbeth commanded.

Whimpering, the whipped girl obeyed, raising her sand-crusted arse high, the trembling of her buttocks spewing eddies of powder. Vap!

'Oh! Ahh!'

Lisbeth's thighs rippled and her titties quivered, bouncing as she cracked the flashing leather to Lulu's wriggling bare fesses. Vap!

'Oh! It smarts so!'

'It will, until you confess how naughty you've really been.'

'I can't . . . you wouldn't want to hear it.'

'Try me, bitch.'

Vap! Vap!

Lulu's body lifted from the ground as the whip lashed her thrice in the bum cleft, licking the inner buttock cheeks, anus and cunt.

'Ahh!' she screamed, her wealed fesses clenching madly.

Vap! Vap! A stroke to each welted haunch made her buttocks squirm.

'Ooh . . . ahh . . .' Lulu sobbed. 'It hurts.'

Lisbeth lifted the whip high over Lulu's naked back. Vap! The tongue snaked between her shoulder blades, leaving a long red weal.

'Ah! No, not my back,' Lulu pleaded.

Vap! The whip curled across her back to lash her breasts.

'Ooh!'

Vap!

'Ahh! Please, no, Lisbeth, don't scar my back!'

'Then own up,' hissed Lisbeth.

Vap! The tongue thrashed Lulu's armpit.

'Ah! Ahh! All right . . . the master paid me to seduce you. He gave me sperm from his own slave boys. But, truly, Lisbeth, you're so beautiful, I'd have seduced you anyway. There, I've admitted, please stop my whipping.'

Panting, Lisbeth laid down her whip and knelt to cover Lulu's buttocks with kisses.

'Oh, Lulu, I'm sorry,' she gasped. 'But why?'

'He has plans for you,' Lulu sobbed. 'I don't fully

understand, but . . . but he doesn't want you to forget your sapphic nature.'

'You . . . a lesbian?' Lisbeth gasped.

'Aren't all girls, sometimes?'

'Aren't all girls *what*?' rasped the voice of Emmeline.

Both Lisbeth and Lulu gaped, Lisbeth's hand flying to her mouth, and Lulu groping for her girdle. Emmeline kicked it from her hand. She bent down and ran her finger along the whip weals on Lulu's back, then savagely clawed the bright crimson welts on her bare bum.

'Ooh!' Lulu shrieked.

'I know what you are, vile lesbian,' Emmeline hissed. 'Poor defenceless Lisbeth, a mere slave, putty in the hands of vicious predators.'

She grasped the whip.

'Did she hurt you, Lisbeth, my sweet? She made you slake her filthy thirst?'

'Please, mistress, I was obliged to whip Miss Lulu, at her command,' blurted Lisbeth.

'I'll show her a *real* whipping.'

Vap!

'Uhh . . .'

Vap!

'Ooh.'

Vap!

'Oh! Oh!'

'You insolent cow,' Emmeline hissed.

Lulu received the most savage flogging Lisbeth had ever seen. She did not resist, but lay squashed to the sand, whimpering and writhing with little jerks and squirms of her lashed nude body as Emmeline's whip covered every inch of her thighs, buttocks and back. Watching the girl's bare body wriggling under whipstrokes, Lisbeth began to stroke her quim, oozing come. She touched her clitty, already throbbing and swollen, and gasped aloud as electric pleasure jolted her cunt and belly. The sun beat down and sweat poured from the three girls' rippling naked bodies, as Emmeline whipped her revenge on her rival's bare.

Lisbeth masturbated openly, come sluicing from her cunt over her wrist as her fingers stabbed her wombneck and her thumb mashed her throbbing clitty. Her come trickled down her thighs into the sand. Emmeline's massive gash flaps were also wet with come, spraying shiny droplets with each twirl of her hips. Lulu wriggled, sobbing helplessly, her bare bum jerking at each whipstroke to the wealed arse melons. Emmeline's powerful strokes lifted Lulu's bottom clean off the sand, showing a damp patch beneath her quim – the flogged girl's cunt drooled come under the lash. Gazing at the striped bare croup, Lisbeth frigged herself off to a gasping, belly-churning climax, her juices spraying over her fingers. When the girl's body was a mass of stark whip weals, Emmeline, panting, lowered her weapon. Lisbeth knelt and licked Emmeline's feet.

'You are so powerful, mistress,' she panted.

'Get up, slut,' Emmeline barked. 'You think I didn't hear? How you want to be crushed, and a slave? A fine trick for wrestling – you submit to every bone-crunching lock or hold, relishing your pain and, when your opponent is off guard, thinking you can't take any more, you spring up and make your move. I should have guessed Lulu would enthral you. Submissives! How I hate them.'

'Are you going to beat me, mistress?' Lisbeth whimpered.

Emmeline fingered her whip, scanning Lisbeth's breasts, quivering against her thighs.

'No. You'd like that, wouldn't you? I've a worse punishment. I'm taking you off the sperming detail. In future you will rank as whipping slave. Here, take your girlfriend's whip.'

'I, a whipper?' Lisbeth gasped. 'I don't think – ouch!'

Emmeline pulled her up with a wrench of her hair.

'You aren't meant to think,' sneered the mistress, 'only to whip bare bottoms. You'll be given the hardest miscreants to crack until you hate submissives as much as I do.'

Emmeline picked up Lulu's whip and draped it around Lisbeth's neck with the tip and handle flicking her nipples. Then she delivered a savage kick to Lulu's arse cleft. Lulu

218

shrieked and her head sank to the sand, muffling her gulping sobs.

'*She* won't be needing it, for I'm reducing her to slave.'

'Mistress, I'm awfully confused,' Lisbeth blurted, stroking the hot leather tongue. 'I hated having to whip Lulu. Now you want me to discipline other slaves. It awakens my past nature and I'm scared. Oh, mistress, won't you crush me with your bottom? Let me tongue you to a spurt and swallow your come and we can be friends again.'

She placed her fingers on Emmeline's cunt lips and Emmeline slapped her breasts, hard.

'Whipping slaves must be chaste,' she snarled. 'You can wank yourself off, like any slave, but no more. Celibacy gives vengeful fire to your lash.'

Being a whipping slave was even worse than being a rude bitch. Although Lisbeth had the right to address the guards, few wished to speak to her. To the slaves she was a hated tyrant. Her ration of sperm now came in gallipots from the sperm mistress and, deprived of cocks to suck, she abandoned herself to incessant masturbation, frigging at every available moment, especially before slave girls, whose nude bodies she was forbidden to touch. Daily she used her whip on the bares of prime miscreants, the discipline given in the secluded punishment shack.

These were low, naughty slaves, who would not aspire to kinship with the red folk. Reserved for the dirtiest work, their only hope of betterment lay in being sold at auction to an understanding slavemaster from another island or, often, to a discerning European voluptuary who precisely desired a wilful, sluttish girl as a flogging slave, no stranger to baring up for the cane, and her nymphomaniac or sapphic lusts guaranteed to earn her frequent chastisement. All recidivists, the girls constantly reappeared although, after each punishment session, their faces contorted in tears and agony, they swore never to offend again. Lisbeth grew hardened to their screams of pain and protest and avowals of reform, knowing she would be flogging the same bare buttocks, breasts or gashes a few days later.

219

Girls were whipped in classic pose, strung by the wrists and hair with their toes dangling an inch from the floor; flogged on the rack with nipple and cunt pincers attached; caned on the bare while lashed to the impaling stool that Lisbeth remembered with shudders. Those girls writhed and squirmed, gagged and bound, with a huge horned dildo impaling their cunts or bumholes, while the cane sliced their buttocks. Her coppery nude body glistening with slave's butter, Lisbeth fastened her victims in zippers of clothes pegs, then filled their slits with spiky choke pears, ripping the pegs from the raw flesh after a sound scourging on teats, belly and quim.

The bound girls wriggled in agony as molten candle wax was dripped into their welts and bruises. Lisbeth tortured her victims in the nude, not disdaining to masturbate openly at their pain, and slapping palmfuls of her own come to their faces for them to swallow, gurgling and writhing, as hot wax filled their squirming gashes. She often had to chastise an English girl whom she had vanquished at wrestling. She was blonde and frightened, tight conical breasts quivering in apprehension, anus writhing around a painful choke pear, and her buttocks squirming, even before the application of the cane.

'How cruel, to lace such soft, ripe fesses,' Lisbeth murmured before the girl's fifth or sixth chastisement, stroking the quivering skin as the girl writhed on the impaling arse-prongs; then, lifting her cane to lash the girl a stinger on the fleshy buttocks, making her shriek.

The girl's wrists were strung above her, exposing her back and buttocks as a sheer wall of skin. Lisbeth frigged off as she caned the croup, watching the quivering arse jellies redden into a blotch of welts, and panting as her come flowed.

'Truly, this hurts me more than it hurts you,' she blurted. *The poor girl! She's my image. I wish it were me being flogged. Frigging's not enough; I should squirm under a lacing. Even a choke pear in the bum ...*

'Oh, miss, that's what they said at school,' whimpered the whipped blonde, 'when I had to lift skirt and lower

220

panties for a dozen stingers on my bare bum. That Dorcas Gunn was such a brute, and I thought there could be nothing worse. Now *this* . . .'

'Worse than *Dorcas*, you beastly slave?' snarled Lisbeth. Vap!

'Ohh! Worse even than her penance board. This is fabulous submission. I never dreamed of such joy.'

'Why, you cheeky –'

Vap! Vap!

'Ahh!' screamed the blonde, as the whip lashed her cleft, slimed with come from her spurting cunt. 'Yes . . .'

'You lucky bitch. It's been so *dreadfully* long since my bum was laced,' Lisbeth panted.

'Really, Lisbeth?' purred a silky male voce.

Lisbeth spun round.

'Master!' she blurted.

The master stood, whip in hand, in his silken robe, with Emmeline behind him. His groin bulged with the proud half-swell of his risen tool. Lisbeth fell to her knees and clutched his robe, vainly trying to part the folds, to bare his cock.

'Oh, please, master,' she babbled, 'do me, whip my bare, let me have your cock in my bumhole. I need it so much. It's been so long, frigging myself to come without cock or a lacing.'

The master slapped her breasts and she sank to the dirt, sobbing.

'I had come to congratulate you on your prowess as a hardened chastiser,' he said. 'It seems you have regressed to your submissive state.'

'Why not, master?' Lisbeth wailed. 'For weeks I have made naked girls scream and weep and wriggle, knowing it was *my* body that deserved the shame of punishment, as my lesbian lusts made me masturbate over their weals. Please punish me, master. Take me back as your slave, I beg you.'

The master clapped his hands.

'You'll do, Lisbeth,' he purred. 'The eternal, adorable female! Two teats, two fesses, two holes, and two faces –

one moment a dominant bitch, the next a submissive slut. You *shall* be enslaved, Lisbeth, for the perfect slave is one who *craves* enslavement. But not by me.'

'Please, master!' Lisbeth sobbed, licking his boots.

While Emmeline undertook the punishment of the English girl, the master bared his cock to Lisbeth's eager lips. The massive tool stiffened to full, throbbing erection.

'Suck, bitch,' he commanded Lisbeth.

Vap! Vap!

'Ohh! Thank you,' groaned the blonde, as Emmeline's whip lashed her squirming bare buttocks and tears streamed down her face.

Crouching, Lisbeth took the master's cock to her throat and began to fellate him with rapid, bobbing swoops of her head. Vap! Vap! Emmeline's whip striped the English girl's shuddering back until all of her exposed flesh glowed with savage crimson weals. Lisbeth sucked the master's cock for several minutes while the English blonde's back and buttocks were whipped raw. The slurps and gurgles of Lisbeth's lips on the rigid tool were drowned by the squirming blonde's screams.

'Give me your sperm, master,' Lisbeth gurgled. 'Spunk in my mouth, let me swallow your cream.'

The master wrenched her head by the hair, baring his cock, dripping with her drool. He dragged her, whimpering, to the flogged blonde, and Emmeline took his swollen glans between finger and thumb, beginning a delicate frottage of his cock, stroking the peehole and corona of his glans until the master grunted, smiling.

'Yes,' he said.

A huge jet of sperm spurted from his peehole, soiling the blonde's hair. Emmeline caressed his glans for several seconds until he had delivered his whole cream and the girl's tresses were a sticky, glistening tangle. He thrust Lisbeth's face into her hair.

'You want my spunk, slut,' he hissed. 'So suck it.'

Sobbing as she crouched with spread thighs, Lisbeth took hanks of the blonde's hair into her mouth, sucking them of the master's spunk. Vap!

'Ooh!' she moaned, as Emmeline's whip lashed her on her open cooze flaps.

Emmeline withdrew the whip, its tongue dripping with Lisbeth's come. Vap! She lashed again, this time on the anus.

'Ahh!' Lisbeth gasped, sucking hard on the blonde's come-slimed hair.

Vap! Her parted buttocks trembled, as inky red bruises spread across her arse cleft.

'Oh, no,' she groaned, and Emmeline and the master laughed as a powerful jet of steaming golden piss spurted from Lisbeth's cunt.

The cleft-whipping continued until Lisbeth had sucked the hair dry of sperm and swallowed it.

'That's what they called you at school, wasn't it?' purred the master. 'The Bedminster bedwetter.'

Lisbeth blushed furiously.

Those dreadful punishment mornings, strapped to my rubber sheets, with my bottom slopping in my lake of pee, and Dorcas licking her cane, ready to lace my wet bare . . .

'How did you – ooh! Ahh!'

A whiplash to the cunt silenced her.

'Lick up your mess from the floor,' the master commanded. 'You may masturbate your clit as you do so.'

Whimpering and sobbing, Lisbeth crouched low to obey, masturbating her come-spraying cunt until she had swallowed her lake of piss. At her last gulp of the acrid liquid, she groaned as her belly fluttered, and her cunt spewed come in a quivering orgasm.

'Humiliance becomes her,' the master said. 'This slut –' he gestured towards the sobbing blonde '– another old Bedminstress, indeed, may go back to the sperming room, as reward for her connivance. As for Lisbeth, the bitch is conveniently naked, Emmeline, so you may fit her with the blonde slut's choke pear and take her at once to auction.'

15

Bumworthy

The spiky cylinder, slimed with the blonde's come and filling Lisbeth's cunt, hurt awfully during the boat journey to the slave market at Flogger's Cay. On disembarkation at the jetty, seawater dripped from her body as she waited to be hobbled and roped to the other nude girls by the cane-wielding Lucayan guards. Their ankles were clamped in bilboes, individual wooden hobbles roped together; their nipples clamped in pincers, fastened likewise. So painful was the choke pear that she stumbled, thighs apart, the half mile to the slave auction, where the slave girls mounted a low stage. Emmeline parted Lisbeth's cunt lips to unlock and remove her choke pear, its egress as agonising as its presence.

'These local buyers want a good scrunt at your insides,' said Emmeline. 'You're lucky – you won't be leaving the master's domain. When we sell slaves afar, there is no auction. Our overseas clients will pay anything.'

Their nip clamps were removed and wrists unbound. Still hobbled, they joined a melee of sumptuous nude girls from other suppliers. Beside the dais stood a gibbet, suspending one black and one white girl, naked with their bare backs facing the audience. Their arms were clamped behind their backs in rubber gauntlets, and their suspension was from single pincers on each nipple, roped to the gibbet crossbar, holding the girls on tiptoe. A muscular, bare-chested youth holding a bull-whip stood behind the suspended girls.

An auctioneer in eighteenth-century scarlet coat and white breeches wore a scarlet tricorn hat that said 'Jumentos Auctions'. He stood at a lectern, amid the slaves, who were marshalled by tall, long-legged and barefoot ebony guard girls, their breasts and cunt mounds bulging under one-piece swimsuits of scarlet nylon. The buyers were all in finery, one tall young European perspiring in a white suit and panama hat. Bare-breasted ebony slave maids offered trays of champagne flutes, the maids wearing white nylon stockings, scarlet stilettos and scarlet sussies, with a tiny, transparent plastic apron covering their shaven quims, leaving their buttocks bare. Several gentlemen gave the maids playful spanks on the fesses, to which the maids curtsied deftly.

At a signal from the auctioneer, the audience – males and females – thronged the dais to inspect the girls. Like the others, Lisbeth had her breasts and croup prodded and squeezed, and was obliged to bend over, parting her bum cheeks to show her anus, and endured repeated probing of her cunt, which began to seep come.

'*There's* a proper juicy slave wench,' drawled one male.

'Pity we can't whip her,' said a lady. 'I'm sure she'd fill buckets.'

Lisbeth's breasts heaved, as her gash moistened. *I'm a naked female animal, a slave in pure submission.* Vap! Vap! Bidding was announced by whiplashes to the buttocks of the strung girls, and the buyers left the stage. First slave up was a pouting black girl, her bubbies and buttocks waggling coquettishly. The auctioneer called for bids to open at ten, receiving a nod; two whipcracks rang out on the strung girls' buttocks. There was a further nod, up to twelve – more lashes to the dangling bares, with the whipped girls squirming on their nipple leashes – then to thirteen, fifteen, seventeen, each bid accompanied by the licking of bull-whip on naked girlskin.

The slave girl was sold at nineteen to a lady, with a flurry of whipcracks to the flogged scapegoats. Next up was a European girl, sulky, raven-haired and slender with heavy teats and buttocks and long, pendant cunt flaps, moist with fluid. She tossed her head and gave a wiggle of her bottom as a first bid of twelve was recorded. Vap! Vap! The whip cracked on the gibbettees' buttocks as this girl's bidding went to twenty-five. The suspended girls' croups glowed with long crimson whip welts; they dangled, quivering and sobbing, on their teat ropes, come dripping to their twitching bare toes and into the dirt.

Lisbeth ached, biting her lip – she would soon be bursting to pee. She watched girl after girl preen and pirouette, opening their gash flaps or bending to spread their buttock cheeks and show succulent velvet anus puckers. The bidding carried to twenties, with a couple of ebony girls fetching over thirty; then a blonde with jutting pale breasts and big strawberry nipples sold for forty-four, and a ravishing ebony slave girl, over six feet tall, went for fifty, raising cheers, with lashes to the strung girls, wriggling in agony. Both girls pissed themselves, oblivious to their shame, and Lisbeth felt sympathetic pain in her belly.

As each girl was bought, she hobbled off the stage towards her new owner. Fuelled by champagne, the buyers cheered each sale and the accompanying lashes to the gibbettees. At last, a scarlet-swimsuited guard thrust Lisbeth forward and she hobbled, holding her gash flaps open. She turned to waggle her bottom, with a wink of her anus bud, to loud applause. Her bidding started at twenty, followed at once by a bid for thirty, then rapid bids at forty, forty-five, fifty-five and sixty. *The power of my nude body!* Breasts and buttocks thrusting, she pouted at the audience, rubbing her nipples and cunt lips while tweaking her enlarged clitty to shiny wet stiffness.

Come spurted from her slit, and she dipped her fingers in her pouch, raising them to her mouth and licking before smearing come over her breasts. The bidding went to seventy-five. She daubed a palmful of come into her arse cleft, smearing her inner fesses and anal pucker, while the whip cracked on the squirming bare bodies strung beside her, their whimpers scarcely piercing the hubbub. The bidding rose to eighty. Thighs parted, Lisbeth vigorously masturbated while pinching her rock-hard nipples.

'And ninety,' cried the auctioneer. 'Who'll say a hundred?'

Lisbeth frigged hard, her belly trembling with impending come, and her bladder bursting in agony. She panted, as she masturbated, bringing herself off with come spraying from her gash. After her yelps of orgasm, her bladder burst and her come mingled with a heavy spray of golden piss, wetting the faces of the ladies and gentlemen gazing at her cunt. Vap! Vap! The whip lashed the nude gibbettees, and their cunts spouted fresh piss.

'I have one hundred!' crowed the auctioneer. 'A record, ladies and gentlemen! Yes, a hundred and twenty – a hundred and forty!'

Lisbeth's cunt basin writhed, squirting droplets of come and piss over the giggling watchers, who'd opened their mouths to catch her golden shower. Her face wrinkled in shame as another, heavier pressure clamped her belly. *No . . . not that . . .* With a groan, she spread her legs, squatted, turning her buttocks to the crowd, and released a spray of dungs, the heavy pellets plopping from her anus.

'A hundred and fifty!' shouted the auctioneer. -

Vap! Vap!

'Ahh!' screamed the whipped girls.

'A hundred and eighty!'

'Vap! Vap!

'Ooh! Ahh!'

'A hundred and ninety!'

Face crimson, Lisbeth pressed her fingers to her cunt and slopped a palmful of come, then thrust behind into her arse cleft and wiped her dung-smeared anus with the come. The crowd roared cheers.

'Two hundred!' cried the auctioneer.

Vap! Vap! The whipper delivered two vicious strokes into his victim's bum clefts; the two girls howled, then began to writhe, their cunts spurting come, and shrieked in high staccato yelps as both orgasmed. The bidding ceased.

'Sold, slave Lisbeth, to our good friend Mr Charles Gee-Toole, for an auction record,' declared the auctioneer, 'at two hundred cents! That's two whole dollars, ladies and gentlemen, for a prime cut of English gash steak!'

The lanky man in the white suit and panama hat nodded acknowledgment, and Lisbeth hobbled towards him.

'I'm awfully sorry, sir, that I . . . you know, lost control,' she blurted.

'Never mind, Lisbeth,' said Charles Gee-Toole. 'You *are* the Bedminster bedwetter, after all.'

He led her, hobbled, to his boat for the short crossing to Whips Island, Mr Gee-Toole's property where, he explained, his 'wenches' wore school uniforms, just like those at Bedminster – the green pleated skirts, white stockings and sussies, black patent leather shoes and tight white blouses. They disembarked on an island lush with flowers and jacaranda trees, dominated by a white sugarcake mansion, amid rolling green parkland, irrigated by numerous rivulets. A girl with a prefect's badge took her, through corridors reeking of girlsweat, cabbage and carbolic soap, to her dormitory, the image of her chill remembrance. To her dismay, her bed was fitted with latex sheets. She peeked at the others to learn that they all had crisp cotton ones – she was the only 'bedwetter' in the dorm. When Lisbeth tried to explain that it was *ages* ago, the 'prefect' smiled coldly and tapped the short cane dangling at her waist.

Lisbeth showered, laced herself into a beastly tight white corset, then donned her 'school uniform', proudly looking into the glass at the image of herself of a few years before. The landscaped grounds, with watered lawns, were filled with smiling English girls, all tan, who picnicked, sunned themselves or played volleyball in the nude, by ponds shimmering with fish. Teatime in the refectory was scrumptious with her favourite tuck – Lisbeth fell back into old school parlance – sausage and mash, toad in the hole, roly-poly pudding. Her companions were friendly but reserved, answering her with knowing smiles.

Her uniform was hot and her corset uncomfortable, squeezing her waist thinner than she had thought possible, but outside nudity was normal, except for the cane-wielding prefects. Lisbeth passed a pleasant two days

228

relaxing by the pool, sunbathing – not that her copper-bronze body really needed to tan – and drinking cups of good English tea. Watching the firm brown bottoms waggling before her at volleyball or swimming, she felt her quim juice, yet had to stifle her urge to masturbate, as she imagined being caned for it. Instead she'd go to the gurgling lavatory and discreetly peek at girls showering while she wanked off.

Sometimes girls would disappear for an hour or two, returning all flushed, but without comment on their absence. Lisbeth wondered what she and the other 'school-girls' were here for. In the distance she saw bare-chested male slaves at work, but there was no contact. Before bed there were games of ludo, cribbage and the like. Her initial nervousness at lights out – for she knew what games schoolgirls played in the dark – proved unfounded, and no one bothered her, although she heard the telltale rustles and whimpers of mutual masturbation all around her.

Her lime-green school nightie was deliciously short and cool, perfect for discreet masturbation, and she always wanked herself to sleep, half hoping one of the girls *would* bother her. She awoke, slippery with sweat on her rubber sheets, and endured the prefect's inspection of her sheets and nightie to make sure she hadn't wet herself in the night. She blushed as, each morning, the prefect sniffed her nightie. Lisbeth knew it must pong of her wanked come, but the prefect smiled and said nothing. After breakfast on her third day – proper bacon and eggs – she received a summons to Mr Gee-Toole's office.

It was just like the headmistress's at Bedminster – sunny but mellow with old wood and leather. Beside the book-shelf was a glass case where several canes hung on a rack. Mr Gee-Toole wore his white suit and mopped his head with a turquoise kerchief. Lisbeth curtsied, and stood with her head lowered and her hands behind her back.

'I expect you're wondering why I've called you,' he said, rather nervously. 'You're settling in all right?'

'Yes, thank you, sir,' Lisbeth replied.

'Probably wondering what it's, ah, all about, eh?'

'It is not a slave's place to wonder,' she said.

'Good answer. But here, you're a wench, a *schoolgirl*. The headmistress – my dear wife – that's the way she likes it. Now, Lisbeth, would you mind awfully, ah, lifting your skirt, and, ah, lowering your knickers? I'm afraid I must cane you on the bare.'

Come spurted from Lisbeth's slit, soiling her panties. Heart thumping, she obeyed as Mr Gee-Toole opened the cabinet and selected a three-foot English school cane.

'Would you like to take me over the chair, sir?' she said.

'That's awfully thoughtful – yes, the chair will do.'

Lisbeth leaned over the leather armchair, with her skirt lifted, bare buttocks raised and panties stretched between her stockinged thighs. She gasped as a trickle of hot come smeared her thighs, sliming the leather beneath her cunt.

'I say, you obviously know the drill,' he panted, lifting his cane. 'Don't you want to know what you're to be caned for?'

'Slaves are beaten, sir,' blurted Lisbeth.

She observed his turgid cock.

'So are schoolgirls,' he said. 'The boss – my wife – says so. Your first beating is to remind you. Comfortable?'

'Sir,' she retorted, 'a flogged girl is not *supposed* to be comfortable.'

He flushed.

'Spirited filly, an't ye?' he hissed.

Vip! The cane lashed Lisbeth full on the bare; she winced, clenching her melons. Vip! A second stroke sliced her first weal.

'Ooh,' she gasped.

'Hurt much?' he said.

'Just a bit, sir,' she panted.

'That's the spirit.'

Vip!

'Ooh!'

Vip!

'Ahh!'

Vip!

'Oh . . . ohh . . .'

Outside, there was the lapping of the ocean, jacaranda trees swaying in the breeze, and the laughter of girls at play. Lisbeth knew only the searing agony in her bare bottom, the tears that blurred her eyes and the come seeping from her slit. Vip! Vip! As the cane sliced, her buttocks squirmed faster, her titties heaving, her breath rasping hoarsely and tears streaming on her crimson face. Vip! Vip!

'Ooh . . .' she whimpered, her bare nates wriggling and clenching, come spraying from her gash.

Her caner's crotch bulged with a full erection.

'You haven't asked your tariff,' he panted, after the sixteenth cut.

'Slaves may not ask, sir,' she sobbed. 'Nor schoolgirls.' Vip! Vip!

'Ahh!' Lisbeth yelped, as two strokes took her in the arse cleft, lashing her anus and wet cunt flaps.

Vip! Vip!

'Ahh . . . no . . . please . . .'

The caning continued to forty strokes, Lisbeth's blotched purple bare jerking under the dry taps of the cane. Vip! Vip!

'Ooh! I can't take any more!'

'Going to piss yourself, bedwetter?'

'Oh, sir, please – the shame . . .'

Vip! Vip!

'Oh! Oh, no!'

Her belly swelled – she could not retain it – and a fierce jet of hot piss spurted from her cunt, spraying her stockings and the polished floorboards.

'You gorgeous pissing hussy,' cried Mr Gee-Toole. 'I must have that arse.'

'Ooh!' gasped Lisbeth, as she felt his throbbing, naked cock pressed to her anus. 'Oh, sir, what . . . ahh!'

Grunting, Gee-Toole impaled her bumhole on his stiff cock and, straddling her, began a rapid buggery.

'Does it hurt, you cheeky mot?' he panted.

'Yes sir, ' she squealed. 'It hurts more than caning. Oh, please, not so hard.'

'Liar,' he spat. 'Your cunt's wet. You're gagging for it.'

His hands clawed beneath Lisbeth's blouse, ripped open her bra and began to knead her bare titties.

'Uhh ...' Lisbeth whimpered, her buttocks rising to meet his thrusts, slapping wetly on his thrusting, piss-soaked balls. 'Oh, yes, sir ... oh! Ahh! It hurts! You brute! Fuck me harder! How did you know ...?'

Her thighs rippled as her wealed buttocks powerfully clenched his cock, her rectum sucking the glans.

'I know all about you,' panted Gee-Toole, between thrusts to her rectum, 'from my wife and Roger de Hazebrouck. The fellow is her lover, and I'm a compliant wretch, for it's the only way I can spunk in her cunt, thinking of another cock poking her before me. The whore won't let *me* bum her, yet I have to watch as her slave boys bugger her, one after the other. Gad, you've a tight arse, you luscious bitch. I'm going to fill your bumhole with my spunk. Yes ... yes ...'

'Gee-Toole!' drawled an imperious lady's voice. 'You vicious whelp, withdraw this instant. How you disgust me – tasting my present before I have the chance. Lisbeth, dear, the liar can't even *stiffen* unless he sees me fucked beforehand.'

Gee-Toole stood, his cock dripping with Lisbeth's arse grease.

'I ... I was testing her for you, darling,' he whined.

'Down, whelp, and lick my boots,' drawled the head-mistress. 'My whip's still warm from its last arse.'

Lisbeth looked up and saw a tall, tan girl in a shimmering turquoise corset of thick ribbed latex, zippered at the front and thrusting her bare teats to full jut, her buttocks and hairless quim bulging beneath, scarcely covered by a narrow satin thong, also turquoise; sussies and nylons of the same hue, sheathing her rippling thighs; her feet in white rubber jackboots with pointed steel toecaps and spiked heels. A white rubber mask covered her upper face and she carried a rubber quirt of short thongs, tipped in metal. Charles crouched at her feet, his bum in the air, and began to lick her toecaps. She lifted her arm;

her face caught the sunlight, and Lisbeth gasped. Vap! The quirt's thongs lashed his bare bottom and he jerked, clenching the buttocks and drooling over his whipper's foot. Vap!

'Ooh, darling . . .' he moaned.

His cock trembled, rigid beneath his wealed arse. Vap! Vap! The whipper's breasts heaved as she flenched the drooling, whimpering male, slapping his squirming bare with rapid, vicious strokes.

'Sabrina . . .!' Lisbeth blurted.

The whipper pouted.

'Welcome, Lisbeth,' Sabrina Stuart-Bossi said, still whipping Gee-Toole's buttocks. 'My, what splendid fesses – you *are* bumworthy.'

Vap! Vap!

'Ooh! Darling, please!'

'Gee-Toole is incorrigibly smutty,' she drawled. 'Look at that beastly organ. So tiny, compared to the master's, and the cheeky worm dares to suggest bumming me!'

Vap! Vap!

'Oh! Ooh! Please stop, darling.'

'I need a *real* man to pleasure me. Don't I, darling?'

Vap! Vap!

'Yes, dear,' he whimpered, his flogged arse squirming.

Sabrina lit a cigarette and puffed luxuriously.

'On our wedding night,' she drawled, 'he could only do me *in cunno* after watching three slave boys bugger me, then cuntfuck me in turn while I fellated three more.'

Sabrina pushed aside her thong and squatted; a stream of piss erupted from her cunt, splashing her husband's buttocks. She lifted her boot and kicked his swollen glans, then began to rub his frenulum with her spiked heel.

'Ooh . . . ooh . . .' he gurgled, as spunk spurted from his cock, all over her boot.

She continued to frot him until his spasm ceased, then ordered him to lick her boot clean.

'Don't you want to go, bedwetter?' drawled Sabrina.

Her blush revealed that Lisbeth did want to go.

'Well, then,' Sabrina said.

Lisbeth sighed in relief as her jet of steaming piss spurted over Mr Gee-Toole's face. He lapped up the golden liquid, babbling thanks.

'How do you know so much about me?' Lisbeth asked.

'I was at Bedminster, too,' replied Sabrina. 'Different year, house and form, but I knew all about you. Dorcas Gunn – the beast of the sixth form – was my best chum, you see. I never had the chance of whipping your luscious bottom, though.' She licked her lips.

'My bottom is yours to flench, Sabrina,' Lisbeth blurted. 'I *am* a slave. Is that is really why you sent me here?'

'To free your true nature, Lisbeth. The red folk helped – I've never seen you so beautiful.'

Sabrina suddenly crouched, plunging her face into Lisbeth's arse cleft, and began a vigorous licking of her anus and cunt, getting her tongue between the lips and tongue-swiving her pouch, with nibbles on Lisbeth's throbbing clitty. As she tongued, she spanked Lisbeth's wealed bottom with vigorous slaps, making her bare squirm. Lisbeth's cunt spewed come while Charles stared, sobbing, his cock tumescent.

'Please don't, darling,' he whimpered. 'Oh, the shame.'

Sabrina masturbated her dripping cunt while gamahuching Lisbeth to a rapid spend, and both girls yelped, coming together. Sabrina rose, licking her lips of Lisbeth's come.

'I've *always* wanted that to happen,' she murmured.

'Me too, Sabrina,' blurted Lisbeth.

'Roger is so sweet,' she said, 'giving you as my birthday gift. Follow me, and I'll show you what *really* pays for LaBo Associates.'

They went down into a gloomy cavernous cellar, lit by flickering turquoise candles, casting a ghostly glow over rows of punishment frames. The huge chamber was filled with the tapping of canestrokes, and the whimpers and groans of the tortured. Imperious, Sabrina, with Lisbeth following meekly behind, walked the ranks of naked males, contorted in excruciating bondage, or roped to flogging horses for canings by uniformed schoolgirls, their skirts swirling as their canes striped squirming bare arses.

234

Occasionally she sliced a bound male's already-wealed buttocks, his clamped nipples, or the tip of his erect cock, and received a groaned 'Thank you, mistress.' One bound male, pinched in a woman's corset and stiletto heels, with his balls harnessed in rubber, steel clothes pegs pinching his nipples and cock, and his spread bare buttocks blue with welts, stuck out his tongue from his rubber pixy hood, begging to lick Sabrina's arse. His reward was a canestroke to the anus.

'Mm . . .' he sighed.

'Recognise him?'

'Sort of – but he's masked.'

'Wearing his own creations. That's Giulio Ferracci. *Dear* Giulio . . .'

They came to a cluster of bound females, squealing under the lash of nude, erect slave boys, or else writhing as one after another buggered them. Tanya Bonslitt's nude body quivered, face up, her wrist and ankles roped at each end of a board, in whose centre a wooden slab bit into the small of her back. Three clothes pegs clamped each of her cunt lips, the pegs fastened to the edge of the slab holding open her glistening pink cunt. Hilary Warmduff, nude and quimshaven, poured molten wax into her stretched gash and over her erect nipples. She smiled at Lisbeth.

'I'm having such an awfully good holiday, miss,' she murmured coyly.

Tanya's breasts, belly and cunt hillock glowed with canewelts. Beside her, Jeremy groaned, arse up, in a similar rack; the twins, Vimella and Femella Culbutt lashed his bare buttocks with steel-tipped quirts, their bare bodies gleaming with sweat as they masturbated each other. Melanie Nave crouched beneath him, squirting hot wax over his harnessed balls while, between whipstrokes, Sapphire buggered him with a horned dildo. Vimella murmured a shy hello to Lisbeth.

'This is better than flying,' she panted as she flogged.

'Better than anything,' groaned Tanya, her eyes streaming with tears. 'The shame! The pain! The sensation! So kind of the master to refer us.'

Vip! Sabrina lashed her naked breasts.

'Silence, bitch,' she snapped.

'Ooh!' Tanya panted. 'Thank you, mistress.'

'My slaves,' Sabrina said, 'pay huge amounts – *shame-fully* huge – for their oppression. They are young, rich and handsome, yet our neurotic western society damns their submissive needs as perverse. Here they endure not a paltry hour's flogging by some Bayswater dominatrix, but real torture, of uncertain end. You, Lisbeth, have crushed and been crushed, and may now play your role as a vengeful schoolgirl.'

She handed Lisbeth a cane.

'I . . . I don't know if I can,' Lisbeth blurted.

'Don't dare defy me,' hissed Sabrina. 'I need you.'

'I've changed, rather, I've discovered things about myself . . . my *own* needs.' Lisbeth said. 'When punishing slaves, I always fantasised that it was *my* bottom squirming under the cane.'

'You claim to be submissive?' Sabrina gasped.

Lisbeth nodded helplessly.

'Pah! After you find what real submission is,' Sabrina snarled, 'you will be pleased to obey me.'

She snapped her fingers; green Bedminster school uniforms surrounded Lisbeth. She was seized and did not resist.

'You wouldn't play at Bedminster, you beastly bedwetter,' rasped a girl's voice, eerily familiar, from Lisbeth's dim, suppressed memory. 'Now you've no choice. I've waited ages – you're so *bumworthy*.'

Lisbeth looked up to see a tall, tan blonde, breasts and bum bulging under her clinging school uniform, thighs rippling in white stockings. She flicked the tips of her nine-thonged rubber quirt in Lisbeth's face.

'Dorcas!' she gasped.

'Girls,' leered Dorcas Gunn, 'take Miss Lache to the penance board.'

In a solitary dungeon, Lisbeth was stripped of all clothing before the convex wooden penance board, tilted on its central hinge. Dorcas laced her in a turquoise nylon corset; Lisbeth squealed, sobbing, as the crushing corset squeezed her waist to impossible, agonising thinness.

'Sixteen inches, bitch,' hissed Dorcas.

The corset thrust her bubbies up into hard parcels of bursting flesh. Femella clamped Lisbeth's nipples in circled metal flanges, tightening the clamp until they were bursting white bulbs inside the biting metal. She was pressed to the penance board and the teat flanges screwed into holes on the shiny surface, until her titties were flattened against the board. Femella cuffed her wrists at each side of the top board, while Dorcas clamped her ankles at the bottom, with her legs splayed wide and her soles facing outward. Pincers bit into each cunt lip, to be screwed to the board like the nipple clamps. Her hair was knotted to a chain hanging from the ceiling and wrenched taut, while her neck was fastened in a steel collar fixed to the board. Lisbeth was helpless, squashed to the penance board, gasping for breath, naked but for the cruel corset biting her flesh.

'You wouldn't play *my* games at Bedminster – too snobbish for a bumming from the hunky rugger team,' hissed Dorcas, 'so now I'll play games with *you*, bedwetter.'

'I can take it, bitch,' Lisbeth spat.

Uniformed schoolgirls, brandishing canes and quirts, clustered round her, beside nude slave boys with cocks erect. Vap!

'Ahh!' she gasped, her bottom wriggling as the nine tongues of Sabrina's quirt lashed her bare.

Vap!

'Ooh!'

Vap!

'Oh . . . oh . . . yes . . .' she moaned.

After twenty more strokes, Dorcas paused. Lisbeth sobbed helplessly, her bottom on fire and throbbing with weals. Dorcas's fingers kneaded the wealed flesh of Lisbeth's buttocks, viciously clawing her welts, and Lisbeth squirmed, whimpering. Hard male fingers parted her cheeks.

'Ooh!' she squealed, wincing, as a huge stiff cock penetrated her anus.

The male began to bugger her vigorously. Lisbeth wriggled beneath his body as his balls slapped her smarting fesses, and come began to spurt from her gash. His cock filled her rectum, slamming at her arse root, and she felt the first jet of sperm from his peehole, hot and wet inside her anus.

'Oh ... you're bursting my bum ... yes ...' she groaned, her cunt squirting hot come.

The slave boy spunked in her, filling her rectum with copious cream, that dribbled down her thighs, in a mingled flood of come and spunk. No sooner had he withdrawn than another cock impaled Lisbeth's anus, slamming hard and filling her rectum in new, savage buggery. Orgasm welled up in Lisbeth's fluttering belly, and, after two minutes of fierce fucking, the slave spunked in her and she came, yelping and wriggling in her corset, with her flailing teats wrenched against the screwed nipple flanges.

'The submissive bitch *came*,' snarled Dorcas. 'Flench her.'

Quirts and canes lashed Lisbeth's bare buttocks, thighs and calves, and, agonisingly, her naked soles. Thongs basted her shoulders, thudding on bare skin and corset. The beating continued for an hour – Lisbeth, swooning, lost track of time – with strokes timed every twenty seconds, for maximum agony.

'Think, Lisbeth,' purred Sabrina, smoking a cigarette, 'it could be you chastising another girl, some filthy sub who really craves it. This must hurt *awfully*.'

'Oh, Sabrina,' Lisbeth sobbed, 'no matter how much a girl craves the whip, it always hurts, yet she still craves it. I do.'

The flogging stopped, and hard cocks pierced Lisbeth's rectum. Come gushed from her clamped cunt as she wriggled on the tools impaling her; as spunk spurted to her colon, she squealed in the flooded pleasure of orgasm. Flogging gave way to buggery and to further flogging, until Lisbeth's body glowed in a mass of livid purple welts, ridges an inch high, and her thighs streaming with come and spunk from her wriggling arse cleft. Crouching beside

Lisbeth's flaming bare, Dorcas rammed her fist into Lisbeth's cunt.

'She's soaking,' she snarled.

Lisbeth's bladder gave way and squirted a hissing jet of hot piss, drenching Dorcas's face and school uniform.

'Ooh! Urrgh! You've soaked me, you fucking bitch,' snarled Dorcas.

'But merrily done, I think.'

It was the master's voice.

The penance board tilted, Lisbeth's roped hair wrenching her face up, and she gagged as the master's erect cock plunged between her lips. She sucked the massive tool, licking the peehole and glans, before sliding the cockshaft deep in her throat while a new flurry of whipstrokes laced her bare buttocks and soles. She sucked the master for three minutes and then a new cock pierced her rectum. Buggered hard, she licked and tongued the master's giant cock until she tasted his spunk at the peehole. Gurgling, she swallowed his powerful jet of sperm while the slave boy spunked in her own anus and her belly convulsed in an orgasm that filled the dungeon with her squeals and whimpers. The master withdrew his dripping cock.

'So, Sabrina, do you win this one, or do I?' he purred.

'Scarcely fair, Roger,' said Sabrina, 'giving her a slave's taste.'

'*Droit de seigneur*, darling,' Roger replied, patting her bottom. 'Just like *those* lovely fesses.'

'Which is it to be, Lisbeth?' Sabrina said. 'One of Dorcas's squad of schoolgirl dominas, enjoying life as a whipping prefect with *lashings* of tea and tuck – or a slave of the master?'

'Dorcas is a pussycat,' said Lisbeth.

'Why, you –' spat Dorcas, but was restrained by Miss Comington who stood beside the master.

'Regrettable, but true,' he said. 'Does that mean you wish to return to Rum Hole, Lisbeth?'

'Yes, master, please,' Lisbeth whimpered. 'I'm submissive. I know it. I shall always be.'

'Very well. It seems I win this one, Sabrina. You know what that means. Our little wager . . .'

Sabrina lit a cigarette, exhaling through pursed lips. 'You bitch, Lisbeth,' she glowered. 'You've earned me sixty strokes of the cane on my bare bottom. *Me!*'

'For that petulance, my sweet, *Lisbeth* shall deliver them,' said the master. 'Then, after Charles has watched me bugger your blistered arse, Sabrina, it is home to Rum Hole.'

Lisbeth was released from the penance board and permitted to watch her flogged bottom in a mirror held up by the smiling Elvira O'Malley. She rubbed her crusted weals and, gazing at her body, began to masturbate, tweaking the engorged marrow of her clitty, rubbing her breasts and corset and licking her drooling lips as her copper-bronze body rippled in the glass. Coolly, she pulled the cigarette from Sabrina's mouth and began to smoke as she masturbated. Sabrina flushed, speechless.

'Master, I think Miss Comington is being rather lax on discipline,' Lisbeth said.

'How so?' asked the master, watching with approval her vigorous frig, and the streams of come flowing on her flogged thighs.

'I'm wearing turquoise, Miss Comington's colour,' she said, exhaling plumes of blue smoke. 'I deserve a *very* severe bare-bottom caning.'

'Slaves are so demanding,' sighed the master. 'You shall have what you crave, Lisbeth – bare-bottom caning, harder than you imagine. Henceforth, you will be laced on the bare every single day, so painfully, that your delicious bottom will *never* be free of weals.'

Lisbeth took a last drag, then stubbed out her cigarette on Sabrina's corset.

'*Thank* you, master,' she gasped, come gushing from her cunt as she exploded in orgasm.

NEXUS BACKLIST

This information is correct at time of printing. For up-to-date information, please visit our website at www.nexus-books.co.uk

All books are priced at £6.99 unless another price is given.

- - - - - - ✂ -

Please send me the books I have ticked above.

Name ....

Address ....

....

...:..

.... Post code....................

Send to: **Virgin Books Cash Sales, Thames Wharf Studios, Rainville Road, London W6 9HA**

US customers: for prices and details of how to order books for delivery by mail, call 1-800-343-4499.

Please enclose a cheque or postal order, made payable to **Nexus Books Ltd**, to the value of the books you have ordered plus postage and packing costs as follows:

UK and BFPO – £1.00 for the first book, 50p for each subsequent book.

Overseas (including Republic of Ireland) – £2.00 for the first book, £1.00 for each subsequent book.

If you would prefer to pay by VISA, ACCESS/MASTERCARD, AMEX, DINERS CLUB or SWITCH, please write your card number and expiry date here:

....

Please allow up to 28 days for delivery.

Signature ....

Our privacy policy

We will not disclose information you supply us to any other parties. We will not disclose any information which identifies you personally to any person without your express consent.

From time to time we may send out information about Nexus books and special offers. Please tick here if you do *not* wish to receive Nexus information.   ☐

- - - - - - ✂ -